If you feel a little strange
When you gaze up at the full
If you sense some greater pow
With the skies arching above y
If you're touched by the presence of something unseen
When walking in the woods,
Then come with me
And enter the world of Stonewylde ...

# THE STONEWYLDE SERIES

# MOONDANCE
# of STONEWYLDE

by

## KIT BERRY

MOONGAZY
PUBLISHING

Published by Moongazy Publishing Ltd
22 Cross Hayes
Malmesbury
Wiltshire SN16 9BG
United Kingdom

First published in Great Britain November 2006
Reprinted January 2008

ISBN  978-0-9551439-1-5


Cover design Big Blu Design Bristol

Printed in Palatino by Cox and Wyman Ltd
Reading, Berks

www.stonewylde.com
www.moongazypublishing.com

The Stonewylde Series
is dedicated to the memory of
Jean Guy,
my best owl aunt.

STONEWYLDE

# ACKNOWLEDGEMENTS

Thanks again to Clare Pearson of Eddison Pearson Ltd, for her professional and personal involvement in the Stonewylde Series.

Thanks and love to my three wonderful sons George, Oliver and William for their great faith in me and their patience with my obsession.

Thanks to all my friends, family and school colleagues who encouraged me constantly and bought so many copies of the first book that I was able to go ahead and publish this one. I've been overwhelmed by everyone's enthusiasm and kindness.

Thanks again to the gorgeous Rob Walster at Big Blu Design for his outstanding skills and professional generosity in creating another brilliant cover.

Thanks to all the readers I've never met who contacted me after reading the first book in the series and clamoured for the second one – their enthusiasm has really inspired me.

Thanks to Sue Andrew and the team at the Three Hares Project for their source material. Further information about their research can be found at www.chrischapmanphotography.com

Finally, all my love and thanks to my beloved Mr. B for his unfailing support and passion for Stonewylde, and for once again "doing the business" with such expertise.

# MOONDANCE
## of STONEWYLDE

**BOOK TWO
IN THE
STONEWYLDE SERIES**

MOONGAZY
PUBLISHING

Swathes of silver light streaked the north-eastern skies, and in the cool dewy twilight Stonewylde slept soundly. On the dirty flagstone floor of a tumbledown cottage an old crone hunched stiffly, rocking as she crooned her incantation. Five points were marked on her circle with stubs of candle and symbols of the elements. A large leather-bound book lay open, the spidery writing faded on the parchment. The glossy crow sat in her lap with eyes shut. Mother Heggy muttered and poked at the small fire. With a shrivelled hand she flung a quantity of dried essence onto the smouldering sticks. A foul-smelling smoke billowed into the air and hung in wreathes about her. Her other clawed hand was clamped around something soft and malleable. Something vaguely human in shape, fashioned from wax, pig fat and a few ginger hairs. This mommet had a strange heart. In its centre lay a crescent of human toenail, yellow and horny.

Smoke choked the cottage and the crow fidgeted in the crone's lap. Her mumbling invocation gathered in power. The mommet became softer, the heat from her leathery skin transferring its energy along with that of the spell she cast. She scraped the remaining dry powder from a dish; all that was left, after her cake-baking, of the concoction she'd prepared one Dark Moon as the boy had sat here, his body bruised and battered and his heart seething with dark hatred. The crop of Sickener from the beech grove was unrecognisable as this desiccated essence which she now used to empower her spell.

She uttered the final words, no longer legible to her in the Book of Shadows, but known in her heart. She traced the five-pointed shape of magic in the smoke about her, and with a cry pitched the mommet into the fire. Instantly the pig fat turned to grease and the wax melted to nothing. The gingery hairs shrivelled and the crescent of nail lay in a viscous pool of thick tallow. Mother Heggy raised the crow gently from her lap, kissed its head and flung it into the air. With a frantic flapping it landed on the floor outside the cast circle.

"Fly, my lovely one! Fly to him now!" she croaked.

The crow hopped out, launching itself into the glimmer of dawn.

# CHAPTER ONE

Magus sprawled across the vast four poster bed gazing at the bright latticed windows. His sheets lay in a tangled heap, kicked off in the heat of the night as he'd slept fitfully. The sun was well up but he lay spread-eagled, magnificent body dark against the pure white sheets, his eyes glittering with fury. That damned boy!

His thoughts spun around like a vulture circling a carcass. Yesterday, Midsummer's Day, should have been a day of glory. His birthday, and a special one this year as he had much to celebrate. Instead – ruined. The arteries in his temple pounded as he remembered the look of triumph in the dark haired brat's eyes. The green magic had eluded him, the Magus, the rightful guardian of Stonewylde and recipient of the goddess' bounty. Normally he'd have been teeming with power and energy after receiving her gift. Today he felt only a flicker of his accustomed vitality. And it was all Yul's fault for fumbling with the torch and allowing the sacred flame to extinguish. The boy would suffer for this latest example of insubordination.

He recalled how all day yesterday after that disastrous sunrise ceremony Yul had excelled at the games held on the Village Green. Despite those gruelling weeks spent at the quarry, which should have broken not only his body but also his spirit, the boy had outstripped many others in countless competitions. Magus had been angered to see Sylvie watching with shining eyes, cheering him on – not that he'd needed it. Magus had a horrible suspicion that not only had the Earth Magic failed to empower him, but had somehow gone instead to Yul. That would explain the boy's brightness and energy.

Magus smiled grimly as he recalled how he'd put an end

to the boy's apparently unstoppable success. He'd waited for the right moment. Yul stood alone under the shade of a tree on the Village Green, still flushed from the exertion of winning a race. Magus recalled with pleasure how the boy's deep grey eyes had clouded with fear as he noticed his approach.

"Solstice Blessings, Yul!"

"Solstice Blessings, sir."

"You're doing remarkably well for someone who's been through such an ordeal so recently."

"Yes, sir."

"And for someone who shouldn't even have been here today. I don't recall giving you permission to leave the quarry."

"No, sir."

Magus' lips twitched as he felt the boy begin to tremble. He was hot and full of energy, but that trembling said it all.

"So why take it on yourself to leave Jackdaw and your friends at Quarrycleave and return to the heart of Stonewylde?"

"I ... I was told you had given permission, sir."

Yul fidgeted, sweat beading his upper lip and beginning to trickle down his flushed face from beneath the heavy mass of dark curls. Magus nodded slowly, looking beyond the boy to where a crowd gathered around the trestle tables of drink. He noticed Sylvie standing slightly apart, covertly watching as he addressed the boy. Anger welled unexpectedly.

"You completely fouled up the Solstice Sunrise ceremony this morning," he spat. "Never before have I witnessed such fumbling incompetence!"

"I'm sorry, sir," mumbled Yul, his heart thudding. This was the moment of truth – would Magus send him back to the horror of that white, dusty quarry?

"How dare you not only ruin the whole ritual by sheer clumsiness, but then have the effrontery to speak *my* words? Who the hell do you think you are?"

Yul shook his head helplessly. Who was he? Someone special and magical, as Mother Heggy had him believe, or just a worthless Villager at the mercy of his enraged master?

"I'll tell you then," hissed Magus, "as words seem beyond you. You are nothing … less than nothing. You've been a thorn in my flesh for too long, and I shall pluck you out and grind you underfoot. You are forbidden to have any contact whatsoever with Sylvie from this moment on. You should never have left the quarry without my express permission. I'm very tempted to send you straight back there, especially in view of your appalling clumsiness this morning at the ceremony. However, I think you'll be of more immediate use up at the Hall, where I find we are a little short-staffed. You'll report to Martin in the morning, first light, and do whatever work he directs you to for the duration of the Midsummer holidays. I'm sure there are plenty of dirty pots and pans to keep you busy. That will be all, boy."

Magus watched as Yul loped off back towards his cottage. All his earlier vitality and spark seemed to have been doused, and Magus sighed. He wasn't finished with Yul yet, not by a long way. But he must be careful. Justice must always be seen to be done, and he'd sensed the boy's popularity amongst the Villagers today during the races. Whatever happened, his own hands could not be dirtied. But there was another option. Magus' dark eyes scanned the hordes of people on the Green, drinking cider and elderflower champagne, laughing and chattering on this, the most special day of the year.

The vertical lines that grooved the skin on either side of his mouth creased further into a grim smile as he spotted the one he sought. Alwyn was quaffing cider outside the Jack in the Green, his bloated face tipped back as he poured the liquid down his throat. Magus noted the tanner's heightened colour and increased girth, his great belly ballooning over his trousers. Here was the means of keeping Yul down – and maybe even finishing him off altogether. Alwyn hated the boy with a vengeance and just a few words of encouragement from Magus would add fuel to his raging desire to punish. Magus resolved to speak to him later. Alwyn was his instrument and only needed a little fine-tuning.

Magus had then turned his attention to locating Sylvie again. It was her birthday too today and he had a gift for her.

3

He thought of the box waiting up at the Hall. Inside the layers of white tissue lay a dress so beautiful and perfect for her that his heart lifted at the memory of it. She'd wear it tonight for the Midsummer Dance and would eclipse everyone, Villager and Hallfolk, with her radiance. Sylvie was special and needed delicate grooming. She was fifteen today and although birthday gifts weren't usually given at Stonewylde, Magus had decided to make an exception. She'd never had much, if Miranda's pathetic life story were to be believed, and the exquisite dress would be worth its cost if it made the girl happy.

He saw Sylvie talking to Dawn, one of the older Hallfolk girls, and watched as they joined a group of youngsters heading apparently for the beach. He decided against speaking to her yet – the dress could wait till later. He recalled her promise to him on Solstice Eve to stay away from Yul. He'd be keeping a very close watch over her in future. It seemed that the Village brat had stolen his Earth Magic this Solstice; Magus didn't intend for him to steal Sylvie as well.

As he lay on the vast bed with the sunlight streaming in on him, Magus' thoughts jumped again to an event that had happened a little later in the day, as people were wandering off the Green. The Midsummer Dance would be starting a little later, with a feast laid out on the Green, and music and merry-making in the Great Barn. He'd noticed Alwyn stomping off up the lane towards his cottage, and had called over to him. The tanner's porcine face had lit up with pleasure at being singled out by the master.

"Midsummer Blessings, sir!"

Magus had looked away from the man's features in distaste. He'd become monstrous. Close up, the ruddiness could be seen as a myriad of engorged veins just under the surface of his fleshy skin. Even his piggy eyes were bloodshot. He wheezed from the tiny exertion of walking a few steps along the lane and his massive bulk gave out a hot, sour odour.

"A word with you, Alwyn. I'm sure you can guess the subject."

The tanner nodded grimly, sweat running down into the

folds of his neck.

"Aye, sir, I can that. The brat – he's back."

"He is, Alwyn, and already mischief-making. Did you see the mess he made of the ceremony this morning?"

Alwyn's face flushed a deeper shade of crimson.

"Little bastard!" he spluttered, spittle flying and almost landing on Magus, who took a quick step back.

"I want him held in check this time, Alwyn. You understand me? You've been lenient with him over the years, which is why he's so out of hand now."

"But sir, I …"

Magus held up a hand, his face stony.

"No excuses. The boy is out of control and I'm sorry to say the blame must lie at your door. Why else is he the only one at Stonewylde to constantly defy me and cause such trouble? I'm afraid, Alwyn, that I can only assume you've allowed him too much leeway. But no more. I'm holding you personally responsible for the boy's behaviour. Don't let me down. I expect you to be as harsh as is necessary. Is that perfectly clear? As harsh as you think fit."

"Aye, sir."

Alwyn's breathing was now so streperous that Magus wondered whether the man was capable of administering any form of beating at all.

"Have you seen Yul yet since his return?"

"No, sir. He's not been home at all. 'Twas a shock to see him at the Solstice Sunrise this morning. I didn't know you'd brung him back."

"Yes … the less said about that the better. But he is back. He'll be working up at the Hall for the holiday and I'll make sure Martin works him hard. But when he comes home at night time – that's up to you. I hope you won't disappoint me this time, Alwyn."

The tanner's eyes, so buried in puffy fat as to be almost hidden, filled with tears and he grasped Magus' hand in a flurry of distress.

"No sir, never. I'm so sorry, sir. I won't let you down again. He'll wish he'd never been born!"

Magus had nodded and disengaged himself from the man's sweaty grip, turning away in disgust.

"Him and me both," he'd muttered, heading back towards the Green.

But now, as Magus kicked away the twisted sheets and rose from his bed, white hot fury flooded him yet again. It seemed that once more Yul had foiled him, though he was at a loss to see how. What had happened? Was the boy responsible? For Alwyn lay now in this very building and looked as if he'd never raise a whip again in this life. Angrily Magus padded through into his black marble bathroom and wrenched the shower on full blast. He groaned as the cool water hit his body, letting it drench his blond hair and run down his face. He stood for several minutes under the great showerhead until the heat inside him had subsided. He had six months. Six months until the Winter Solstice when Yul would reach adulthood. The boy would be dealt with. Turning off the shower, Magus smiled grimly to himself. As he rubbed his body briskly and reached for his exotic cologne, he met his own velvet-black eyes in the mirror.

"Mirror, mirror on the wall..." he muttered and then chuckled to himself. He needed no reassurance, for he knew with absolute certainty the answer. He was the strongest of them all. Even without the Earth Magic.

Earlier that day, wearing rough work clothes, Yul had stood in the vast cobbled yard at the back of the Hall waiting for Martin to appear. It was pearly grey in the twilight, the sun not yet risen. Yul shivered. He'd had no breakfast for he hadn't wanted to wake his sleeping family. He yawned in the chill air as all around him the birds sang their divine dawn chorus. After what seemed like a long time, Martin opened the wide oak door and scowled out, looking quite surprised to find Yul ready and waiting. Yul had never liked Martin. He was about forty or so, clearly a Hallchild with his thin blond hair, but had never made it to the Hall School. He was dogged rather than quick witted, relentless rather than efficient. Martin had served at the Hall since he was a lad and enjoyed a special status there. He had no humour or warmth and was intensely loyal to Magus.

"Ah, there you are," he grunted sullenly, as if Yul was late. He came outside into the yard and looked Yul up and down. He knew the boy, for everyone at Stonewylde knew everyone else, but acted as if Yul was a stranger.

"Master has warned me about you," he muttered. "Don't try any of your tricks with me, sonny, I'm telling you. Just do your job and you'll be alright. But mess me about or try to skive off and Magus will hear about it. He particularly wants to know if you haven't pulled your weight. Understood?"

"Yes, sir," said Yul wearily.

"Right then, I've got you for the next five days, which is just as well seeing as we're so short staffed. There's extra Hallfolk here all needing to be served, and served well, mind you. Get in the kitchens and see what Marigold wants doing. And after that, get yourself down to the stables and report to Tom. Remember boy – no slacking or you'll be very sorry."

At the old butler's sink in the scullery, Yul scrubbed hard trying to remove some baked-on grime from a huge saucepan. His thoughts turned to the events of yesterday, Midsummer's Day. It had been one of the most amazing days of his life – a turning point he was sure. First that incredible experience as the sun rose over the Stone Circle and the Green Magic pierced his soul. He'd never, as long as he lived, forget the look of bewilderment on Magus' face.

He'd felt the effects of that magic all day as he won race after race. He sparkled with it, and every time he looked up there stood Sylvie, her silvery-grey eyes dancing with joy. He recalled the kiss they'd shared the previous night under the yew tree on the Village Green. He relived that moment when he knew with absolute certainty that they belonged together. The sight of her smiling at him as he competed filled him with happiness, and then she'd beckoned to him. They'd managed to find a quiet corner round the back of the Great Barn, and she'd grasped his hand desperately.

"I've brought the cake for you, Yul!" she'd said hurriedly, gazing up into his eyes. "You know, the cake Mother Heggy made.     I've hidden it just outside your gate in the undergrowth.  She said only Alwyn must eat it and nobody else. That's absolutely vital."

He nodded slowly, doubt clouding his intent now that the moment had come. Sylvie had seemed to sense this.

"He'll kill you, Yul," she said quickly. "Remember the last time?  Remember what Mother Heggy warned?  Please, don't back down now.  You have to go through with this."

Yul nodded again.  He kissed her slim hand and then joined the other lads for the next race.  Not long after this, Magus had taken him to one side and informed him that he was to work all during the holidays.  His heart seething with bitterness, Yul had made his way home, the celebrations ruined.  As he walked up the lane, a path he'd trodden every day of his life, his resolve stiffened.  He deserved better than this.  He was not going to spend the rest of his life at the mercy of the two men who for no apparent reason hated him to the point of destruction.  He recalled Mother Heggy's words all those months ago and felt a surge of power.  Now was the time.

"But Yul, my love, where's it from?"

His mother's deep grey eyes were puzzled as she took the package from him.  Yul shrugged, not wanting to lie.

"Some Hallfolk girl just gave it to me," he said.  "She said it was a special gift for Alwyn and him alone."

"How strange!  Must be from Marigold up in the kitchens I suppose.  I know he's been going up there for meals, though Goddess knows why seeing as I feed him well enough.  The man has the appetite of a bull at the moment.  Oh well, if it's come from the Hall it must be special."

"And only for Alwyn, Mother.  Nobody else must eat it, she said."

"Aye, I understand that, my boy.  Well, he'll be back soon enough for a nap no doubt, after all that cider he's been putting back.  Maybe he'll have a slice of the cake then.  And you better make yourself scarce, my boy.  'Twill be the first time you've been under the same roof for a while and I don't want trouble today of all days.  You go back to the Green, my love, and

8

enjoy yourself. And Yul ... I thought my heart would burst this morning at the ceremony, I was that proud of you."

Maizie took her eldest son in her arms and hugged him fiercely, the fears and unhappiness of the past months forgotten for a moment. Yul felt her shudder with suppressed emotion and squeezed her tightly. He'd missed his family a great deal during his exile first in the woods and then up at the quarry, and especially his mother.

They heard laughter and chatter and the front door was flung open. The rest of his family piled into the small sitting room: Rosie, with little Leveret in her arms, Geoffrey and Gregory almost as tall as their older sister now, and Gefrin and Sweyn fighting as usual. The children swarmed around Yul, delighted to see their oldest brother home again. Yul took Leveret from Rosie and laughed into her mop of black curls.

"Rosie, where's your father now?" asked Maizie quickly. "Is he on his way or ..."

Too late they heard the tuneless whistling and everyone froze. Alwyn walked into a still life. In the total silence he allowed his bulk to fall heavily into his armchair. Nobody moved. Alwyn's heavy breathing filled the room and he peered around at the group of statues until his gaze fell on the one he sought. Maizie jerked into action.

"A bite to eat, Alwyn my dear?" she gabbled. "There's a fine cake here, sent up from the Hall special, just for you. I'll cut you a nice big slice, shall I?"

Alwyn grunted, his belligerent stare unbroken. Carefully Yul handed Leveret back to Rosie and straightened his back. Very slowly the children shrank away from the armchair until Yul stood alone, facing the man who'd almost beaten him to death not so long ago. His heart thudded but he found himself lifted with a strange courage. He looked Alwyn square in the eye, his cool grey gaze unwavering, his chin raised in defiance. He'd never looked into Alwyn's eyes before. They were buried almost completely in bloated skin, but Yul stared hard into the tiny pools of blue rage, feeling a thrill of power. At this unheard of insolence, Alwyn's face suffused with blood. A great vein throbbed at his temple.

"Here you are then, my dear!" Maizie's voice was shrill. "A lovely bit of cake from the Hall! And a nice bite of cheese. You enjoy that, and ..."

Alwyn glanced at the plate she'd laid on his lap and picked up the slab of dark cake. He growled and aimed a kick at his wife, who scuttled out of reach, trying to block Yul from his sight. Everyone remained rooted as Alwyn contemplated the cake in his hand. Gently Yul moved his mother to one side and stood again directly in the tanner's line of vision.

"You can fetch the strap off the hook," grunted Alwyn. "When I've done with eating this, I'll do for you. Just like the master said. There'll be no getting away with nothing this time round, you little bastard. You're in for it now, coming back like this and upsetting him. Got to do my duty by him, right enough."

He raised the slice of cake towards his mouth, but then paused.

"You hear me, boy?" he bellowed. "I said fetch the strap!"

He bit hugely into the dark cake, his jowls swinging as he masticated. Yul folded his arms and remained where he was.

"You'll never lay a hand on me again," he said quietly, his voice as shattering as a pebble thrown into a lake. Next to him Maizie jerked with terror, then her eyes widened as she watched. Alwyn's skin was crimson, the veins now bulging in both temples and his neck. His eyes were bloodshot and his mouth was working, trying to speak through the mass of half-chewed cake. He began to splutter and cough. There was a tapping at the window and Yul flicked a glance towards it. The crow sat on the sill surveying the scene with a round eye. Alwyn's coughing turned rapidly into a fit of choking. He struggled to suck in breath, the violent rasp and wheeze in his constricted throat sickening to the ear. His eyes rolled up in his head and he pitched forward, crushing his plate and thrashing his arms. A strange noise came from his mouth, along with the dark mangled-up cake and a great foam of saliva. His body heaved and jerked in violent spasms. Then he threw himself back in the armchair and was still, soft wheezing the only sound in the crowded sitting room.

Everyone looked on in appalled silence, hands over mouths and eyes enormous. Nobody breathed. It was unthinkable; too shocking to comprehend.

Then unbelievably, Leveret broke the horrified hush. Her gurgle of laughter split the stillness.

"Quiet, child!" moaned Maizie, shaking her head in bewilderment. She sent the family from the room back to the Village Green with instructions to find the young doctor. Only Yul remained with her, and they stood together contemplating the tyrant slumped in the armchair, his eyes lifeless and breathing slow and loud.

"Goddess, I don't believe this," she sobbed. "What's happened to the man?"

Yul put a strong arm around his mother and kissed the top of her head.

"Don't you worry, Mother," he said softly. "I'll take care of the family now."

But as he stared at the bulky mass sprawled helplessly before him, his eyes hardened and he whispered into his mother's curls.

"Those who stand against me shall fall, one by one."

The crow launched itself from the window sill and up into the sky, heading back to the tumbledown cottage.

As Yul scoured the pan in the scullery, he permitted himself another smile of pure pleasure. He felt as if shackles had been removed after a lifetime of chafing his skin. He felt as free as a swift on the summer thermals. For Alwyn lay somewhere in the Hall right now, tucked away in the hospital wing and unable to move at all. It appeared he'd had some sort of seizure, possibly a stroke, and the young doctor who'd arrived just before the Solstice said he may never recover. Yul recalled the stab of joy he'd felt on hearing this, and the difference in the whole family's enjoyment of the Midsummer dance that evening. Maizie had hesitated at joining in the celebrations at such a time, with her husband lying up at the Hall and maybe at the gateway to the Otherworld. But Yul and Rosie had managed to persuade her that it would be wrong not to honour the festival in the proper way. Maybe the

Goddess would give their poor father strength to recover, they'd suggested. Reluctantly Maizie had agreed to her family bathing and dressing in their finest festival clothes to attend the feasting and dancing that night.

Yul wiped the pan dry with a coarse linen cloth and smiled again. What a good thing they had attended the dance, for otherwise he'd have missed the sight of his beautiful Sylvie sparkling like the brightest star in the heavens.

Sylvie lay on the coarse sand, her fingers idly sifting through the grains as she gazed at the blue sky overhead. The sun was scorching hot on her skin and she sighed deeply. She'd hoped to spend some time with Yul over the week-long Midsummer Holiday, but he was nowhere to be found. She hadn't seen him since the night of the Solstice, when they'd managed to snatch some moments together at the dance. She smiled as she remembered that evening. For the first time in her life, she'd felt like a fairy-tale princess. When she'd returned to Woodland Cottage later in the afternoon, a large white box had been waiting on her bed. Miranda had stood in the doorway, a strange expression on her face.

"I don't understand, Mum. You said now we're at Stonewylde we'd follow the customs here and not give birthday presents."

"It's not from me. It's from Magus. There's a note."

*For a beautiful girl on her fifteenth birthday – wear it tonight!*

Sylvie looked up and was shocked to see her mother in tears.

"Mum! What's wrong?"

Miranda wiped her eyes and sniffed, shaking her head.

"I'm sorry – I'm just being silly. It's nothing."

"You don't mind that Magus has given me a present, do you? I'll send it back if …"

"No, of course I don't mind," Miranda said quickly. "It's stupid, I know. It's just that … when I think back to my fifteenth birthday, it was all so different. I was so naïve, so sheltered. My parents treated me like a child. And then not long after my birthday I fell pregnant with you and that was

12

that – my childhood over."

"I'm sorry, Mum," said Sylvie gently. "I know I'm so lucky compared to you. You had a rotten time of it."

Miranda shrugged and tried to smile.

"Well, it's all in the past now. And I've never regretted having you, Sylvie. Come on, let's see what's in the box. Something to wear tonight – sounds interesting."

Sylvie untied the silver bow and lifted the lid from the box. Carefully she pulled aside the layers of white tissue paper to reveal the most beautiful dress she'd ever seen. She found it hard to breathe as she lifted the dress from its soft nest, gasping as the layers of exquisitely fine material fell from their folds. The dress was of gossamer silk, silvery grey with thin silver ribbon straps. The bodice flared out into a cloud of skirts, which ended in little points all the way round the hem, each point tipped with a tiny silver bead. But the most amazing thing was the embroidery; the diaphanous fabric was shot with silver threads depicting small crescent moons and five-pointed stars. The effect was a glint and shimmer that gave the dress a light of its own. As Sylvie held it to her it seemed to dance with a subtle silver sparkle which perfectly mirrored the strangeness of her eyes. She couldn't speak, but stroked the dress against her body as if it had become her skin. Without a word, Miranda turned and went downstairs.

Sylvie raised herself on an elbow and gazed out to sea. Many other Hallfolk youngsters had come to the beach today, walking together along the path by the river that flowed through the Village and down to the sea. Her first sight of the beach had filled Sylvie with excitement, for it was a beautiful spot. Swans sailed grandly amongst the reeds where the river widened its mouth into a great freshwater pool, before dispersing over large pebbles and into the waiting salt water. The beach itself was a mixture of smooth shingle and coarse sand, shelving quite sharply into the sea. But the unusual aspect of the beach was its shape. It formed an almost perfect lagoon as if someone had etched out a scoop of the sea shore just to provide the people of Stonewylde with safe bathing. The water within the lagoon was very clear, for a huge low rock at the neck guarded the private bay and kept the rough seas out. The choppy waves could be seen out to sea crashing against the rock, but inside the shelter the water was calm. About twenty young people were on the rock, looking like a herd of seals as they basked and played. Sylvie squinted against the brilliant diamonds that danced off the water. Holly and her friends were out on the rock making a great deal of noise. They'd already crowded out the Villagers who'd been there first, much to Sylvie's dismay. She'd been hoping to see Yul there.

At the dance he'd told her the bad news about his extra work duties, but nevertheless she'd hoped that he may have managed a little free time. As she lay so indolently on the beach, Sylvie thought sadly of how unfair life was at Stonewylde. Here she was, pampered and spoiled, idling away yet another afternoon in the sun with the other Hallfolk teenagers. Whilst poor Yul was toiling away up at the Hall for no reason at all other than to keep the visitors who'd flocked back for the Solstice in luxury. Given his ordeal at Quarrycleave, Yul more than anyone at Stonewylde deserved a holiday. He was still so thin, his face chiselled into new planes and hollows. She thought back to the obscene defilement of his back that she'd witnessed less than a week ago in the white marble bathroom at the Hall. The sight of those deep wheals on his skin had filled her with a pity and anger that she knew would prevent her from ever trusting Magus again. For she knew it had been Magus who'd overseen the cruelty. But at least the actual perpetrator had got his just desserts. Sylvie knew that Alwyn lay in the hospital wing at the Hall hovering somewhere between paralysis and death.

She smiled grimly at the thought, remembering the fuss his collapse had caused on the Solstice. Hazel, the young doctor who'd brought Sylvie and her mother to Stonewylde, had recently taken up residence on the estate. She'd rushed off the Village Green to Yul's cottage after his brothers and sisters had arrived breathless and distraught, gabbling that their father had thrown a fit. Sylvie had smothered a smile of triumph, guessing that Mother Heggy's cake had worked its dark magic. She'd had to retain her composure again later on, when Magus had shot her a look like thunder as he'd heard the news. She'd been close by when Hazel returned to the Green much later and sought out Magus to give him an update.

"You're positive it was a stroke?"

"No, not positive. I'll need to do more tests. But I believe so."

"It couldn't be anything more sinister?"

"In what way? I don't understand."

"I mean foul play. Deliberate."

"No, I doubt that very much. He presents the symptoms of a stroke victim. And he's grossly overweight, unfit and he'd been drinking heavily. If anyone's to blame, it's himself."

Magus mouth had tightened at this, and then looking up, he'd caught Sylvie's eye. His expression changed but she couldn't read his dark eyes other than to recognise his anger. Did he really suspect Yul had had a hand in his father's collapse? Sylvie hoped fervently that whatever Mother Heggy had put in the cake was undetectable.

However Magus was back in fine form by the evening and had been delighted when Sylvie and Miranda arrived at the Barn for the dance. The Village Green was lit with hundreds of tiny lanterns. They hung amongst the branches of the trees, strung on lines around the trestles set up for yet more feasting and drinking. Light poured from the Barn and the sound of lively music filled the warm evening air. Sylvie felt as if she were floating on a carpet of magic as she walked shyly next to her mother along the cobbled street leading to the centre of the Village. Her long hair hung like a silver veil around her bare shoulders. The dress twinkled as she moved, the silver moons and stars catching the light with every step.

"Perfect!" breathed Magus, emerging from the vast open entrance into the Barn. "It fits just as I'd imagined and you really are the most beautiful girl at Stonewylde. I knew you'd do justice to such a dress."

Sylvie had stood awkwardly whilst her mother remained silent. His gaze was warm and approving and she prickled with embarrassment as his eyes swept her from head to toe.

Miranda prodded her sharply.

"Sylvie!" she hissed. "Where are your manners?"

"Oh! Thank you, Magus, thank you so much. I'm sorry – it's so special I don't know what to say. I feel overwhelmed."

"A moongazy dress for a moongazy girl," he murmured, leading them across the grass to get a drink. "Happy Birthday, Sylvie. I will expect at least one dance with you tonight. And you too, of course, Miranda."

The dress had proved to be a mixed blessing, for it had aroused a good deal of attention. The Villagers gawped openly, their smiles full of admiration for the sparkling girl from the Hall. Several of the younger children had been awestruck enough to forget protocol and actually stroke the shimmering material and Sylvie's silky hair. She felt too the approbation of many of the Hallfolk boys who seemed unable to take their eyes off her throughout the evening. But Holly and her gaggle of friends were another matter, and Sylvie felt their envy like a hail of arrows. The one person whose approval she sought was nowhere to be seen. Sylvie spent the first part of the evening trying surreptitiously to locate him. As she endured dance after hot dance with an endless stream of sweaty partners, her eyes constantly scanned the crowds.

Eventually she managed to leave the revelry and escape outside into the comparative coolness of the Midsummer Night air. Even though it was late, the sky still retained daylight on this, the shortest night of the year. The sun seemed to have barely dipped below the horizon and the stars struggled to be noticed in the cerulean sky. The fairy lights all around in the encircling trees gave the Green an atmosphere of enchantment. Sylvie's heart jumped as she sensed a movement behind and felt a light touch on her hair. She smelt Yul's unique scent and her stomach melted with excitement. He stood close, barely touching, but all her senses jangled. She felt him stoop and whisper into her hair.

"I've been waiting all evening for you to come outside, Sylvie. And it was worth it. You've fallen out of the sky, a beautiful flying star that came to earth and landed at my feet."

She smiled at this poetry, her heart thudding. She felt his

breath on the back of her neck and shuddered as he gently ran his fingers down the sides of her bare arms.

"You're so lovely, Sylvie. Your dress ... it's full of moonlight and magic. You must wear it when you dance at the Moon Fullness."

She nodded and turned around to face him, gazing into his deep grey eyes. She longed to stroke his face – or better still, to fling her arms around him and bury her face in his chest. But there were far too many people milling around the Green. She read the same longing in his eyes as he lifted a strand of her hair and felt the silkiness between his fingers.

"Come with me, Sylvie. Come with me under the yew tree where we were last night. We have unfinished business there, you and me. I want to kiss you again ..."

"You know we can't, Yul," she said softly. "Last night I made a promise to Magus that we'd stay apart. We must wait until all the fuss has died down. We can't risk anything that'll make him angry with you again."

He groaned and looked away.

"I can't stand it, Sylvie. How can we stay apart? I think of you all the time, every second of the day and night. All I want is to be with you. It's unbearable knowing you're nearby but not being able to even talk properly."

"I know, but maybe ..."

She stopped abruptly as the unmistakable silhouette of Magus appeared in the light flooding out from the Barn.

"He's looking for me, I'm sure – checking up that we're not together. I'd better go back inside. Maybe I'll see you at the beach? Everyone seems to go there in the afternoons."

He shook his head sadly.

"No, he's ordered me to report to the Hall every day for extra work, the bastard! But soon, Sylvie. Next week at the Moon Fullness I'll be waiting for you in the woods and we'll go up to Hare Stone together. You can dance and ..."

"I'll be there, I promise."

She turned away reluctantly and made her way back towards the Barn, where Magus stood washed in light. His eyes narrowed as she drew closer and he reached to grasp her arm.

"I thought we had an agreement, Sylvie? Stay away from him and so will I. Surely you haven't forgotten the consequences if you disobey. Must I remind you? Or him?"

"No, Magus," she said quickly. "Not at all."

"Good. Because you're far too special for a lout like him."

His fingers released their grip and stroked her arm idly.

"You really are absolutely stunning in that dress, Sylvie. Now come back inside and dance with me again. I think we make rather a striking couple."

Sylvie gazed out to sea but Holly and July were making so much noise over on the distant rock that she found it impossible to daydream. With a sigh she stood up.

"Coming for a swim, Dawn?"

They went in together and Sylvie gasped as the icy water lapped around her shins. Dawn laughed at her dismay.

"Freezing, isn't it? And it's warmer here in the lagoon than the open sea. But it's only June, remember. By Lammas in August it's lovely and warm. Come on – plunge in and swim fast. It's the only way to warm up."

Soon Sylvie's skin was tingling as they swam the distance to the rock. She was reluctant to reach it, dreading any confrontation with Holly today. It had been bad enough the night before, trying to avoid her gang and their snide remarks about her fairytale dress. But the girl with the bobbed hair and pretty feline features noticed them and called out.

"Hi there! Come and join us on the rock! It's so hot up here."

Dawn swam towards the smaller rocks where it was possible to climb up onto the natural platform. Unwillingly Sylvie followed. It would cause more trouble if she didn't.

As they sat dripping onto the warm stone, hair in a wet tangle, Sylvie kept quiet. Maybe today Holly would call a truce to her unpleasantness. Sylvie hugged her knees, feeling self-conscious in front of so many people. She was pleased that Buzz was away on holiday with his mother until Lammas. She could just imagine the scene if he were here now, giving her unwanted attention whilst Holly looked on in jealousy. Holly messed about with July, Wren and Fennel and his gang, diving into the sea and ducking each other. Sylvie kept her eyes averted from their antics. She looked instead at Rainbow, who was uncharacteristically quiet today. The younger girl was basking on the rock, her sea-blue eyes faraway. She wore a bikini which shone like silver scales in the bright sunlight, with a turquoise and silver sarong wrapped loosely around her waist. Although only thirteen, she had a lovely figure, her skin already tanned to a soft apricot. Her hair was darker blond than most Hallfolk's, the heavy waves glinting with natural highlights. She'd be stunning when she was older, Sylvie thought. Curled on the rock, her hair fanned out to dry, Rainbow stared dreamily up at the sky. Then she glanced across suddenly and caught Sylvie's gaze.

"Why are you staring at me, Sylvie? What is it?"

"Nothing. I was just thinking that you look like a mermaid."

Rainbow burst out laughing at this.

"Do I really? How nice! I love mermaids."

Wren overheard the conversation and flung herself wetly next to Rainbow.

"A mermaid? They lure men away from their homes and into the depths of the watery underworld."

Rainbow laughed again.

"Well I won't be doing any of that today. None of the boys here are worth the effort."

She slipped off the silky sarong and dived gracefully into the lagoon, her silver scales sparkling in the sunlight. Sylvie shivered, and not just from the drops of water that splashed onto her hot skin. There was something about Rainbow – a kind of sinuous, calculated perfection – that disturbed her more than Holly's blatant antagonism and bullying. She thought again of Yul, trying to conjure him up in her mind. She could imagine him here, brown and lithe, putting all the pale Hallfolk boys in the shade. How he must be rejoicing today, free at last from his father's reign of tyranny.

Whilst Sylvie and the Hallfolk youngsters swam and sunbathed, Yul continued with the seemingly endless chores that Martin had lined up for him. After the pans in the scullery had been dealt with to Marigold's satisfaction, Yul was sent across to the stables. Tom was pleased to see him and smiled his welcome at the tousle-haired boy.

"I were going to clap you on the back, son, but I weren't sure if 'twas still painful."

Yul looked up at the old ostler sharply, his grin fading.

"So you know about what happened to me?"

"Aye," he muttered, "I do. I heard every single damn stroke, every crack of that whip. Magus got me to rig up the byre with that electric light afore he came and got you. I was outside while it all happened, battling with myself what to do for the best. I ended up doing nothing. I been wanting to say to you ever since how bad I feel about it."

"No need for you to feel bad, sir. It wasn't your fault."

"Well, it was partly, I'm sorry to say. 'Twas me as told Magus about you riding Nightwing that day, when the gentleman was thrown and hurt hisself. Not to get you into trouble, you understand. I thought the master'd reward you. You showed great courage riding that horse back to get help quick. Anyhow, I feel bad that I told Magus, and for not coming to help you in your suffering."

"But you couldn't have, not without disobeying Magus."

"Aye, well maybe I should have done. Starving you like that was downright cruelty. 'Tis not something I'd have believed of Magus, treating a Villager so bad. And as for that Alwyn ... I tell you, if that man hadn't been taken sick, I'd have gone for him myself. All that bragging and boasting about what he done to you, every night down the pub."

Tom shook his grizzled head sadly.

"No, I won't forgive myself for not helping you. I could've got some food to you or something. Truth is, I was scared, and I'm ashamed of that."

"I never expected any help. Magus can't be disobeyed."

"Aye, but if you're ever in any trouble, you come to me, Yul. What the master did to you weren't right and I feel I owe you. I won't rest easy till I've made it up to you somehow."

Yul looked at Tom speculatively and nodded.

"Thank you, sir. I'll remember that."

"So why are you here now, lad? You should be down the Village enjoying the holiday with all them other young folk, not up here working. What have you done this time?"

Yul shrugged, and Tom remembered the boy doing the same last time he was sent here as a punishment, way back in March

"Like that is it, son? Right, well you'll have to put your back into it. We're rushed off our feet with all them Hallfolk visitors wanting to ride every day. Half the daft buggers don't know one end of a horse from t'other."

He tossed Yul a pitchfork and the work began. By sunset Yul was exhausted, although he decided he'd much rather be in the stables with the horses than up in the confines of the Hall itself. The place made him uneasy, and he hated dealing with the visiting Hallfolk. He resented being treated as a servant. How Harold put up with it he couldn't imagine.

It was late that evening when Martin finally released Yul from his duties, with an admonishment to make sure he was back good and early the next morning. He trudged back to the cottage wearily, ignoring the sounds of fun and merriment that drifted down the lane from the Village Green and Great Barn. The festivities would last all week, but Yul was far too tired to get washed and changed and go down to join in. All the other Villagers who had to work during the holiday were given a rota, so they could at least take part in some of the fun. But Yul knew Magus wanted him kept hard at it all week long until it was time to return to his work in the woods with Old Greenbough. Yul opened the door to his cottage and looked around. The place was as clean and tidy as ever, and his family nowhere to be seen. They must all be in the Barn, Yul decided. He breathed deeply, realising that the feeling of dread he usually experienced when returning home had completely disappeared. Except for one detail.

His mouth a thin line of bitterness, Yul went over to the door and tugged the hateful strap off its hook. Next to it, hanging on a new nail, was the whip. Coiled like a malignant snake, it hung dark against the whitewashed wall. The plaited leather handle was thick and solid, the tail long and viciously thin. Shuddering as he forced himself to touch it, Yul pulled the whip off the wall and took both instruments of punishment outside to the chopping block. Taking a deep breath, he raised the axe above his head and swung it down hard. It felt good as the sharp blade sliced through the leather. He raised the axe again and again, overcome by a sudden destructive frenzy as the hated objects of subjugation were chopped into ever smaller pieces. The memories swarmed in his head like angry wasps, the years of pain and humiliation reaching back as far as he could remember. The strange light in Alwyn's eye as he went on and on with the punishment; he'd never forget that particular look as long as he lived. As the leather which had bitten so mercilessly into the soft skin of his back became now a jumble of tiny pieces on the block, Yul found himself screaming with fury. He dropped the axe, his body heaving. Tears streamed down his flushed face as the rage overwhelmed him. He sank to the ground. Kneeling in the dust, he cried into his hands. Harsh sobs shook him, dragged out from the dark place where he'd locked them away. All those years of injustice and fear were released. Never again would he have to face Alwyn. A lifetime of abuse had finally come to an end.

Later and a little calmer, he wandered down the long back garden looking at the masses of fruit and vegetables growing, and the dripping combs inside the bee hives. Maizie tended their produce well. He thought of how much happier her life would be now, free from Alwyn and his cruel domination of the family. He wasn't the only one who'd benefit from Mother Heggy's magic. Yul stooped and picked a few luscious strawberries, savouring the explosion of sweetness in his mouth. He thought instantly of Sylvie and felt the familiar tugging at his heart. She'd probably be in the Village right now along with everyone else at Stonewylde, and he longed with every cell in his body to go and find her. To take her in his arms and smell her, feel her silky hair and smooth skin, drink her beauty with his eyes. And more than anything else in the world, he wanted to kiss her again. He was in a fever for her since their first kiss only two nights ago under the yew tree. But the Village was crawling with Hallfolk and Magus was everywhere. Yul must not risk angering him at any cost.

Yul stormed out of the garden and down the lane, tears welling up again in a hot, angry flow. He loved Sylvie but how would they ever find a chance to be together? Now he must work every day at the Hall, he wouldn't even be able to get a glimpse of her during the holiday that everyone else was enjoying. How could Magus do this to him? Hadn't he suffered enough? Darkness had fallen and Yul headed down to the river and sat on the grassy bank, watching the sparkling water as it flowed to the sea. He should have expected this. Had he really thought he'd get away with leaving the quarry with Sylvie? Or climbing onto the Altar Stone so defiantly and taking the Earth Magic from Magus? He tried to swallow his disappointment at losing the holiday he needed so badly, and with it his only chance of seeing Sylvie.

The willows whispered all around him, offering their sympathy and comfort. The waxing moon shone brightly again, fuller than last night. Everything gleamed in the moonlight. By the silver reeds of the river bank, fish came up to the surface, their mouths circles as they gulped at the gnats just above the water. There was a movement upstream. Yul saw the glossy head of an otter, its blunt skull clear against the water as it headed in a V shaped ripple towards the fish. It dived smoothly, long body sinuous and slick in the moonlit water, and disappeared. Yul stood up and gazed at the stars, the noise and merriment from the Village seeming very distant. He felt, as ever, alone and on the outside. The only one who'd broken through his isolation to touch his soul was forbidden to him. Alwyn might have fallen, but happiness seemed no closer.

A week later Miranda had just finished teaching her class when Magus walked into the schoolroom.

"Are you free for a while?"

"Yes!" Miranda said breathlessly, shoving her things into a pile and standing expectantly. He smiled and took her arm, leading her out through the French windows and onto the stone terrace outside. They stood and looked over the lawns, watching the swallows soaring and swooping up in the blue skies. She leant against him and he put an arm around her, holding her close. She closed her eyes in bliss, unaware that Magus was surreptitiously looking at his watch on the other wrist. A group of children ran onto the lawn with a ball, breaking the silence.

"Let's go into the formal garden," he suggested. "We can be more private."

She nodded eagerly. As they strolled around the raked gravel paths, Magus took her hand.

"Did you enjoy the Midsummer Holiday?"

"Oh yes, it was lovely."

"And still no sign of your period?"

She looked up at him quickly.

"No. I'm never usually late. I really think I am pregnant."

"That's wonderful, Miranda. Our young doctor can do a pregnancy test, if you like."

"Yes, I'd like to know for sure. I'm a little scared and worried, and …"

He stopped and turned her to face him, tilting her chin so she had no choice but to look straight into his dark eyes.

"Why? Do you think I won't take care of you? You know how it is at Stonewylde, Miranda. Babies are considered a blessing, something to celebrate."

She tried to look away.

"What?"

"It's just … what about us? Our relationship? I don't know where I stand with you. I know you like me and when we're together it's wonderful. But then you don't come near me for days on end, and …"

"Oh Miranda," he sighed, "you must understand - I can't have normal relationships like other people. I'm the magus here and you know now what that means. I have to look after everyone in the community and there are hundreds of people here. I can't commit myself to one person - it wouldn't be fair. I'm afraid that's how it is. But we can be together sometimes. And I promise that when we are, I'm all yours. This baby will be loved and wanted. Of course you could terminate the pregnancy ..."

"Oh no! I want to have your baby," she said. "As long as I know you care for me, I'll just have to accept that I must share you with the rest of the community. I suppose I have no other option really. But I am special to you, aren't I?"

He hugged her, taking the opportunity to check the time again, and chuckled.

"Of course you are. Very special. So how is Sylvie taking the news that you might be expecting a baby? She obviously knows it's mine?"

"Oh yes. She seems fine about it. Not that bothered at all. She's quite distracted at the moment."

They'd come to one of the alcoves in the clipped hedging and Magus took her in to sit on the wooden seat. He put his arm around her, his long fingers brushing her breast idly. She closed her eyes and sighed.

"Are you keeping a close watch on her to make sure she doesn't mix with that boy?"

"Yes I am, and she hasn't."

"Mmn. I still want her watched. I'm going away in a few days' time. You must ensure they stay apart while I'm gone."

"How long for? Where are you going?"

"Just business. And for less than a month."

"A month?" she squeaked.

"I have a company in London to run, remember. But I'll be popping back now and again. You must promise me you'll watch Sylvie closely and keep her well away from Yul."

"Of course, although I think you're worrying needlessly."

"Let's hope so. The other thing I need to talk to you about is the full moon business. Tell me, has she always been affected by it?"

Miranda shrugged, wanting to talk about the baby and their relationship, not Sylvie and her moon madness.

"More or less. But it was becoming worse as she got older.

25

I didn't realize it was happening here. I thought it was all part of her illness in London and that she'd got over it. I thought she was fine here."

"Well she clearly isn't, and I can't have her wandering around Stonewylde in the dark meeting up with unsuitable boys in the woods. Anything could happen, couldn't it? So tonight I'd like to keep an eye on her myself."

"Yes, of course, Magus. It's a full moon tonight then?"

"Yes, and I want you to let her go. In fact, come up to the Hall for supper and stay here till after the moon rise. Leave her on her own in the cottage. I promise I won't let her come to any harm. I just need to see how she behaves, what she does. I might be able to help her, of course, like I did with her other illnesses. And I also want to see whether she'll try to meet the boy in secret behind our backs, despite her promises."

He stood up briskly.

"I must be off. That's settled then, about tonight? I'll bring her home when it's over. You're not to worry, Miranda. I'll look after her."

"Of course, Magus," she said trustingly.

"Sylvie will always be safe with me," he said softly, leading her back up the garden path.

All day the tension rose within her until by early evening Sylvie thought she'd explode with it. She felt the familiar tingling inside; the increasing sense of being trapped indoors and needing to get outside and up somewhere high. She was also excited at the prospect of seeing Yul alone. It had been so long since they'd been together. She was relieved when, at six o'clock, Miranda announced she was leaving for the Hall and would be there for the whole evening.

"Are you coming too, darling?" Miranda asked innocently.

"No, I'm not hungry. I'll have a sandwich and stay here."

"Sure you'll be alright?"

"Yes!"

"You know it's the full moon tonight?"

"Do you really think I'd be unaware of that?"

"No need to be rude, Sylvie. I want to make sure you understand you're not to go out gallivanting with that boy."

"I know."

"Magus wanted me to remind you that you're forbidden to see each other."

"That man makes me sick! Who does he think he is - dictating who I can see and who I can't!"

"Don't be so rude! And anyway, I'm your mother and *I'm* telling you not to see Yul. You're only just fifteen and he's not suitable company for you - running around the woods and getting up to goodness knows what. It's not just Magus telling you, it's me too. I have every right to stop you seeing that boy."

Sylvie glared sullenly at her mother, hating her at that moment. She was so unfair, judging Yul only by what Magus had told her. The Miranda from the old days would have made up her own mind. And would have liked Yul.

"Actually, I'm quite surprised you're not off gallivanting yourself up at that horrible rock on the cliff with your picnics and incense. You're such a hypocrite, Mum! All *I* want to do is watch the moon rise in the company of someone I like. *You're* the one going off having sex with a man you barely know and getting yourself pregnant."

"How dare you, Sylvie! You make it sound sordid."

"Well it is sordid!"

"No it's not! Magus cares for me and he's really pleased there might be a baby. I have a special relationship with him. He told me so today in fact. Anyway, we don't know yet for sure that I'm pregnant."

"So why isn't he seeing you tonight if he cares for you so much? What happened to the moonlight picnics in the tent? The rugs and cushions on the rock? Maybe he doesn't want you so much now he's got you pregnant."

Miranda looked at her coldly, picking up a jacket for later on.

"Magus has business to attend to tonight so he won't be free to see me. I'll speak to you tomorrow about this rudeness, when you've calmed down. I won't have you talking like this,

Sylvie. You must accept Magus and stop being so hostile. You liked him when we first came here and I don't see why you've changed your opinion of him. If I'm going to be the mother of his baby he'll be a major part of our lives and you'll just have to get used to it. Have a nice evening, Sylvie, and remember to stay away from that boy. Or there'll be serious consequences."

"Good riddance!" snapped Sylvie as the door closed behind her mother. But she cheered up at the news that Magus was busy for the evening. She could enjoy Yul's company without fear of being found out. She decided to get ready now and change into the beautiful moongazy dress as Yul had suggested. She wanted to look lovely for him.

By eight o'clock Sylvie was ready. She felt a sharp thrill of excitement deep inside that was nothing to do with the lunar cycle. Half an hour later she could barely sit down. She'd eaten nothing, food being the last thing on her mind. She paced the room, her feet padding up and down the floor boards, the gauzy grey and silver dress floating out around her in soft webs. It was a warm evening, the sky almost clear but for a few small clouds melting to gold as the sun began its descent. Sylvie was frantic to get outside. Finally, she could stand it no longer. She opened the front door and stepped into the evening, breathing in the balmy golden air.

*Soon I shall dance with the hares and the magic will sparkle in me like quicksilver. I shall be with Yul, the darkness to my brightness, the earth magic and moon magic joined as one.*

She skipped down to the gate, her bare feet hardly touching the ground. Her hair flowed around her bare arms and shoulders like a veil of silvery-white silk. She fumbled with the gate and then she was free, speeding up the path towards the woods. But something loomed ahead blocking her way; a tall shape that grabbed her by the arms, smiling grimly into her face as she tried to wriggle away.

"Going somewhere, Sylvie?" asked Magus.

# CHAPTER TWO

Yul sat under a tree listening to the soft call of wood pigeons, the peace of the golden evening like a mantle around him. He thrilled with anticipation. She'd be here soon, dancing up the path on light feet, hair rippling about her. He smiled to himself and felt a knot of excitement in the pit of his stomach. It seemed ages since they'd been alone together properly; not since the eve of the Summer Solstice under the yew tree. He wondered if their new intimacy would make tonight any different from the other Moon Fullnesses they'd spent together. Maybe afterwards, when she'd danced and sung and the desperation had calmed, they'd be able to talk. He wanted so much to hold her close and perhaps even kiss her again. He'd spent the past week dreaming about kissing her. He closed his eyes at the thought of it and sighed deeply. Not long now.

Sylvie tried to free herself from the iron grip, her hair flying about her face as she pulled and wriggled.

"Not so fast, Sylvie! I think you've forgotten our deal, haven't you? You're off to the woods to meet up with a certain young man whom you've been forbidden to see, aren't you?"

"Set me free! I must go!"

"Oh no you don't! You're staying with me, young lady."

"No, no, I cannot stay here! I must go; I must go up there now! You let me go, you let me go …"

Magus picked her up bodily and clamped a hand over her mouth as she struggled and shrieked. He hauled her back to the gate and in through the open front door of the cottage, kicking it shut behind him, and dumped her on the sofa. She sprang up immediately so he pushed her down and sat next to her. He turned to face her, holding her wrists in a manacle-like grip.

"Stop it! Stop it, Sylvie and listen to me!"

Still she struggled, trying to stand and escape his grasp.

"Sit down!" he shouted, thinking she'd damage her wrists if she carried on like this. "Sylvie, can you hear me? If you don't calm down now I'll have to slap you. *SYLVIE!*"

But she didn't seem to hear him, kicking out and shaking her head violently from side to side. She began to shout but the words didn't make sense. She was clearly hysterical. He released one of her wrists and slapped her sharply round the face. Her head snapped to the side, hair flying, and she went limp and pliant. She slumped down into a huddle, crying piteously.

"Sylvie, stop it. There's no need to cry. It didn't hurt that much."

He put an arm around her and she flopped against him, all the fight knocked out of her. A strange little sobbing noise came from deep within her but after a moment she started again.

"Please, please let me go. She is coming, she is rising. I must be up there to greet her, to honour her. Please let me go. I beg you. Please, please ..."

"Alright! We'll go outside and you can show me what you do. Come on then."

She leapt up, her eyes wild, and he held on to her hand tightly. They went up the garden path, but at the gate when she tried to turn towards the woods, he pulled her round and bundled her in the other direction.

"The woods, the woods, my Yul ..."

"Oh no, Sylvie! We're not going anywhere near him. I'm going to show you somewhere far better for moongazing."

In the woods, Yul's excitement had turned to anxiety. It was almost time for the rising. The sun had already set. Where was she? He knew she'd come if she could, so something must have happened. Had they locked her up? Was someone with her preventing her from leaving the cottage? He decided to go and have a look for himself. The light was fading amongst the trees as he moved silently along the path, eyes scanning and ears pricked, ready to melt into the shadows if Magus or anyone else appeared. But nobody did, and at the cottage no lights were on. He crept in through the wide open front door, hoping he wasn't walking into a trap. It was soon obvious that the place was empty. Now what should he do? Frowning, he left and started down the lane away from the woods, unsure of where to look next.

Sylvie skipped along, still tethered to Magus' hand but tugging him forward.

*She is coming, she is rising! I can feel her. Quick, quick, quick! I must be ready to dance for her. I need wings like an angel. I need to fly. Quick!*

Magus was mystified by the sounds she made, which were like speech but didn't make any sense. She was desperate, rigid with tension and quivering with suppressed energy. She tried to pull him into a run, clearly frantic to arrive at their destination. As they began to climb the path leading to the cliff top Magus held on to her tightly. The drop was treacherous in places and he didn't want her running ahead.

*Let me go, let me go! She is here, she has come in her beauty - the Triple Goddess! I must dance and sing and feel her quicksilver magic. She is giving and I am not there to take her gift. Let me go!*

With a sudden twist she freed her hand from his and flew up the path. Her bare feet skimmed the stony surface, her long gauze skirts brushing the grasses and flowers at the side. He called after her but in vain. She was so fast, haring ahead until she reached the top of the cliff. He was fit and strong but couldn't keep up with her. When he reached the top a few minutes later she was already dancing. She spiralled joyfully, springing across the grass with pointed bare feet, arms outstretched to the heavens. Magus stood at the head of the path, out of breath from the rapid climb and now breathless with wonder. The great moon had risen, a glowing orb that hung brightly just above the sea. And Sylvie glowed too with a strange silvery light which arced around her in shining threads, lacing her body and making her sparkle.

Yul had reached the Hall. Keeping to the shadows, he skirted the main building trying to see inside without being seen himself. Maybe Magus and her mother had dragged Sylvie up here and shut her in one of the rooms. He could see Hallfolk sitting around on big sofas watching a large coloured screen. The lighting was different here from the candlelight he was used to, for the Hallfolk used electricity from the wind-farm. The harsh light reminded him of the one in the byre, its bright glare making him shudder. He crept around the walls looking into windows. In other rooms people sat talking and reading. He saw servants working in the kitchen, washing up and preparing more food for the next day. He found Marigold sitting in a small room talking to Martin, and stepped back quickly from the lighted window in case they saw him. But there was no sign of Sylvie or Magus. His hopes soared at one point when he spotted Miranda curled up in a chair with a book on her lap. But Sylvie wasn't there. So where could she be? What had Magus done with her? If she was trapped upstairs in the Hall he'd never find her.

Magus walked across the grass to the great stone, the one where he'd celebrated the Moon Fullness with Miranda under a tent in the rain. This was the place where he liked to honour the Moon Goddess every month with a different woman from the Hall or Village. He sat on the disc of rock and watched the incredible sight before him as Sylvie danced, arms upraised like wings. The silvery light coursed around her body and then disappeared down into the earth, shooting off her feet as she leapt and skipped. She sang too, a weird unearthly sound. Her face was turned to the great golden moon as it climbed steadily, turning more silvery the higher it rose. Magus watched in fascination, trying to understand where the silver threads of light came from and what they could be. He could see them earthing, like lightning in a storm. He wondered if they were some sort of electrical or magnetic energy generated by the moon. Sylvie crackled with the force; even her hair, normally so silky, stood out thick and stiff with strange static.

32

He felt a churning in his stomach as he watched her; a sharp excitement as if on the verge of a special discovery.

Sylvie was oblivious to everything other than her dancing. Magus watched for what seemed like ages; he couldn't tell exactly for his watch had stopped. He thought she must surely be exhausted by now; she'd danced energetically for a long time. He noticed she was beginning to slow down and called to her. She appeared to listen and stepped delicately on tip-toe over to where he sat on the white stone. Her dress glinted in the bright moonlight, the silver embroidery catching the moonbeams.

"Hello, Sylvie," he murmured. "That was an amazing dance. Is this what you usually do with Yul?"

But she ignored him as if she hadn't heard him at all. He could see in the moonlight that her eyes were blank. They were strange under normal circumstances; a pale grey with a darker grey round the edge of the irises. But now they were like full moons themselves; silvery and reflective, seeing nothing, but beaming out moonlight. In one graceful leap she sprang onto the great stone. As she landed she froze, her fingers outspread in shock. She uttered a piercing cry. The silver filigree threads still laced her pale limbs, but now they poured downwards into the rock in a cascade of energy. Magus felt it with a jolt. The feeling was similar to that jolt he'd experienced on the Altar Stone at the recent Solstice sunrise. That surge had been so powerful and unexpected it had made him drop the torch. Now he thrilled as the force of the silver energy pulsed up through the stone into his body, filling him with tingling euphoria.

He looked up at Sylvie in awe. She remained frozen, her face anguished and her song silenced. Her eyes rolled towards him and focussed. She gazed at him in sorrow as if begging for help. The rock around her feet glowed slightly; Magus leaned over to feel it but couldn't get his hand close enough. The energy field was very powerful, like the repelling power of two identical magnetic poles being forced together. Yet his hand, spread above the glowing rock, was absorbing the energy. Magus could feel it coursing into his body, a strange icy sensation that tingled and burned. He felt strong, powerful. He laughed with delight, ignoring Sylvie's beseeching eyes. This was in some ways even better than the energy he received on the Altar Stone during the festivals. That was a brief, albeit powerful, flash of irradiation. But this moon magic went on and on, pouring down through her body and streaming up from the white stone. He stretched out flat on the rock as close as he could get to the force field around Sylvie, feeling the energy flow into every part of him. He heard a small sound. Her lips were moving.

"Please! Help me get off ..."

"Oh no, Sylvie! I don't know what's going on here but we're staying put. You're the moondancer. You keep at it, my moongazy girl. I'll just lie back and enjoy it."

He closed his eyes and concentrated on the powerful sensations flooding through him.

It occurred to Yul that Magus might have followed Sylvie up to the Hare Stone. He couldn't understand how, for he'd been in the woods waiting and would have seen them. But he had to check. If she was up there with Magus, who knows what might happen. He hated the thought of Magus seeing her moongazy and defenceless. So he ran at full speed from the Hall, into the woods and up the hill through the boulders to Hare Stone. He saw immediately that they weren't there. The hares raced around the stone and the barn owl sat on top of it. But there was no girl with silver hair dancing like a bright fairy, and no dark-eyed man either.

He flung himself down on the grass in disappointment, chest heaving and lungs burning. He'd run a couple of miles mostly uphill, and to no avail. Where on earth were they? And then the dreadful thought struck him like a thunderbolt. He cursed himself for not thinking of it earlier. Mooncliffe! That was where Magus always went for the Moon Fullness. He'd imagined Sylvie leading him, but it would of course have been the other way round. Yul didn't think Magus would harm her. She was still a child and he'd always treated her so gently. But nevertheless he started to panic, knowing well the significance of that round disc of stone. Leaping to his feet he raced back down the hill again, through the dark woods, past her cottage, and onto the long path that led up to Mooncliffe. The moon was now high and bright in the sky, a silver coin flecked with tiny grey clouds. If anything bad was going to happen at Mooncliffe, it would by now have done so. But that didn't stop him running as fast as he could to find her.

It was late and Miranda had been waiting at the cottage for some time. She was worried about Sylvie. And also about Magus. She didn't like the thought of them being alone together. She knew it was stupid to be jealous of her own daughter, but she had no control over it. She paced up and down the small cottage in a fret of impatience and growing anxiety. She should have asked to join Magus in keeping an eye on her daughter, not leave them alone together like this. Sylvie was her responsibility after all. What on earth could they be doing all this time?

Sylvie stood in exactly the same position on the great stone as if rooted. The glowing area of rock had spread. Her eyes were now shut, her face still agonised. Her outspread fingers had drooped and her arms hung by her sides. She stood like a closed-eyed carving in the moonlight, a strange statue with silver threads travelling down her body and into the rock at her feet. Magus still lay spread-eagled as close as he could bear. His eyes too were shut, but the expression on his face was one of bliss.

"Please, Magus, please let me go," Sylvie whispered. She was aware of what was happening but couldn't move at all. She felt exhausted, drained of everything. Her legs trembled and were barely able to support her. Magus ignored her pleas. He'd worked out that somehow her body was channelling energy from the full moon into the stone. Just like at the Altar Stone in the Stone Circle, he was able to soak it up from the rock itself. He wasn't sure if the energy would remain in the stone once she'd got down. He was loath to let her go quite yet. Another few minutes should do it.

She crumpled almost in slow motion onto the pale rock,

her legs finally giving way. Reluctantly Magus sat up and stretched, glancing at the girl lying next to him. He felt as if he could perform any feat in the world. He jumped to the ground and leaning over, scooped Sylvie up in his arms. She was as light as a feather and he felt so strong, almost superhuman. Her hair hung over his arm in a long silver swathe, the static gone. Her arms and legs gleamed in the moonlight and she was cool to the touch. Her beautiful dress shimmered, the silver moons and stars reflecting the real moonlight. He stood on the cliff top, a tall figure gazing at her as she lay motionless in his arms. Her eyes were closed and she seemed to be asleep. A moongazy girl indeed, he thought tenderly as he looked down into her silvered face.

Yul, his heart pounding with exertion, had arrived just in time to see Sylvie fall. He thought at first that she was alone on the great stone, but then made out the dark figure of Magus lying there. Was the man unconscious? But at that point he moved and effortlessly picked Sylvie up, then stood staring at her. Yul's instincts screamed to run over and make sure she was alright, but he didn't dare do anything to attract Magus' attention. Instead he crouched down in the tall bracken, his legs pulsing from the punishing run. He was only just in time, because Magus turned and began to walk towards him and the path leading down the cliff. It was a striking sight – the tall, powerful man, blond hair gleaming in the bright moonlight, carrying Sylvie's limp body. She lay like a wounded bird in his arms. They brushed past where Yul hid; he steeled himself not to leap up and challenge Magus. He waited until they were well down the path before moving. Magus was obviously taking her home, whatever had happened up here now finished.

When he was sure it was safe Yul went over to the great stone and was shocked to see it glowing a ghostly blue-silver, luminous in the moonlight. He reached over to touch it and received the same jolt that Magus had experienced. Yul's eyes widened in surprise. Was this why Magus had been lying on the stone? The same reason that he himself went on the Altar

Stone at sunrise and sunset? He climbed up onto the great Mooncliffe disc and lay down. He too felt the energy soaking into him and closed his eyes. All around him the stars twinkled like bright diamonds in the warm June night, the only sounds the distant hooting of owls and barking of foxes.

Magus tapped the front door of the cottage with his boot. It was opened immediately by Miranda, her face twisted with concern.

"Thank goodness! I've been so worried! Magus, what's happened? Is she alright?"

"She's fine, just a little tired. I'll take her straight up to her bed."

He climbed the narrow stairs and laid Sylvie down. She opened her eyes drowsily as her head hit the pillow, but was asleep again almost instantly.

"You must get her out of that dress," Magus said to Miranda, who'd followed him up. "She'll spoil it if she sleeps in it, and it cost a fortune."

"I'm sorry, I didn't know she intended to wear it tonight."

"No matter. She'll probably be very tired tomorrow so let her miss school. Take the day off yourself so you can look after her. She'll need to sleep."

"But what happened? Did she meet that boy? Why is she so exhausted?"

"She's been cavorting about in the moonlight, that's all, although it did go on for quite some time. And no, she didn't meet him. But she was on her way to the woods, presumably to find him. Naturally I stopped her. She'll need to be guarded at the next full moon to protect her from him. They'd obviously arranged to meet despite all my instructions to the contrary."

They went downstairs and Magus headed straight for the door. It was the Moon Fullness and he had other things to do before he could eventually go to his bed. At the door he stopped and kissed Miranda. She melted into his arms, desperately hoping to keep him there. Sylvie's words earlier in the day played through her head. Maybe he didn't want her any more. He let her fawn over him for a few minutes, wanting to make sure that Sylvie stayed put in bed. Then he extricated himself from Miranda's embrace.

"Listen, Miranda. I think Sylvie has some special sort of … illness, sensitivity, call it what you will. I believe I can help her but it'll take time," he said. "It's linked to the full moon, that's for sure."

"But I thought she was getting over her illnesses. I thought she'd been healed at Stonewylde."

"Yes she has, but this is different – lunacy in the true sense of the word. It's going to take me some time to cure her and I want her where I can keep watch on her. And of course I want to have you close too. So when I come back from my business trip, you are both to move in to the Hall."

Miranda was delighted at this and kissed him again, hugging him tightly. She could feel a difference in him. He was shimmering with energy, almost glowing with it. She felt such an attraction to him, as if he was pulling at her soul. All she wanted was to be with him and bask in his thrall. But he smiled and once more disentangled himself from her arms.

"So we'll be moving in with you?" she said excitedly, still trying to cling to him. "That'll be wonderful! Especially with the baby coming."

He frowned at her.

"No, I didn't mean move in with me. Not in my rooms. I'll have a suite made available for you and Sylvie, and the baby when it arrives. I've already told you how our relationship has to be and it doesn't entail us living together in that way. I'm sorry, Miranda. I thought you understood that."

She stared down at the floor, her excitement crushed.

"Of course. I thought … I thought maybe you'd changed your mind. You just said you wanted me close."

"Close, but not that close. I need to keep an eye on Sylvie and this moongaziness. She's not well and she's a danger to herself. You can't possibly manage her on your own. She needs protection and I want to help her. As the magus I feel it's my responsibility to take care of her when she's so clearly in need of guardianship. Now I'm sorry, but I really must go.

I have things to do. I'll be back later tomorrow to check she's alright. Goodnight, Miranda."

As he walked back to the Hall, Magus smiled to himself. What a successful night! And it wasn't over yet. He now had the key to the future of Stonewylde. He felt himself pulsing with power and energy, all thanks to Sylvie and her moongaziness. She was the channel for the moon magic and he could receive it every month through her. He could fill himself to the brim with her gift. The lack of Earth Magic at the Solstice no longer mattered. He now had an additional power source. He would be invincible.

He strode down the corridor and tapped on a door, entering at once.

"Are you ready?" he asked, his voice deep and inviting. "I'm all yours now. Sorry it's so much later than I said. There were unexpected developments with my earlier engagement. But I'm here now, and I'm sure you'll feel it was worth waiting for. It's a beautiful night out there. Let's go!"

The young doctor smiled and left the room with him, shaking with excitement as they went down the wide stairs to the entrance hall. Magus' eyes gleamed as he led her out through the great front door and into the moonlight. It was indeed a beautiful night.

"What on earth are you doing here? You're not allowed any contact with us!" said Miranda sharply. She glared at the dark haired boy standing on her door step in the bright morning sun. He wore the rough spun clothes and heavy leather boots of the Villager. He looked down guiltily, long curls falling over his face.

"I'm sorry to trouble you, ma'am," he mumbled. Then he looked up and she was struck by the beauty of his eyes; a deep, clear grey, long lashed and slightly slanted. He was a very good looking lad and she could quite understand why Sylvie found him attractive.

"If Magus knows you've been here ..." she said, shaking her head.

"I know. Please don't be angry. I was worried about

Sylvie. I just wanted to know if she's alright."

His eyes were beseeching and she had to steel herself to resist him. Magus had said he was manipulative and cunning.

"I don't see that Sylvie's welfare is any concern of yours," she snapped. "In fact, it was thanks to you last month that she was so ill. So if you don't mind …"

She started to shut the door but he took a step forward to stop her. She frowned at his hand holding her front door. It reminded her of Magus' hands; long fingered and square nailed.

"Let go! I'm warning you, Magus will hear about this."

"Please, ma'am, just tell me if she's alright. That's all I want to know. Then I'll go."

"She's fine. She's very tired and she's still asleep. But she's absolutely fine."

His relief was almost comical. He smiled and his whole face lit up.

"Oh thank you, ma'am!   When she wakes up please would you say that I asked after her? I won't bother you again and I'm sorry I did, but I had to know. Thank you. Blessings on you."

He smiled at her again and despite herself, she warmed to him slightly. He did seem a very sweet boy, although Magus had warned her to beware of his ability to charm.

"Just don't come here again or I will tell Magus."

She shut the door firmly and sighed. She hadn't strictly told the truth, for although Sylvie was tired and still asleep, there was a little more to it than that. The girl was totally exhausted, drained of every gram of energy. She was deathly pale with great dark rings under her eyes, and she'd been whimpering in her sleep. Miranda had tried to wake her and give her a drink, but she was limp and unresponsive. She hoped that Magus would call soon for she was worried. She'd never seen Sylvie like this after the full moon, however strangely she'd behaved at the time. Nor was it anything like the previous month when she'd had a fever after being out in the rain. This was almost more worrying as there seemed to be no good reason for her awful lethargy.

Magus had every intention of visiting to check on Sylvie, but at that moment was busy in his office at the Hall. A servant had just brought in a tray of coffee and pastries. Magus paced the large room, looking impatiently at his watch, now functional again. The office was in one of the wings at the rear of the Hall. It overlooked a beautiful sunken stone garden full of white flowers, their scent wafting in through the open windows. The room was lined with many books, some of them old and valuable, and several paintings. One side was devoted to a humming network of computers. Magus looked out of the French windows, not noticing the bright butterflies dancing in the white garden below. His fingers drummed edgily on the woodwork; he was full of restless energy. When the heavy oak door finally swung open behind him he spun round and exclaimed loudly at the sight of his brother.

"About time too, Clip! I thought we'd agreed to meet first thing this morning."

The thinner, wispy-haired brother ambled over to the old leather sofas and sank down in one, stretching out his long legs and laying his head wearily against the backrest.

"You sent me a message to come, Sol. I don't think I actually agreed to be here first thing. You know how I am the day after the Moon Fullness."

Magus sat down on the other sofa and poured coffee, watching as his older brother gulped it down. Clip had clearly been out all night and still wore his summer cloak, full of burrs and twigs. His blond hair was wild and his grey eyes faraway.

"Good journey? I assume that's what you've been doing all night."

"Extraordinary. I was at the dolmen up past the heath. Remember it?"

"Oh yes, I remember it," smiled Magus, recalling boyhood adventures at the strange place. The massive stones made a small chamber, with a roof formed by a huge flat stone. It was in this place of Neolithic construction that Clip often spent the nights of the Moon Fullness and festivals. Here he travelled on shamanic journeys with the help of an aromatic fire and various herbs and spices.

"You're looking full of yourself today, Sol. In fact, you're quite radiant with it. What's happened? I take it last night went well, with our little moongazy newcomer? You stopped her meeting up with the Village boy?"

Clip helped himself to a pastry and Magus joined him.

"I'm so damn hungry this morning," he said. "Yes, it was amazing. You won't believe what happened. You may have to help me. I'm off to London soon and we've got to get certain things in place before the next Moon Fullness."

As the two men wolfed down the plate of pastries and drained the coffee pot, Magus told Clip about his experience at Mooncliffe the night before and Sylvie's incredible ability to channel the full moon energy.

"It sounds as if the stone's acting like a kind of battery storing the power," said Clip thoughtfully.

"That's right! I went up there early this morning and the rock is still full of it. Not as strong as last night, of course, but still powerful. You must come up yourself and feel it."

"And you say that she couldn't get off once she was standing there?"

"No, it was strange. She danced around on the grass like some sort of weird bird, but once she'd jumped up on the stone she froze, almost as if she'd petrified. I could see that she wanted to get off, that it was ... uncomfortable, maybe even painful for her. But she was completely unable to move, let alone get down."

"And you forced her to stay up there? You're a sadistic bastard, Sol. Always have been, ever since you were a boy."

Magus smiled sardonically and raised his eyebrows.

"But I get results, don't I? I tell you, once you've experienced that moon magic you'll want more. I've never felt like this before, not even after the Solstice energy. I've been making plans this morning and I've had some good ideas."

"Just so long as I don't have to do anything," yawned Clip.

"I may be a sadistic bastard, but you're a lazy one," said Magus, an edge to his voice. "Yes you do have to do something. Because you'll benefit from this too."

"How? I'm not interested in your empire building. I don't want to be any part of your schemes and dreams, you know that. I've always made it clear that you must leave me out of your grand plans."

"You're the owner of Stonewylde, Clip. You're a part of it whether you like it or not."

"It's nothing to do with me, Sol, all this expansion business. *I* didn't want you to open up the quarry and bring in van loads of illegal immigrants to risk their lives quarrying the stone. I don't want you to build a new school to cope with the population explosion you've encouraged, nor build holiday homes for rich visiting Hallfolk and charge them a fortune for the privilege of staying here. I don't want any part of the investments or the stock market scams or the off-shore trusts, nor the fortune you're earning from your company's wheeling and dealing. I don't want to father children all over the place. I don't want to be treated like some sort of god. I don't want any part of the whole empire thing, which is why I let *you* be magus instead of me. All I ask is to live at Stonewylde when I want to and to travel when the need takes me. And to feel the Earth Magic, honour the Goddess, and take part in the rituals and ceremonies."

"You're a fool, Clip. This moon magic is part of Stonewylde too, as much a part as the Earth Magic. Look at you this morning - worn out and looking old and tired. And look at me. You come up to the rock now and you'll see just how good it makes you feel. I've never felt stronger in my life."

Miranda held a glass of water to Sylvie's lips, her other arm supporting the girl as she lay propped up in bed. She took a few sips, then her head fell back weakly against the headboard.

"Try to drink a bit more, Sylvie. It's nearly lunch time and you've had nothing today. You didn't eat last night either, did you? You know you must look after your health or you'll go back to how you were in London. Please, darling."

"I'm sorry, Mum," whispered Sylvie through pale lips. "I just want to sleep."

Sighing, Miranda gently laid her down, making sure she was warm enough. Where was Magus? She couldn't leave Sylvie to go and find him. She wished now she'd asked Yul to take a message to the Hall when he'd called earlier. Why was there no phone in this place? She thought of her old mobile phone lying useless at the bottom of a cupboard; there was no signal at Stonewylde. Why didn't Magus come?

Clip lay spread out on the huge round stone, the midday sun beating down on him. Magus towered over him impatiently.

"Well?"

"It's unbelievable, Sol! I've never heard of anything like it, but I can see why it's possible. If a battery works by converting chemical energy stored inside it, why not a stone storing magnetic or maybe gravitational energy from the moon? What a wonderful sensation! I feel completely re-energised."

"What we need is to find out exactly what this stone is made of," said Magus. "I'll bring up a mallet and chisel and knock a bit off. Then we can send it off somewhere for analysis."

"You can't knock bits off it! It's an ancient stone placed here thousands of years ago by our ancestors. Look, they even made it disc shaped like the full moon, and smoothed it. They must have been able to channel the energy too."

"It makes me wonder whether only Sylvie can do it, or if others could too. Remember our mother? She was moongazy, wasn't she? I don't remember too well, but now I come to think of it I'm sure there were tales about her and this stone."

Clip frowned, sitting up on the rock.

"Yes, you're right. I've heard she used to dance and sing at the Moon Fullness."

"That's what Sylvie was doing!"

"And I know Magus – I mean your father, not mine – would bring her up here every month. I followed them once. He saw me and shouted at me to go home. So maybe our mother could channel the energy too. And maybe he used it to power himself up. I wonder if my father brought her here too?

We'll have to find out. Some of the older Villagers might remember."

"That crone Heggy would know," said Magus speculatively.

"You can ask her. I'm not going anywhere near her. You know how she hates us. She terrifies me. Maybe Violet could tell us. Ask her next time she bakes the ceremony cakes. It would be interesting to know if both our fathers brought Raven here and whether she channelled the moon magic for them."

"I'll speak to Violet soon. Get off now, Clip. You'll use it all up."

"Oh come on, Sol. Just a few more minutes."

He lay down again and stretched out. Magus sat next to him and closed his eyes.

"I'll have to take a sample but I'll take it from underneath the edge so it won't show. When we know what the rock is we can do some geological surveying of the estate and find out if there's any more of it. It's an unusual stone, isn't it? It's very sparkly which may mean that there's quartz in it perhaps. It's certainly different from the stones at the Stone Circle, and the dolmen stones, and even that single one up on the hill by the woods, the one where the hares run wild. Can you think of any others?"

"Near the dolmen there's another small circle. I can't remember what sort of rock they are. And at the quarry – there's that enormous stone at the cliff end looking down over the place. Remember we used to climb on it and you'd threaten to push me over the edge? Goddess, I used to hate it there!"

"Oh yes! I'd forgotten that one. The serpent rock, the one where they say I was conceived. I think it may be the same composition as this. I remember it glittering in the sun just as this one does. I'll phone the Gatehouse and leave a message for Jackdaw. He can get one of the men to chisel a piece off and then we can compare it."

"But why do you want to find more stone like this? I don't understand. You can get the girl to channel the moon energy here every month and then we'll come and soak it up," said Clip, still lying sprawled on his back, eyes closed in the sun.

"So you do want to be part of it now?" Magus' voice was cynical. "Changed your mind about joining me, have you?"

"This is different. This is Stonewylde magic, not your scheming. Of course I want some of it. It'll help me on my journeying into other realms, this moon magic. We both knew all along that Sylvie had come here for a purpose and now we know what that purpose is. Clearly it's to channel the moon energy for us. But I don't see why you want to find more stone like this. Surely this is enough."

"I've been thinking about it all night," said Magus excitedly. "This is fine in the summer, but what about in the winter, or when it's foul weather? She was ill last month after being out in the rain at the Moon Fullness. She's not really that strong or healthy, despite the healing. I thought if we had some small pieces of rock, we could make her channel the energy into those. Then we can store them and use the energy when we want it. She can still come up here when the weather's fine, but that way we'd have a portable power source too."

"That's brilliant, Sol! But be careful with Sylvie. I don't want her to suffer. She's a sweet girl and it wouldn't be fair."

"No, we don't want to kill the goose that lays the golden egg, do we? Talking of which, I must go and see how she is. And keep Miranda happy too. You know she's pregnant?"

"Already? You didn't waste any time, did you? Has she told you yet who Sylvie's father is? He must be Hallfolk. Sylvie's so like everyone here and she's moongazy, which is a Stonewylde phenomenon as far as I know."

"No, Miranda won't tell me; there's some dark secret she feels she must hide. But I'm going to put pressure on her and find out. I've got her where I want her now. Surprising how quickly she's knuckled under, given her initial independence. Although she's said she's never come across anyone from Stonewylde before, I agree with you Clip - the father must be Hallfolk. Probably a random coupling with someone who left here to live in the Outside World. There are a lot of them out there. And what about Sylvie's amazing likeness to our mother? Do you remember when you first saw her, how striking the resemblance was?"

"Yes, at the Story Web back in March. She's got to be related. Do find out from Miranda."

"I will. Come with me, Clip, down to the cottage. I need to see how Sylvie is today. She was a little weak last night after the moon dancing."

"Of course. It's amazing! An hour ago all I wanted was to crawl off to bed and sleep. But now I feel I could run a marathon. That moon magic is powerful stuff."

Miranda almost wept with relief when Magus arrived at the cottage, although she wasn't so pleased to see Clip standing on the path behind him. The two men were bursting with brightness and energy as they stood in the small sitting room.

"She's in a terrible state, Magus," she said. "Come and see for yourself. She won't wake up, won't drink anything, and she's been whimpering in her sleep. What did happen last night? I've never seen her like this before. And there're awful bruises on her wrists too, and a mark on her cheek."

"We'll talk in a minute when I've seen her," he said, brushing past her. "You stay down here, Miranda. There isn't room for all of us in that tiny bedroom."

The two men filled the room as they stood one each side of the narrow bed looking down on the sleeping girl. Her skin was translucent and the dark shadows under her eyes were shocking. Her arm lying on the white coverlet looked frail and delicate, the bruising round the wrist stark. Her breathing was quiet. If they hadn't known she was alive, they could well have believed they were looking at a corpse.

"This is no good at all, Sol. We can't go on with this if it makes her ill. I won't be a part of anything that harms her. Why is she bruised?"

"I had to restrain her when she attempted to meet that damn boy again. But she's alright. She's not harmed, just tired."

Magus sat on the side of the bed and picked up Sylvie's limp hand.

"Sylvie, Sylvie, wake up. Wake up!"

He shook her slightly.

"I know you can hear me. Wake up!"

With a visible effort she opened her eyes and looked straight into his. She flinched slightly as she recognised him. He leant over and kissed her cheek, for she was unable to move away from him.

"That's a good girl. How are you feeling?"

"A bit tired," she whispered.

"See I've got Clip here too, to visit you."

His grey eyes watched her more compassionately than Magus' and she smiled weakly at the brother whom she'd always preferred.

"Do you remember what happened last night, Sylvie?" asked Magus softly.

She nodded slightly.

"Tell me then."

"I was dancing up at Mooncliffe. And then ..."

"And then what?" he prompted.

"And then I went on the great round stone and I couldn't move."

"And do you remember anything else?"

She looked into his handsome face, glowing with vitality. It all came back to her.

"You lay on the stone and you wouldn't help me. You made me stay there for ages. You knew it was hurting me, but you wouldn't help me."

She began to cry. She had no energy to sob, but tears spilled onto her cheeks. Magus frowned down at her.

"For Goddess' sake, man!" said Clip, fishing a piece of cloth from a pocket. "Show some human kindness."

He leaned over and wiped away her tears.

"It's alright, Sylvie. It wasn't Magus' fault. He was frozen too, just like you were."

"No he wasn't," she whispered. "I remember it all now. He loved it. I'm not going up there again. It hurt and it still hurts today."

"You'll do as you're told!" said Magus, his eyes glittering.

"Ssh, leave this to me," said Clip. "Sylvie, what you did last night was amazing. You're such a clever girl. We're so proud of you."

She closed her eyes, shutting them both out.

"You're a magical girl, Sylvie. You must share your magic. It's wrong to keep it all for yourself."

She opened her eyes and gazed at Clip, who'd sat down on the narrow bed next to her and was staring at her intently.

"I don't keep it for myself," she mumbled. "It's for Stonewylde. I give the magic to Stonewylde."

"And we're Stonewylde," said Clip gently. "We need to share the magic too. That's why you must dance at Mooncliffe for us."

She shook her head slightly and shut them out again. She couldn't bear the pair of them staring down at her like this, overwhelming her with their intensity and air of urgency.

"I won't go up there again. It's horrible, all wrong. I won't do it."

"Sylvie …" began Magus, but his brother waved him to silence.

"Open your eyes, Sylvie," Clip said softly. "Just look at me a minute."

Reluctantly she gazed at him. His grey eyes shimmered before her, luminous and strange. She felt herself drawn to him, pulled in to his will. She tried to look away but found she couldn't. He took her unresisting hands in his and she sensed his power, a gentle but insistent force that locked her into his command. She felt her free will melt away under his unrelenting eyes.

"You love to dance at Mooncliffe," he said. "At the Moon Fullness, you love to dance at Mooncliffe."

"No," she moaned. "I want to be with Yul …"

"Sylvie, you know you love to dance at Mooncliffe. Look at me, Sylvie. That's better. We understand each other. You're a special moongazy girl and you want so much to serve Magus. It's why you were brought here and you know this in your heart. You love to dance at Mooncliffe."

Slowly she nodded, and Clip felt Magus twitch with barely controlled suspense. Ignoring this, he smiled kindly, holding the girl in his thrall.

"You love to dance at Mooncliffe for Magus. You want to give him your magic on the great stone. Isn't that right, Sylvie?"

She nodded again, her face impassive. Clip sighed.

"Good girl. We're very pleased with you. This is the right thing and you know it. You're going to rest now and you'll feel much better when you've had a sleep. There's no problem at all. You're not ill."

"No, I'm fine," she whispered. "Only tired."

"Before you go back to sleep, Sylvie, tell me one thing. What do you like to do at the Moon Fullness?"

"I love to dance at Mooncliffe for Magus."

As they went down the stairs, Magus turned to Clip.

"You're a bloody genius, brother."

Clip grinned.

"No, just a good shaman."

# CHAPTER THREE

June slipped into July and the weather became increasingly hot and sunny. The hay was harvested and the honeycombs dripped with sweet bounty. Scores of hives were moved around the estate following the nectar; bean fields, wild flower meadows, clover. The Meadery was busy, inundated with the quantities of honey that were sent in daily from the hives dotted across the estate.

The Villagers spent every available hour of daylight gathering in the crops as they ripened. All the soft fruits and many vegetables were picked, with the entire Village school trooping across to the various fields daily to join in with the harvesting. This was also the time of year for the flax harvest, which was grown extensively at Stonewylde for its fibre. It was spun and woven into linen cloth, which along with wool and leather provided most of the Villagers' clothing. The crop was rotated with cereals; by July it was over a metre high, and the fields of pale blue flowers were beautiful. It was a labour intensive crop that couldn't be harvested in the usual way by cutting, which would damage the fibres. Instead, wearing strong leather gloves, the workers pulled it from the ground by hand. Every Villager available was taken from their normal duties for this back-breaking task of pulling the flax. After the flax harvest and retting, all women and girls in the Village were busy at home spinning thread that would be dyed and woven into cloth. Most families had their own loom, men and women sharing the weaving later when the autumn nights started to draw in.

During July the boys of the Village were sent out rabbiting every day, for the rodents had to be controlled if the crops weren't to suffer. There were thousands of rabbits on the downs and it was the job of all boys over the age of ten to cull them using snares, nets, cudgels and slingshots. Nothing was wasted. Rabbit meat was eaten several times a week by the Villagers. The bones were processed into glue and also used in the traditional building materials. The fur was made into warm winter covers, cot liners, hats and mittens. Rabbits were an important crop at Stonewylde, and despite the boys' efforts their numbers seemed to remain undiminished.

The fields given over to cereal were rippling with wheat, corn, barley and oats. The oil seed rape had been harvested and the sunflowers turned their glorious heads to track the blazing sun each day. The hemp, grown to make ropes and nets, had been gathered in. The smaller, more specialised crops such as woad and madder for dye, and the exotic poppies for use in the ceremony cakes, were all ready for harvest.

The farm managers were a band of trusted Villagers who organised the farming system at Stonewylde. Magus left the smooth running of the estate entirely to them and at this time of year they worked from dawn to dusk and often beyond. They worked closely and cooperatively, pooling labour and machinery. Tractors, combine harvesters and any essential machinery were used, for Magus had long since seen the economic sense in abandoning the old horse drawn methods of farming. Nothing that could be grown in the fields of Stonewylde was imported, so farming had to be productive and efficient. But even with mechanisation and the need for high yields, there was no exploitation of the Earth Mother. There was no bleeding the land dry of its goodness and then pumping it back artificially with infusions of chemicals. Stonewylde used only traditional organic methods, and the ultimate testimony to its success was the good health and fitness of all the people who lived there.

Magus left Stonewylde a few days after the full moon at the end of June, taking with him to London several of the older students for a cultural visit. To him the young Hallfolk were an investment; another crop waiting to be harvested. Although given every educational opportunity and encouraged to follow lucrative careers in the Outside World, Magus instilled in them the idea that their hearts and souls belonged to Stonewylde, and with it the obligation of the ancient practice of tithing. When grown up, in return for a portion of their income they could visit the estate for holidays or extended stays and also send their children to the Hall School, paying expensive fees like any other boarding school. A healthy tithing revenue was gradually building as successive children grew up, graduated and settled into professions in the Outside World. The drawback was that the great Hall was now hardly big enough to cope with the influx of visitors at festival times.

Clip too had left Stonewylde to stay with an alternative community living near ancient stones in Ireland, where he was always in demand as a storyteller. The majority of the visitors who'd come for the Midsummer Holiday had now returned to their homes in the Outside World. From being crammed full and bursting at the seams, the Hall was suddenly very quiet.

With both Magus and Clip absent and many of the resident Hallfolk away on holiday in the Outside World, the atmosphere at Stonewylde was relaxed, despite the extra hours of work in the fields. Yul felt free with Magus away. He worked harder than ever before, spending hours every evening pulling flax after a long day working in the woods. He ate Maizie out of house and home as his body grew taller and stronger with all the extra labour. Rosie was working all hours at the dairy, for milk production was at its peak. Much of the excess milk was made into the great wheels of cheese that were part of the feasts at both Lammas and the Autumn Equinox festivals. Geoffrey and Gregory were busy rabbiting and helping with the flax harvest. Maizie was up to her elbows in preserves and wine making, and trying to keep the two younger boys, Gefrin and Sweyn, under control. Without their father's subduing presence they were running wild and constantly into mischief. Their favourite occupation was tormenting their little sister Leveret. Maizie had to be extra vigilant and make sure her youngest child was safe from their spiteful pranks.

Alwyn still languished in the hospital wing with no power of speech or movement. Unable to eat solid food, he was losing much of his bulk and had taken on a wasted look. Maizie went to see him weekly but it was a duty visit, and she spent less and less time there. She always returned very quiet, feeling guilty for enjoying her life so much more with her husband out of the way.

Yul visited the hospital wing just once, and spent only a little time with the man who'd bullied and beaten him for as long as he could remember. He went one evening before starting work in the fields and approached the Hall with trepidation, despite knowing that Magus was away. He went round to the kitchen wing where he'd worked so hard during the Midsummer festival. He knew Marigold would welcome him, although she'd barely had time to speak to him when the visitors had been around.

"Come and have a little bite to eat first, Yul my love," she said warmly, sitting him down at the over-sized scrubbed table where the servants ate.

"I've already eaten," he protested, smiling at her insistent kindness. She cut him a generous slice of gooseberry pie and smothered it with cream.

"Aye, well you're not greedy like that father of yours, but a working lad like you needs to keep his strength up."

"It's him I've come to see," he explained. "I won't be a regular visitor but I wanted to see him just once."

She shook her head and folded her arms.

"The day that man was taken ill was the best day for your poor family," she said. "I should think your mother's glad to see the back of him, nasty brute."

Yul was surprised at this. He'd heard from Maizie how Alwyn had been a constant visitor to this kitchen during his time at the quarry, piling on the fat as he was overfed daily by Marigold's generosity. She laughed at the look on his face.

"Aye, I know what you're thinking. We all knew what he'd done to you, Yul, and what he'd been doing to you for years. I saw him that week Magus had you locked up by the stables. Starving you was a terrible thing to do, and making you watch your father eat when you were so hungry ... Magus should never have done that. 'Twas downright cruelty. And that Alwyn! Nasty piece of work, greedy as a pig after weaning. I said to myself – if that man wants food, I'll give him food. I'll feed him till he bursts. He'd sit in my kitchen like a great porker at the trough. But I thought if I stuffed him up enough he'd get heavier and slower. Maybe find it harder to beat you. Looks like it worked, eh? They don't come much slower than Alwyn is now!"

Yul laughed at this, pleased to know he had another ally.

"There's one thing I want to ask you, boy. I heard some gossip the other day, something one of the men up at the Gatehouse let slip in the pub. Now 'tis all round the Village. He's denying he ever said it of course. Rabbit-scared he is. But you'll know the answer. Is it true that Jackdaw's back, working up at Quarrycleave?"

She stared at him intently and Yul swallowed. Magus had been insistent that Yul was to tell no-one about Jackdaw's return to Stonewylde. He understood why Marigold was so concerned; Jackdaw had been married to her daughter. It was only his banishment that had stopped Marigold organising a lynch-mob after the death of his young wife. Marigold nodded slowly, her face darkening.

"No need to answer, Yul. 'Tis plain you been told to keep quiet and Goddess knows you've enough reason not to anger the master again. Well, if that Jackdaw ever steps foot in the Village he won't last long. What is Magus thinking of, bringing him back here? I never thought I'd see this day. My poor girl Lily – what she suffered at the hands of that man when her front door was shut don't bear thinking about. Death was a release for her, I can tell you. And their little boy, Jay. Why didn't Magus let me take care of him afterwards? I'll never forgive him for that. My own daughter's son, my grandson. I should have been given the care of him, poor little mite. But oh no, Magus sends him to his other grandmother, that sow Vetchling. No more fit to bring up a child than hatch an egg. I'll never understand the reason for that as long as I live.

I ..."

Yul was saved from any more of her diatribe by the arrival of Harold in the kitchens. The young servant grinned at Yul and rolled his eyes, knowing all too well what Marigold was like once launched into her favourite subject. Harold was pleased to see Yul again. Yul had made his life a lot easier during the Midsummer Holiday doing many of the jobs that would otherwise have fallen to him.

"Could Harold take me to the hospital wing?" asked Yul, needing to get on with this visit for the flax was still waiting to be pulled. "I'll never find my way alone."

"Aye, you do that, young Harold. And come and see me again soon, Yul," said Marigold, taking his empty bowl and ruffling his hair. She smiled as he stood up, towering over her.

"Sacred Mother, but you've grown lately! Thriving now, aren't you, without that brute around. Give my blessings to Maizie. Tell her next time she's up visiting Alwyn to pop in to the kitchens and see me. Always did like your mother."

Harold led Yul out of the kitchens and both boys burst out laughing.

"Goddess but she can talk, that one!" said Harold.

"She's kind though," said Yul.

"Too kind! So how's life treating you now?"

"Life's good. Very busy, of course. It's that time of year. I haven't seen you up in the flax fields, Harold."

The boy shook his head.

"Come on, Yul. You know what it was like here over the holiday. I was worked to the bone. I think I deserve a break. Anyway, with all the Hallfolk away I've been doing something ... special. Something Magus wouldn't like if he found out."

He glanced furtively around as they climbed a short flight of back stairs and went along a corridor. Yul looked at him in surprise. He'd always imagined the servants at the Hall to be, like Martin, intensely loyal and obedient. But it seemed he was wrong.

"What have you been doing?" he asked, intrigued by Harold's secrecy. The boy was bubbling with excitement.

"It's amazing! I can't believe I'm doing it. You know all

them computers they have here? Maybe you don't. They're these machines, like televisions but different. And there's this thing called the Internet. Well, I've been doing it!"

Yul looked unimpressed.

"Why do you want to do that? Doing what exactly?"

"Oh Yul, you don't understand! It's brilliant! I play games and visit websites, and it's a whole different world! I'm learning to read. I've got some books from their school and I've been visiting this old dear in the Village who still remembers how to read. It's great! I can type things now, and read some of the stuff on the websites. I practise every day. I use a computer in one of the Hallfolk's bedrooms while he's away. I'm up there every night!"

Yul eyed him suspiciously.

"You're not turning into Hallfolk, are you Harold?"

"Don't be daft – why would I want to be one of them? But it's a new world, I can tell you. I could show you the computers sometime. They're the best thing in Stonewylde. You should learn to read too, Yul. I'll teach you if you like."

They'd reached the entrance to the hospital wing and stopped by the door. Yul frowned, remembering Sylvie offering the same thing. Maybe they were right. He was amazed that Harold was learning to read and write. It was unheard of at Stonewylde, although he'd always known at the Village School that Harold was bright. He should have passed the tests and come to the Hall School. But he had no Hallfolk blood and Yul reckoned they'd failed him deliberately. He nodded.

"I don't know, Harold. But I'll think about it. Thanks for bringing me up here."

He opened the door to the hospital wing and was hit by the different smell. A nurse took him into a small room where something sat in a great wheelchair facing the window.

"I'll leave you alone with your father, shall I?" she asked quietly, her blond head cocked in sympathy. "You won't get anything out of him, I'm afraid."

"Will he get better?" asked Yul, his voice trembling slightly at the thought of Alwyn sitting only a couple of metres away. The nurse shook her head, her face concerned.

"You'll have to speak to the doctor," she said. "But it seems very unlikely. They've done tests and sent him for a scan at a private hospital in the Outside World. There's nothing much going on in his head. All we can do is keep him comfortable. But he's losing weight rapidly and his muscles are starting to atrophy. You could always ask the Goddess for a miracle."

*I already have,* thought Yul. *And this is it.*

The nurse left the room and quietly shut the door. Yul went round the high wheelchair and gaped at the sight before him. So this now was the hated man. The one who'd frightened Yul all his life and made sure that any happiness he felt was soon crushed out of him. The one who would have beaten him to death if he'd been allowed to continue his cruelty. How long did it take to whip someone to death? Yul pondered this as he stared at the shrunken, sallow effigy before him. He shuddered, recalling the violence in the byre. Or maybe not the whip; it could have been blows that killed him. Alwyn had been just as fond of this form of punishment. Punches and kicks to the kidneys, the head, the spleen; maybe that would have been his end.

Yul found to his horror that his eyes had filled with hot tears. He blinked them away angrily, glaring at the pathetic huddle that gazed sightlessly out of the window. Alwyn smelt strange, his gingery hair had thinned to wisps and his skin hung loosely in empty folds. He was disgusting, almost less than human in his rapid decay. The vindictive speech of revenge, the glory and hatred that Yul had thought to enjoy as he finally faced his helpless tormentor faded now to nothing. He stood looking at the man propped lifelessly in the chair, the evening sunlight on his sunken face. In his pocket Yul's fingers closed round the pieces of leather he'd brought to toss contemptuously at his father – the remains of the whip and the strap destroyed so frenziedly with his axe. He thought of the words he'd dreamt of saying at this moment. But instead of revelling in triumph and gloating at his father's fate, he cried. Standing in the small room next to the man who must have hated him so much, Yul cried for his lost and trampled childhood, now gone forever.

Hazel the doctor gave Miranda a pregnancy test and confirmed that she was expecting a child. Sylvie wasn't the only one who'd changed since Hazel had first met them both in the London hospital. She remembered Miranda as a pale, worn out teacher, over-worked and worried sick about her daughter. The woman before her now glowed with good health, her skin and hair sleek, her figure curvier and softer. Her green eyes shone and her movements were slow and calm. Hazel felt a twinge of jealousy knowing that Miranda was carrying Magus' child. Not that she begrudged Miranda this pregnancy; she was delighted for her. She just prayed to the Moon Goddess as Mother that she would conceive too, even though there were now already two women at Stonewylde expecting his babies. Hazel knew that Magus rarely fathered more than one child a year, so she'd have to wait. But she was in favour and remained hopeful. Maybe next year she'd be honoured. She knew Magus was pleased with her for introducing the newcomers to him. And more than anything Hazel wanted to please him.

Miranda was ecstatic on learning she was expecting Magus' baby, seeing it as a way of binding him to her. Hadn't he said he'd love and care for the baby? It could only strengthen their relationship. She visited the store where the baby equipment was kept. Marvelling over the lovely cribs and prams woven from wicker, she chose some pretty linen to make covers for hers. Luckily Sylvie felt no resentment towards this new life that was claiming her mother's attention. She was just pleased to be left alone.

Sylvie had gradually recovered from her experience up at Mooncliffe and was nearly back to normal. She'd spent a couple of days in bed, totally exhausted, but then Magus had called before leaving for London. He'd told her to get up and stop malingering; he'd been quite sharp which had upset her. He glowed with energy and she'd wondered if he'd offer to heal her again. But that seemed to be the last thing on his mind. He'd sent Miranda downstairs to make coffee and shut the bedroom door. Sylvie had felt confused when he'd sat down on her bed smiling, having just reprimanded her for being there at all. Her first reaction had been to shrink from him. But there'd been something else pulling against this feeling; a compulsion that she didn't understand.

"Remember the last Moon Fullness, Sylvie?" he'd asked softly, aware of Miranda moving about downstairs. He'd stroked the black bruises circling her wrists with a gentle finger. Sylvie had met his dark gaze and felt a strange sensation inside. She recalled the white disc of stone up on the cliffs. She knew that she must share her magic with Magus; it was why she'd been brought here. She nodded, her eyes luminous and intent as she returned his gaze. Despite himself, Magus had shivered at her strangeness.

"I do," she said. "I stood on the rock at Mooncliffe."

"That's right. You were a good girl. And what about the next Moon Fullness, Sylvie? What will you do then? Go running off with Yul?"

She swallowed. Of course she wanted to be with Yul up at Hare Stone. She knew this in her heart. But she found herself speaking differently.

"I want to dance at Mooncliffe for you," she whispered.

Magus had smiled at this. She felt the full blast of his charm and vitality as he leant across the bed to kiss her forehead, his exotic scent filling her nostrils.

"I'm very pleased with you, Sylvie. I shall come back specially and you can dance for me again. Don't forget now. Remember what Clip told you."

She nodded, her throat aching with unshed tears. She knew this was wrong. She knew how ill she'd felt since the full moon. She wanted to be with Yul. And yet …

"You must share your magic with me," he said, squeezing her hand. "But don't talk about it, will you? It's just between us."

He then went downstairs and made Miranda's day by hugging her and telling her how beautiful she looked expecting his baby. He kissed her deeply before leaving, teasing her for becoming so weak and submissive at his touch. He promised to spend time with her when he returned and reminded her of the imminent move up to the Hall. His final words, though, were concerned with Sylvie.

"I expect to come back and find her completely well again. I will not be pleased if I return and find she's still moping about. I'm counting on you, Miranda, so don't let me down. I want Sylvie strong and healthy."

A few days after Magus left, Sylvie and Yul came across each other in the woods where they both walked regularly in the hope of such a meeting. They were a little shy and both wished they could get back to their previous easiness with each other. Both also remembered the magical kiss on Sylvie's birthday under the yew tree, which made them slightly nervous about being alone together now. They climbed up the hill to the Hare Stone and Sylvie ran over and rested her cheek against its rough warmth. She breathed deeply.

"I love this stone. It makes me feel safe."

Yul flung himself down on the short grass carpeted with white clover and sky blue speedwell. He looked out towards the sea, hazy in the July sun. His deep grey eyes were startlingly clear in his tanned face as he narrowed them against the glare of the sun.

"So tell me what actually happened at the last Moon Fullness, Sylvie. I was really worried about you."

"Oh yes, of course," she said brightly, sitting down on the grass next to him. He wore a thin, sleeveless jerkin; she noticed how brown he was and how well defined the muscles in his arms had become. "I went to Mooncliffe with Magus and I danced on the moon stone there."

"What? You danced?"

"I went to Mooncliffe with Magus and I danced on …"

"Yes, I heard you. But why did you go there, Sylvie? Did he force you to go with him? What happened?"

She frowned, feeling confused.

"Yes, he was waiting for me, I think. I don't … I don't remember that bit too well. He took me up to Mooncliffe and

... I'm not sure. I danced on the cliff for a while I think, and then I went on the white disc of rock."

"I thought he must've been lying in wait for you. The bastard! I waited for ages in the woods, and then I wasted time looking all over the place trying to find you. I should've realised straight away he'd taken you up there. Was it awful for you?"

"Yes, it ... no, it was fine. I don't know. I'm going there next month. I love dancing at Mooncliffe."

"*What*? I thought you liked coming here with me and dancing with the hares."

She wrinkled up her face, looking puzzled.

"Yes, I want to be with you, Yul. But ... I love dancing at Mooncliffe for Magus."

He stared at her in consternation. She didn't sound like herself at all.

"Sylvie you really didn't dance on the stone. Don't you remember? You were standing still and then you collapsed."

"No, I think ... I don't know. I can't remember. I love it there. I know that for sure. I think you're wrong, Yul. I was fine. I want to go there again."

Yul shrugged, swallowing his hurt. He'd thought that moongazing up at Hare Stone with him was special to her. But if she preferred to be with Magus at Mooncliffe, he wouldn't make a fuss.

Her strangeness made their time together awkward and Yul couldn't shake off his disappointment. They watched the young leverets playing below them on the hill for some time, and lay on their backs amongst a patch of pale blue harebells that grew in the grass, following the swallows arcing in the sky overhead. They could smell the delicious, sweet fragrance of honeysuckle wafting up from the hedgerow bordering the woods. It should have been idyllic; a rare chance to enjoy each other's company without being disturbed or overlooked. After their passion in the moonlight under the yew tree, they should have fallen into each other's arms. But despite being acutely aware of the other's proximity, they were careful to avoid any contact. There was an uncomfortable constraint between them and neither knew how to banish it.

Sylvie could see how much Yul had changed since Alwyn's departure. He'd lost the hunted look; he no longer jumped if taken by surprise, or constantly looked over his shoulder at every noise and movement. At one point his top had ridden up his back a little and she could see where the terrible lashes still marked him, the skin now mended. He would carry the scars for the rest of his life, she was sure, but it was good to see that he was healing. He was obviously sleeping and eating well, and she imagined his mother must be fussing over him. Sylvie could only guess at how the woman must have felt over the years, watching her husband crush her son so brutally at every given opportunity. Yul's eyes and skin were clear and glowing, and he'd had his hair cut so it no longer flowed onto his shoulders. The dark curls sprang round his face, glossy and soft. Sylvie wanted very much to run her fingers through them.

He could see a change in her too, but it wasn't for the better. She'd lost weight and looked more delicate than ever. Her face was sharper and her eyes different. He couldn't quite pinpoint what was wrong but knew she wasn't herself. She seemed brittle and nervous, as if she might crack at any moment. What he didn't know was that Sylvie suffered from nightmares every night, and awoke drenched in sweat with her heart pounding. In her dreams she'd frozen into stone and couldn't move, whilst slowly she died inside, her life force draining away. And Magus was in the dreams too. Sometimes he stood there laughing. Other times he lay at her feet groaning with pleasure. And the worst dream of all - once he stood very close touching her and she couldn't move away to stop him doing it. She'd told nobody about the nightmares. In the daylight she tried to forget them, but the evidence of their damage was plain to see.

After a while, they wandered further along the Dragon's Back ridgeway, both remembering the last time they were here escaping from Quarrycleave, and the time before that when Yul had ridden Nightwing. Recalling how happy they'd been together made them feel sad now, for something had changed.

Sylvie reached across and took his hand in hers, too shy to look at his face. He smiled and linked his fingers with hers, careful not to crush her bones. What he longed to do was scoop her up and kiss away her strangeness until there was no awkwardness, only passion and that glorious feeling of being part of the same whole. Yul sighed and contented himself with the warmth of holding hands.

A little later on they were surprised to see a horse and cart approaching. As it drew nearer they recognised Tom at the reins. He pulled the cart to a halt.

"Blessings!" he called. "'Tis good to see you again, boy. And you, miss. But should you two be out together? I heard that's what all the fuss was about before."

"Yes, but Magus and Clip are both away. You won't tell on us, will you?" said Yul.

The old man chuckled.

"Not me. Anyway, best be getting this lot back to the Village."

"What have you got in there?" asked Sylvie, peering into the cart. She saw a pile of small rocks and shuddered. "Have you been to Quarrycleave? The place where Yul had to work?"

"Aye, that's the one. And I seen Jackdaw there too. You won't know him, miss, but I reckon you do, Yul."

"Oh yes."

"Thought he'd been banished from Stonewylde. There's talk in the Village but I didn't believe it till today. Never thought Magus'd bring Jackdaw back, not after what he done. Turns out he's up there working with a bunch of Outsiders who don't even speak our tongue. You must've known that Yul, but I expect you weren't to tell us. What is Magus thinking of? I don't know ... I don't like it."

"What are these rocks for?" asked Sylvie. "They're rather pretty, sparkling in the sun. Oh!"

She'd reached in to touch one but drew her hand back sharply.

"What's wrong? Did you cut yourself?" Yul took her hand but there was no mark on it.

"No," she said, frowning. "No, nothing like that. It just

gave me a funny feeling."

"Don't know what this lot's for. Magus just said to go to the quarry where they'd have it ready to collect. I've to take it to the stonecarvers in the Village. One of his new schemes I suppose. You still do stonecarving in the evening, Yul?"

"No, not since I worked at Quarrycleave," Yul's tone was terse. "It put me off stone."

"Reckon it would, after what you went through. Anyway, 'tis good to see you looking so fit and healthy now, lad. Drop by the stables some time if you're up that way. I know old Nightwing would be pleased to see you."

As soon as he'd moved on, Yul turned to Sylvie abruptly. He pulled back the sleeves of her blouse and stared at her wrists. The fading purple bruises still clearly encircled them. Yul looked her in the eye and she flinched from the blaze of his sudden fury.

"I noticed these when I thought you'd cut your hand," he said tightly. "What happened? Why are you marked like this?"

She looked away, staring over the downs where the sky met the curve of the land. She shook her head.

"I think ... it was when I was struggling, I think. When I was trying to get into the woods to meet you."

Yul swallowed hard and she could feel him shaking. Reluctantly she met his eye again and recoiled from his expression. She'd never seen him so full of rage.

"And you *want* to be with him at the Moon Fullness? You're telling me he isn't forcing you to go with him against your will? This is proof, Sylvie. Proof that he's forced you."

He almost spat the words at her.

"Please, Yul, stop being so angry. I don't know. I feel so confused. I didn't want to go with him. I fought him, I seem to remember, and he held on to me. This isn't as bad as it looks. I bruise very easily. I don't remember him actually hurting me, just holding on to me so I couldn't go to find you. Please don't look like that at me. I can't bear it."

"But *why* do you want to go to Mooncliffe again? I don't understand! Tell me, Sylvie. Explain it to me so I can try to make sense of it."

But she shook her head and pulled away from him.

"It's just something I must do," she said quietly. "I don't understand it either. But I want to go there, Yul. You're upsetting me by going on about it and getting cross. It's between me and Magus. I don't want to talk about it any more."

Yul and Sylvie walked for some way that day, but the awkwardness between them remained as impenetrable as the boundary wall. Later when they came to say goodbye, Sylvie felt immensely sad. She still wanted nothing more than to be with Yul, but he was different with her; angry and cold. She looked up at his sun-tanned face, his deep grey eyes as beautiful as ever. She had a horrible feeling she was going to lose his affection.

"When can we see each other again?" she asked diffidently. "We can make the most of Magus and Clip both being off the estate, can't we?"

He shrugged and looked away. He felt uncomfortable with this different Sylvie. How could she prefer to be with Magus than with him?

"Whenever you like, Sylvie. You know I'm always here. You know how I feel about you. And I'll still wait for you in the woods at the next Moon Fullness in case you change your mind."

Her hesitant smile faltered at this.

"But Yul, I've already told you. I go to Mooncliffe now for the Moon Fullness. I love to dance on the moon stone for Magus."

His eyes clouded with pain.

"If that's what you want, Sylvie, don't let me stop you. See you around."

He walked off without looking back. Her eyes followed him, her heart like lump of stone. She was going to lose him and she didn't even know why.

# CHAPTER FOUR

A few days later Sylvie made a new and unlikely friend; a strange man called Professor Siskin, and it was he who unwittingly instigated her next encounter with Yul. The professor had arrived with the influx of visitors just before the Summer Solstice but had remained at Stonewylde after they'd all left. He was a dapper little chap in his seventies with straggly white hair, slightly outlandish in velvet jacket and pointed shoes. His glasses hung on an ornate chain. When he remembered to put them on his nose, he spent most of the time peering over them, his faded blue eyes blinking owlishly. He carried a silver topped walking stick and wore a large panama hat to keep the sun from his pink tonsure. He chattered like a small bird, usually to himself, but was quite happy to latch on to anyone within earshot. This was how Sylvie had come to befriend him.

One morning in the Hall, Sylvie was helping herself to breakfast from the long sideboard that ran the full length of the cavernous Dining Hall. She was still trying to regain the weight she'd lost during the days after the full moon when she'd felt so weak. She noticed the funny little man sitting at one of the long tables surrounded by Holly and a group of her friends. He was more conspicuous now that the other visitors had left. Many of the older students were away with Magus but Holly wasn't yet an adult and had been left behind. She'd quickly gathered a new gang around her.

Sylvie couldn't help but hear Holly, with her abrasive voice, being rude to the old man. He was a strange old thing and dressed in an odd fashion, but Holly was unnecessarily offensive. She was showing off as usual to the silly group who seemed to find her remarks entertaining. They laughed with her, making fun of the old man almost openly.

"So are all the teachers at Oxford like you?" Holly demanded. "I'd thought of going there one day, but on second thoughts, maybe I won't bother."

"No, my dear, I'm no longer a don," twittered the professor, seemingly oblivious to her rudeness. "I've long since retired, although I keep rooms there as a research fellow."

"Don? Fellow? What are you on about?"

She rolled her eyes and tapped the side of her head, much to the gang's amusement.

"Titles, my dear, mere titles. What were you thinking of reading?"

"What? I'm not talking about reading! Are we on the same planet, I wonder?"

The professor gazed amicably at her as he chewed on his toast.

"Oxford, like many other universities, is a place of jargon. I apologise, my dear. One always assumes that everyone is au fait with the terminology. I wondered which subject you were thinking of studying."

She frowned at him, annoyed that her needling was having no effect.

"I'm only fifteen. I have no idea. But nothing that you teach, I'm sure of that."

Sylvie could stand it no longer – she had to stop Holly before she said something really offensive. She took her plate over to the old man and sat next to him at the long table, opposite Holly and her crowd. Her cheeks burned with indignation, giving her the courage to face Holly.

"Excuse me, do you mind if I sit here? There's no danger of Holly turning up at Oxford, Professor. She's nowhere near intelligent enough."

"Ooh look, it's little Miss Sparkle herself, the girl with the fairy dress and big ambitions."

"I wonder if Magus knows how you treat the visitors, Holly? How rude you are to them?"

"Not still after Magus are you? You've got another year to

wait before he'll look at you, and running to him telling tales won't change a thing. He won't touch you till you're sixteen."

"I won't even bother to reply to that. But I might tell him how you spoke to the professor. You're just like some of the horrible kids I knew at school in London. I thought Hallfolk were above that sort of behaviour."

"What would you know, you silly cow? You're a newcomer here, an Outsider. What would you know about Hallfolk? You go ahead and tell Magus and we'll all deny it, won't we? Come on, let's leave her to it. She seems to want the silly old fool's company, even though she said she's not interested in older men."

Holly stood up noisily, leaving her breakfast things littered all over the table. The others followed like sheep, subdued now at the thought of Sylvie telling Magus. She sighed – it wouldn't help her popularity but she felt so ashamed of how Holly had spoken to the elderly man.

"That was kind of you, my dear," he murmured, popping a heavily buttered and jammy cube of toast into his mouth and beaming at her. "She was a little strident."

"She's a disgrace. I'm sorry she was so cheeky to you. I'm Sylvie, by the way," she said, "and I'm quite new here so I'm afraid I don't know anything about you. Do you come every year for the Solstice?"

"Oh yes, without fail. Just for the six weeks until Lammas, that's all Magus will permit. But I'm grateful for that and I've been doing it for many years, ever since he took charge. Before that I used to spend the whole summer at Stonewylde, right up until the Autumn Equinox. But I understand that he needs to regulate the amount of Hallfolk living here at any one time. Stonewylde would become another St. Petersburg in the final days of the Tsar if all the aged retainers were permitted to cling on."

"I see," said Sylvie. "And have you had a nice holiday this year? We've had wonderful weather."

"Oh I don't come here for a holiday, my dear. No, no. I'm researching, you see, researching the history of Stonewylde. Writing a book in fact. Fascinating. Never been done before.

Magus has kindly given me access to all the manuscripts and diaries, all the artefacts and letters. Whether or not he'll ever allow me to publish is another matter. In fact I doubt it very much, given the ... er... nature of Stonewylde, the insularity of the culture here. But we could probably publish an account for the Hallfolk to read and that would suffice. For me at least, it's the journey that's so pleasurable. Whether or not there's a published book at the end is almost irrelevant."

He stopped for breath and popped another cube of toast into his mouth, his pale blue eyes twinkling at her. She smiled, wondering how she could now extricate herself for there was no stopping him from ceaseless chatter. But she was also interested. She guessed this was the person Buzz had mentioned once; the one who'd taught the older students about how Stonewylde had stayed intact over the centuries. It would be fascinating to find out about the history of the estate, and she told him so. He patted her hand and beamed at her again.

"You are a lovely girl. New to Stonewylde you say? Indeed, I would have remembered if you'd been before, for you are somewhat striking. Such unusual beauty. And yet strangely familiar. You must tell me your genealogy some time. Would you care to accompany me this afternoon down to the Village Green, my dear? It's Sunday and there should be cricket practice for the Villagers. I always enjoy watching that. So delightfully bucolic and traditional."

She was just about to decline when it occurred to her that Yul might be there, so she agreed to meet him later in the porch.

The old professor hobbled slowly up the great staircase. He headed for a locked room in a distant wing, in which were stored Stonewylde's oldest and most valuable documents. He was in the middle of some interesting reading in the library but had to check this first. He was sure there was a silver-framed photograph in that archive room of Clip and Magus' mother Raven. He wanted to see if his memory was playing tricks. Or whether the wild, moongazy girl who'd wrought such havoc all those years ago between his brothers really had returned in a new incarnation to Stonewylde.

After lunch Sylvie sat in the vast entrance porch waiting for the professor. The porch was bigger than the average family sitting room with a cobwebby vaulted roof. Tiny stained glass windows were set all along the thick walls, and it was lined with stone benches big enough to seat two football teams. A jumble of riding boots, umbrellas and wellingtons lay under the benches. Being summer, the heavy oak front door to the entrance hall stood open, its thick wood bound and riveted with black wrought iron. Opposite this, through the pointed stone arch, the gravel drive with its flanking lines of beeches looked bright in the hot afternoon sunshine. It was cool and shady inside the porch. Sylvie gazed down at the floor's massive flagstones, worn down shinily in the areas of heaviest tread. She imagined the feet that must have walked across those stones over the centuries. Hundreds upon hundred of pairs of feet, slowly wearing away the stone. She thought of Professor Siskin's research and how she'd love to read what he'd written. Stonewylde must be unique in its history. Where else could have been cut off from global and national influences in such a way and have kept itself completely intact?

She was awoken from her reveries by the arrival of the little man himself, complete with panama and stick. They set off down the long gravel drive leading onto the track to the Village. Their progress was slow and Sylvie wondered how they would make it back up again. Siskin seemed to sense her concern and assured her that Tom from the stables was sending down a pony and trap later on to collect him.

"I've just met your mother, I believe," he told her. "Fine young woman, hair like chestnuts. English teacher, she tells me. Welcome addition to the gene pool, I've no doubt. But your father – who is he?"

Sylvie was a little thrown by his directness but replied with the same vague response she always gave. The old man shook his snowy head.

"You know, don't you, that you are Hallfolk?" he said. "Whoever it was that fathered you was without doubt one of us, and a close relation too. This morning I managed to locate our one photo of Raven, Magus' and Clip's mother. You are almost identical to her. Quite extraordinarily so. Everyone here is inter-related and the girl must have had a great deal of relations, one of whom was undoubtedly your father."

"I've been told before how much I look like her," Sylvie said. "Mother Heggy especially thinks so."

"Ah yes, the venerable Wise Woman. Haven't seen her for years, poor creature. Not too keen on us Hallfolk, especially my generation. Understandable too, when one considers how she was treated."

"So what's your relationship to Magus, Professor?" asked Sylvie.

"I'm his half uncle, if there is such a thing. His father, Elm, was my half-brother. As was Clip's father, Basil. Both men older than me. Elm, Basil and I all shared the same father – the magus as was then, of course – but different mothers. Our father was … liberal with his favours, fathered many children. My half-brother Basil was the eldest, and the one entitled to inherit Stonewylde. The rest of us were just excess siblings. Although after Basil's death, Elm stepped in and took over until Clip was old enough to don the mantle of magus. But he never did, and one can't really blame him, given the responsibility and what he was up against. Sol was ever the dominant one, just like his father before him. It's fascinating tracing the family lines. Not just Hallfolk but the Villagers too. So much inter-breeding, which is why Magus is keen to get new blood here. He encourages Hallfolk to go Outside for their partners. It's also why he's brought your mother here I would imagine. As I said before, an addition to the gene pool."

Sylvie was quiet at this. It seemed so cold and calculating. But she knew that Magus was like that. The professor glanced at her.

"Not the only reason, though. I should think you played a major factor in the unusual invitation too. For as the old saying goes - a moongazy girl is hard to find."

Sylvie stared at him in amazement.

"How do you know I'm moongazy? And Magus didn't

know that when he invited us. He only found out recently."

The old man smiled.

"I know it because of your eyes, Sylvie. I remember Raven well, and you have the same moonstone eyes as she did. That girl drove those two half-brothers of mine, Basil and Elm, wild with longing for her. There was something about her, a flash of quicksilver, a coolness that would not be warmed by their passion. They were both utterly obsessed with her to the exclusion of all else. I wonder if you'll have the same effect on men as you grow older."

"I do hope not!" said Sylvie in horror. "I'm not like that at all."

Professor Siskin chuckled.

"Neither was Raven. She wasn't interested in the slightest, which made her even more alluring to them. All she wanted was to moondance, roam Stonewylde wild and free, and learn the craft with Mother Heggy. But anyway, that's another story which I'll tell you some other time. Don't let it trouble you, Sylvie. You may look uncannily like the poor girl but I'm sure you're very different inside. Raven was a strange creature and you seem perfectly sane."

They'd left the gravel drive now and turned towards the Village. Sylvie loved coming down here, feeling as if she was entering the very heart of the community. The Hall was lovely of course, but had a totally different atmosphere to that of the Village. She smiled as she saw the thatched roofs nestling in the distance and the smoke curling from the chimneys. Even in the height of summer the ranges must be alight for cooking. The track became a cobbled way and a group of children ran past chasing an errant chicken.

"I love the Village," she sighed. "There's something so safe about it."

"It's terribly old, you know," chattered Siskin. "Really old. We're talking Bronze Age, with evidence. There's been jewellery, a dagger, belt buckles and such like dug up in the Village gardens. In fact I have a theory it was here before the Stone Circle was built, which would make it Neolithic. But there's no proof of that. Never been a proper archaeological dig. Of course the river was a big factor, and the meadows so fertile, with woods too. Near the sea, but not exposed."

"I don't understand. Why would the Village have been here before the Stone Circle? What makes you think that?"

"I've spent a lifetime researching this era, early peoples and their religions. The Village Green, this one at least, is the clue. The circular clearing in ancient woodlands was the earliest temple of all. Woodland deities, the tribe worshipping at the very trees themselves. The circular area inside, living and worshipping in the same place. Interchangeable to those people."

Sylvie looked at him in puzzlement. He spoke so fast and missed out words in his sentences so that she couldn't be sure what he meant.

"Are you saying that the Village Green is what's left of an ancient woodland temple?"

"Indeed, indeed. Most people would see the green and imagine maybe a meadow, with the trees planted around it for protection. But in fact the trees were there first, and the green is the clearing made in the middle. Not of course those trees themselves, although possibly the yew. Did you know the yew tree regenerates itself? Grows out of the old bole from the original root, and gives birth to a new bole? But it's as old as the root, and in fact there's one in Perthshire in Scotland which is estimated to be about nine thousand years old. Many of the yews in churchyards are well over a thousand years old, often much older than the church itself, which was probably built on a pagan place of worship anyway. I don't know about our yew by the Village Green because I'm no tree expert. But it could be thousands of years old, given that Stonewylde didn't hack down every yew in sight for longbows during the Middle Ages. Far too sacred for that. And of course there's the funerary yew too – another ancient tree."

Sylvie stared at him in fascination. What an interesting man he was. She remembered her kiss with Yul under the yew tree. Knowing that the tree was maybe thousands of years old made that first kiss even more special. They had now arrived at the Green and saw a large group of Village men spread out in the familiar pattern of cricket.

"Let us sit outside the Barn for a while and watch," suggested Siskin. He led the way around the grass to one of the wooden seats sheltered by the flint and stone walls of the Great Barn. Sylvie sat down next to him and looked across at the figures on the grass. Her heart jumped when she recognised Yul – his dark hair always made him stand out. He stood with a group of men, part of the batting team, and she noticed how much he'd grown. He no longer seemed a boy amongst men but was virtually one of them; in fact taller than some of them. She noted the brown skin of his arms, face and throat, the length of his powerful legs, and shivered. Siskin said nothing but smiled.

"The other clue, of course, is the Village pub. Jack in the Green."

"That must mean the Village Green," said Sylvie, eyes fixed on Yul as he swung his muscular arms in mock bowls. He hadn't noticed them yet and was behaving unselfconsciously.

"Strangely enough, it doesn't," said Siskin, "although it would seem to. Jack in the Green is a medieval term referring to a May Day figure, the one who was encased in a green frame of shrubbery and boughs. The sacrificial male at the centre of the fertility dances and rites. But in fact the Beltane reference was merely a later interpretation of something far, far older – namely the Green Man. Jack in the Green, therefore, actually means the Green Man. I'm sure you know that he is literally the embodiment of the spirit of the woods, the woodland deity - Lord of the Greenwood. Which is what this Village Green is all about – an ancient woodland temple!"

He smiled at her triumphantly and she smiled back, nodding her understanding. It was interesting, of course, but nowhere near as interesting as watching Yul in action. He was batting now and Sylvie, although no expert at cricket, could see that he was good. He swung the bat strongly, whacking the ball with incredible power and precision. When he ran it was beautiful to watch. He was so fast and well co-ordinated. His team cheered him on as he ran, taking a risk, and made it to the crease just in time. Sylvie sighed.

"So who is he, the fine young man with the dark curls?"

Sylvie looked at the professor sharply but he twinkled at her.

"His name's Yul. He's a woodsman."

"Of course, of course. A woodsman. What else could he be? And he feels the same about you?"

She nodded, a sudden lump in her throat.

"At least, he did. I'm not sure - something's gone wrong between us."

Siskin patted her hand kindly.

"The course of true love never runs smooth. But it will be alright, my dear. Nobody could resist a moongazy girl like you. Look at him run! Poetry in motion."

The Village Green was becoming quite busy as many people had turned out to watch the cricket practice. Sylvie realised that apart from the evening when she'd wandered down looking for Yul, this was the first time she'd been here for a normal visit and not with the Hallfolk as part of some festival or organised event. She felt, as she'd done when she'd blundered into the Barn that evening, conspicuous with her Hallfolk hair. Everyone else here today apart from the professor was Villager.

"Come, let us drink a glass of cider at the Jack in the Green."

He rose creakily and Sylvie dragged her eyes away from Yul, still batting skilfully and running superbly. She walked slowly by the elderly man's side as they ambled around the edge of the Green towards the pub. Sylvie had never really looked at it closely before. She could see now that it was very old, built of the same stone and flint as the Barn, with a lopsided roof of slate. The building was long and low, the upper-floor windows right up under the eaves. The entrance too was very low with a massive piece of ancient wood, practically a whole tree, forming the lintel. The sign swinging on a post did indeed depict a Green Man; leaves sprouting around his green face, his hair a halo of foliage. It reminded her of Magus at Beltane with his face paint and head-dress of leaves.

Sylvie and the professor entered the cool, dark pub and she looked around with interest. It was large and yet snug inside due to the low, heavily beamed ceiling. There was a long counter, its wood black and smooth with age. Tankards hung on hooks all along the walls and great barrels lined the space behind the bar. There were many dark bottles too and several smaller casks. The place smelt very strongly of cider and mead. Small tables and stools filled the open area, and around the walls were benches and high backed pews. The uneven floor was flag-stoned and brought to mind the floor in the porch that she'd been studying earlier, for this too was very worn down in places. She could feel the age of this building, imagining that even before the present walls were built, an older structure must have stood here.

They went to the empty bar and a burly Villager stood up from where he'd been playing a dice game with a group of old men. He moved round behind the counter and served Siskin with a tankard of cider and Sylvie a glass of apple mead. They sat in a window seat and Siskin sipped at his cider appreciatively.

"Nothing beats the taste of this," he mused. "You can keep your vintage wines and fine champagnes. Give me Stonewylde cider any day. Do you like the apple mead, Sylvie?"

"Delicious! I didn't realise mead came in different flavours. I've only had the stuff at the ceremonies and it's nothing like this."

He chuckled.

"Ceremony mead is something very different, my dear. Magus puts a special ingredient into that brew. But honey mead is one of the staple drinks here. You must visit the Meadery and see how it's made. And the Cider House too. To make the mead, they use honey gathered in different months and from different locations – such as the apple blossom honey, the willow honey, the clover honey, the rose petal honey. It all depends from whence the bees have collected the nectar. So the honey is flavoured before the process even begins. But then other fruits and flavours can be added, either before fermentation, during, or after it. Your mead is made with apple-blossom honey. After the mead is fermented it's mixed with some vintage cider, which gives it that lovely heady, apple taste. You'd like the cherry mead too, I expect, and blackberry. They're all delicious. I'll inform Magus of your new taste for mead and I'm sure he'd be delighted to bring some bottles up from the cellar for you to try."

Sylvie felt very grown up sitting in a pub and wasn't sure if she should be here at all, but Professor Siskin assured her that nobody would mind on a Sunday afternoon. She was also fretting that Yul was outside and she wasn't there to watch him. That dilemma was overcome when suddenly the two cricket teams burst in through the door and crowded around the bar, clamouring for cider. Sylvie immediately picked out Yul. He was handed a brimming tankard and stepped back from the bar to give the others room. He was very surprised to see Sylvie sitting in the window seat drinking mead. He came over straight away, smiling as if his face would split in two.

"What are you doing here?" he asked, desperately trying to quench his thirst and be sociable at the same time. Sylvie watched his throat in fascination as he swallowed the cool cider in long gulps.

"We've been watching you practising cricket, and Professor Siskin here has explained some of the history of Stonewylde to me," she said.

She moved up on the pew so he could sit next to her. She could smell him as soon as he got close. He was very hot and had been running fast; he smelt of fresh male sweat. The aroma made her feel quite weak with an almost animal recognition. She could see the beads of sweat on his forehead and upper lip, the way his dark curls clung damply to his flushed face. He seemed so much bigger next to her. She felt again that somersault of longing in the pit of her stomach, and was shocked at the intensity of her feelings. They alarmed her, belonging to another phase in their relationship for which she wasn't yet ready. She took a deep breath and tried to control the drumming of her heart.

"How do you do, Yul," said Siskin. "I hear you're a woodsman. No wonder you're so fit and healthy. And I remember now. You were the Herald of the Dawn at the Solstice. A fine job you made of that, I recall."

Yul smiled at him politely, accepting the compliments but not accustomed to making small talk with Hallfolk. He wished the old man would clear off so he could have Sylvie to himself. She was still looking a little delicate but nowhere near as bad as the last time he'd seen her. He wondered if her recovery had anything to do with the fact that Magus was away at the moment.

"I didn't know you played cricket," said Sylvie, smiling at him. Sitting so close, she was very aware of the heat he was giving off as his body cooled from such hard exercise in the hot July afternoon.

"Oh yes, I love cricket! But this is the first year I've played with the men and not in a boys' team. We're coming up to the big match at Lammas and I'm really hoping I'll get chosen for the Village team. We play against the Hallfolk. See Edward over there?"

He pointed to an enormous man resembling a mighty oak tree, who was downing a pint of cider in one.

"He's the captain and it's up to him. But he's pleased with me today, so there's a chance."

He finished his drink and stood up, noticing the other men beginning to make their way to the door. He brushed Sylvie's shoulder longingly with his fingertips when he was sure Siskin wasn't looking, towering above her and staring deep into her eyes. She felt his love in that gentle touch. Her heart leapt as she was pulled into the intensity of his burning grey gaze. She poured her love back to him and hoped he read her message as clearly. His lips mouthed a tiny kiss and then he was gone, and the pub was suddenly empty.

"What a charming young man," murmured Siskin. "I can quite understand your attachment to him."

Sylvie sighed, wishing Yul could have stayed longer. Clearly he was no longer angry with her. If they'd had the chance today they could surely have overcome the awkward constraint of their last time together. She hoped desperately to get another opportunity soon to put things completely right. The sight of him today and his proximity to her on the seat had brought everything flooding back. Without him she was only half of what she was destined to be. Her heart ached for him. Why had they wasted the other day up on Dragon's Back? It could have been perfect.

"Please don't mention it to Magus," she said quietly. "He's forbidden us to see each other and he's really got it in for Yul."

"That doesn't surprise me," chuckled Siskin. "Our Magus has serious competition there and he's not the sort of man to take kindly to that. And now Sylvie, we ought to be leaving. Tom will be coming to collect me soon. But before we go I want to show you something."

They stood up and Siskin took her over to one of the back walls. Inlaid amongst the huge blocks of stone was a massive slice of wood. It was almost circular, well over a metre in diameter and clearly the whole cross section of a once enormous tree trunk. Like the counter it was black and shiny with age, but Sylvie saw that it had been carved upon. It was dark at the back of the pub and she found it difficult to see exactly what was carved on the wood. She gently felt with her fingertips and began to make out shapes – mostly leaves.

"Can you feel it, Sylvie? It's a Green Man, a Jack in the Green, a Lord of the Greenwood. Feel the face and the foliage radiating from it. And there's writing too, carved all around the edge of the circle. Can you see it?"

She bent and looked carefully, making out the face and some letters, although she couldn't read what they said.

"It's written in Old English which dates it way back to very early medieval or even late Saxon era. Not much writing survives from that period for few people could write. And apart from stone there wasn't much to write on. That's why this yew tree bole is so unique. Translated, it reads, 'When the Green Man returns to this place, all will prosper and thrive.' I've always felt it to be some kind of prophecy, a message from our ancestors."

Sylvie felt a shiver trickle down her back at the feel of the wood beneath her fingertips. It was so ancient. All those hundreds of years ago someone at Stonewylde had gone to such trouble to carve this message.

"Stonewylde is still waiting for its Green Man to return," mused Siskin as he led Sylvie out into the bright, hot afternoon. "Maybe then all will be right with the world."

They blinked in the almost blinding sunlight outside and looked up the track, but there was no sign yet of Tom with the pony and cart. They wandered over to a great beech tree and stood in its cool shade.

"Are these trees really the descendents of the ancient ones?" Sylvie asked.

"Most likely. The people of Stonewylde would have collected the seeds and grown saplings, then eventually replaced the old trees as they died. Except for the yew, as I said, for that replaces itself in the most extraordinary phoenix-like fashion. That splendid specimen could well be the original tree from the woodland temple. There would have been a wood-henge here too. A great circle of tree trunks erected into post holes, with lintels joining the uprights together."

"Like Stone Henge?"

"That's right. Henge simply means an enclosed circular structure. They would without a doubt have built one here before the Stone Circle. Wood henges preceded stone ones. I've begged Magus to let me organise a dig but he refuses. He doesn't want any Outsiders here, putting the place on the map. And it would be, believe me. There are many important archaeological phenomena at Stonewylde. The place is utterly unique and we'd be over-run by the media if the Outside World were to learn just what we have here. So until there are trained Hallfolk archaeologists, we'll have to wait for proof of a wood henge."

"But what would you find? Surely the wood would have rotted away by now."

"True, but there's usually indication of post holes and sometimes certain fibres remain. There must be a wealth of artefacts and evidence buried beneath our feet."

Professor Siskin removed a large white handkerchief from his pocket and mopped his brow. He smiled kindly at Sylvie and patted her arm.

"I would dearly love to know if I'm right – just a small excavation would suffice. But it's all a dream and maybe Magus is right. One shouldn't desecrate a sacred place out of idle curiosity. Remember this, though, Sylvie, whenever you're on this Green or under these trees. You are in a place of ancient worship and potent magic. You are in a place where the spirit of the Green Man is at its strongest."

# CHAPTER FIVE

When Magus returned to Stonewylde, Sylvie's nightmares began all over again. In the sky the moon grew fatter each night. But as the Hay Moon of July loomed closer Sylvie lost her appetite. She withdrew into herself, beset by fears but not understanding why she was so scared. Magus wasted no time in moving her and Miranda out of Woodland Cottage and into the Hall. This only added to her sense of entrapment. He put them in a suite of rooms at the end of a long Tudor wing of the building. Sylvie's room had its own little staircase leading down to the floor below, where an outside door opened straight into the gardens. The suite led into a long Tudor gallery, which connected to the main body of the Hall. The adjoining rooms were kept free for visiting Hallfolk, so were not always in use. Miranda was delighted with the move; she loved her four poster bed, and Sylvie guessed she was imagining nights of passion with Magus. The tiny room was to be the baby's, and Miranda was in raptures about that too. Sylvie's bedroom, at the very end of the wing, was light and airy for a Tudor room with diamond-paned windows all around. She was pleased that she had access to the garden. Without that she would have felt completely imprisoned.

Clip came back from his trip to Ireland, and as Lammas drew nearer, the Hall began to fill once more with visitors. Sylvie wanted only to retreat from the bustle and noise, unable to face so many people. Holly and her group continued to make her life unpleasant at every opportunity. Sylvie found she had no fight in her and avoided them wherever possible. She knew Buzz was due back soon and dreaded his return, for it could only make Holly worse. She longed to see Yul, but now she was living in the Hall there was little chance of that.

As the end of the month drew closer, she became quieter in the day and more disturbed at night, the nightmares growing steadily worse.

Just before the full moon, Sylvie had the worst nightmare yet. She woke in the middle of the night in a blind panic, her body trembling and heart pounding with terror. It was all the more terrifying because she could never quite remember the dream. She lay in her bed, damp with sweat, too scared to move. What had happened? She vaguely remembered being buried alive on the moon rock, unable to move or even breathe as a great weight of stones pressed down on her, crushing her lungs. And there was something else. Something sucking, leeching the life from her, a great snake with gaping jaws. It punctured her skin and coiled around her as it drank her magic. But above all this, swimming in and out of focus, was Magus' face. His chiselled features were hard, as if carved from stone themselves. His silvery blond hair glinted in the moonlight; his dark eyes glittered, cruel and implacable. He watched her suffering, her feeble struggle to breathe. He just stood and looked on with a greedy smile on his face.

In the morning she didn't want to get out of bed and face the world. She was overwhelmed with a sensation of dread. She knew that tomorrow was the full moon and thought desperately of Yul. He'd said he'd wait for her in the woods. More than anything she wanted to be with him, protected and loved, dancing around the Hare Stone in honour of the Bright Lady. But when she thought of that a fog rolled in blocking everything. All she could think of was her compulsion to visit Mooncliffe and give her magic to Magus. It was why she'd been brought to Stonewylde and she must do it without question. There was no doubt in her mind – only a deep sense of trepidation. She dragged herself out of bed and got ready for breakfast. Food was the last thing she wanted, but she knew she must look after herself if she wasn't to become ill again. Miranda was still in bed feeling queasy as Sylvie left their rooms. She made her way down the long gallery of the Tudor wing towards the upper landing, subdued and full of foreboding.

The first person she saw was Magus, glowing with vitality after an energetic early morning ride. He was on his way up the wide staircase, his long legs in tight jodhpurs taking the stairs two at a time. He stopped on the stair below her, still taller than she was. Sunlight shone through the great stained glass window behind her full onto his handsome face, staining his silvery hair with the royal colours of red and purple. His skin was golden from the summer sun and his dark eyes danced with energy.

"Good morning, my moongazy girl!" he said, his voice smooth as mead. He couldn't see her face clearly for the light was streaming in behind her, throwing her into silhouette. He did notice that she seemed taller and longer limbed, no more a young girl but now coltish and leggy. When had that happened? She was growing up so fast. He reached forward and took both her hands in his, surprised to find her trembling violently.

"Sylvie, what's the matter?"

He took a step up onto the same level as her and turned her so the coloured light washed her face. He could see the strain and fear in her eyes, the way her lips quivered.

"What's wrong, Sylvie?" he asked softly. "Why are you so frightened?"

She shook her head silently, unable to articulate her fears, her pale grey eyes enormous and pleading. Magus cocked his head, frowning at her.

"Has anyone hurt you? Upset you?"

"No," she said. "It's nothing, really. Just ... I had a dream. A nightmare."

He stared at her, watching the expressions chasing over her face.

"Yes?"

"There were stones, rocks, crushing and suffocating. It was horrific."

He stroked her cheek gently.

"Just a dream, Sylvie. Forget it. Look – it's a beautiful day. Go for a walk and chase the darkness away. And you know it's the full moon tomorrow night? I've come back from

London especially for you. You remember why?"

Her face clouded over immediately, like a shadow passing across her.

"You've come to take me to Mooncliffe," she whispered. "I want to dance on the stone for you."

He smiled at her and bent to kiss the top of her head.

"And so you shall. I've been looking forward to it all month. See you later, Sylvie. And forget the nightmare."

He patted her arm and bounded up the stairs, heading for his rooms. He needed a shower after his hard ride on the spirited Nightwing. Sylvie continued down the stairs feeling close to tears but not sure why. The hall below was full of people moving around, heading into or out of breakfast in the Dining Hall. She noticed Rainbow standing at the foot of the stairs, her hands idly caressing the carved newel as she watched Sylvie with her bright sea-blue eyes. Sylvie found that her appetite had gone completely, and ignoring the speculative look Rainbow cast her, she wandered outside into the balmy morning.

Sylvie walked around the grounds of the Hall looking at the great trees in full July robes, their greenery at its thickest and best. She thought of the woodland nearby where Yul would now be working. She wished she could go and find him. She hadn't seen him since the cricket practice on the Village Green, when she'd felt that maybe things would be alright between them after all. But she had no idea where in all those acres of woodland he'd be, and felt too listless and downcast to walk far today. Instead she made her way to a beautiful sunken garden she'd recently discovered around the back of the Hall. Climbing down the stone steps, she found a lichened bench carved into the rock walls and tried to let go of her tension. The garden was lined with dark grey stone furred with emerald moss, and every flower growing down here was white: roses, lilies, jasmine, alyssum, clematis, marguerites, asters and even white snap-dragons. Great lush green plants and ferns offset the whiteness, giving the garden an exotic feel. The scent of roses and jasmine and the soothing sound of water trickling from a mossy frog's head in the wall caressed the senses. Sylvie closed her eyes, soaking up the heat and languid calm. She sighed deeply. Bees hummed drowsily in the somnolent peace. She tried to cast off the heavy sense of oppression that blanketed her mind, making her want to cry. The sunken garden was too beautiful for unhappiness.

"Mind if I join you, my dear?"

It was Professor Siskin, who picked his way carefully down the stone steps and into the warm enclosed garden. He raised his panama in greeting and lowered himself onto the stone bench next to her. He too closed his eyes in appreciation of the fragrance and heat.

"Ah, that scent! As one gets older, one appreciates the simple pleasures in life. The Earth Mother is indeed bountiful with her favours. Blessed be!"

Sylvie sat in silence, still close to tears but pleased of his company. She felt an affinity with the elderly man and she liked the way he'd spoken to Yul in the Jack in the Green. He hadn't shown the condescension with which most Hallfolk treated the Villagers, that automatic superiority they claimed as their right.

"Are you feeling a little fragile, my dear?"

She nodded and he patted her hand.

"Magus has that effect on some people. I don't know what's going on, but I would warn you to be very careful. To be on your guard."

She turned and looked at him but he stared ahead, gazing at the white velvet roses.

"I don't understand, Professor. What should I be on my guard against?"

"I'm afraid I don't know. I wish I could help you, but I shall be leaving soon. Lammas approaches and after that my welcome has been outstayed for another year. But there *is* something. I can feel it. And I know Magus of old."

"Has he ever done anything to you?"

The old man shook his head, refusing to be drawn.

"It's all in the past now. But remember, I watched him grow up. I saw him as a boy and then as an adolescent. He was … powerful, even then. He's always enjoyed exercising control and making others obey him. Only then he was far less subtle about it. His father, my half-brother, was a nasty piece of work. Hardly a good role model for a young boy growing up, especially a motherless boy."

"But Clip isn't like that, is he? He's always struck me as being gentler and kinder than Magus."

"Oh yes, that's true. They have different fathers, remember. Clip's father Basil, another half-brother of mine, was hardly a good man but seemed almost an angel compared to Elm. Both the boys, Clip and Sol, take after their respective fathers. Clip means well and isn't a bad chap, but he's weak-willed and easily led astray. Whereas Magus ... single-minded to the point of obsessive, utterly ruthless, some would say sadistic in his determination to dominate. Magus has always had Clip under control. Clip jumps when he's told to jump. He's struggled to maintain any independence. That's why he goes away so much; to try and establish some sort of autonomy. But anyway, I've said more than enough, my dear. I'm very grateful to Magus for allowing me to return each summer. I don't wish to sound disloyal."

"Yes, but this was your home, the place where you grew up," said Sylvie. "You shouldn't have to feel grateful for being allowed to visit. Magus had no right to send you away in the first place. He's not even the owner, is he?"

"No, the estate belongs to Clip. Although it will be Magus' one day, I imagine, as Clip has no children and never will have."

"Why not?"

Siskin raised his eyebrows delicately.

"I gather it wasn't originally from disinclination. But Magus early on discovered a weakness ... how can I put this? ... an unreliability there and exploited it, teasing and humiliating relentlessly until Clip found himself incapable of any act of passion. Completely impotent it was always said. And now of course Clip is the shaman, who must lead a celibate life if he wants to keep his powers strong. Clip was one of Magus' earliest victims of control and he's never managed to break free."

"Yet Magus can be so kind too."

"Oh yes, and that is half his strength. He excites loyalty and devotion, even slavish obedience. The vast majority of people here are only too happy to serve him, anxious for his praise and approbation. It's not until you defy him that you come up against his steel. And then Goddess help you if you don't submit to him. He is not one to tolerate being crossed, or to ever accept second place. Ruthless doesn't even begin to describe him."

He stood up slowly, leaning on his silver-topped stick.

"Just be careful, as I said, my dear Sylvie. Moongaziness is not necessarily a blessing."

She nodded, the heaviness still pressing down on her.

"I will be careful, Professor Siskin. But I feel I'm in a thick fog. I have no idea what's out there waiting for me."

He looked down at her, his pale blue eyes kind, and patted her shoulder.

"Maybe that's just as well, my dear."

The day of the full moon dawned bright and clear. Yul sat crossed legged on the Altar Stone in the Circle facing the rising sun. As the golden disc cleared the tops of the standing stones and the shimmering warmth fell on him, he breathed deeply and prayed to the Earth Goddess that all would be well for Sylvie tonight. He felt the now familiar surge of force flowing up through the stone into his body. He tingled with the power; alchemy of earth magic and sun energy. The ancestors had known where to place their stones, where to mark the points where the dragon lines in the earth surfaced. They knew the places where the fecundity of the Earth Goddess rose up to meet the inseminating power of the sun. But it took a special conduit to make the magic happen; someone with the ability to channel the energy, to transform it within themselves. A magus, a wise one, a magician. Few had these alchemic, transformative powers. Yul was one of the few.

He stayed there for some time in silent meditation as the sky turned from pink to blue and the sun rose higher. Then he opened his eyes and sprang lightly from the stone. Back home for breakfast, then off to work in the woodland. He'd wait for Sylvie tonight in the woods, but in his heart he knew that she wouldn't come to join him. Something had happened to her. Somehow she'd changed and now felt an allegiance to Magus. Why did she want to go to Mooncliffe with him rather than Hare Stone where she belonged? He felt the deep sadness of late fill his soul. She was slipping away from him and he didn't know how to get her back. He'd thought after the Solstice that the world would be his. But apart from Alwyn's demise and his own growing strength, nothing else had changed. Magus was still in power. Sylvie was still out of his league. He was still a Villager in a society where that was not a desirable thing to be. He swore vehemently and ran as hard as he could back to his cottage.

Later that morning Magus called Miranda into his office. He was pleased with their new living arrangements. He now had Sylvie in the Hall close at hand so he could keep an eye on her. The fact that she was in a room with outside access was no accident, for he wanted to be able to get her in and out of the building without Miranda prying. He'd organised the pieces of rock, taken from the great snake-carved stone overlooking the quarry, to be smoothed into egg shapes at the stone carvers' workshop in the Village. These were now ready up at Mooncliffe in a great sea chest. There were twenty-eight of them, one for each day of the month. He had no idea whether his plan would work; whether they'd hold the moon energy in the same way as the great moon stone. He'd had the rock analysed. The round stone at Mooncliffe and the tall stone overlooking the quarry were indeed identical, and were a very unusual form of oolithic limestone. The geologist who'd undertaken the analysis of the samples was excited and had asked to visit the site to investigate further. Magus had refused, for he didn't want anyone snooping around. And particularly not near the quarry where the gang of immigrant workers were tearing stone from the earth, working in conditions not complying with any Health and Safety Act.

"Come and have a word in my office," he said casually to Miranda, when he'd located her in one of the school rooms. Although the students didn't have a complete summer holiday there were fewer lessons at this time of year, with emphasis on personal study and coursework. Magus led Miranda into the wing overlooking the sunken white garden. She'd never visited this part before and looked around with interest. She was impressed by the sheer size of his office and the old books and paintings that mingled with the very expensive, up-to-date looking bank of computers. She sat down on one of the leather sofas and Magus sat back on the other, surveying her. Being pregnant suited her; she was soft and curvy, her eyes bright. He smiled at her, noting her eagerness and excitement at being summoned to his presence. He found the energising effect of the moon stone had gradually worn off during the month, but when he looked at the woman before him he felt a surge of power. Miranda was completely in his thrall and would do whatever he demanded of her. The baby growing inside her was his and would make her even more dependent on him. And maybe this baby would be as special as Sylvie. Next week, once this Moon Fullness and Lammas were over, he'd get to work on her and find out exactly who Sylvie's father was.

And Sylvie herself - she'd knuckled down since the Summer Solstice. He remembered her arguing with him when Yul was at Quarrycleave, challenging him and disobeying him by bringing the boy back to the Village. He'd watched Sylvie at breakfast this morning and couldn't imagine her now standing up to him at all. She'd sat quietly in the Dining Hall, her silver hair falling over her shoulders like a curtain that shielded her from the world. She looked delicate and meek, not strong at all. He knew that with a little help from Clip she would now obey him without question. Thinking of her now, and looking at her mother sitting expectantly before him, he felt that familiar melting sensation in his abdomen. He was in absolute control. Even that thorn in his flesh, Yul, seemed to have faded into the background. He was sure that Sylvie hadn't been seeing him. He smiled; everything was working out perfectly to plan.

"Have you settled into your new accommodation?"

"Oh yes thank you, Magus. It's lovely. And wonderful to be here in the Hall."

"Good. I knew you'd like it. I just wanted to have a quick word with you about tonight. You know, the Moon Fullness."

"Oh, that's tonight is it? I lose track."

"Remember I said I wanted to keep an eye on Sylvie? I need to make sure she's not attempting to meet that boy."

"I'm sure she wouldn't do that. She's changed recently. She's lost some weight, which is worrying, and she isn't herself. She's so docile and passive."

"That's a good thing. She was becoming rude and defiant and I won't stand for that. As for her weight – that's up to you to make sure she eats properly and rests. I won't be pleased if I find she's becoming weak again. I shall take care of her this evening at the moon rise. I want to observe her again. This apparent lunacy is rather perturbing and I need to see exactly how the moon affects her. She's clearly distressed and psychologically disturbed when the full moon rises. I intend to care for her personally each month so you don't have to worry about her. All you need to do is make sure she eats, sleeps and generally stays healthy. Is that clear?"

Miranda gazed at him, loving everything about him. She'd never met a man like Magus before and knew he was one of a kind. She was lucky to have him, even though she must share him with Stonewylde. She was sure that as their baby grew their relationship would strengthen. Maybe one day he'd want to make a commitment to her and the child, if she could just keep him happy in the meantime. She knew he found her attractive and he was good to take such an interest in Sylvie and her problems. She smiled at him.

"It's really kind of you, Magus. I used to worry terribly about her behaviour during the full moon. She was so wild and strange. Thank you for taking this on. When we were in London, I thought she was actually going mad, losing her mind. Will you keep her in the hospital wing under sedation or what?"

"No, no, I'll take her out in the open and watch her, like last month."

Miranda frowned.

"What – let her free? Is it safe? I don't know about this dancing business that she's always insisting on doing. Are you sure it's not going to harm her like last time? Remember how exhausted she was?"

Magus sighed, his mouth tightening.

"The reason she becomes exhausted is because she's not looking after herself properly and you're not doing your duty as a mother. Why do you think I'm telling you to make sure she eats and rests? Use your brain, Miranda."

She flushed and became flustered at his sharp tone.

"Yes, I'm sorry, Magus. I just thought …"

"Well don't! I'll do the thinking. All you have to do is to take her up to bed now and keep her there until tonight. I'll come and collect her at about eight o'clock. Make sure she's ready. And make sure she eats plenty of food today. I don't want her weak. Do you understand?"

"Yes, of course. Shall I come with you tonight, just to ..."

"Absolutely not!" he snapped, his black eyes flashing. "Clip and I will take care of her. That's all, Miranda. Find Sylvie now and take her straight up to bed."

Miranda stood up looking awkward and unsure of herself. The phone buzzed suddenly making her jump. Magus reached across and barked into it.

"What? *What?* The quarry? Well what sort of accident?"

He glanced across at Miranda. She hovered hesitantly, uncertain if she'd been dismissed or not. His face was hard and closed as he listened to the voice on the other end of the line.

"No! On no account call anyone. Drive back there and I'll come up right now… I know, Jack, I understand, but we can't have anybody seeing anything. I'll meet you there. Do what you can and hold tight till I arrive."

He slammed the phone down and stood up.

"An accident?" asked Miranda. "What's happened?"

"Never you mind. Just some trouble up at Quarrycleave.

I'll be back for this evening, whatever happens."

"What about my classes today, Magus? Should I still teach or not?"

"No, cancel them. Sylvie's far more important. Have meals sent up to your rooms and make her eat."

"Thank you, Magus. I'm sorry if I annoyed you or …"

He shook his head impatiently, waving her away.

"Just make sure she's in a fit state for tonight, that's all I ask of you."

As the afternoon wore on, Miranda noticed a change in Sylvie. She'd been kept in bed all day despite her protests, and had been plied with food she didn't want. Miranda had been upset by Magus' attitude towards her that morning and had taken it out on Sylvie. It was all her daughter's fault for worrying him in the first place with this silly moon dancing. Sylvie had just lain in bed staring up at the ceiling or out of the window, eating what she could force down. She'd let Miranda's flood of chivvying and scolding wash over her. She was filled with dread, her mind chasing round in circles thinking one minute of Yul up at Hare Stone and the next of her duty to dance at Mooncliffe. She felt torn in two, utterly confused, and frightened too by the memories of her nightmare which crowded in whenever she dropped her guard. She recalled the sensation of being crushed by heavy rock and Magus' smiling face. It made her shudder.

As the afternoon passed, Sylvie began to feel the old, familiar rising of tension. She sat up in bed and started fidgeting.

"Lie down, Sylvie," said Miranda, looking over from the chair where she was reading.

"I can't. I want to get up."

"Lie down and do as you're told. You know what Magus said."

Sylvie lay down but within a few minutes was up again.

"Please, Mum, let me get up. I can't keep still."

"Why can't you just do as I tell you? Magus said you must rest. He'll be furious with me if you don't."

"I have rested. I've been lying here all day. I'd like a bath. Please let me have a bath."

"I don't think Magus would want that."

"I don't give a damn what he wants!" cried Sylvie, some of her spirit returning. "Who the hell is he to say whether or not I have a bath?"

She flung the bed covers off and marched out of the bedroom, locking herself in the bathroom and ignoring Miranda's mingled pleadings and threats.

When she emerged later clean and refreshed, she found the moongazy dress and put it on. She remembered Yul saying she should wear it for the Moon Fullness. As she thought of him she felt the sadness seeping in, overlaying the jitteriness. She had a sudden image of the Hare Stone and walking up there holding Yul's hand. She thought of him sitting with his back against the stone, watching as she transformed into a moon angel. She remembered the feelings of relief and fulfilment after the dancing and gazing were done. The joy of pouring her moon magic into the earth where it belonged, to mingle with the Earth Magic of Stonewylde. The Hare Stone marked the spot where this could happen, where the circle could be danced and the spirals of energy and force could interact. All this flooded into Sylvie's mind as she put on the gauzy dress and brushed out her long, silver hair. She felt a tingle of anticipation.

But then dowsing it, blanking it completely and utterly, came Clip's commands, rolling in like dark clouds blotting out the sunshine:

*"You want to dance at Mooncliffe every Moon Fullness, Sylvie. You must dance for Magus and share your moon magic. It's what you were brought here for."*

She stopped brushing her hair and sank down into a chair, gazing blankly out of the window. When Miranda came in a few minutes later, she was delighted to see Sylvie had returned to her passive state. She smiled and stroked her daughter's hair affectionately. Magus would be so pleased to find Sylvie calm and obedient, and he'd know it was all her doing. Maybe he'd stay for a while when the moon dancing thing was over. She longed for that more than anything.

Yul could feel the evening drawing in. Although he wasn't moongazy himself, he was very much in tune with the forces that underlay Stonewylde and could feel the setting of the sun and the rising of the moon in his soul. He thought hard of Sylvie, trying to reach her with his mind.

*Sylvie, Sylvie, come to me, my moongazy girl. Come to me at the Hare Stone tonight. Come and dance like a moon angel with the hares and the barn owl. You belong with me, Sylvie. We are two sides of one, the darkness and the brightness. Come to Hare Stone!*

He could feel no answering call, no tremor that might be her mind connecting with his. All he felt was a black fog blanketing everything. He sighed and walked up the path past her old cottage to the woods. It was the gossip of the Village: the two newcomers had moved out of Woodland Cottage and into the Hall. He now had no opportunity of seeing her unless she came to find him. And there seemed little chance of that, especially after he'd become angry with her that last day they'd spent together up on Dragon's Back. He should have hidden it better; not shown her how hurt he felt that she chose to be with Magus and not him. He felt bitterly sad for what had been lost, and for no reason that he could fathom. He also blamed himself for Magus' interest in Sylvie. It was he who'd blurted out her secret to Magus in the byre; he who'd revealed that Sylvie was moongazy. And all for a mouthful of pie.

"Is she ready then?" asked Magus brusquely, walking into their rooms with a cursory knock.

"Yes, she's waiting in her bedroom," said Miranda quickly, jumping up. "Magus, I …"

"Sorry, not now. I must get on. She's been fed and she's rested?"

"Yes. She insisted on having a bath, and …"

"That's fine. I'll take her down the back stairs and I'll bring her back that way too, so as not to disturb you. So don't wait up. I really don't want to see you tonight when I get back."

Her face crumpled.

"Oh come on Miranda! You know I didn't mean that like it sounded. I was thinking of you getting over-tired. We must remember the baby. I'll come and see you first thing in the morning, I promise. I meant that if Sylvie's tired, it's best if you're not around worrying and upsetting yourself. All she needs is sleep, so I don't want you fussing and getting in the way. Clip and I will take care of everything. Alright?"

"Yes, alright. I'm sorry."

"No need to be."

He strode into Sylvie's bedroom where she still sat in the chair gazing out of the window. Her arms, legs and feet were bare, and the soft shimmering fabric of the dress fell from the narrow silver straps on her shoulders. Her freshly washed hair hung like a curtain of silk around her face and down her back. She turned to him, her eyes pale and enormous in her pointed face.

"I want to go to Mooncliffe and dance on the moon stone for you."

"Good girl, Sylvie, that's right. We're going up there now. You can dance all night for me if you want. Come with me, then."

He took her hand in his and led her to the little arched doorway. He lifted the latch and they climbed down the steep wooden staircase. The outside door opened easily and they were out in the glorious evening, where the late July sun was beginning its descent. Birds sang in the soft golden light as Clip stepped out from behind some trees and joined them. Miranda watched them from the window above; her daughter like a delicate silver flower fairy flanked by the two tall men. They disappeared round the corner of the building and Miranda turned away, trying to swallow her hurt and jealousy.

"How are you this evening, Sylvie?" asked Clip.

"I want to dance up at Mooncliffe," replied Sylvie, fixing her moonstone eyes on his. She seemed to be in another world, her eyes strange and face expressionless. She moved like an automaton.

"We want you to dance at Mooncliffe too," he smiled.

Looking over her head at Magus, he winked. "Still working, then."

"Certainly is," Magus replied.

"I'll reinforce it again later on," said Clip. "She's so receptive. She's easy to command and very obedient once it's in her subconscious."

"Strange, seeing as how spirited she is normally."

"That's something entirely different. That's her personality and conscious mind. But this is all linked to her magic, her ability to pick up signs and forces. You told me you thought she had the sight. That's why I can get her to do anything I want. She's incredibly compliant and open to suggestion."

"Could be useful," murmured Magus. "I think I'll carry her there. I want her as fresh as possible."

He scooped Sylvie up in his arms and she lay quietly against his chest, staring up at the sky.

"So tell me what happened up at Quarrycleave," said Clip as they walked the couple of miles to where the cliff path began. "I gather there was some kind of accident today?"

"Goddess, it was awful!" said Magus. "Jackdaw phoned down from the Gatehouse in a panic this morning. They'd been blasting and there was an unexpected rock-fall. A whole section came down that shouldn't have. Don't know if it was that bloody Portlander's fault or not. Maybe just bad luck. Several of the men were trapped."

"That's terrible. Was everyone alright?"

Magus shook his head, his face dark.

"No. We got a couple out but three of them were buried. Crushed. Not a hope in hell. The Portlander had disappeared by the time I arrived. Taken his truck and gone. The other men were hysterical. You know how emotional these foreigners can be. We dealt with the injuries as best we could. I didn't want to get Hazel involved for obvious reasons. Jackdaw's taken the minibus and got them all off the estate. He'll have dumped them back in Dover where he found them by now."

"But what about the ones who were buried?"

"Still buried. They're not going anywhere, so they're best left where they are, under a ton of rubble."

"Sol! I can't believe it! You can't just leave their bodies there!"

"The worst of it is I'll have to shut the quarry up again, for the time being at least. And just when it was going so well. It's a bloody nuisance."

"*It wants lives.*"

They both stared at Sylvie. She gazed up at the skies, her eyes faraway, her voice sing-song.

"What?"

"It's hungry. It wants lives. But now you've fed it there'll be no end. It will not be satisfied."

"What is she on about?"

"I know what she's talking about," said Clip quietly. "I've felt it too. It's the beast that stalks."

"Oh please! Come on, Clip! That's just a load of superstitious Village rubbish!"

In his arms, Sylvie shuddered. Even in her strange state, she recalled the despair and lure of whatever it was that walked the stone labyrinth at Quarrycleave. Those men had been crushed to death to feed the hunger. No saviour, no owl or raven to turn them away from the jaws of death. And if he'd stayed there as Magus and Jackdaw had wanted, Yul too could now be lying under a ton of rubble.

Yul sat up in a tree in the woods. He still clung to the tiny ray of hope that Sylvie would come skipping up the path, her eyes strange and faraway, her body taut with the imminent rising of the moon. But his heart was heavy. He knew she wasn't coming tonight, and tried not to imagine her with Magus going up the path to Mooncliffe. It wasn't only jealousy that was upsetting him so much. She'd insisted that she loved to dance on the great round stone, and yet he knew what he'd seen that night in June. She'd stood as if frozen and it was only when her legs gave way that the spell had been broken. Surely that wasn't good for her? It was nothing like the joyous dancing with the hares. And she'd been absolutely silent, not singing her strange, celestial music. Why did she want to go with Magus? There was something wrong.

Up at Mooncliffe, the sun was still visible low over the hills. The great round stone glittered in the rosy light, all the tiny crystals within picking up the dying sun's rays. It was a breath-taking sight, almost unreal.

"So how are going to do this?" asked Clip. "Put her on the stone now?"

"I'm not sure," replied Magus. He sat Sylvie down on the grass facing the sun. She was passive and unresponsive, the antithesis of her normal behaviour so close to moonrise.

"Last time, she ran up the path and danced for ages on the grass. She must have wasted so much of the energy doing that. This time I want all of it fed into the stone, so there'll be no dancing around. Once she's on the stone she can't escape. We'll keep her there as long as we can."

"Alright, but we must be careful, Sol. She doesn't look strong and we mustn't hurt her."

"It won't hurt her – how could it? It may tire her a bit, but she can sleep for a week after this so there'll be no permanent damage. Don't go soft on me, Clip. You know how good that moon energy feels. We must get as much of it as possible. We're still learning how to get the best out of Sylvie. See the stone eggs I've had made?"

He showed Clip the chest full of the smooth carved ovoids.

"Sacred Mother, how many have you got there?" exclaimed Clip. "She can't possibly charge all those up!"

"There are twenty-eight, one for each day of the month," said Magus. "And she may be able to charge them all – we just don't know. Better to have too many than too few."

"How's she going to charge them?"

"I thought maybe put one in each hand? Or maybe lie her flat on the rock and put the stones on top of her? I don't know. We'll see when the time comes what works and what doesn't. But you can tell when it is working because the stone glows."

"Look, she's stood up."

The sun was sliding down behind the hills. The sky was beautiful, the few clouds on the horizon turning blood red and the higher ones a deep purple. Sylvie was washed in the pink light. Her hair fanned slightly about her in the soft breeze as she watched the sun disappear. She closed her eyes when it had gone and started to tremble. Magus and Clip began to unload the stones from the chest and lay them around the moon stone. As the dusk deepened they waited. Normally at this stage Sylvie would be restless and full of wild tension but tonight she was calm, although still trembling.

At last there was that expectant hush at the moment before moon rise. They now looked out to sea at the spot exactly opposite where the sun had set; the full moon always rises there. With the warm breeze wafting her dress and hair, Sylvie's arms began slowly to rise like great angel wings. Her mouth opened, pouring forth the strange ethereal song. Both men stared, mesmerized by such unearthliness. Then Magus broke the spell.

"Quick, let's get her on the stone now before she runs off to dance."

The two men lifted her up and placed her in the centre of the enormous disc. They stood on it together, one on either side of her, all three facing the sea. Sylvie's song had been silenced the moment they put her there and her wings had dropped. She stood transfixed, her eyes locked onto the horizon.

A soft pinkness appeared over the sea, turning the layer of low cloud draped along the horizon to flamingo gold. Then there was a tiny sliver of deep pink which quickly grew. A strange noise came from Sylvie at the sight of the rising moon, a strangled mewing. Her trembling turned to a violent shuddering that racked her body, almost like a fit. Her hair rippled in silver waves, her eyes fixed wide open. Then they felt the force coming up through the rock into their feet. It seemed as if the moon rock was moving beneath them, although they knew this couldn't be possible. The quaking was so powerful they felt they might lose their balance and fall. The power was too intense for them. Both jumped off the stone feeling a little frightened. Sylvie was rooted in the centre as the moon bloomed before her, huge and deep red-pink, hanging over the silver sea. Her body juddered and jolted, her hair flying around her, and then they noticed the light. It chased itself around her in tiny worm-like strands, flickering all over before heading downwards into the rock beneath her feet.

"I have never in all my journeys in this world or the other, seen anything remotely like this," whispered Clip in wonder. "It's something you have to see to believe."

"Think of that energy going in!" hissed Magus. "This is much, much more powerful than last time. I suppose because then she'd wasted so much of it dancing. Shall we get her to hold two of the eggs now?"

"No, I'd leave it for a bit," whispered Clip. "She's shaking so much I think she'd drop them. And I don't know about you, but I don't want to get close enough to touch her. She's jerking like there're ten thousand volts passing through her."

So they left her on the rock and sat down on the grass to watch.

Yul sat with his back against the Hare Stone also watching the moon rise over the distant sea. The hares arrived from the long grass and the woods as he watched. They started to run in a great circle around the top of the hill and the stone, marking out the spirals. Bats flickered in the deepening darkness and then the barn owl appeared silently. Huge white wings outstretched in ghostly flight, it glided from the woods towards the stone.

"Oh Sylvie, why aren't you here where you belong?" whispered Yul, wiping the tears away angrily with the back of his hand. "Why aren't you here with your creatures and with me?"

As the moon climbed higher and lost its pinkness, Sylvie's violent jerking became less, settling down to a deep trembling shudder. The mewing sounds had ceased. She stood fixed to the spot where they'd placed her, still staring at the rising moon. The stone around her feet glowed a luminous blue-silver. Magus picked up two of the eggs and knelt on the stone. Clip could see from the way he jerked as his knees touched the rock how powerful the force was. Magus crawled across and put an egg in each hand, closing her fingers around them. She kept her fingers curled as he'd left them, so the eggs seemed secure. Then he felt his way back off the stone.

"I don't want to lie there right now," he said softly. "It's still much too strong a sensation, not pleasant at all."

"How long's she been up there? Twenty minutes?"

"Don't know. My damn watch has stopped again. Must be something to do with the energy pulses. Last time I kept her up there until the moon was really high. We'll see how it goes. Oh look at the eggs! It's working! They're starting to glow already!"

He then began a relay of egg holding that went on for a long time. As soon as two of the eggs were glowing strongly he'd replace them with fresh ones and put the charged ones in the chest. He noticed it was taking longer as the moon rose higher. Every time he knelt on the rock to change the eggs he received a blast of the energy. Soon he was buzzing with it. Clip lay on the grass with his long legs stretched out, feet just touching the moon stone. This way he too was drawing the moon power.

Sylvie shuddered only gently now, although the silver light still danced over her body and chased into the stone. She was becoming aware of her surroundings as the moon slowly turned bright silver and grew smaller in the sky.

"It's been a good hour," said Clip. "Shall we take her off?"

"Whatever for? She's fine. The energy's still pouring into the rock through her. And besides, we've only done about half the eggs. No, she can keep it going for a lot longer."

Yul rose from the grass and stretched his legs. He'd recovered from his earlier emotional outburst, the tears long since dried. He now felt hollow with sadness. The hares had stopped their wild cavorting and sat upright, their long ears laid back and lozenge eyes gazing up at the silver moon. They'd marked out the paths and honoured the Bright Lady. They could now moongaze in peace. Yul stepped delicately around them and made his way down the hill through the boulders and back into the woods. He wondered whether Sylvie had enjoyed the Moon Fullness up at Mooncliffe with Magus. He hoped not, for then she may come back to him in August for the next one.

"I really think she's had enough now," said Clip. "Look, the eggs are taking ages to charge up."

"Yes, but they *are* still charging. She's alright, I tell you. She can take it. Stop fussing."

Clip shrugged. He wouldn't argue with his brother; there was no point. Magus always got his own way. Then Sylvie's eyes blinked, and when Magus changed the eggs over again she gazed at him with the same beseeching look as last time.

"Let me go now, please," she mouthed silently.

Magus ignored her and glanced down at Clip, who lay oblivious on the grass with his feet on the stone, soaking up energy and staring at the star-spangled sky above.

A while later Magus noticed tears on her cheeks, like diamonds in the bright moonlight.

"Please let me go," she whispered.

"What was that?" asked Clip. "Did she say something? I really think she's had enough, Sol. She's been up there for at least two hours. You must've got all the eggs charged now."

"Not quite. Four to go. She can take a little more. Last time I left her until she fell down."

"Yes, because you're cruel. For Goddess' sake, she must be exhausted. Haven't you got any feelings?"

"You'll be grateful when you have these eggs all month to keep you buzzing with energy. Just shut up and leave it to me, like you always do."

Not long after this, Sylvie's legs gave way and she crumpled onto the stone.

"There, that's it! She's coming off!" said Clip, jumping up. "She can't take any more."

"Hold on! She's okay. She's lying down now. There are only two more eggs to do. Just watch. She'll be fine for just a little bit longer. She can take it, I know she can."

He climbed onto the stone with the last two eggs. He straightened Sylvie out so she lay on her back, arms by her sides on the stone and palms upwards. He placed an egg on each hand and sat back to watch. The silver threads still ran over her body, but faintly now. He could feel an immense swell of power pulsating in the stone beneath him. It was far, far stronger than last month's. His insides felt molten with energy and power. He felt as if he could jump off the cliff and fly. He laughed with exhilaration.

Sylvie's eyes turned in her head and locked onto him.

"I need to get off this stone," she croaked. "It hurts so much. Please let me go now. I've given you my magic."

Clip stood up and came over, sitting on the rock next to his brother. He too laughed in amazement when he felt the force shooting up into his body, but then looked serious as he caught sight of Sylvie's huge staring eyes.

"What did she say? I heard her say something."

"She's fine. Look, the eggs on her hands are just starting to glow. I want all the magic this month with nothing wasted. Only ten more minutes and these last eggs will be charged. Then we'll take her off."

"Take me off now!" she groaned. "It's hurting me."

"That's it, Sol," said Clip, leaning across and pulling her upright. "You're being unnecessarily cruel. Poor girl! She's had more than enough."

He lifted her off the stone and she felt like a little rag doll in his arms. As he looked down at her, something inside him stirred. She was so vulnerable. What had they done to her?

"You really are an insatiable bastard, Sol," he muttered, laying her down gently on the grass. "Look at her. She's exhausted. You've drained her completely. Why did you make her go on for so long?"

"Never mind that! You've lost one of the eggs, picking her up like that. It rolled off and I can't see it anywhere."

"For Goddess' sake, Sol, stop it! She looks terrible. Look! She's unconscious now. I can hardly hear her breathing."

He laid his head lightly on her chest.

"Sacred Mother, she's barely breathing at all!" he cried. "You greedy, selfish fool! If you've killed her ..."

"Let me see," said Magus harshly, pushing him aside and feeling her neck for a pulse. "Stop fretting, she's fine. This is what she was like last time. She'll be alright once we've got her home. You head back to the Hall with her while I padlock the chest. I'll have to come back in the morning to look for that missing egg."

They climbed the wooden stairs to Sylvie's bedroom and put her into bed. Her breathing was still shallow but steady.

"See? She's absolutely fine. A few days of rest and she'll be up and about as good as new. I want you to make sure she remembers the commands, just like last time, and wants to do it again next month. It was so much better this time without her struggling. She's not bruised or marked at all. Really drive it into her head. I want her desperate to dance for me again."

Clip shook his head, looking at his brother with distaste.

"I can't believe you sometimes, Sol. You remind me of your father, you know."

Magus shrugged. "Are you coming then? It's getting late."

"I know. I'm going to stay and sit with her for a while. I'm still not convinced she's alright. What's the great rush?"

"Clip, it's the Moon Fullness! You know what I like to do under the full moon. And especially now I'm so charged up."

Clip rolled his eyes and shook his head again.

"So you're going next door to visit Miranda?"

"Goddess no! She's far too clingy and dull. I may visit her during the month but certainly not tonight. No ... I've got one of the Lammas visitors waiting. Camellia, remember her? She's a lawyer now and doing very well for herself in the Outside World. Infinitely more exciting than Miranda. Camellia told me she's been waiting a long time for this, so I mustn't disappoint. And thanks to little Sylvie's gift, there's no danger of that!"

"You disgust me, Sol," said Clip quietly. "Close the door behind you."

# CHAPTER SIX

Clip was seriously concerned for Sylvie's well-being the next morning when he and Magus visited. He insisted that Hazel was brought in to take a look at her. Miranda hovered anxiously, still upset by Magus' brusqueness the evening before. She resented the attention he was bestowing upon her daughter, but at the same time was worried herself. She hadn't heard them return the previous night but had looked in around midnight and had been alarmed to find Sylvie lying ashen and motionless under the bed covers. This time there was none of the fitful sleep or whimpering. Sylvie lay like a corpse. This morning she was no better. For once Miranda sided with Clip and privately agreed that Hazel should be called, although she was very careful not to anger Magus by showing this. He was in high spirits this morning, bubbling with energy and verve. He glanced at Sylvie and felt the pulse in her wrist, but it was only a cursory examination. Clip knew what he wanted: a further dose of the hypnosis to ensure her continued obedience. He shook his head at Magus, who frowned ominously.

Miranda fiddled with Sylvie's covers, for the pale girl was cool to the touch.

"I really think we …"

"For Goddess' sake shut up, Miranda!" Magus barked. "Get out of here! You're driving me up the wall this morning with all this fussing. Go down to the Dining Hall and find Hazel. Tell her we need her up here, but it's not urgent. Let her finish her breakfast first. Go on!"

When a crestfallen Miranda had left, he turned to Clip.

"Do it now," he commanded. "Before they come back."

Clip shook his head and Magus took a step towards him.

"What the hell's the matter with you? We don't want her blurting it out in front of both the women! Quick!"

"There's no point," said Clip. "I won't be able to wake her when she's like this. Don't worry – I doubt she's capable of speaking to anyone in this state. And if she does they're hardly going to believe her, are they?"

"Mmn, I suppose you're right. But you must do it later."

"You are the most selfish, unfeeling person I've ever come across," said Clip with unusual temerity. "The girl is ill because of what you've done to her, yet all you can think of is covering your own back."

"What *we've* done to her, Clip. You were as much a part of it as me. And she's not ill. She'll be fine in a few days, you'll see. You know what you need? A visit to Mooncliffe. I've been up there this morning and believe me, I feel on top of the world. Go there later on and you'll stop this whingeing and realise that a little suffering on Sylvie's part is nothing if it means a constant source of moon magic for us. A small sacrifice on her behalf for the good of Stonewylde."

Hazel was mystified at Sylvie's condition, and Miranda didn't help with her attempts to explain Sylvie's strange behaviour during the full moon. In the end Magus lost his temper and dismissed both Clip and Miranda, wanting only to ensure that Hazel did what was necessary for Sylvie without knowing too much. She may be in his thrall but she was a doctor too; he didn't know where her loyalties would lie.

"Her pulse is weak but steady," said Hazel, releasing Sylvie's thin wrist. "Her heartbeat's slow but regular. She just seems exhausted, that's all."

"Exactly!" said Magus. "I knew those two were fussing unnecessarily. Like a couple of old women. All she needs is rest."

"And fluids maybe, if she doesn't wake up. I could put a drip in later on if she's the same. But what happened to her? I've never seen her like this before, even when she was so ill in London."

"Hazel …"

Magus' dark eyes regarded her steadily across the room and he gave a small smile. He watched Hazel's expression change under his glittering gaze. He held out his arms and she flew across the room to be crushed in his embrace. He bent his head and began to kiss her. Soon the last thing on her mind was the sleeping girl lying only a couple of metres away.

"You didn't come to me last night at the Moon Fullness," she whispered eventually, her body on fire for him. "I waited for you."

"I never promised, Hazel," he said thickly, holding her head between his hands and looking intently into her eyes. "You shouldn't wait unless I've told you to."

"But I thought ..."

"No you didn't. You know how it is. I've always made that perfectly clear. Anyway, I was caught up in this." He jerked his head towards the girl. "I'll need your help with Sylvie. She has a strange kind of moongaziness. You may have heard of it before. Sometimes the girls and women at Stonewylde are affected by the full moon. I believe my own mother was. It's all part of the magical forces at work here. It's cruel to keep them locked up when the madness is upon them. Poor Sylvie is desperate to dance when the full moon rises, and you know how over-protective Miranda is. In London she used to shut the girl in a small room under lock and key to restrain her. I'm trying a different, kinder tack – letting Sylvie dance to her heart's content. That's why she's so exhausted today. She danced for hours. I don't want Miranda getting herself in a state about it, not in her condition. Do you understand me?"

"Yes," breathed Hazel, returning his caresses. "I understand perfectly."

"I knew you would, Hazel. I knew I could count on you to help me. So just under-play it, would you? Sylvie will be fine. Put in a drip if necessary but make light of the whole thing to Miranda so she stops fretting. I'd be so grateful to you, Hazel. So very grateful."

The young doctor looked up at him, her eyes glazed with longing. He smiled at her and she saw in his velvety eyes a fiery intensity that made her shiver. He crackled with it today; she could feel it in his touch.

"Let's go for a walk up on the hills, shall we?" he asked lightly. "I'm free for a couple of hours. I know a lovely spot smothered in sweet clover where the butterflies dance. I think you'd like it there, under the blue skies with the swifts and swallows flying overhead and the sun beating down on your skin. Just as good as the moonlight. Unless you're too busy, of course."

"No, no," she gasped. "I'm not busy at all. I'll sort the drip out later when we get back. There's no urgency. You're right. Sylvie's fine, just tired. Sleep is what she needs. I'll make sure Miranda understands, I promise. I want you to show me the sweet clover where the butterflies dance. Take me there now, Magus. Please."

He smiled as waited for Hazel to pack her things away in her doctor's bag. Now he knew exactly where her loyalties lay.

As the Hall filled with visitors and the Village bustled with Lammas preparations, Sylvie spent the next days recovering in bed. Hazel hydrated her with a drip and Miranda had to keep her warm even though the days and nights were hot and sticky. Under Magus' black gaze Clip hypnotized her again, reinforcing the same mantra as before. At Magus' insistence, he emphasised how she must dance again at Mooncliffe for the next Moon Fullness. She repeated this obediently, her moonstone eyes startling in her wan face. The dark shadows under her eyes emphasised their silvery softness as she dutifully reiterated how much she longed to give all her moon magic to Magus. Privately Clip had his doubts whether she'd be able to take it again, particularly with the added burden of charging the eggs. He was sure she was worse this month because the eggs had taken every last drop of her energy. He felt guilty about forcing her to obey, knowing this was an abuse of his gift. But Clip had always given in to Magus and this episode was no exception. However he did visit Sylvie regularly, much to Miranda's annoyance. He liked to sit in her room, regardless of whether she was awake or asleep, and slip into one of his meditations. He hoped that maybe he could pass some positive energy back to her just by being close. The extent of Magus' concern was to barrage Miranda with instructions about feeding Sylvie and making sure she regained the weight she'd lost. Miranda seemed depressed and Clip felt sorry for her. She was desperate for Magus' affection, returning like a kicked puppy again and again.

"For Goddess' sake be kind to her," muttered Clip after one particularly impatient remark Magus had made.

"Yes, I know. I will. As soon as Lammas is over I'll visit her and make it up to her. It'll be easier to fit her in now she's under the same roof."

Meanwhile, as Sylvie languished in her bed, the community prepared themselves for the rituals and festivities that would take place at the beginning of August. Lammas was the festival celebrating the abundance of the crops ripening in the fields ready to be harvested, and some of it was already gathered in. It was a time for honouring the Corn Mother, the spirit of the grain, and as a farming community Lammas was very important to the people of Stonewylde. At school the children had made corn dollies tied with red and gold ribbons or wool. The women wove larger corn dollies from the ears and stalks of the crops harvested already, plaited into intricate patterns and designs and interwoven with red ribbons. They now adorned the rafters of the Barn and the great stones in the Circle. The decorations painted onto the stones were of grain, fruits and flowers. Yul had once again helped to build the great bonfire which always played a part in the ceremonies. This one was a far simpler affair than that of the Solstice; all that was required of the Lammas fire was that it burn brightly. At the appropriate moment the corn dollies would be thrown in and consumed by the flames, representing the sacrificial element of the festival.

On the first of August the bright dawn bloomed in the sky as the people of Stonewylde gathered in the Lammas Field up high above the Village. Under the pink sky they stood strung out like a necklace around the crop of wheat that rustled, golden and heavy-headed. Everyone held hands around the large field and the giant human circle began to chant. Magus, glorious in his robe of gold, led the ceremony. Voices raised, they started to move widdershins facing outwards and looking across the vast expanse of fields all around them. There were crops growing and ripening as far as the eye could see; gold, ochre and burnt sienna in the clear light. This particular field was chosen for the Lammas ceremony because it commanded such magnificent views across the miles and miles of flourishing fertility that was Stonewylde in August. As the red sun burned its fiery arrival above the horizon, the people turned inwards and began to move deosil, making another complete circuit of the field and chanting to the drumbeat. Overhead circled a pair of buzzards, enormous wings outstretched, the air plaintive with their high-pitched mewing cries.

At a signal from the drums everyone released hands and stepped forward, plucking an ear of wheat from the crop. All was silent as the people reflected on the bounty of the Corn Mother, the figurative spirit who lived amongst the grain. Every year she sacrificed herself for the community, yet held within herself the seed for next year's abundance. The drums began a different rhythm and the people picked the grains off their ear of wheat, thanking the Corn Mother for her generosity, throwing the individual seeds back onto the soil. Symbolically they returned some of her bounty to the darkness of the earth, where it must lie dormant through the long winter months until spring quickened it with new life. The ritual struck a chord in the hearts of the people of Stonewylde. They were still in touch with a knowledge so primeval that most others in the western world had long forgotten it. This knowledge was the very source of survival: without the Earth's gift of fruitfulness, all would perish.

The sun was by now well risen and everyone cheered at the sight of two carts being driven by decorated horses up the track to the gate of the field. One carried the Lammas cakes, special flat cakes as big as dinner plates baked from corn, honey and butter and flavoured with nutmeg. The other brought great churns of milk, creamy and frothy, straight from the dairy. Breakfast was served at Stonewylde. Afterwards the younger men of the community were presented with sharp sickles decorated with red ribbons and favours. Once again the singing began as they stepped forward and began to cut the crop in time-honoured fashion. This was a ritual, for the combine harvesters reaped all the other fields. But at Lammastide this one field was reaped in the old way, just as their ancestors had done for thousands of years ever since hunters became gatherers.

The women, the very young and the old went home at this point, the neediest riding in the empty carts. The women would be busy all morning preparing picnic lunches and food for the feast tonight. In the Lammas field the reapers worked steadily, their sickles slicing the stalks of wheat close to the dry earth, hands grasping bundles which were then laid to the side for the binders. The binders were younger boys and girls who tied the bundles with a long piece of reed into a sheaf. The stookers followed the reapers and binders, gathering up several of the sheaves and stacking them into stooks, roughly pyramidal in shape. By mid-morning there were many stooks standing proudly in the blazing August sun, and the uncut area in the centre of the field was dwindling rapidly. Even for the hardy outdoor Villagers this was tough work requiring a great deal of bending and stooping. There was water and cider available to quench thirsts, and as the morning progressed the atmosphere became increasingly merry. By mid-day there was only a circle of golden wheat left standing in the middle, and this rustled and moved strangely. Everyone had their nets and clubs ready to hand.

The band of women, small children and older ones returned up the track. Some came on horse and cart and some carried their own wicker baskets; all were laden down with the picnic lunch. Once they'd arrived the last part of the field was reaped. As the men cut into the wheat with their sickles, rabbits started to fly out, their final refuge no longer a haven. The boys were waiting. Nets were thrown and clubs whacked.

Before long the stubble field became a rabbit graveyard. The unfortunate creatures were lifted by the ears and flung into one of the carts. The women would spend the afternoon baking special Lammas rabbit pies, enough for the whole community to feast upon tonight. When the final handful of wheat was cut, it was carefully carried over to Magus who wrapped it in a golden cloth and presented it to the Corn Mother. She was the girl who'd been chosen for the Lammas festival to represent the spirit of the corn, and like the May Queen she was always young and pretty. She must take this last sheaf and during the afternoon weave it into a special corn dolly. This great dolly, symbolically harbouring the spirit of the corn, would take pride of place on the Altar Stone at tonight's ceremony in the Stone Circle.

Now with the whole field reaped, sheaved and stooked by so many willing pairs of hands, the picnic lunch could begin. Yul took his sickle and trudged over to where the women were spreading out the cloths on the stubbly ground and laying out the food from the baskets. His back was aching, his arms were throbbing, and he had a thirst on him that would have drained the duck-pond. But he was very happy; it had been a good reaping and it was immensely satisfying to see the golden stooks stacked all over the field. He always enjoyed Lammas and this was the first year he'd been allowed a sickle. Before he'd only been a binder or stooker. He put the sickle into one of the carts where they were being collected and joined the queue by the cider cart. There were several barrels on board and older people who weren't able to help with the reaping handed out great tankards of cider to the thirsty workers. Tom was in charge of the carts and horses and greeted Yul, handing him a brimming tankard with Lammas blessings. Yul stood gulping down the cool, tangy cider, his eyes shut at the pleasure of the liquid sliding down his parched throat. He was clapped on the back by Edward, the farm manager and cricket team captain, and nearly choked.

"Good reaping, Yul! Well done, lad. Let's hope you do as well tomorrow in the match, eh?"

"Hope so, sir," grinned Yul, feeling like a man amongst

men. Since the Solstice when Alwyn had been carted away, he noticed that people were treating him differently. He was now the head of his family and enjoyed the honour and responsibility.

He refilled his tankard and found Maizie and the family already seated on their rug and tucking into the picnic.

"You two did well at the rabbiting," Yul said to Geoffrey and Gregory, both over the age of ten and now experienced rabbiters. They grinned at him as they devoured their food. Gefrin and Sweyn poked at the ground as they ate, digging up insects with sharp stones. Rosie kept Leveret well out of their reach as the little girl ate her lunch and gazed dreamily up at the sky, watching the swifts darting and swooping overhead. Maizie poured everyone some redcurrant wine, diluting it with water for the younger ones. Yul looked around at the other families enjoying their picnics under the brilliant blue August skies and felt a surge of happiness. The only blight on the day was the absence of Sylvie. He'd established early on that she wasn't with the Hallfolk, and he wished she was here today. He was becoming increasingly worried about her and knew something wasn't right. Whilst reaping he'd devised a plan to get to see her later on, assuming that she was up at the Hall.

The Hallfolk sat together, not mixing with the Villagers. Most of them had only come for the picnic lunch, not taking part in the morning's reaping. Yul noticed the funny old man whom Sylvie had been with in the pub the week before. The professor saw him watching and raised his panama in greeting. Yul nodded back, pleased to have been acknowledged by a polite member of the Hallfolk. Magus sat on a large rug with the Corn Mother, who this year was Hallfolk. Yul knew that Magus tried to alternate the May Queen at Beltane, Corn Mother at Lammas, and Bright Maiden at Imbolc with girls from the Hall and the Village. Wren had been chosen for the honour this year and Magus was making a fuss of her, feeding her titbits from the delicious picnic spread before them. Yul's stomach clenched with anger as he watched Magus in the distance, laughing and teasing the girl. Where was Sylvie? Why wasn't she enjoying this glorious day? He was sure it was all Magus' fault for taking her up to Mooncliffe four nights ago at the Moon Fullness.

When the picnic was over, everything was packed up and carried back down to the Village. Then large farm carts arrived pulled by the shire horses. Their manes and tails were plaited and be-ribboned for the special occasion, their bridles and harnesses decorated. They trundled across the Lammas Field and men with pitchforks tossed the sheaves into the carts. It had been a long, hot summer and the wheat was dry enough for the Lammas threshing. Some years it wasn't, and then this part of the ritual would be abandoned as the stooks remained in the field to ripen and dry out. Yul worked with the men flicking the sheaves expertly with his pronged pitchfork into the waiting cart, and then moving on to the next stook. A great buzzard perched on the gatepost watching the proceedings with golden eyes, his beautiful tawny feathers glowing in the blaze of the sun. Finally all the sheaves were loaded and the carts rolled towards the gate heading back down the track to the Village. The buzzard launched himself from the post, the clumsy flapping of his immense wings belying the grace of his high altitude flying. The men trudged behind the carts, pitchforks over their shoulders. Yul felt quite light-headed from the cider.

Back in the Village the newly harvested wheat was taken to the Great Barn for threshing. Every year the women hoped this event wouldn't happen, for if the weather was poor and there was no threshing they had more time to clean the Barn and lay out the food and drink for the evening. But this year there was no danger of that. There wasn't a cloud in the hot sky and the threshing went ahead. This was another ritual that echoed the farming customs of their ancestors; before mechanisation, all grain had been separated from its stalk in this laborious way. The men split themselves into teams of four, with four youngsters to help. Each man had a flail consisting of two pieces of wood joined with a leather hinge. One piece of wood, the handle, was of strong ash. The beating piece was holly, for this didn't split. Yul himself had helped cut the wood to make these tools. Each team had their own patch on the clean flagstone floor of the Barn, and several sheaves of wheat. The sheaves were loosened and then beaten with the flails, the team working in a peal, one after the other thrashing the wheat as it lay on the ground. As the grain became separated from the stalks, the youngsters would run in and pull away the straw, shaking it well to dislodge any remaining seeds. They would scoop up the grain into a pile to be put into a waiting sack. It was a competition to see which team could fill a sack first, the winners each receiving a specially brewed bottle of Lammas Mead to take home.

More cider was consumed to slake this latest thirst, and then each team carried their sack on the strongest man's back down to the mill. The grain would be ground into flour at the old watermill where all the cereals were still milled under the ancient quern stone. The resulting flour from the afternoon's hand-threshing was given that evening to the bakers. Overnight they produced Lammas rolls in the shape of a plait, dusted with poppy seeds. They baked enough for every person in the community, to be eaten the following morning for breakfast on the Green with butter and honey or new strawberry jam.

After this most Villagers went down to the beach to swim, for there wasn't enough hot water at the Bath House for everyone to wash away the day's sweat. Yul thought his back was probably alright now to expose, although he felt embarrassed at people seeing how badly he'd been beaten back in June. Down at the beach he joined everyone else and stripped off to his underwear, running into the sea, splashing and making a great deal of noise. Nobody said anything about the terrible marks although he could feel the stares. Several times he looked up to catch the expression on people's faces before they quickly turned away. Everyone in the Village knew about Alwyn and the beating in the stone byre, for Alwyn had boasted about it to anyone who would listen. Yul was pleased that Magus wasn't around. He'd have felt humiliated all over again if the master had been there to see the scars. In fact there were very few Hallfolk about, which was a relief. He could imagine what Holly and her silly gang would have said. As he swam in the warm water of the lagoon and lazed on the great rock further out to sea, he thought what a better place Stonewylde would be if there were no Hallfolk at all. They put a dampener on the Villagers' high spirits and fun with their airs of superiority and stupid comments. Except Sylvie of course. He wished she was there now, slim and silver-haired, lying next to him on the rock and diving into the sparkling blue sea. She would have enjoyed this.

After the swimming and games on the beach, most people went home for a rest before the evening's events. Everyone was exhausted and sunburnt. Yul's skin, already tanned from working outside all summer, was now a deeper shade of brown and the whites of his eyes and teeth were startling in his dark face. Back at the Village Green he decided not to go home, where he knew it would be noisy with his six siblings running around. Instead he flung himself down in the cool shade of the yew tree and lay thinking. The thick dark branches almost blocked out the sky and it was very quiet under the canopy. He felt at once peaceful and yet stimulated. There was a strong feeling of magic here and it wasn't just the memory of his and Sylvie's first kiss on the eve of the Summer Solstice. He could sense something else. It was part of the Stonewylde supernatural, linked to the Earth Magic, the Moon Goddess and the Green Man. He felt its presence strongly today at this primeval festival, under the phoenical tree of regeneration.

Yul closed his eyes and slowly drifted to sleep under the enchantment of the ancient yew. His young, strong body relaxed from the hard labour of the morning as his soul danced in the magic that permeated the woodland temple. Professor Siskin, sitting on a bench outside the Jack in the Green sipping cider, had seen Yul disappear under the spreading boughs of the yew. He nodded wisely, his heart more gladdened than it had been for many years. This was as it should be. The magic calls to its own.

That night before sunset, the people of Stonewylde took part in the Lammas ceremony up at the Stone Circle. As the great bonfire crackled, they joined in the singing, dancing and chanting. Magus and the Corn Mother stood by the Altar Stone leading the rituals. On the altar lay a great corn dolly, beautifully woven in an intricate circular design with ears of wheat radiating out like the sun's rays. This Corn Mother dolly would be burnt on the altar at Imbolc the following February. The ashes would then be ceremoniously ploughed back into the cold earth of the Lammas field to ensure the never-ending cycle of fertility.

Wren looked solemn dressed in green and gold robes, a huge crown of woven cereals and poppies on her head. Magus too was magnificent, sparkling with energy. Yul resented him bitterly, standing up there looking so pleased with himself. The ceremony continued and then came the sharing of mead and saffron cakes, which heightened everyone's perception of the festival. Yul was now ready to embark on his plan, and made sure he was up near the front of the queue. He knew this part of the ceremony took ages, especially with all the extra visitors around. Even when it was over there was still the burning of the children's corn dollies, more dancing, and then the procession down the Long Walk back to the Great Barn for feasting and dancing whilst the Rite of Adulthood took place up here. Nobody would miss him for quite a while if he were to leave early, but he knew he must first go up to the altar and receive the cake and mead. Magus might be looking out for him.

He bowed his head to Magus, glorious in his beautiful robes with the massive barley, corn and wheat crown on his head adding to his stature. Magus looked down on Yul and smiled in satisfaction, amused that not so long ago he'd perceived this boy to be a threat. At the last ceremony Yul had confounded him by appearing on the top of the Solstice Fire with the crow on his shoulder, and had made him drop the torch. But since then everything had changed. True, he'd felt an ebbing of the power he received from the Altar Stone. In fact tonight at sunset and the lighting of the fire, when normally he would have received the Earth Magic, he'd felt

119

nothing at all. But that was more than compensated for by the new energy he was getting from the round stone up at Mooncliffe and his supply of moon stone eggs. This was a different sort of energy, more thrilling and quicksilver than the deep and throbbing Earth Magic. With the supply of eggs safely stored in the chest on the cliff, he could re-energise himself as often as he wanted. The eggs were holding their charge superbly. He'd found that if he slept with one of them touching him, he awoke brimming with vitality. One egg had lasted three days in this way. He felt like a squirrel with a vast hoard of acorns stored up for winter. Twenty-eight eggs would keep him pulsing with power whenever he wanted it, and at the next Moon Fullness Sylvie would perform for him once again. He could drain her moon magic every single month. It was evolution, he'd decided, when trying to understand why the Earth Magic no longer blessed him. He now had the Moon Magic instead. Since Sylvie had come to him, he'd moved forward. Sylvie was the answer. She was the catalyst for this evolution.

Magus watched as Clip ladled the measure of mead into the boy's open mouth, feeling a great bursting of power as Yul swallowed and bowed. He'd well and truly crushed this impudent and disobedient upstart, and it felt good to see him bowing now in subservience. Yul was unaware of this, keeping his head down to hide his exultation. The power sizzled from the Altar Stone, finding its way to him even though he wasn't even touching it. In the flickering firelight Magus failed to notice the green flash as the energy merged with its host. The almost daily visits up here, as Mother Heggy had advised, had strengthened Yul's connection with the energy spirals. The Earth Magic now sought him out whenever he was nearby. His mind raced, picturing the daring plan that he was about to undertake. He relished the strong mead and the spreading heat as it hit his insides. As he held out his cupped hands to receive the ceremony cake he looked up, and in that split second caught Magus' eye. He felt another rush of exultation as the Earth Magic swirled inside him. His cool grey gaze carried unmistakeable challenge. He suppressed a grin as he saw the arrogance in Magus' black gaze turn to surprise and then anger as he read the look in Yul's eyes.

*The fight's not over yet. You haven't beaten me. You never will.*

Yul moved on, shuffling in the long queue away from the Altar Stone, and slipped out of the Circle through the throngs of people. Still wearing his green and gold tunic of Lammas and with barley woven into his hair, he ran as fast as a leaf in the wind up to the Hall. He'd managed to find out from Harold which wing Sylvie lived in, and the fortuitous fact that there was an outside door and stairs leading straight into her bedroom. He'd already been up there at night time to locate it and had checked the door and stairs. Now, out of breath but alive with vigour from his run, he arrived at the Tudor wing. He looked up to the windows at the very end which he knew to be Sylvie's. He'd seen Miranda at the Stone Circle so he knew he was safe from bumping into her. It was now completely dark as he opened the side door from the garden and crept barefoot up the wooden stairs, silent as an assassin. Carefully he lifted the latch of the arched oak door at the top of the stairs and found himself in her bedroom, lit only by a soft lamp. He saw Sylvie lying in the white bed, her long silver hair spread over the pillow and spilling onto the sheet. She was apparently asleep and he tiptoed over, gasping as he got close enough to see her clearly. She looked like death.

In the tiny room of the hovel, the crone muttered to herself as she peered through nearly sightless eyes into the dark glass. She found scrying almost impossible now, but she grunted with satisfaction as the black glass clouded over. A scene began to emerge from beyond the smokiness. But as she squinted at the image, her heart grew cold.

"No, no, no!" she screeched, making the crow squawk in alarm. "Not again! I never saw this! All the dark spirits come down and witness this horror! It's happening again. Oh, dear Mother!"

She shoved the dark glass away from her, rocking frantically in her chair whilst the crow scrabbled to maintain its grip on the chair back. After a while she calmed down but continued muttering to herself, shaking her wispy head. Then she turned and spoke to the crow. He hopped onto her shoulder and she craned to kiss him with her toothless mouth. With a flurry of black feathers he flapped across the room and out of the tiny open window to do his mistress' bidding.

Yul knelt by the side of the bed gazing down at Sylvie as she slept. It was now four nights since her ordeal up at Mooncliffe and yesterday Hazel had removed the drip, judging her to be improving. Her skin was still translucent and the violet shadows under her eyes remained deeply defined, but she had slightly more energy now and could sit up in bed to eat and drink a little. She needed infinite amounts of sleep, and when she did wake was confused and disorientated. Yul knew nothing of this. All he saw was his beloved Sylvie, normally so bright with quicksilver magic, now as lifeless as a corpse.

Gently he stroked the hair away from her forehead and traced the contours of her beautiful face, still lovely despite its delicate thinness. His throat ached at the sight of her. He whispered to her, telling her how much he'd missed her and how he thought of her every minute of the day. He could sense her struggling to surface from a heavy slumber.

"I'm here, Sylvie. That's right, open your eyes."

She recognised his voice and smiled slightly. Then her eyes opened and she smiled properly.

"Is it really you, Yul? Am I dreaming?"

"No, I'm here."

She reached out to embrace him, pulling his head down and rubbing her cool cheek against his.

"Oh Yul, I've missed you so much. Don't leave me again, ever."

The crow flew over the Stone Circle, looking down with bright eyes at the people below spiralling in corn dances. The great fire sent forks of heat lancing up into the night sky. He flew on and finally reached the Hall. He circled for a while, then landed with a flap and a flutter on a window sill. He preened himself and peered through the diamond-paned window at the boy and girl inside, cuddled together in a gentle embrace.

Sylvie released him after a while and tried to sit up. He helped her, propping her against a mound of pillows and cushions, and passed her a drink of water. She smiled at him, trying to act normally, but it was obvious just how weak she was. Her eyes were enormous in her face, pale grey pools of suffering. It broke his heart to see her like this.

"What's happened to you?"

She shook her head.

"I don't know."

"Was it anything to do with the Moon Fullness?"

A strange look passed over her face and she stared at him.

"I danced on the stone up at Mooncliffe for Magus."

"And that's what's made you so ill?"

She shook her head and shrugged, her face screwed up in puzzlement.

"I can't ... when I think of it I feel muddled. It's not ... I don't understand what happened."

"Can you tell me about it?" Yul asked gently, trying not to show his resentment.

"No ... I don't think I can. But I love dancing on the stone."

"How can you love it when it does this to you? Did he force you to go up there?"

Bewildered, she shook her head. He took her wrists and examined her for bruising, but this month there was none. Only the marks from the needle of the drip.

"If he didn't force you, why did you go? Why didn't you come to Hare Stone with me? You know that's where you belong. Why do you go to Mooncliffe when it makes you so ill, Sylvie?"

"I DON'T KNOW!!"

With that she burst into tears, sobbing piteously. He held her in his arms, comforting her, stroking her hair, whispering to her that he would help her. After a while she quietened down and sniffed into a hanky.

"I'm sorry. I'm so frightened, Yul. I don't understand what's happening but I know something isn't right. I have these awful dreams…"

She shuddered violently.

"What happens in them?"

"I don't know! When I wake up I can never remember. Sometimes I remember just as I'm dropping off to sleep but then it's gone as soon as I wake."

"Is it anything to do with Magus?"

He noticed that she shuddered again at the sound of his name.

"I must share my moon magic with him. It's what I was brought here for. I have to do it. Yet …"

She shook her head in confusion and he frowned at her. Just then there was a tapping on the window and they both jumped. Sylvie clutched at him in terror. Yul walked over slowly and saw the crow. Laughing, he opened the window. The crow hopped inside and let out a polite *caw!*

"Look, it's Mother Heggy's crow, Sylvie, come to say hello."

She smiled wanly. He could see that she was exhausted.

"I'd better go soon," he said reluctantly, sitting on the edge of her bed. "Someone could come back at any minute."

For the first time she noticed his tunic and bare limbs, and the ears of barley and corn fastened in his hair.

"Why are you dressed like that?"

"It's Lammas! We've just had the ceremony in the Stone Circle. Now it's back to the Great Barn for the feast and dancing. I wish you were coming."

"Me too. I'd love to dance and have fun. Yul, please come and see me again. I miss you terribly. I don't know what went wrong between us but I still feel the same about you."

He stretched over and kissed the top of her head, wanting more than anything to kiss her properly.

"So do I, Sylvie. You must remember that, whatever happens. I'd do anything for you. I'd give my life for you. When you're well again we'll sort this out, I promise. I'll help you, you know I will."

She nodded, stroking his brown cheek with delicate fingers. Unwillingly he rose to his feet and crossed to the arched door. The crow hopped after him, then flapped up onto his shoulder. He blew her a kiss and shut the door carefully after him.

The crow wouldn't get off Yul's shoulder so he abandoned his original plan to join the feast and decided to pay Mother Heggy a visit. He'd seen her a couple of times since the Solstice but not recently. He'd been so busy with the harvesting of flax, fruit and vegetables and the extra responsibilities at home as the head of the family. He needed to speak to her about Sylvie's terrible condition; he hoped she could help with some of her restorative potions. Yul skirted the Village carefully, not wanting it known where he was going. He carried on up the path leading to the cottage and the crow took off and flew on ahead. When he arrived, the door was already open and the wizened figure of Mother Heggy was waiting for him.

Yul was put into the hard chair while the old woman fiddled about at the range, filling tiny bottles with various liquids from jars and saucepans. Every time he tried to speak she hushed him. She seemed agitated, muttering to herself and ignoring him. Finally he decided he'd sat there for long enough. If she wasn't going to speak to him he might as well go to the feast. He hadn't yet eaten and the thought of Lammas rabbit pies made him very hungry. But she turned and glared at him.

"How did you let it happen, you stupid boy?"

"What?"

"The bright one, the girl. He will destroy her if you don't stop him. The prophecy will never be fulfilled and you will walk alone. You need Sylvie by your side if you are to take your place. You were meant to be guarding her but you let him take her."

"I don't understand what you're on about, Mother Heggy. Do you mean the Moon Fullness and her moongaziness?"

"Aye, of course I mean that. He has taken her to Mooncliffe and made her dance on the glittering snake-stone.

And now he has strength again, just when he should be weakening. History repeats itself. She must dance with the hares. Always with the hares up high on the hill where the tall stone marks the place."

"I know that, Mother Heggy. It's not my fault. How can I stop her? She wants to go to Mooncliffe with him."

"He is forcing her, like his father before him. He is an evil man with a craving for power. Such a lust for power I have never seen, not even in his father. This one is worse. Aye, much worse. This one is the strongest, the cruellest. And the cleverest."

"But she's told me that she loves to go there. He didn't force her to say that."

"You're a fool, boy! I tell you, he is forcing her against her will. Her heart cries out but nobody hears. I have heard her cries in the night, heard them in the skies as she sleeps. But not till tonight would the dark glass clear and show me the truth. Then I saw it, the horror of it. Just like my little Raven before her. History repeats itself, aye it does. He drinks up her life, feeds on her magic until there is no more left to give. He is so greedy, this one. He will never have his fill, always wanting more and more, bleeding her dry. He will destroy her."

"I don't understand. She wants to dance at Mooncliffe."

"'Tis a spell he's put on her. She speaks as a puppet."

"But I didn't think he had any magic of his own. After the Solstice, the magic has become mine. It's getting stronger and every day I visit the Stone Circle. Magus has no power from there. How can he put a spell on her?"

She nodded at this.

"You speak right, boy. 'Tis the brother; he is the one who casts the spell. You must beware of him. He creeps like a snake and you won't know he's about till you put a foot on him. Beware of him and his spells. He is powerful, and 'tis not earth or moon magic like yours and Sylvie's. His is a different sort, a wisdom he has learnt. He is a strange man; he has gifts. He can walk with the spirits. And there is some secret, something not clear."

Yul nodded as he thought about it. That would all make

sense. A spell forcing her to go to Mooncliffe, yet making it sound as if it were her choice. And Clip! Yul remembered the night of the Story Web when Clip had called him up on the stage to touch the Rainbow Snake. He knew the man had strange powers. He could've put a spell on Sylvie and that would explain everything. But his immediate concern right now was her health, for he had seen how weak she was.

"I know, I know," muttered Mother Heggy, before he could say anything. "I have it ready here."

She showed him the bottles she'd prepared.

"Morning, noon and night, a draught for each until it is all gone. 'Twill help the girl get her strength back. But the best thing, once she is up and about, is to take her to Hare Stone for the magic there. You come back here next week and I will speak to you again. Here, put the bottles in this bag. And mind you bring them back, boy. 'Tis not easy to get good bottles and corks."

Quite when and how he was going to get the remedies to Sylvie, or take her up to Hare Stone, Yul had no idea. She was closely watched and looked after. He ran back to the Village, and after concealing the bag of tinctures at his cottage, joined the rest of the community in the Great Barn. There was little food left by this time but he could still enjoy the music and dancing. It had been a long and strenuous day and he needed to relax now. He felt a great deal happier knowing that Sylvie was under a spell and not choosing to go with Magus. He could fight a spell, but he couldn't fight Sylvie not wanting him.

He stood chatting to his sister Rosie as they watched their mother dancing around the Barn. She could at last enjoy herself without the prospect of a drunken Alwyn to mar the event. She'd always had to be so careful in the past for his possessiveness was legendary.

"It's good to see her having such fun," said Rosie. Her own cheeks were as flushed as their mother's as she too had been dancing. She looked very pretty and Yul felt proud of his sister.

"Where's Robin then? Not abandoned you here?" teased

Yul, sipping his cider.

"Just gone to get some more drinks. He wouldn't abandon me," said Rosie. She was madly in love with Robin, who also worked at the dairy. "And anyway, Yul, where's the girl you were so keen on? You never did tell us who she was."

"She's not here," said Yul sadly. "I just wish she was. Hey, look at Mother now! She's dancing with Magus!"

They both watched as Maizie swung past them, her dark curls flying and eyes sparkling. She was linked to Magus, handsome in his festival clothes, who seemed to be enjoying the dance as much as she was. They made a striking pair and many people turned to watch them.

"Always did have a passion for each other, those two," laughed a Village woman, eyeing them both. "Remember that long summer?"

"Aye, quite an item they were, as young 'uns," agreed another. "Alwyn was so mad and jealous, for he had his eye on her too. Remember how spirited Maizie was when she was just coming into her prime? Alwyn wanted her bad, but he had to play second fiddle, I seem to recall. 'Twas Magus she'd set her heart on. Moonstruck for him, she was."

"Aye, right enough. He'd come riding into the Village for her right under Alwyn's nose. And off she'd go with him! Jump up on his horse without a second glance or by your leave. She was a real wild one, that Maizie, with her dark hair and rosy cheeks. Had Magus in her pocket for a while, no mistake."

"And now Alwyn's safely tucked away, the first fiddle can come back and play another tune!"

"Get away with you! 'Tis only a dance, nothing else."

Yul was shocked to overhear such gossip. He'd had no idea that Magus and his mother had once liked each other. The thought was repulsive to him. He turned to discuss it with Rosie but she'd joined Robin on the dance floor and he was left standing alone. Holly, Rainbow and a couple of other girls were now the closest people to him, and their giggling and shrieking was hard to ignore. He stayed in the shadows, not wanting any of Holly's attention. He disliked her all the more for having once found her attractive.

"Look at Magus tonight! Cavorting with another Villager. And an old one at that."

Yul felt his fists clench but kept silent and out of sight.

"Well, he has to keep the peasants happy. He told me that once when I asked him how he can bear having to mingle with them at every festival. He always spreads himself around and he said that's one of the main purposes of all these dances and things. Makes them work harder for the rest of the year. At least that stupid Sylvie's out of the way tonight."

"Yes, else she'd be monopolising him right now. We all know the little cow's got her sights set on Magus."

"I saw him kiss her on the stairs the other day."

"Did you? And have you heard she was with him at the last Moon Fullness? You know, up at Mooncliffe."

"But she's not an adult yet! That's not allowed!"

"Well she was definitely with him. Fennel saw them going up the path just before sunset. I don't know what they were doing up there but she's been in bed ever since. So … what happened that night, I wonder?"

They giggled and Yul gritted his teeth, his stomach hollow with disgust. He longed to challenge them. If they only knew why Magus really took her to Mooncliffe and how she suffered because of it. He felt sick with suppressed rage.

"And with any luck she'll be out of the way tomorrow too, when Buzz gets back."

"Do you think she'll still be after him as well?"

"Well, you know how he was about her before he left. He followed her around like a puppy dog. She's got him well and truly hooked, the bitch."

"She certainly knows how to pull the men, doesn't she? And she looks so sweet and innocent too. You'd never think it of her. I hate her."

"She'd better watch out with Buzz, though. You know he's got that … side to him. He can turn very funny if he thinks he's being messed about. I'd laugh if she pushed him too far and upset him. That'd serve her right."

"And he's back tomorrow for definite?"

"Oh yes, sometime in the morning in time for the Lammas cricket match. Remember how mad he is about cricket? You know he's on the Hallfolk team this year? He phoned tonight and said he's bored at his mother's. He's got loads of new clothes and music. I can't wait to see him again."

"Will you go out with him again when he gets back, Holly?"

"You bet! With madam safely tucked away up in her tower, I'll remind him of what he's been missing all summer."

The girls laughed at this. Yul slipped away and went home, sickened by their talk, the evening now spoilt. Sylvie and Magus, Sylvie and Buzz; he didn't believe a word of it. The girls were vindictive with jealousy. Sylvie was beautiful and special; of course she'd attract other men's attention. He'd have to accept that. There was something about her, maybe her quicksilver moongaziness, that made her so desirable. But she belonged to him. Yul knew this deep inside, despite the apparent impossibility of such a union. Mother Heggy had recognized it – the darkness and the brightness. And like any prize worth having, winning her wasn't going to be easy. He'd have to fight for her.

Reaching his cottage, he looked up at the stars. Eternity patterned in the sky and echoed in his soul. Yul knew he and Sylvie were destined to be together one day. An owl called from the woods nearby and he shivered suddenly. He'd told Sylvie this evening he'd give his life for her. But that was only a part of it. He'd also kill for her.

# CHAPTER SEVEN

Yul left the Stone Circle once the sun had climbed a little in the sky. He now felt energised and strong and knew he'd need this today. It promised to be a scorching day for the annual cricket match. He wanted desperately to play well for the Villagers' team and not let Edward down. At his age it was an honour to have been chosen to play with the men, for he was not yet an adult. Crackling with Earth Magic, both from this morning's sunrise and from the Lammas festival yesterday, Yul decided to go to Mooncliffe. Mother Heggy's words yesterday had been a revelation. He wanted to understand exactly what was going on up there with Magus and Sylvie. Clearly the man had somehow discovered how to take moon magic from her, and it had to be the disc of rock that enabled him to do this. Yul remembered how it had felt before back in June when he'd laid down on the rock after they'd left.

Luckily he moved silently up the path, because when he reached the top he was shocked to find Magus there lying spread-eagled on the massive round stone. He'd taken off his shirt, revealing his tanned, well-muscled torso and the silver disc on a chain around his neck. His eyes were shut and his body relaxed as the sunlight glittered on the rock. He reminded Yul of a viper sunning itself on a stone to warm its cold blood. Yul crept off the path and hid behind the tall bracken that grew so thickly on the hill, watching Magus. His heart beat slow and hard with hatred for the great man who lay glowing like a golden god. This was the man who was responsible for Sylvie lying now in bed, white, exhausted and barely able to move.

After a while, Magus sat up and stretched. His muscles flexed under the tanned skin.

"Sacred Mother, that feels good!" he said huskily.

He leapt off the rock, clearly brimming with energy, and stood on the cliff edge looking out to sea. Yul hated everything about him. The way his silvery hair curled slightly as it reached his neck. The length and power of his legs. His smooth broad shoulders. The bronzed satin of his bare skin. The feelings rose unbidden and almost choked Yul in their violence and intensity. He had a sudden urge to run over and shove Magus hard in the back. To watch him fall and smash his golden body on the sharp rocks below. He swallowed hard and clenched his fists to stop the shaking. He'd never felt such hatred before, not even for Alwyn after his worst excesses. He wanted to destroy Magus and the feeling frightened him in its overwhelming passion. Sylvie was so delicate – this man so powerful. How could he force her to give him all her moon magic? How could he steal something so precious?

Magus chuckled to himself and turned from the sea. He strolled over to a large wooden chest that Yul hadn't seen up here before. Taking a key from his pocket he unlocked it and looked inside, his face breaking in a smile of pure delight. He bent over and took out what looked to Yul like a large goose egg, cradling it in both hands against his chest. He groaned and at first Yul thought he was in pain. But then he heard what Magus muttered and realised that actually the man was in ecstasy. Yul frowned in bemusement. Magus locked the chest and picked up his shirt from the rock. As he turned, the egg caught the sun and sparkled. All became clear to Yul. He could barely swallow for his mouth had become suddenly dry. He had to steel himself not to leap up and attack Magus there and then. He knew it would be pure folly. The man was far larger and stronger than him, and it wouldn't help Sylvie at all if he was beaten to a pulp. As Yul watched, Magus grasped the egg like a ball and made a mock bowl, his arms rippling in perfect co-ordination. He chuckled again and tossed the egg in the air, catching it and laughing.

"Howzat!" he said softly as he started off down the path past where Yul was concealed.

Once he'd gone, Yul went over to the chest but of course it was locked. He tried to move it but it was extremely heavy and must be full of the stone eggs. Stone eggs that Sylvie had been made to fill with her magic. Then he sprang onto the stone disc and was struck as before by the force emanating from it. He could feel the power pulsing into his body. Magus was right – it did feel good. But it was Sylvie's magic and not his to take. He wanted none of it. He jumped off and stood on the short grass of the cliff top just as Magus had done, looking out to sea at the gulls riding the thermals. He vowed that Magus would suffer for this. He didn't know how, but that man would pay for what he was doing to her.

During the morning everyone was busy putting the final touches to the Village Green in readiness for the cricket match. This was a major event at Stonewylde and one of the few times that Villagers competed directly against Hallfolk. It was always a fiercely contested affair and evenly matched, as there was strength, stamina and skill on both sides. Yul could see both Magus and Clip on the Green and decided to chance a visit to Sylvie. He needed to deliver the potions from Mother Heggy and help her begin the process of recovery. He raced home to collect the bag and walked in to a major row. Leveret was in his mother's arms, scarlet-faced and screaming, whilst Gefrin and Sweyn stood silently in the middle of the room looking down at the floor.

"Yul! Thank Goddess you're here!" cried Maizie. "You sort this out. Rosie and the boys aren't here and I've enough to do helping get the cricket match tea ready without this."

"What's happened?" asked Yul, wanting to face his responsibilities at home but anxious to get to Sylvie while he knew Magus and Clip were safely on the Green.

"Those two again!" said Maizie angrily. "I don't know what's been going on but they've done something to Leveret and look at the state of her. She can't tell me of course, and they're denying everything. Since Alwyn's gone they've been terrible. You deal with them. And make sure it sticks. This isn't the first time they've hurt her."

Yul glared down at the two little boys, both looking sheepishly at their feet. He felt a bubbling of anger. Sweyn particularly annoyed him, and Yul knew it was because he looked so like Alwyn.

"Well?" he said. "What did you do? I want the truth now!"

"Nothing!" cried Gefrin. "We didn't do nothing, Yul!"

"She's just a cry-baby," muttered Sweyn, his jaw stubborn.

Yul took a deep breath. He had to get up to the Hall now; it really was urgent. Maizie had calmed Leveret down a little and watched her oldest son struggle to deal with the situation.

"Smack them, Yul," she said firmly. "They've obviously done something nasty to her."

Yul rounded on her, his face white.

"I don't smack children," he said quietly. "Nobody in this house is to be smacked, or hit, or beaten. Not ever."

She stared at him and swallowed. Leveret held her arms out and Yul took her, hugging her close. She clung to him, hot and tearful, her little body still shaking with the aftermath of sobbing. He turned back to the two boys who were eyeing each other hopefully. They weren't to be smacked. Maybe they'd get off altogether.

"If you won't tell me the truth, then you must have done something horrible," he said. "I won't stand for it. Smacking is wrong, but you'll be punished. I'm taking you down now to the nursery and you can spend the day there. You'll miss the cricket match and the tea. Daisy never comes to the match and she'll be there looking after the babies. She can keep you in the naughty room for the whole day. Don't you ever do anything nasty to your little sister again. You should be looking after her, not hurting her."

He kissed Leveret and handed her back to his mother, then collected the bag of remedies from his room. Grabbing each of the boys by an arm, Yul marched them quickly down into the heart of the Village to the nursery. Their legs could barely keep up with his long strides and both snivelled all the way. He saw Clip and Magus in the Barn and breathed a sigh of relief. With a final admonishment to his youngest brothers,

134

he bundled them into the care of Daisy and ran towards the track leading to the Hall.

On the way he heard voices around the corner and dived into the bushes. He recognised Buzz's voice and didn't want to risk a confrontation now, not with the bag full of precious medicine for Sylvie. Soon Buzz came swaggering into sight surrounded by his old gang of friends, as loud and ebullient as ever. He seemed bigger than before and more adult. His face was freckled and his blond hair now very short. Yul's skin prickled with dislike at the sight of him and the memory of the beatings Buzz had given him over the years. He had a score to settle with this large blond youth, and the sooner the better.

As luck would have it, he saw Miranda sitting outside on the terrace as he skirted the Hall and made his way round to the Tudor wing. Quietly he climbed the stairs, knocking gently on the arched door at the top. He went in to find Sylvie out of bed and sitting in a chair by the window. She leapt up and flung her arms around him. He grinned at her, delighted to see her up and looking a little brighter today.

"Mother Heggy has sent you some of her potions to help you get your strength back," he said, showing her the bottles inside the bag. "You must drink one – see, they're quite small – every morning, noon and night she said, until they've all gone. And keep the bottles and corks because she wants them back."

Sylvie looked dubiously at the assorted glass bottles and their murky brown contents.

"Do you think it's safe?" she asked. "It won't poison me, will it?"

"Sylvie, Mother Heggy is renowned for her remedies. She's brilliant. I promise this will make you feel better. Have one now, if fact."

She did so, and felt the effect of the strange medicine as it slid down her throat. They hid the bag in the fireplace behind the decorative summer fire-screen. She smiled at him and sat down again in the chair.

"You look wonderful today, Yul," she said softly. "You're shimmering."

"It's the Earth Magic," he said. "It comes to me now so strongly. Last night at the Lammas ceremony – I didn't even have to stand on the Altar Stone. It sought me out."

"What about Magus? Did he notice? Isn't he angry that he doesn't get it?"

Yul's face darkened at the memory of what he'd seen on the cliff top earlier.

"No. He doesn't need it any more. Sylvie, I know what's wrong with you now. It's all Magus' fault. It's that stone up at Mooncliffe. It …"

"No!" she cried. "I don't want to talk about it! When I think of it all my head hurts. Please … just leave it, Yul."

"Alright," he said softly. "We'll sort it out when you're stronger. At least you're safe from him until the next Moon Fullness. I'm sorry."

He knelt before her and took her hands in his, gazing up into her thin face. She flinched, her eyes widening with shock, and pulled her hands away.

"What?"

"I can feel the Earth Magic in you, Yul! It's so strong. It feels like when Magus healed me back in the spring."

"Really? Then take it, Sylvie! Take it now. I can heal you too!"

She looked uncertain.

"Are you sure? Magus said he had to be careful or it would be too powerful. Can you control it?"

He shook his head. She looked down at him kneeling at her feet, his deep grey eyes full of concern for her. It seemed every time she saw him he'd changed. He looked so grown up nowadays, more a man than a boy. She thought back to the Yul who'd dug her back garden and looked at him now more closely. He was different; the thin defiant face now filled out into strong planes and hollows. He was so good looking. She reached forward hesitantly and stroked his angular cheek bone, tracing the thin scar.

"Just hold me," she whispered. "That will be enough."

He stood up and helped her to her feet, wrapping his arms around her and holding her tight. She felt thin and frail and he was careful not to crush her. Tentatively he tried to free just a little of the energy burning inside him and let it pass gently through his fingertips where they touched her. He felt her tremble but he held on, and slowly felt the release. It was a strange sensation but not unpleasant, and he was pleased to be able to do something to help her.

Eventually she pulled away and held him at arm's length, looking deep into his eyes.

"Thank you, Yul. I feel stronger already."

He could see a faint tinge to her cheeks that hadn't been there before, though whether that was due to him or Mother Heggy's potion he couldn't be sure. Her eyes sparkled slightly, no longer dull and clouded, and she smiled. His heart filled with compassion for her. She was so brave, not complaining about what had happened to her, not making a fuss at all.

"I have to go, Sylvie," he said reluctantly. "It's the cricket match and I'm on the Villagers' team. Edward did pick me after all. I'm so excited! That bastard Buzz is back and I would love to bowl him out. I wish you could be there to watch and cheer me on."

"Me too. Good luck, Yul. I'll be thinking of you."

"I'll come and see you again as soon as I can, I promise. You can take some more of the Earth Magic next time. I'll learn to control it properly and then I'll share it with you until we can get your moon magic back."

She smiled and reaching up, kissed him softly on the lips.

"The moon magic isn't mine to keep. I must give it all to Magus. It's what I was brought here for."

The Village Green had been transformed for the special event. A cricket pitch had been marked out, with bunting strung around the trees in the colours of Lammas – green, gold and orange. A platform had been erected with a scoreboard on it, the whole thing decorated with corn dollies and the great silver cricket cup. Tonight the winning team would drink specially brewed Lammas mead from it to celebrate their victory. Chairs and benches were positioned all around and many families were staking claim to their places with rugs and cushions. Long trestles had been set up for lunch, and later on, tea. Children ran around excitedly; when they started to get bored later in the day, games would be organised for them on the Playing Fields with their own junior cricket match.

The two teams were changing into their whites ready for the match, the Hallfolk in the School House and the Villagers in the Great Barn. Yul was excited but nervous. Both Magus and Buzz were in the Hallfolk team. He would love to personally beat them if possible but realised that was only a dream. His fear was that one of them would get him out at the very beginning and make him look a fool. He felt the energy rushing through his veins and prayed silently to the Goddess to help him play well today.

As the two teams led out onto the Green, the community cheered and whooped. All the players wore proper whites and used best quality equipment for this match meant a lot to Magus. He was very skilled at cricket, being both strong and fit. Although his team didn't always win, he himself played well every year without fail. Yul stood out from the rest of them with his dark curls, now almost shoulder-length again. Most of the Hallfolk team were very pale blond and the Villagers tended to be darker blond or brown-haired. There were very few black haired people in the community. Maizie and the children cheered especially loudly as Yul walked past grinning at them. Maizie was so proud of her eldest son. He was turning into a fine young man, strong and handsome, and a different person since Alwyn had been struck ill and taken away. She knew that Yul wouldn't have been striding out confidently as part of the Villager cricket team if Alwyn had still been around. Her husband would have taken pleasure in ensuring that Yul wasn't fit to play on the day, rather than have the boy doing well and feeling good about himself. Maizie shuddered at the thought of it. She thanked the Goddess that Alwyn was no longer around to blight his life.

The two teams stood beneath the platform and the captains climbed up the steps for the toss. Magus of course captained the Hallfolk team, and Edward the farm manager, the Village team. The Hallfolk won the toss and chose to bat second. Under the blazing August sun, the Lammas cricket match commenced. The Villagers batted well, scoring many runs. Yul himself scored a respectable forty or so before being bowled out. He felt he'd acquitted himself fairly well and his family cheered enthusiastically as he came off. Magus was in fine form, bowling superbly, and Yul was very pleased he hadn't had to contend with any of those bowls. Buzz was so busy showing off to all and sundry that he missed several catches and often bowled wide. Magus was clearly becoming annoyed with his behaviour, which was letting down the Hallfolk team. As they stopped for lunch with only two Villagers still in, Yul noticed Magus hauling Buzz off for a private word. He smiled to himself. He liked the idea of Buzz being on the receiving end of Magus' wrath.

Everyone enjoyed a good lunch, and then a minor stir was caused when the Landrover appeared. Clip, who was not on the Hallfolk team, got out and waved to everyone. He went round to open the passenger door. Yul stared in joy as Clip helped Sylvie out of the car and ushered her solicitously over to a comfortable seat near the platform. Magus looked taken aback and strode over to talk to them.

"Hello, Sylvie! This is a pleasant surprise. I hope you're well enough to be out."

"She was desperate to come and watch and I thought it would do her good," explained Clip. "You're feeling a great deal better today, aren't you Sylvie?"

She nodded. "Yes, thanks. I think I'm getting over whatever was wrong with me. I feel much stronger."

"Good, that's marvellous news," said Magus. "You're just in time to watch us Hallfolk bat. We're going to thrash the Villagers this year, I'm sure."

"Now, now," said Clip. "It's the playing not the winning that matters."

"That, dear brother, is why you're not on the Hallfolk team. Of course it's the winning that matters. Isn't that right, Sylvie?"

But Magus was in for a nasty surprise. His team were playing reasonably well but then the Villagers seemed to up their performance a notch. There was some excellent bowling and fielding and several Hallfolk were bowled or caught out in quick succession. When Buzz came to bat he swaggered onto the pitch, saluting the bevy of Hallfolk girls led by Holly who screamed and waved at him. He stood, bent in the batting position by the wicket, an expression of smug confidence on his face. He whacked the first bowl with a lazy swing and started to run. But he faltered half way along as a great roar rose from the crowd. Yul had hared across the grass and dived in an impossible leap. Somehow he'd caught Buzz out. He sprang up from the ground and threw the ball into the air, whooping with triumph. Buzz's face flooded crimson as he stomped off the pitch, cursing loudly enough for many to hear. Yul looked across at Sylvie and saw her clapping wildly. He gave her a discreet wave and she beamed at him.

Magus liked to bat near the end and was becoming increasingly annoyed at the way the Hallfolk team were playing. Their score was way behind the Villagers' and it meant there was now considerable pressure on him to perform. He knew just how much every person in the community looked up to him. He felt he had both a duty and a right to play spectacularly, to show them that their adulation was indeed justified. The game was stopped for afternoon tea just before Magus' turn to bat. Everyone enjoyed sandwiches and cakes and some late raspberries and cream. Magus ate heartily for he found that lately his appetite had increased. As he ate he held a stone egg in his lap and could feel its effect pulsing through his body. He looked across at Sylvie nibbling on a sandwich. She seemed slightly stronger, not quite so pale and exhausted. It proved that she was perfectly capable of recovering almost fully within a week or so. One week of every month wasn't too much to ask of someone, not when it meant serving him in such a special way. Self-sacrifice was after all part of living in a community. As the magus, everyone depended on him. His needs must come first.

He looked around at the crowds of people, his people, and

felt a swelling of pride. They were all here looking so healthy and happy because of his expert leadership. He did an excellent job of running the estate and keeping both Villagers and Hallfolk contented. Nobody else could do the job he did. He glanced over at the Villagers who sat on the grass on their rugs. He noticed Rowan, the delightful young May Queen who now carried his child, the fruit of their Beltane union. He caught her eye and she gave him a beautiful smile that lit her lovely face. He smiled back and saw her flush with pleasure. Scanning across the crowd he saw Maizie with her family and she nodded at him, her pink cheeks dimpling. Magus couldn't see Yul's face for the boy had his back to him. He was holding the youngest child, little Leveret, and whispering into her dark curls. Magus frowned; Buzz should never have let the boy catch him out on his first bat. It was typical of Buzz's form today. He'd been far too complacent about the whole match.

Magus's gaze moved on to the Hallfolk. Buzz was nowhere in sight; Magus imagined he'd gone back to the Hall in shame. The group he hung around with were particularly noisy; he'd have to speak to them. They had no idea how Hallfolk should conduct themselves. Wren was with them and smiled a little knowingly at him. He noticed Professor Siskin, sitting on a deck chair enjoying his cucumber sandwiches. The old man raised his panama in greeting and Magus nodded.

Then he saw Hazel sitting next to Miranda and smiled broadly. He knew Hazel would do whatever he asked. Both women were looking across at where Sylvie sat with Clip, and Hazel was talking earnestly whilst Miranda nodded. He was pleased with Hazel and must make sure he showed his appreciation. He knew exactly how to keep her happy. Someone was waving at him and he realised it was Camellia, the charming young lawyer he'd visited only a few nights ago. She'd be returning to the Outside World soon and he must make sure he saw her again before she left. He sighed as he bit into another scone. Life was good and he intended to keep it that way. He put his hand on the stone egg and accepted another cup of his favourite Lapsang Souchong from Marigold.

Tea over, the teams returned to the pitch. As Magus

walked across the Green to bat, the whole community circling the Green stood and cheered. He acknowledged the adulation with a slight incline of his head, his long legs in the cricket whites carrying him gracefully across the distance to the wicket. His blond hair gleamed in the sunlight and he nodded at the Village bowler to indicate he was ready. His face took on an expression of concentration. This mattered to him and he was going to excel himself today.

Almost an hour later Magus was still batting. He looked magnificent; tall, powerful and shimmering with vitality. Yul knew where his strength had come from and felt a flash of white-hot rage shoot through him. Magus sweated in the heat, his bronzed face gleaming with perspiration. He was playing superbly, never better. He felt amazingly strong and wondered how much money professional sports people would pay for access to such special energy. He smiled to himself. He hadn't thought of Sylvie's gift in terms of making profits, but here was another way he could use her. He could make a great deal of money out of the eggs, the joy being that it was a renewable resource. Sylvie could be made to channel the moon magic every single month. Thirteen loads of eggs a year! She'd managed the twenty eight eggs fairly easily. With practice and training she could do considerably more. He smiled broadly and whacked the ball to score another six.

When Yul's turn came to bowl, Magus' features broke into a sardonic smile. In his dark eyes, Yul read all the arrogance and superiority in which this man luxuriated. He truly believed that he was a god. That he was invincible. As the boy faced Magus across the cricket pitch, something within Yul snapped. With a tiny skip and a thudding heart, he started his run towards the wicket. Magus adjusted his grip on the bat and narrowed his eyes in concentration, confident in his outstanding skills to deal with anything the boy could offer.

The cricket ball felt like a missile in Yul's hand as he flew along his run, gathering tremendous speed, well-muscled arms and legs perfectly in synchronisation. He kept the gleaming, supercilious face in his sights as the ball launched hard from his hand like a rocket, flying in the fastest bowl ever towards its target. Magus seemed to move in slow motion. His eyes widened in surprise at the speed and velocity of the red ball hurtling towards him. He started to react, adjusting himself to intercept this unexpected and deadly marksmanship. But fast as he was, he wasn't fast enough. Yul's deadly shot had found its target. The bails went flying from the wicket in a great arc and the Villagers exploded into a roar of triumph that shook the trees and scattered the pigeons to the skies.

Across the expanse of grass, Yul's grey eyes met Magus' black ones. Yul nodded. Magus nodded back.

"Excellent bowling, young man!" he called down the pitch. "I congratulate you."

As Magus walked off in dignified style to great applause, Yul glanced again at Sylvie. She was laughing with delight.

The celebration in the Village pub that night was riotous. Yul sat amongst the group of men and felt on top of the world. The great silver trophy cup was filled to the brim with Lammas mead, brewed extra strong and with a heavy taste of malt. It was handed round from man to man, mouth to mouth, each sipping then passing it on. Very soon Yul felt the effects of the powerful drink. The speeches began and Yul became increasingly embarrassed by the over-effusive praise.

"But it wasn't just me!" he protested. "We all batted well, and loads of you got them out when we were fielding."

"Aye, but you caught out that puffed up Buzz on his very first bat!"

"Did you see his face? Hah! Cocky little bastard! That burst his bubble, right enough! Never did like him."

"And that bowl you done at Magus! I never seen anything like it, lad."

"Yes, but …"

"But nothing! Magus was on a winning streak, all set for another century. If you hadn't bowled him out the Hallfolk would've won."

"Yet again! I hate it when the Hallfolk win."

"Three cheers for Yul!"

Yul had never in his life received so much adulation. At

one point he fell asleep on a pew, but woke up later and it started all over again. The earlier rowdiness had calmed down a little and there was more chance to talk. Yul was pleased when Tom from the stables came over and patted him on the shoulder.

"Well done, young Yul! A great catch and a great bowl!"

"Thank you, sir."

"Tom, not sir. We're all friends and equals in this pub. None o' that cap doffing rubbish here."

Yul grinned.

"Thank you, Tom."

"You're very brave, lad, challenging Magus the way you do. Today you could've let him carry on scoring. Every year there's always a bother about getting Magus out. I seen men many a time deliberately fumble catches and give him easy bowls because they don't want to be the one who gets him out. It takes a good deal of courage to stand up to a man as powerful as him. Especially after what he's put you through in the past. I reckon you're the only one at Stonewylde who'll do it. Can't think of anyone else, Villager or Hallfolk, who'd challenge him like that. It hasn't gone unnoticed, you know. People talk of what you've done."

"Really? I haven't done much."

"You've defied the man – look at that time at the Solstice ceremony! He dropped that torch and 'twas you as picked it up and lit it again – I saw it. You used your fingers and nothing else. I saw the blue flames. You've got something in you and he don't like it. But we do. Us Villagers. 'Tis about time somebody broke that man's power."

Yul stared at Tom in amazement. He had never, ever heard anyone talking like this. He'd thought he was the only one who resented Magus' arrogance and domination.

"Anyhow, enough of this," said Tom, resuming the heartiness of earlier. "You drink down this last bit of mead, my boy. You earned it. Right enough, everyone? Let's hear it again for Yul, the Villager who took on the master and beat him!"

It was very late when Yul finally decided he must go home to his bed. Yul said his farewells to much cheering, and staggered out onto the Green. He stood swaying slightly at the scene of his earlier glory. He remembered the two high spots of the match: Buzz's crimson face as he was caught out on his first bat, and Magus' expression of shock as he realised the ball coming towards him was going to stump him and there was nothing he could do to stop it. Yul savoured those moments again and knew he'd remember them all his life.

He looked around the great circle of the Green, shadowy under the sparkling stars and tilted yellow moon. He felt the magic of the place, a different magic to that of the Stone Circle. This was a power from within, something deep in his soul emerging. A magic that the Village Green brought out of him rather than put in. He stopped before the yew and thought of what he intended to do there one day. He smiled picturing himself and Sylvie lying entwined under the protection of the sacred boughs. Then feeling a little uncoordinated from the strong mead, he headed along the track to his home. He wanted to lie flat on his bed for everything had started to spin.

A fist flew out of nowhere and cracked him full on the cheekbone. He went flying into the hedge and lay sprawled and confused, his head ringing from the blow. His initial thought was that Alwyn had come back, but he shook his head. Alwyn was out of action; a living corpse up at the Hall. Then he was yanked out of the hedge by his shirt and shoved hard in the back. He fell forward onto the stony track and the weight of someone heavy thudded down, crushing him. Straight away he knew it was Buzz, who liked to use his bulk to pin down his victims. Buzz then bumped his full weight hard on Yul's back. He felt an excruciating pain and vomited as the strong mead was forced out of his stomach.

"Oh shit, he's puking!" yelled Buzz, hastily scrambling off. Yul dragged himself up onto all fours and continued to heave. He was aware of a circle of feet surrounding him and judged there were five or six of them. He was sobering up quickly in the face of danger. Lying on the ground amidst all those feet was not a good position to be in. He staggered upright, barely able to stand, surrounded by the Hallfolk youths.

"I'm going to teach you a lesson once and for all!" growled Buzz. His speech was clumsy and garbled. "I came back especially for that cricket match. I organised my whole summer holiday so I'd be able to play today. I never even had a chance to bat, thanks to you, you little bastard. You need to learn your place, boy. Isn't that right, lads?"

They chorused agreement. Yul smelt the drink on them and it was no drink that he'd ever come across at Stonewylde. Buzz must have brought it back with him from Outside. Yul tried to think straight; with all of them so drunk he was in considerable danger. If they got him down on the ground and started kicking, they might even kill him. He had to escape and fast.

"You're going to regret catching me out like that," slurred Buzz. He shoved Yul hard into one of the others, who thrust him back equally hard. "I am going to beat the shit out of you, boy! I am going to smash you to a pulp, you ignorant bloody peasant! When I've finished you'll never play cricket again!"

They flung him back and forth across the circle, yelling insults and trying to unbalance him. As he was thrown around, Yul deliberately fell harder than he needed into each one. This made them step back each time, unsteady as they were, widening the tight circle a little. As soon as he saw a gap, he pretended to fall, then sprang out through the space between them and ran full pelt up the track.

"Quick, he's got away! Catch him!"

But Yul was much faster than any of them. He'd brought up the contents of his stomach and was feeling better than they were. Buzz in particular was out of condition after being away for much of the summer. Yul raced ahead into the woods, and soon lost them. He could hear them way behind him, crashing about in the undergrowth and calling obscenities at him.

He ran lightly through the woods and decided to go up to the Stone Circle. All he wanted was to lie down and sleep, but he didn't dare go home in case they were waiting for him again. In the yellow light of the waning moon, now tipped very low on the horizon as it set, Yul approached the sacred stones. He felt the sheer grandeur and magic of the silent

146

place. He apologised to the powers that walked there for his intoxication, trying to clear his thoughts as he entered the sacred space. He felt an almost tangible presence – not exactly benign, but not hostile either. With a straight back and upheld chin he carefully stepped onto the soft earth of the ancient arena and walked across to the great Altar Stone. He'd been coming here now almost every day for the past few weeks, but familiarity didn't make the place any less awe-inspiring. He vaulted up onto the waist-high altar and lay down. Immediately the force spiralled up; pure, green energy. All the places that hurt from Buzz's ambush throbbed less painfully.

He looked at the bright stars above, the familiar patterns in the sky. He picked out the great arch of the Milky Way, so beautiful it made the breath catch in his throat. Buzz and his friends faded into insignificance. Yul was acutely aware that he was just one tiny human being lying under such vast beauty. He felt the energy of the Earth Mother pouring up, greeting the starlit dome of the heavens with spirals of movement and power. He was caught in between the glorious interaction of sky and earth, lying on one of the points where the forces met. Like Sylvie at the time of Moon Fullness, his body and spirit were in harmony with these forces; a perfect receptor and conduit through which they could pass. He fell asleep on the great stone as the stars danced their stately patterns above him.

Yul was awoken the next morning long after sunrise. The sun was warm on his skin as he opened his eyes. He could see nothing at first for the light was blinding, but then a dark figure moved and blocked it out. The silhouette was unmistakeably Magus'. Yul's heart began to thud – what now? He sat up quickly, blinking, scrambling upright. Magus moved round slightly and Yul saw his face. The man had obviously come straight from Mooncliffe for he too was glowing with energy. Yul sensed it pulsating through him and wondered whether Magus could sense the green energy swirling around him. They faced each other and Yul held his gaze, determined not to show any fear or subservience. Why should he?

"Why have you been sleeping on the sacred Altar Stone?" asked Magus, his voice neutral. Yul was aware that Magus too may feel he had a score to settle from yesterday, but he might as well tell the truth. If Magus had already decided to punish him, nothing he said would make any difference anyway.

"I was hiding from Buzz and his friends."

"Why?"

"Because they said they were going to beat me to a pulp."

"Why would they do that?"

"Because I caught Buzz out on his first bat."

"I see. And when did this happen?"

"Late last night. I'd been celebrating in the pub with the other Villagers and I was on my way home."

"And was Buzz waiting for you, or was it pure chance?"

"He was waiting with his gang. They jumped out at me."

Magus moved a little closer, his face expressionless but his eyes hard. Yul could feel just how much the man resented him. He steeled himself not to flinch at what must come next.

"I can see the bruise on your cheek. Have they done anything else to you?"

"No, not really, they just shoved me around. And Buzz sat on me which made me throw up. I managed to escape before they could do anything else. They were very drunk and I was worried they'd go too far."

As he spoke, Yul realized the futility of these words. This was the man who'd had him whipped so severely that he could no longer stand, and who'd then starved him for five days. Magus wouldn't understand the concept of going too far. But to his surprise, Magus looked concerned.

"That's plain bad sportsmanship on Buzz's part. He will apologise. Hallfolk don't go around beating up people just because they lose a game. Buzz is forgetting our code of behaviour. Villagers must be allowed to win with impunity or there's no point to the match. Go back home and clean yourself up. Tell your mother that Buzz will be dealt with for this. You'll receive an apology later in the day."

# CHAPTER EIGHT

That afternoon Yul was helping the Village men to dismantle the platform on the Green when they heard the clatter of hooves on the cobbles. Magus rode into the Village on Nightwing, accompanied by Buzz.

"Here they come," muttered one of the men. "Watch yourself, Yul."

The men had noticed the swollen bruise on Yul's cheekbone. They'd heard the details of the previous night's events, and the Villagers had been furious to learn that Buzz was responsible. There was a groundswell of feeling against the young Hallfolk and their arrogant ways, and Buzz was the least popular of them all.

Magus trotted over on the great black horse, whose eyes rolled at the sight of the group of men. Nightwing's mouth was foaming and he champed at his bit, sidestepping impatiently. Magus reined him in sharply and tapped the whip warningly against his neck. Nightwing tossed his head in defiance, flecks of foam flying. Buzz was astride a smaller, quieter horse, who tried to crop the grass at her feet as they stopped in front of the Villagers. The men had closed protectively around Yul, shielding him from view. His performance yesterday had been spectacular and not likely to endear him to the Hallfolk. Both Tom and Greenbough had spoken openly in the pub of all that had happened to Yul over the past few months. Everyone knew of Yul's ordeal at the quarry and the extra work he'd been forced to do over the Midsummer Holiday. It was now common knowledge that Magus seemed to abandon his usual code of justice when it came to Yul, and the thin scar on his cheek was a constant reminder of this. Yul was becoming a popular figure in the

Village, something of a martyr because of Alwyn's cruel abuse, and now a hero after the cricket match.

"Blessings to you all," said Magus briskly.

"Blessings, sir," the Villagers replied, nodding their heads in automatic deference.

"I believe you have Yul there. Come here, boy."

The men parted reluctantly and Yul stepped forward. Nightwing bobbed his head and gave a little whinny of recognition. He tried to come forward but Magus reined him in viciously, cursing under his breath. The horse danced on the spot, haunches bunching up under him. Yul tilted his chin and looked up at Magus towering above him on the stallion.

"Yes, sir?"

Magus gazed down at him coldly, black eyes glittering.

"You told me earlier that Buzz lay in wait for you last night. That he attacked you as you walked home after celebrating the Villagers' victory at the cricket match."

There was an immediate murmur and grumble of disapproval amongst the men. All eyes turned to Buzz who stared at the ground, his face burning scarlet.

"You said it was he who gave you the bruise on your cheek and made you sick."

Magus shifted in his saddle, still trying to control Nightwing who pranced and shook his head, jingling his bit noisily.

"You said Buzz was not alone but had a gang with him. He wanted to punish you for catching him out at the cricket match. Is that correct?"

"That's correct."

"Buzz, get down off that horse!" Magus commanded. "Come here where we can all see you."

Buzz dismounted and stomped round in front of Magus, still staring at the ground. Nightwing reared up slightly and one of the Villagers stepped forward to take the reins of Buzz's horse, walking it away so it couldn't upset Nightwing further.

"I will not tolerate bad sportsmanship in any form," said Magus curtly. "Nor will I tolerate Hallfolk abusing Villagers."

At this hypocrisy, Yul could barely contain himself. He

glared up at Magus, grey eyes blazing, his nostrils as flared as Nightwing's. Magus regarded him with a black, steely stare.

"Buzz has seen the error of his ways and now wishes to apologise."

There was a pause, the tension almost palpable. Yul's angry breathing was clearly audible as everyone waited for Buzz's words. Nightwing cavorted to the side and almost knocked Buzz over. Magus swore viciously, fighting to control the stallion. The blond youth stumbled and tried to get out of the great horse's way, frightened of the terrible hooves that drummed the ground in a tattoo of impatience. Yul stepped forward and reached up to Nightwing's bridle, holding him and stroking his long nose. Immediately the horse pushed his head into Yul's chest, rubbing against him and snickering with pleasure. Magus' mouth tightened dangerously at this but he said nothing. At least the horse had stopped fretting.

"Buzz?" Magus barked.

The youth looked up for the first time and Yul saw a long slash across his freckled cheek. The thin line was raised in a swollen red wheal just like the one Magus had given him, the skin broken and sore. Buzz's pale blue eyes locked into Yul's. The Hallfolk youth was shaking and his lips trembled; the blood had drained from his face. The expression in his eyes was one of pure hatred.

"I apologise for attacking you."

"And?" prompted Magus.

"And for my bad sportsmanship. The Villagers won the cricket match fairly."

The speech had obviously been rehearsed. Yul held his gaze, a feeling of triumph welling up inside him at Buzz's public humiliation. He nodded.

"Apology accepted."

He broke the gaze and cupped his hand under Nightwing's velvet nose, feeling the prickly whiskers under his chin. He could feel the men behind him nodding their satisfaction. Justice had been done after all.

With a jerk of suppressed anger, Buzz turned away. Grabbing his horse's reins, he heaved himself into the saddle and kicked the horse away into a canter. With a final pat, Yul stepped back from Nightwing and Magus wheeled the great beast around.

"You see that I will not tolerate any Villager being unfairly treated. Now that's an end to the matter. Blessings to you all."

With a squeeze of the thighs he galvanised Nightwing into action and left with a thudding of hooves and flurry of dust.

But if Magus thought he'd dealt with the matter, he was wrong. Buzz was too much his father's son to let it rest there, ego dented and superiority in doubt. The revenge on Yul he chose was the one he thought would hurt most of all. A couple of days later, the Lammas holiday over and everyone back at work, Yul was on his way to the hazel coppice. It was mid-afternoon, another sunny day, and Yul jogged along the woodland path shaded by the leafy canopy. He wore the usual woodsman clothing – a sleeveless jerkin, old trousers and leather boots, all an indeterminate shade of green-brown. He was hot and dirty, his curls full of bits of the woodland. He'd been making hazel hurdles all morning and longed now for a drink. He knew that nearby was one of the large pottery jars of water that the men had stashed all over the woodland for just such a time. He slowed down and left the path, stepping through the undergrowth of ferns and hart's tongues to the foot of a great lime tree where he knew the bottle to be laid.

The lime tree was ancient and beautiful. Its late blossom attracted the bees and it buzzed and hummed with life. The heart shaped leaves clustered thickly but sunlight dappled through onto the woodland floor, and Yul sank down with his back against the massive trunk. He sniffed the exquisite sweet fragrance of the lime blossoms, feeling sleepy from his hard, physical work in the woods all day. He raised the stone bottle and drank deeply of the cool water, then splashed some onto his dirty face. The dirt and green lichen that coated his hands smeared all over his clear-cut features, unbeknown to him. He closed his eyes, savouring the moment, knowing that the lime was the tree of soothing justice, the generator of divine knowledge and truth. He felt peaceful here and in harmony with the spirit of the great tree. He drifted into a doze.

Yul was disturbed a little later by a sharp click, followed by another. His eyes shot open and he stared into the lens of a camera. It was Professor Siskin making the most of his last days at Stonewylde. The professor stepped around Yul, sprawled against the bole of the tree with long legs spread out before him, sleepy in the heat. His slanted grey eyes watched the small man lazily and he smiled, his white teeth bright in the smeared green face. Siskin stopped and took another photo, gazing down at the boy intently.

"Extraordinary!" he muttered. "Utterly extraordinary! Do you have any idea of your true identity? Of who you actually are?"

"I'm Yul," the boy replied. "I'm a Villager and a woodsman."

"Yes, that is true. Just a simple boy of the woods, with the leaves and twigs in your hair, the foliage all around you, and the green lichen on your face. You are truly sylvanian."

The white-haired man continued to stare down at him and Yul began to feel uncomfortable under his pale blue gaze. He stood up, brushing bits off his trousers.

"I'd better be getting back to work," he said.

"Yes, of course. Yul. Did you know 'Yul' means 'the wheel'? And now it has come full circle. We are back again at the beginning of it all. The dance continues."

"No, sir, I didn't know that. I must go or I'll be in trouble. Blessings to you!"

Yul stepped back through the undergrowth onto the path and continued on his errand to the hazel coppice. He'd been walking for a while when he heard cries. He stopped and listened intently. The cries were coming from some way distant, in the direction of the track further along which ran parallel to the woods. Yul took off, running like a deer, cutting through the trees towards the sound. He saw the track ahead, the sunlight bright where the canopy was broken. The cries were loud now; a girl calling for help, pleading for someone to stop. With horror he recognised the voice as Rosie's.

He burst through the undergrowth and jumped down

onto the track, looking around frantically.

"Rosie!" he shouted. "Where are you, Rosie?"

Then he saw her. She lay spread out against the mossy bank by the side of the track, her blouse pulled open and skirt bunched up, exposing her legs. Her hair was a tangled mess and her face scarlet, tears streaming down her cheeks. She was hitting desperately at the big, blond youth half lying on top of her, who held one of her hands pinned above her head whilst he tore at her clothing.

With a roar Yul sprang onto Buzz's back, pulling him with such force that a piece of Rosie's blouse, still clutched in his hand, was ripped away. Yul wrenched him off and sent him sprawling to the ground. Buzz looked up in wide-eyed astonishment; his freckled face flushed and mouth gaping in surprise at this unexpected attack. Yul leapt on top of him and punched him very hard in the face. He noted with satisfaction the clicking crunch his fist made as it hit Buzz's nose. A bright geyser of blood spurted out, spraying all over Yul's shirt. Buzz yelled, struggling to sit up. Yul grabbed a handful of his cropped hair and banged his head down hard on the stony track, whilst the other fist punched full force into Buzz's eye.

"What have you done to my sister, you bastard?" screamed Yul, white-faced and beside himself with rage. "I'll kill you for this!"

Rosie was screaming too, trying to pull Yul off as he pounded again and again into Buzz.

"He didn't do anything, Yul! He didn't get that far! Please stop, stop!"

But Yul wouldn't listen. He'd gone berserk and Rosie abandoned her attempts to stop him.

"I'm going to get help!" she cried, and clutching her open blouse together, ran off down the track towards the Village.

Buzz, meanwhile, had managed to push Yul off and stagger upright. His face was a complete mess; his nose a bloody pulp and his eye swollen almost shut. A cut above the other eye was bleeding profusely down his face and his breath was ragged.

"You've done it now, you little shit!" he cried at Yul.

His voice was high and cracked and Yul realized that despite his aggression, Buzz was very scared.

"No, *you've* done it now, Hallfolk scum! You're going to get what you deserve at last!" spat Yul, his eyes ablaze with vengeance.

They circled each other, fists clenched and legs slightly bent, ready to attack.

"I'm going to finish you this time!" screamed Buzz, finding it difficult to see through the veil of hot blood and puffed up eye. His nose was excruciatingly painful.

"Come on then!" called Yul, his voice trembling with adrenalin but feeling very much in command of himself. "Come on, you fat, lazy Hallfolk bastard! Let's see what you can do without your gang of friends to hold your hand! Let's see how you fight one against one!"

Yul launched his offensive in a frenzy of ferocity. He kicked Buzz hard in the stomach and twisted away fast, with a nasty side swipe at his head as he pulled back. Buzz staggered, doubled over in agony from the brutal kick. Yul leapt in again and punched upwards, his fist connecting with Buzz's chin. His lower jaw smacked sickeningly into the upper one and more blood sprayed everywhere. Buzz spat and a tooth flew out with the mouthful of blood. Yul closed in, fists pounding relentlessly, thumping Buzz in the chest, stomach and shoulders. Buzz tried at first to retaliate but he could barely see. His face was one livid mass of swollen tissue and he was winded. He slowly doubled over and sank to his knees, curling up, trying to protect his head. Yul flew in yet again, a whirlwind of snarling rage. His face was contorted with hatred as he roared and screamed abuse, kicking Buzz in the buttocks and kidneys. He knew very well where it hurt most.

"STOP!!"

At first the shout didn't register. Yul continued to lay mercilessly in to Buzz's crouched form, oblivious to the screeches and bellows of pain.

"I SAID STOP!!"

This time Magus waded in and grabbed Yul by the collar, hauling him off. Yul stood there shaking all over, panting and gasping for breath, his face white and hollow with the desire to kill. He was covered in blood. Rosie came running up with Maizie following breathlessly, and both stared at Yul in horror.

"What's he done to you, Yul?" cried Maizie, trying frantically to examine him. "Where's it bleeding?"

Magus, surveying the scene, barked with laughter at this.

"I don't think Yul is bleeding anywhere," he said. "The blood is all Buzz's."

He stepped over to where the youth crouched, huddled and squealing with fear, all self-control gone. He prodded Buzz disdainfully with the toe of his boot.

"Be quiet, for goodness' sake! You sound like a stuck pig. Stand up, boy!"

Slowly, Buzz stopped the noise and tried to straighten up. He was in considerable pain and started to cry with loud, hoarse sobs. The tears mixed with blood and snot to form a cascade of red slime. Yul, his breathing now almost recovered, turned away in disgust. He had never, ever cried like that in all the years of beatings he'd taken.

"Are you alright, son?" Maizie asked him again, still looking for injuries.

"I'm fine, Mother," he replied, shaking with the aftermath of fury but in control of himself. "Is Rosie alright? What did he do to you, Rosie?"

All eyes but Buzz's turned to her. She clutched her torn blouse together trying to cover herself. Her hair was tangled and her hands and cheeks were scratched.

"He ... he tried to force me," she said in a small voice.

Maizie gasped. Yul took a deep breath and stepped towards Buzz again, his fists clenched ready for another go.

"Hold on!" commanded Magus curtly, putting out a hand to stop Yul. "No more, Yul. You've given him a beating he'll never forget. That's quite enough. Are you sure, Rosie? He wasn't just messing about?"

She shook her head, staring at the ground in shame and embarrassment.

"Can you tell us exactly what happened?" asked Magus, more softly. Maizie put her arm around the girl, who burst into tears.

"He was sitting on that stone, like he was waiting for me," she sobbed. "I was coming back from the dairy, as I come back every day along this way. He grabbed hold of me and started trying to kiss me. I thought he was just fooling about at first - maybe he was a bit drunk or something. But he meant it. He said I was going to help him punish Yul. He pushed me down against the bank there, and I tried to fight him off. I didn't give in, but he was so strong. I was trying to stop him but ..."

"And that's when Yul arrived?" asked Magus, his mouth a tight white line of fury. "Did Yul arrive before Buzz had managed to do anything?"

She nodded, sobbing uncontrollably. Maizie held her tight and looked over her head at Magus. The bright spots burned on her cheeks.

"That's enough questions now," she said, her voice shaking. "Thanks to my son she weren't harmed. Though if Yul hadn't come along when he did, I'm sure that this ... this animal would have forced her. I hope you deal with this proper, Magus. No sweeping it under the rug. 'Tis against the laws what that young man was doing and we all know it."

Magus' face was tight as he surveyed the snivelling youth who could barely stand.

"Just so. Buzz will be dealt with appropriately. In the meantime I apologise on his behalf. Rosie was ill-treated."

"And no punishment for Yul," she said, looking straight into Magus' dark eyes. "'Tis plain he was only defending his sister. You can see that."

Magus nodded curtly.

"As you say, Maizie. Yul was blameless in this particular incident."

He flicked a glance to where Yul stood upright and taut, protectively close to his sister. Yul glared at him.

"I would like to say something," he said.

Magus' eyes narrowed.

"Well?"

"Buzz did this to get at me. Rosie's honour and welfare mattered nothing to him at all. So I want this known. If Buzz ever crosses me again I'll finish it properly next time."

"Yul!" cried Maizie in horror. "Don't say such things! I'm sorry, Magus. The boy's upset. He doesn't know what he's saying ..."

"Oh I think he does," said Magus quietly. "He knows exactly what he's saying. And he'd do well to curb his tongue before I do it for him. Take your children home, but send Yul up to the Hall when he's been cleaned up. I want him checked over by the doctor. I think he may have hurt one of his hands."

Yul had indeed hurt his hands; one finger broken and another dislocated, and a sprained wrist as well, all of which were strapped up. But as the doctor said, he would soon mend and it was nothing compared to Buzz's injuries. Hazel frowned at Yul, whom she remembered as a pleasant boy from their encounter in the cottage after Alwyn's seizure.

"It was a really vicious attack. Buzz is much heavier than you. How did you manage to beat him so severely?"

Yul shrugged, shaking the dark curls from his face, his mouth hard.

"He's had it coming a long time. Those who stand against me will fall, one by one."

Word spread around Stonewylde like wildfire. Magus had led Buzz back through the Village after the fight and many people had seen the state of him. At first, the Villagers thought it was Magus who'd beaten him. But then the truth came out – Yul had done it defending his sister. People were shocked. Like the doctor, they found it hard to believe Yul had caused such damage to someone so much larger, and virtually without injury to himself. What they failed to understand was Yul's pent up rage, his desire for revenge, his toughness and fitness, and above all, his first-hand knowledge of exactly where to hit to make it hurt the most. Buzz had never stood a chance. Yul was hailed as a hero for defending his sister's honour so bravely. That night he was carted down to the pub again and toasted with cider. People looked at him with a new respect; it was about time someone stood up to the Hallfolk. They waited to see how Magus would deal with Buzz.

"You are a bloody fool!" spat Magus, standing over Buzz's bed. The youth was back in his own bedroom now, the day after his fight with Yul, and in a terrible state. Both eyes were swollen almost shut, the puffy skin a deep, dark purple like a pair of plums. His nose was in a splint, badly broken, and his mouth too was bulbous and raw. He'd lost a bottom tooth, although with his lips so swollen this hardly showed. He had to keep very still because of the cracked rib and was in agony from the deep bruising all over his body. He wasn't used to pain and made a great deal of fuss, whimpering in distress whenever the painkillers wore off.

"What the hell were you thinking of, having a go at a Village girl? Have you *any* idea of the trouble you've caused me? I'd already had to deal with the other incident, when you jumped Yul with your gang. Don't you understand how much I *hate* having to pander to the Villagers? To go and apologise? Having to stand there and kow-tow to them, demean myself. It's the worst thing, the very worst thing in the world, to have that *bloody boy* looking at me like he's beaten me! Touching my damn horse as if he owns it, not showing any respect to me in front of all those men, and having to let the little *bastard* get away with it! I could have slashed his face to ribbons the other day on the Green. That was all *your* fault. And now *this*!"

He paused for breath, spitting with anger. His eyes sparked as he paced the room, his great body taut with controlled rage as he avoided looking at the pathetic wreck on the bed. Buzz moved a fraction, groaning, and tried to speak through bruised and puffed up lips.

"I'm sorry."

"I should bloody well think you are sorry! Trying to force a girl – who's still a child, remember – is one of the most serious offences. There are only two punishments for it. Public whipping or banishment. I can't make it anything less."

"No, no please, Magus," he whimpered. "Please don't."

"You should have thought of that before you had a go at her. Why the hell did you do it? You can have any of the older Hallfolk girls you want. They seem keen enough on you, although Goddess knows why, the way you behave."

"It was because of Yul. I only did it to get back at him. You shouldn't have made me apologise to him like that. It's your fault."

"MY FAULT?"

"For humiliating me in front of all those stupid, ignorant Villagers on the Green."

Magus growled in exasperation and strode to the window, looking out over the sunny lawns. He saw a group of Hallfolk children running around playing a game and two gardeners working, bent over in the flowerbeds. He turned back to the pulpy face before him.

"*You* are the stupid, ignorant one, Buzzard. I'm ashamed to admit you're my son. How can you be so bloody dense?"

He sat down on a chair next to the bed, visibly trying to calm himself down.

"Look, you idiot boy, do you really not understand how Stonewylde works? The whole community here only functions because of the Villagers. They grow all the food, provide all the labour, keep everything running. They make our lives very comfortable. We need their good will. There are a great deal more of them living here than there are of us. If they wanted to rise up against us, they could. They may not realise it now, but it only takes a couple of bright ones and there could be a revolution just like in Russia, France. You know your history."

"You're not scared of them, are you?"

"Goddess, you are *stupid*! No, I'm not scared of them, but I need their good will. I put a great deal of effort into ensuring they are happy. That they respect me and actually *want* to serve me. That they consider it an *honour* to bend their backs for me. They would all of them willingly do anything I asked, just to please me, but it hasn't always been like this. My father, my uncle and their father before them had run the place into the ground. They'd taken and taken and not given anything back. A bit like you. There almost was a revolution then. I've invested years and years and a great deal of money into building this place up to what it is now. I've worked myself very hard, both here and Outside, to ensure that Stonewylde is a perfect society. That everyone shows me honour and obedience, not because they fear me but because they respect me. And I'm not going to let an arrogant fool like you destroy everything I've achieved over the past years with your thoughtless, selfish actions."

He shook his head, looking disdainfully at his son. Buzz struggled to sit up a bit.

"But I didn't actually force the girl. So you don't need to punish me as if it was rape."

"The intent was there. And with the beating Yul gave you, every person on the estate knows about it. It can't be hushed up. He's once again the bloody hero. Have you seen yourself in a mirror? How could you let him do this? He's given you a professional work over and you didn't even scratch him. There's not a mark on him, other than his knuckles and wrist. And they're only damaged because he hit you so hard."

"He's a madman! *He's* the one you should banish, not me. He's vicious and violent. He's a danger to the community. He's inhuman."

"Oh come off it! He's only fifteen and nowhere near your weight. You should've at least put up a fight. I don't think I've ever seen such a pathetic display of cowardice."

"It felt like I was up against a man. He didn't give me a chance to fight back. And he knew what he was doing, where to hit me."

"Yul's learnt the hard way from his father. I've had several run-ins with that boy over the past few months. I thought I'd broken him but clearly not. He's even tougher than I imagined and I'm going to have to deal with him again once and for all. But to be honest, I can't blame him for beating you. He was defending his sister. He had every right to have a go at you, and more importantly, that's what the Villagers will think. They'll be after your blood."

"I still can't see what all the fuss is about. She's just a stupid Village girl and I didn't do anything to her."

"As I said, the intent was there. And there's the other matter – she's only fourteen. What were you thinking of? You know how important it is to wait until a girl is sixteen.

Nobody at Stonewylde *ever* breaks that rule."

"But what's the big deal? She may be fourteen but she's not a child. I've seen her at the festivals with a boyfriend. In the Outside World lots of people do it before they're sixteen. I should know. I spend time out there every year. Why have you got such an obsession with waiting till they're sixteen?"

Magus sighed and stood up, moving to the window again. He'd calmed down, his anger turned to exasperation and disdain. It was baking hot outside and the brilliant light fell on his face, etching the lines around his mouth, the hollows under his cheekbones. His deep brown eyes gazed at the rolling parkland that fell away from the Hall from this view. The raucous rooks caught his eye, circling above their old nests in the trees, gossiping like a queue of noisy women. He recalled Sylvie once laughing at the way they stole each other's twigs.

"Girls do grow up quickly and look older than they are. But there has to be a cut-off point, a date up until which they are treated as children and are off limits. Else mistakes happen and a young girl could end up being coerced before she's ready. That's part of it."

He came over to the bed again and stared down at the disfigured young man. Buzz obviously imagined that Magus would smooth it all over for him. He wasn't in the least contrite.

"There's another reason I'm adamant about observing the Rite of Adulthood and making everyone wait until they're sixteen. Stonewylde is unique – truly unique. There's nowhere else like it in the British Isles. It's not easy keeping the world at bay outside the boundary walls. We're classed as a religious community and as such are permitted a certain amount of autonomy. But if there was ever even the slightest whiff of underage sexual activity here, even though as you say it goes on in the Outside World, then we could see the end of Stonewylde. Can you imagine the field-day the gutter press would have if there was any sex scandal with underage girls? Although our customs may seem bizarre to those Outside, we're not doing anything illegal. We're not a cult who brainwash people into handing over money. We're not sacrificing animals or advocating sinister sexual practices. Some Christians may brand us as devil-worshippers because we follow the Old Religion and live in harmony with the natural world, but we know how utterly ridiculous that is. The devil is a Christian concept and nothing to do with us. We're clean and not doing anything wrong. And that's why I'm so unwavering in upholding that law and why I can't forgive you for what you tried to do. We both know, Buzz, that if Yul hadn't intervened you would have raped that girl. Raped her knowing full well that she was only fourteen. You're a fool, and you deserve everything that's coming to you."

His stare was unrelenting and cold, showing no sympathy whatsoever for his badly injured son. Buzz's voice cracked with self-pity and fear and his swollen eyes oozed tears.

"Please, Dad, *please* don't have me publicly whipped. Or banish me. You always said I was your favourite son, that one day I'd be magus after you. You were going to teach me all about the estate and how to run it. Don't let that bastard Yul spoil everything. It's all *his* fault anyway for making me so angry. Please, I beg you!"

Magus looked at him with cold distaste, his lip curling.

"For Goddess' sake, stop your snivelling. You have no backbone whatsoever. I've never once said that you'd be magus after me. You may have wished it or assumed it, but I have never said that. And as for it being Yul's fault – you need to take responsibility for your actions. Yes, I shall be dealing with Yul once and for all before the next solstice. But that's in connection with other matters and nothing to do with this. This is entirely your fault, not Yul's, and you need to face that fact and deal with it. You may have reached adulthood, Buzzard, but you're certainly not yet a man."

With a final look of contempt, Magus turned and left the room. He could see that Buzz simply didn't get the point. But he had a while to decide on a course of action as Buzz was in no fit state to be up and about. He'd let him stay in bed and see how opinion was in the Village. Maybe it would all blow over. He'd have to lay off Yul for a while too, for the boy was something of a hero at the moment. That's what really made

# CHAPTER NINE

The talk amongst the Villagers was all of Buzz and his expected punishment. There was much speculation about which Magus would favour; whipping or banishment. Most agreed that whipping was more likely, for Buzz hadn't actually forced Rosie and he was after all Magus' eldest son. Yul had his doubts but kept them to himself. He wasn't convinced that Magus would do anything at all, despite his reputation for justice. In which case, Yul decided, he would have to take matters into his own hands. Amongst the young Hallfolk the sympathy naturally lay with Buzz, particularly after the terrible beating he'd suffered at the hands of a Villager. Buzz had locked himself in his room, taking his meals in there and seeing only Fennel.

"I think it should be both," said Marigold firmly as she dished up the servants' lunch early one afternoon. "A good whipping and then banish him. What that young man done was terrible."

"You're right, my dear," said Cherry, sitting at the head of the table. "Why should he get off lightly?"

The sun streamed into the cavernous kitchen, gilding the heads of the troupe of servants as they ate. The enormous scrubbed table was packed as everyone enjoyed a hearty shepherd's pie, their morning work done. With Lammas over the atmosphere was more relaxed; nobody had time to chat during the festival periods when the Hall was crowded with visitors. Copper pots and pans gleamed on the walls above the enormous cast-iron range. Pots of lavender lined the windowsills to keep the flies at bay during the hot weather, and the huge door was open onto the sunny courtyard outside, where some servants had taken their lunch. Most however preferred to squeeze in at the table and join in the gossip.

"They say 'tis not the first time Buzz has had a go at a Village girl," said Meg, one of the chamber-maids.

"Wouldn't surprise me," said Cherry. "He's got no manners at all, that one. Reminds me of his grandfather."

"Aye, Magus' father was the same. Any girl that took his fancy."

"We're lucky that Magus isn't like that," said Rowan warmly. "He'd never force anyone."

"Wouldn't have to, would he, Rowan?" said another laundry maid with a sly grin. "Not with girls falling over themselves to bed him. Girls just happening to bump into him every time he turns around."

"Now, now!" said Marigold. "None o' that sort of talk at my table, thank you."

"And what about the beating Yul gave him!" said Harold, his eyes shining with admiration. "Have you seen the state of Buzz? Yul did him good and proper!"

"Aye, Yul put him in his place, right enough," agreed Cherry.

"They say if Magus hadn't turned up when he did, Yul would've killed him," said Harold. "They say our Yul was like a mad bull and he'd lost his reason altogether."

"Well, 'twas about time Yul got his own back on them that've bullied him all his life. When they were younger, that Buzz used to …"

"That's enough of your idle gossip!"

All eyes turned to the door where Martin stood glaring at the sea of faces around the table. He walked into the great kitchen and stood with his arms folded, a grim look on his dour face.

"We was just saying about Buzz and …"

"I heard what you were saying, Marigold. 'Tis not our place to question the business of Hallfolk. Magus is the judge and we can be sure that he will be just."

"Well of course!" said Cherry, a little pink. "We know that. We was only saying …"

"I think you've said far too much! I'd like a word with you two women after lunch, in my office."

"Silly old fart!" muttered Marigold as she and her sister made their way to the cubby-hole by the pantry that Martin liked to call his office. "Who does he think he is?"

"He's always been like this, hasn't he?" said Cherry. "Never hear a word against any Hallfolk. Goddess knows why. He's more cause than most. 'Tis plain as your face he's a Hallchild – I reckon it was Master Clip's father Basil myself – but look at him! Never given any Hallfolk treatment. Just a servant like you and me, sister."

When they entered the tiny room, Martin stared sternly at them and indicated for them to sit down

"I was very unhappy to hear the way you were both talking today. You have positions of authority here, as the cook and the housekeeper. 'Tis our duty as the senior servants to set a good example," he began.

"As we do!" said Marigold indignantly. "There's no need for you to get so pompous, Martin."

"Aye, Martin. You'd do well to recall we two've been serving here at the Hall even longer than you," said Cherry. "A good many years longer. We know our duty well enough."

"Your tone was disloyal," said Martin.

"We said nothing against Magus!"

"But you spoke badly of Master Buzz. It's the same thing."

"'Tisn't the same thing at all! What Buzz did was wrong and we can say so if we want."

Martin tapped his pen on the desk.

"As I said earlier, 'tis not our place to sit in judgement. We know nothing of what led up to his ... involvement with the girl."

"Rubbish!" cried Cherry. "What he did was wrong whatever way you look at it. 'Tis against the laws to force a girl and against the laws to go with a girl under the age of sixteen."

"We don't know he forced her," said Martin. "Everyone

knows what that family's like."

"What do you mean by that?" said Marigold, her jowls quivering.

"Oh come. We all remember Maizie as a girl. I expect the daughter's the same."

"I remember you had your eye on Maizie yourself!" said Cherry. "Or maybe you've forgotten that, Martin."

He ignored this, although his ears burned red.

"All I'm saying is, Master Buzz is Hallfolk, Magus' son no less, and she's just a Village girl. A dairy-maid. It wasn't so long ago that we wouldn't even be discussing this. I don't know why there's all this fuss. The girl should feel honoured."

"That's the biggest load of pig-swill I've heard in a long time!" said Cherry.

"Aye! Just because your mother was tumbled by Hallfolk when she were a maid don't make it right now."

Martin stood up and turned on them both, his narrow face furious.

"My mother was proud and honoured to be chosen, and to find she was carrying me. How dare you speak of it in that way!"

"Your mother Violet was hoping to be the Wise Woman back then, all those years ago," said Marigold. "I was a young maid and I remember it well. Mother Heggy was teaching the craft to Raven, but Violet always wanted to learn too. Once Raven was taken by the magus, Basil, and expecting the first baby, Violet thought she'd be trained instead. She vowed to anyone as would listen that she'd never be handfasted, never lie with a man, just as it must be for the Wise Woman. And next thing we know – she's expecting too! There went her chances of ever taking over from Mother Heggy."

"That's all in the past," said Martin quickly. "My mother's skills have been put to good use for the community, especially since Old Heggy went so mad after that Winter Solstice. My mother bakes all the ceremony cakes. She makes remedies for us. It never mattered at all that I was born."

"Pah! Old Violet's never had any real powers. Anyone could bake those ceremony cakes," said Marigold. "If Magus gave me the special ingredients I'd do a better job of it than she does. Mine would melt in the mouth, not stick in the throat."

"Anyway," said Cherry firmly, "I have work to do, Martin. You keep your old-fashioned ideas to yourself. I don't want any of my maids hearing such rubbish and thinking they should put up with any nonsense from Hallfolk men. Magus'll punish that boy of his, you'll see. And I hope it's banishment, because that Buzz isn't worthy of being magus one day. And I don't care if you don't like me saying so."

That evening, Martin himself took the supper tray up to Buzz's room.

"Thanks, Martin," mumbled Buzz. "I hope it's something soft I can manage. My jaw's still so painful and I can hardly open my mouth."

"Of course, sir," said Martin, placing the tray on a side table and helping Buzz sit up in bed. He plumped the pillows and poured some more water for him.

"What's everyone saying?" asked Buzz, eyeing the tray with little enthusiasm. "Are they all laughing at me for getting beaten up by that bastard Yul?"

"No, no, sir, of course not. Nobody's laughing at all. 'Twas shocking what happened. Yul should be punished for what he did."

"Well he's not going to be," said Buzz morosely. "Magus said it's all my fault."

"Maybe he doesn't know all the facts, sir," said Martin. "Whatever happened, a Villager should never be allowed to get away with doing this to Hallfolk."

"You're very loyal, aren't you, Martin?"

"I believe in the natural order of things, sir. I was born to serve the Hallfolk, and especially the magus. To be his right hand man. My loyalty is of course with you, as Magus' eldest, Hallfolk son. I would always stand by you and help you in any way you asked."

Buzz smiled as much as he was able through such swollen lips.

"You're a good man, Martin, and I'll remember that."

Whilst Buzz recuperated alone in his room, Sylvie made every effort to get back to normal after her debilitating ordeal on Mooncliffe. She still had little energy and initially remained in the Hall and the gardens, even though it meant no chance of seeing Yul. Wandering around the Hall one day, deserted because of the hot weather and lack of school lessons, she found herself in the Galleried Hall. She sat down on an oak settle against the wall and stared up at the vaulted ceiling. It was very high, carved in dark wood that curled and swept in curves. There were many stained glass windows set up in the walls near the roof. The sun poured through these beautiful windows in coloured shafts, illuminating the motes of dust dancing like gnats in the light. With craned neck she studied the designs illustrated in stained glass.

She was particularly struck by a great window that glowed green and gold, depicting the Green Man. It reminded her of the carving Professor Siskin had shown her on their visit to the Jack in the Green pub. Looking around the Galleried Hall, she realised just how often the motif was repeated. Many of the ceiling bosses were tiny leafy faces staring down at her. There were faces surrounded with leaves carved into the stone above the arched doorways, and all around the vast room more leafy faces were carved into the cornice of the dark oak panelling that lined the walls. These had been picked out with gilt, and the leaves burned gold in the bright sunlight.

"I see you have discovered the Lord of the Greenwood carvings," called an unmistakeable voice from high up in the gallery overlooking the hall. Sylvie smiled up at Professor Siskin, pleased to see him again. He kept himself tucked away most of the time, buried in his research.

"There are so many of them," she called back. "It's a forest of Green Men!"

"Indeed it is! Wait there, my dear, I'm coming downstairs to join you."

He disappeared from his vantage point up above and reappeared a couple of minutes later through a door opposite her. He hobbled across the flagstones and sat down stiffly on the settle next to her, looking around him with pleasure.

"This is the oldest part of the Hall still standing," he said. "It's probably thirteenth century, with later additions, of course. The floor itself is undoubtedly even older."

They looked down at the large, worn flagstones, and Sylvie shook her head.

"I find it hard to imagine just how many feet have trodden this floor. I was thinking the same thing in the porch the other day. The Hall is so steeped in history."

"Indeed, which is why it holds such fascination for me. I have devoted my life to history and all because I was lucky enough to be born here, surrounded by it. Of course there's my history of Stonewylde, my own small contribution to posterity. And don't forget, Sylvie, it's not just the Hall. Remember I told you about the Village Green and my theory of the woodland temple? The pub and the Great Barn are ancient too, but I would imagine the oldest thing on the whole estate of Stonewylde, including the standing stones, dolmen and barrows, is the yew tree on the Village Green."

Sylvie smiled at the thought of that yew tree.

"I'd love to read your book when it's finished, Professor. I was wondering - has Stonewylde always had a magus?" she asked. "A lord and master who lives here in the Hall?"

"Yes, I believe there's always been a magus. And Stonewylde's always had a lord. But only in fairly recent times have the two roles been held by the same man. Do you know what magus actually means?"

"I thought it meant the master, the ruler."

"Not at all. Although a common misconception. A magus is a magician, a wise one, a learned one. You may remember the Magi in the Bible, the three wise men who visited the infant Jesus, bearing gifts? It's the same word. Magi is the plural of magus. Stonewylde has always had its magus, the one alone who receives the Earth Magic, the one alone who can channel the power. So the magus would be the one leading the ceremonies, and the lord was the person who ran the community. Not the same person doing all of it. I've just been re-reading some fascinating accounts from early

Tudor times describing some of the ceremonies up at the Stone Circle. Magus must have read them too, for I know that when he took over he revived the celebration of the festivals. Thanks to his father and grandfather, the ancient traditions of Stonewylde as a pagan community were almost lost and forgotten. We have a lot to be grateful for with our present magus."

"I suppose so," agreed Sylvie, shivering at the thought of him.

"But interestingly enough, in the documents I read it told of how the magus channelled the Earth Magic during the festivals and shared the power and force with the folk of Stonewylde. Passed the power on to everyone. Our Magus hasn't continued with that practice, but instead gives us a feeling of well-being with the mead and cakes."

"They're amazing. You feel so good after them."

"That's the idea I believe," said the professor, smiling. "Magus is a clever man indeed."

"So why doesn't he channel the Earth Magic and share it with everyone?"

"Who knows? Maybe he feels that he alone needs the energy. But whatever the reason, he ensures that the people leave the ceremonies with a feeling of euphoria. As an act of mass socialisation that is crucial to the community. Ah yes, he is a clever man."

Sylvie stood up and stretched. She helped Siskin stand, for his joints were stiff.

"Yul gets Earth Magic from the stones," she said casually.

"*What?*"

Siskin sat down again abruptly and blinked up at her.

"Say that again, my dear. What do you mean?"

"He goes up there most sunrises and sunsets if he can and stands on the Altar Stone. He comes back charged up with power, full of it. And at the festivals it's even stronger. At the Summer Solstice he made sparks shoot from his fingertips to relight the torch when it went out."

"But it's not possible for two people to receive the magic! It will only go to one person, the chosen one who has the ability within them to channel it. According to the history, there have been times when there is no magus at all. But *never* two. How extraordinary! Unless … unless it has ceased going to Magus. I wonder …"

"I think you're right. I don't think Magus gets it any more. That's what Yul says anyway."

The old man sat there in the dusty sunlight and gazed up at the ceiling.

"Well I never. The Green Man … and now this. I hadn't imagined …"

He shook his head in bewilderment. Sylvie glanced at him; he seemed to have disappeared into a day dream. Then he turned and smiled at her.

"These are exciting times for Stonewylde, my dear. I wish I could be here to witness what is about to unfold."

"What is about to unfold?"

He shook his head again.

"Time will tell. I am only speculating. Best keep it to myself, I think. But I do wish I wasn't leaving."

"Will you be back soon? Do you come at the Winter Solstice?"

"No, my dear girl. I only wish I did. I'm permitted to come merely for the Summer Solstice and stay until Lammas. Magus has been very good to me this year, allowing me to stay on a few extra days. But I'm leaving tomorrow."

"I do wish you weren't leaving," she said sadly. "I have so few friends here, and you're one of the best. Can we keep in touch when you're back in Oxford? Do you use e-mail?"

"Of course, my dear! I might be old but I'm jolly good on my computer. A wonderful invention, the Internet. Invaluable for research. I'd love to correspond with you electronically. You can keep me informed of events … the unfolding."

They sat in peace for a while longer, the professor in his old velvet jacket gazing around wistfully. Sylvie felt so sorry for him. He was an elderly man and Stonewylde had been his home, the place where he'd grown up. Who was Magus to send him away? She sighed and looked up at the ceiling again, noticing this time another motif repeated around the gallery.

"What's that one?" she asked. "The three ... rabbits? Or are they hares?"

"Ah, the triple hare motif! Yes, that's another favourite. This Galleried Hall is positively teeming with hares. See how they chase each other in a circle and share the same three ears? It's a very popular symbol. Quite fascinating, the research that's going on about the hares. There are many churches throughout the country, but especially in nearby Devon, where the triple hare symbol is present. Mostly in ceiling bosses, stone and wood, but sometimes in stained glass or floor tiles. And it's not just this country!"

Sylvie smiled encouragingly at him. He was so enthusiastic and full of knowledge.

"It's been discovered in churches all over Europe – France, Germany, Switzerland – and then even further afield."

"The same symbol?"

"Exactly the same symbol! The three hares chasing around in a circle and sharing the three ears between them. An Iranian coin from the thirteenth century, a Russian reliquary casket, thirteenth or fourteenth century. But the most exciting of all – our triple hares have been discovered in a Buddhist cave temple in China! Dating to the Sui Dynasty, circa the sixth century. Isn't that extraordinary?"

"Incredible! What does the symbol mean?"

"We don't know. The experts think that it was brought to Europe along the Silk Road, when the Mongol empire opened the trading route for silk from the Orient. But I don't know ... I sometimes wonder whether it was here all along. The fact that we haven't discovered any older examples in Britain doesn't mean it didn't exist here. Maybe there are ones yet to be unearthed. It could be a universal symbol. The hare is a sacred animal, remember. Linked to the Moon Goddess. Even the ancient Egyptians had a hare god, and that's going back a great deal further. The hare is a magical creature indeed."

Sylvie nodded, thinking of the hares that danced with her up on the hilltop. But then her head began to cloud and the headache to throb, and she tried to dismiss the memory.

"Ah well, that's enough of the history lesson for today, my dear Sylvie. I hope I haven't bored you? I do get a little carried away in my zeal."

"No, I find it fascinating. I wish you were around to tell me more."

He stood up slowly, a groan escaping his lips.

"I don't mind becoming old but I do wish my body still worked properly. Make the most of yours, my dear, while it's young and supple. Before I go in the morning I wanted to give you something. I have it in my room and I think you'll like it. Will you accompany me there now?"

They left the mediaeval hall with its blazing stained glass and carvings and made their way into the corridor leading to the entrance hall and the main staircase.

"Why are there so many Green Men in the Galleried Hall?" asked Sylvie, as they slowly climbed the wide stairs.

"He's a popular motif everywhere. Many churches have a Green Man tucked away, carved up in the roof or hidden in a corner. Remember most churches were built on sites already used for pagan festivals. The builders – the stonecarvers and woodcarvers – would have felt uncomfortable abandoning their woodland deity completely for the new Christian one. So the Green Man pops up everywhere. The ones here at Stonewylde are in the style of foliate heads, where the head of a man is surrounded by a halo of leaves. This indicates the Lord of the Greenwood. Others you'll see elsewhere show branches and leaves sprouting from the mouth, nose and ears. They're 'masque feuillu', or the sprouting head. Sometimes they symbolise death and sometimes they're to ward off evil spirits."

"But I still don't see why there are so many in the Galleried Hall."

"You've seen that ancient carving inside the Jack in the Green, and I've told you about the wood henge and the woodland clearing that is now the Village Green. The religion here, before mediaeval times, was not only the cult of the Earth Goddess as it is to this day, but also that of the woodland deity, the Green Man. He was the spirit of virility, the inseminator who impregnated Mother Earth and made her bountiful and fruitful. So the Green Man would appear in much of the early architecture at Stonewylde, and the Galleried Hall is of course the oldest part of the building."

They'd climbed the main stairs and were now making their way down corridors into a wing at the back where Sylvie had never been before. She would easily get lost on her own in this vast place. They started to climb another, narrower staircase. Professor Siskin was wheezing and took it very slowly.

"The Green Man isn't important here any more, is he?" said Sylvie, waiting for the professor to catch up. "I know he's celebrated at Beltane, but apart from that nobody seems to mention him much."

"Well observed, my dear!" gasped Siskin, pausing at the top of the stairs to catch his breath. "The Green Man deity was also part of a sacrificial cult, I believe. At least at Stonewylde, if not the rest of the country. I've uncovered some fascinating references to a very old practice here of an annual sacrifice of the Green Man at the time of the Winter Solstice, to ensure the vitality and renewal of the life force for the coming year. I believe this took place at the quarry, for there is mention of it in several documents. The Place of Bones and Death, it's referred to. Rather eerie, I thought. I imagine that's why the custom of deifying the Green Man fell out of practice, for who wants to give up their life? You'd need an endless supply of willing young men to be sacrificed every year, and the community needs its strong men. So you're right, the cult of the Green Man has fallen from popularity and is now only represented by Magus dressing in green at Beltane. It's a shame, though, because I personally feel at my most spiritual in woodland. There is a definite feeling of a deity present, don't you think?"

"Oh yes," she agreed. She'd felt that tingle in the woods, knowing there was an unexplained presence watching her. "I can't wait to read your book, Professor!"

He chuckled, and finally opened a door at the end of a corridor. It had been a long trek for him, and once inside she was surprised at the meanness of the room. Surely Magus could have made him more comfortable during his stay?

"My needs are simple," he said, reading her expression as she looked around the small room in disapproval. "And my rooms at Oxford are very comfortable indeed, so this is only a temporary privation. Sit down, sit down my dear."

He indicated a lone chair, where she sat whilst he rifled through a stack of papers.

"I have it here, and I know you will treasure it. I made you a copy specially. Here!"

He presented Sylvie with one of the photos he'd taken in the woods. It was a close-up of Yul's face smiling out at her, his slanted grey eyes drowsy in the golden sunlight. His face was smeared green and brown, the almost classical features clearly defined. His hair was a wild riot of dark curls, and surrounding his head was a great halo of green leaves and ferns where he lay in the undergrowth against the tree.

Sylvie stared at the photo in surprise.

"Why, it's the Green Man!" she exclaimed.

"Indeed it is," agreed Siskin. "Our own Lord of the Greenwood."

After Professor Siskin had left Stonewylde, Sylvie finally cast off the shadow of illness that had hung over her since the last full moon. She regained her strength and energy and was enjoying the fine weather. She insisted on going for walks every day and found Hare Stone to be a place of healing. Lying on the grass by the tall stone amongst the vetch and harebells filled her with a sense of calm and peace. She loved it up here. When he managed to join her, Yul was very careful to leave her be and not put her under any pressure. He'd mentioned the Moon Fullness once and she'd become agitated and upset. He realized that Mother Heggy was right; she was under some kind of a spell. The next full moon was still a week away and he hoped Mother Heggy would be able to break the spell before then.

Yul wasn't the only one worrying about the next Moon Fullness. Miranda was concerned and quite sure she didn't want Sylvie going up to Mooncliffe again with Magus and Clip. Much as she wanted to please Magus, and even though she was more than a little scared of him when he became angry, she felt that she had to insist on this. But when she broached the subject he lost his temper with her.

"Sacred Mother, as if I haven't got enough to worry about at the moment without you interfering! The girl wants to go there, she enjoys going there, so leave it be. I don't want to hear any more about it."

"But Magus, she comes back so ill. It can't be good for her if it makes her weak and exhausted. She was almost comatose for a week afterwards, and she's only just about back to normal now."

"Have you thought about how ill she might be if she *didn't* go up there? I don't want to hear another word about it."

"But I think …"

"I don't care what you think! Enough!"

He glared at her, black eyes flashing and mouth severe. She was frightened of him and wanted to give in. But a spark of her former self - the Miranda who'd stood up to her parents and fought to keep her daughter from being adopted, who'd struggled as a teenage single mother against the odds and succeeded through sheer determination - suddenly reignited.

"I'm sorry. I'm her mother and I say she can't go. That's the end of it."

She turned and almost ran out of the room, terrified of what he might say or do next. Up in her room she sat on her bed and cried. If she really made him angry, would he throw them out of Stonewylde? What about the baby? He had all the power. He was the magus here. What had she done?

An hour or so later, by which time she'd worked herself into a terrible state, there was a gentle knock on the door of their sitting room. Magus was calm, and as handsome and charming as ever. He walked straight over to her, taking her in his arms and kissing her; a long, passionate kiss such as he hadn't given her for some time. She melted in his embrace, like snow in the glare of sunshine.

"Don't say a word about it, Miranda. You were absolutely

right. You are Sylvie's mother and you have every right to be concerned for her welfare. Please forgive me for my anger earlier on. Come and sit down here with me. That's right."

He held her in his arms as they sat on the sofa together, putting his hand on her belly, already starting to swell slightly. He started to caress her slowly and skilfully.

"How could I ever be cross with you? I am such a fool," he murmured, his face nuzzling at her neck. She closed her eyes in contentment, loving him with all her heart, feeling herself become aroused by his knowing touch.

"You must understand, Miranda," he said, continuing his caresses, "that I only have Sylvie's interests at heart."

"I know, Magus, but …"

"No buts. I really do know best. Moongaziness is something that happens at Stonewylde. My own mother was moongazy. I have experience of it. I know what's best for Sylvie."

"Yes, but …"

"Come on, Miranda," he whispered, his lips brushing her collar bones. "Stop fighting me. You know you want to please me. You know how happy I can make you. Don't make me angry. Let me decide what's best for Sylvie."

"Oh Magus, I do want to please you," she breathed, her eyes half closed with pleasure. "But I really don't want her going up on that cliff again."

"You'll make me so angry if you don't agree," he murmured. "I don't want to be angry with you, Miranda. I want you to stay at Stonewylde and have our baby here, with me to care for you. I want to have you living under my roof. I want you close so I can make love to you. Why are you fighting me?"

"I'm not fighting you," she said tremulously. "You know I love you, Magus. I'd do anything to please you."

"Don't defy me then. Let me decide what's best for Sylvie."

"But I don't want her getting ill again. I can't bear to see her so weak. That's why I don't want you to take her up there."

He sighed and pulled away from her slightly.

"You've brought this on yourself," he said, his voice now cold. "You were given the chance to comply with my wishes. You disappoint me, Miranda."

"Please, Magus," she said desperately, "please let …"

"Clip!" he called sharply. "Come in now!"

The door opened immediately and the thin, long-haired brother walked in. He came straight over to the sofa where they sat and knelt on the floor in front of Miranda.

"What on earth are you doing?" she cried in alarm.

She struggled to sit up but Magus held her firmly in his arms.

"Sit still and do as you're told. It's really not a good idea to go against my wishes. My brother would agree with that, wouldn't you, Clip? Everybody here obeys me and you, Miranda, are no exception."

Clip ignored him and leant forward, looking into her green eyes.

"Miranda, look at me. Look at me."

"No! What are you doing? Stop staring at me!"

She tried to avert her gaze but Magus held her firmly and then she relaxed suddenly, her eyes locked into Clip's.

"Ah that's it, well done. Listen carefully to me, Miranda. When I tell you to wake up, you will do so immediately. Do you understand me?"

"Yes."

"Good." He turned and looked at Magus. "Well she went under quickly. What do you want me to say? I'm getting fed up of being used like this, you know. I'm a shaman, not a bloody party trick."

Magus laughed, releasing Miranda and stretching back on the sofa lazily.

"It's so easy for you to do, Clip. Stop complaining. Just make her obey me and stop interfering with my plans for Sylvie."

"Alright, but I've had enough of this, I warn you." He turned to Miranda again. "Miranda, listen to me."

"Yes."

"You must obey Magus. He has Sylvie's interests at heart and you must not interfere. Magus knows best. You will let him do whatever he wants. Do you understand?"

"Yes."

"Tell me."

"I must obey Magus. I won't interfere. He knows best."

"Well done, Miranda. Don't forget what you've been instructed. Now I want you to wake up."

She blinked and stared at Clip in confusion. Magus stood up briskly.

"Sorry, Miranda, I have to go. Clip came to get me."

"Oh, right. Yes."

"Thanks for your apology. I knew you'd agree with me when you'd thought about it."

"Pardon? I don't know ..."

"About taking Sylvie to Mooncliffe next week. You said I must do whatever I wanted because I knew best."

Miranda frowned and rubbed her forehead.

"Yes, Magus, of course. I'm feeling muddled. But I know you only have her interests at heart. I'm sorry I disobeyed you."

"Just don't do it again, Miranda. I may not be quite so forgiving another time," he said silkily. "See you later."

The two men strode down the long gallery leading out of the Tudor wing and Magus chuckled.

"I wish I could do that. I'd have such fun!" he said. "You don't realise the power you have."

"Yes I do realise the power I have, which is why I'm not going to repeat this, Sol. It's a gift, a wisdom, and I'm abusing it. Don't ask me again."

"Oh lighten up! It's no big deal. You know I need Sylvie to go to Mooncliffe every month and work her magic, and I can't have Miranda constantly interfering. That's all."

"Well actually, I think she's right. I don't think you should take Sylvie up there either. It's obviously damaging the poor girl."

"What?"

Magus turned on Clip angrily, grabbing hold of his

brother's shirt in a swift movement.

"Get off me, Sol!" he cried, his face blanching. "We're not boys now. You won't win with violence any more."

Magus released him abruptly.

"Alright. I'm sorry. It just makes me furious when you talk such rubbish. Of course it's not damaging Sylvie. She's absolutely fine now. You know I need those eggs charged up. And I was thinking of trying smaller pieces of stone, that you could wear around your neck. I could use ..."

"NO!" Clip shouted. "*If* I help you take Sylvie up there this month, it's just going to be for half an hour or so on the round moon stone. She's not going to charge up all those eggs nor anything else you've brought along. She's not strong enough to do it again so soon. You can threaten me all you like, Sol, and even hit me if it makes you feel better. But if you try to force me to do this, I'll reverse the hypnosis on both of them. And then you'll find it impossible. Just for once in your life, you'll have to do what *I* want."

# CHAPTER TEN

It was the last week in August and the day of the full moon. The summer had been long and hot and most of the crops were now harvested. The fields were a patchwork of deep brown, ochre and sienna, stubbly and bare, many already ploughed. The flax had been retted and some of it bleached; now the women of the Village were busy in every available moment spinning the long fibres ready for weaving. The cobnuts ripened thickly on the trees, green and frilly. The great tufted heads of sweet corn, zipped in their green jackets, were almost ready for harvest. In the orchards the trees were laden with apples, their boughs heavy. Early types of apple were already being picked. The swallows were still around but beginning to gather in the skies. There was a feeling almost of sadness, of the summer having nearly gone but no sign yet of the beauty of autumn to cheer the heart.

Yul left the Stone Circle after his sunrise rituals. He was tanned a deep golden brown, his clear grey eyes striking against his skin. He'd managed to keep himself out of trouble since the big fight with Buzz, who was skulking around the Hall avoiding people. Magus had let it be known that he was still deciding on his son's punishment whilst he recovered, but people were beginning to wonder when it was going to be announced. The Villagers were very angry that one of their girls had been attacked by a Hallfolk man. Magus was aware of this and knew he'd have to act soon.

Yul ran down the Long Walk as fast as he could. Legs pumping, he enjoyed the animal pleasure of the exercise and the green coolness under the ancient trees that lined the processional walk. He sprang and cavorted like a young stag, laughing out loud and shouting like a wild thing. Then he saw a figure at the other end standing in the shade, silhouetted against the brightness. His heart leapt – it was Sylvie! He ran full pelt towards her and she smiled as he approached, loving his darkness and wildness.

"I thought I might find you up at your stones," she said. "Feeling good?"

He laughed in reply.

"Do you want to come with me up to mine now?"

They cut through the woods and made their way up the hill to Hare Stone. As they got closer Sylvie felt the familiar tranquillity enfolding her. She touched the stone with her cheek before lying on the grass next to it. The moon magic of the place soothed and nourished her. She closed her eyes. Yul sat next to her on the grass gazing down at her, and his heart melted. She was so very beautiful, so ethereal and perfect. The dark shadows under her eyes were now gone and she'd lost the haunted look of suffering. Her fair skin was tanned to a pale gold, her silvery hair exquisite. He loved the arch of her lips, the tiny line each side of her mouth that crinkled when she smiled. He noted the delicate veins at her temples and the way her white blond hair started to grow there, feathering back into the proper hair. He saw the pulse in her throat beating like a tiny creature. Her small hands, their fingernails bitten, were spread on the grass, her thumbs idly stroking the ground. He bent over without thinking and kissed her mouth; soft kisses like angel wings.

Her eyes flew open, pale grey glass with the dark-ringed irises, and then they dreamily fluttered shut as the kisses became more insistent. She kissed him back, loving the feel of his mouth on hers, the emotion she could sense just under the surface. His lips were soft but demanding, his tongue hard but gentle. She felt herself spiralling away into heaven and wrapped her arms around his neck, pulling him down closer, her fingers twined in his curls.

Their kiss was shattered by a very loud CAW! Sylvie looked up and saw the crow fidgeting on the stone above them. Yul too looked up, his eyes smoky with passion, dark lashes drooping.

184

"Damn crow!" he muttered. "Perfect timing."

But then they heard a voice calling from down the hill.

"Sylvie! Sylvie! Are you up there?"

"Oh no, it's my mum!" cried Sylvie. "What on earth's she doing here? What shall we do?"

"It's alright," said Yul softly. "I'll just go over the top of the hill. Don't worry, she won't see me if I keep low. Sylvie, I ... Sylvie, that was lovely. Your kissing ..."

He gazed down at her and bent his head again. She laughed and pushed him off.

"Go! There'll be so much trouble if we're found here together. Go!"

"And the Moon Fullness tonight? Will I see you here?"

"I love to dance on the great moon stone at Mooncliffe," she told him. "I must dance for Magus."

"Oh Sylvie!" he cried, scrambling away over the hilltop.

Sylvie sat up, hastily smoothing her hair, hoping her face wouldn't give her away. Now she was upright she could see her mother climbing the hill, red hair gleaming like conkers in the sun.

"I'm up here, Mum!" she called, waving. Miranda waved back and continued to make her way around the boulders that littered the hillside. Sylvie assumed that Yul was out of sight. Her mother finally reached the great stone.

"Phew! I'm really out of breath!" she panted. "That's a steep climb."

Sylvie thought of how she and Yul liked to run up the hill together and smiled. Her mother sat down on the warm grass beside her, exactly where Yul had been stretched out only a few minutes earlier.

"This is a lovely surprise, Mum," said Sylvie brightly, trying not to think of the kiss she'd interrupted.

"Well, I haven't been out for a walk for a while. I need to keep fit, for the baby's sake. What a lovely spot!"

"How did you find me?"

"You've spoken about Hare Stone and I thought you might be here. I asked one of the Villagers and they directed me. Didn't seem to know it was called Hare Stone, though.

Just the stone on the hill, they said."

Hare Stone must be Yul's own special name for the place. Thinking of the moonlight and hares made her feel strange, and she remembered what he'd said. It was the Moon Fullness tonight. She thought of how it would be, dancing in the warm August moonlight with Yul watching over her. But then the black fog rolled in over her mind, blanking it out. She saw an image of moonlight over water snaking a path towards her. She saw a great disc of rock where she must stand and send the snake deep within, where it could coil in contentment. There was a man, two men, laughing with pleasure and delight. And the pain, the weariness, the sadness. No hares or moon angel wings or singing heavenly songs for the Triple Goddess. She hung her head in sorrow.

"What's the matter, darling?"

"It's just tonight, Mum. I must go to Mooncliffe and dance."

"Oh yes," agreed Miranda. "I've been worried about that. But Magus says it's what you must do, and he does know best. Did you know that his own mother was affected by the full moon? Apparently some people at Stonewylde are. He'll take care of you. I'm not going to interfere."

She lay back in the grass and closed her eyes, her thoughts a little jumbled. She sighed. It was peaceful up here.

"I love you, Mum," said Sylvie suddenly, squeezing her mother's hand.

Miranda turned her head on the grass and looked into her daughter's clear grey eyes, so beautiful and strange.

"I love you too, Sylvie. My special girl."


"Mother Heggy, you've got to help me!" cried Yul. He stood in the doorway of the hovel and the smell billowed out to hit him. She glared at him from her rocking chair.

"Brought back my bottles and corks, have you?" she squawked. "No! And you didn't come to see me, did you? But now 'tis the Moon Fullness and you realize you have none o' the knowledge yourself, oh aye, *now* you come here with your tail between your legs!"

She glared at him but he doubted she could actually see him at all.

"I'm sorry," he said, worried that she was going to turn him away. "I've been so busy with the harvesting and helping at home. I thought you'd be able to undo the spell before this Moon Fullness."

"Did you now? Well come in and shut the door!" she snapped irritably. "Come and sit down."

He sat down opposite her, trying not to recoil from the stale odour of her. How could Sylvie not be repulsed by her? She cackled, and too late he remembered her uncanny knack of reading his mind.

"Can you sit still awhile so I can read you? Or must I make you as stone?"

He remembered the potion she'd given him on his first visit, when he'd been unable to move, and quickly shook his head.

"No, I promise I'll sit very still."

She cackled again and pushed him back in the seat with a bony claw. She hunched forward in her chair and regarded him intently. He felt the tug of her milky eyes, and something deeper, just behind, something powerful.

"Quiet now," she whispered hoarsely. "Quiet and still. Let your mind float free. Let the white swan glide in the misty waters."

He felt his heartbeat slow down, his mind relax and slip away to the place between waking and sleeping where all is hazy and everything is possible. His breathing became deeper; his eyelids drooped shut. She took his hands in hers …

His head was filled with a sudden vision of dark crimson and black swirling in a vortex, silver light glistening, and then feathers everywhere, black feathers falling and falling, a tiny, white baby and a crow on the cradle. She snatched her hands away, muttering sharply. His eyes flashed open and he stared at her, jolted back into reality. He could see how the shadows had moved across the room, and knew she'd been reading him for quite some time.

"Well, well, so much has happened. Poor Mother Heggy.

Not so many visitors nowadays, nobody to tell me what is abroad. But now I have seen all that has passed. I understand the spell they put on the bright one."

"Can you break it, Mother Heggy?" he asked urgently. "Tonight – she'll go up there tonight if you don't do something."

She nodded, sucking her gums and rocking.

"Aye, I know that, boy. I cannot break the spell for tonight. You must go to Mooncliffe and see what is happening there with that evil man. 'Twill be hard for you. You must watch your girl suffering and you must do nothing. Do not try to stop it tonight. The time is not yet right and you would fail. You must watch but you must be hidden. When you came at Lammas I was afeared. The dark glass showed me what he did to her. I feared for her life, like my precious Raven before her. But now I see more clearly. There is danger, real danger, but you are far stronger than I had thought. I have faith in you, my young Holly King. The Goddess has chosen wisely. The magic will be safe with you."

Magus and Clip strode into the rooms at the end of the Tudor wing as the sun was dropping in the sky. The nights were beginning to draw in, dusk coming earlier as summer came to an end, although tonight it was very warm indeed.

"We've come for Sylvie," said Magus briskly, walking straight through the sitting room and towards the bedrooms.

"Of course," said Miranda. "She's rested and ready, like you said."

"Glad to hear it," said Magus.

Clip gave Miranda a little salute, which she ignored. Sylvie was sitting on her bed, her eyes vacant. Tears rolled down her cheeks but she was silent. She wore the moongazy dress and her hair floated around her bare arms and shoulders in a silver cloud. As the men walked in she raised her eyes to them. The tears spilled over and caught on her dark lashes.

"She is so lovely," said Clip softly.

"Never mind about that," said Magus. "It's late. Let's go" He took her hand from her lap and tugged her upright.

"Come, my moongazy girl. You've work to do tonight."

Yul was hidden behind the bracken slightly down the path. Once it was dark he'd be able to sit up and see everything happening on the cliff top. The still air was oppressive and he was sweating. He was scared, not of Magus, but of being unable to control himself. Mother Heggy had stressed how important it was that he didn't act yet. But could he bear to watch Sylvie suffer at Magus' hands? Gnats danced on the cliff top and swallows swooped, feasting while they could. The stone disc was rosy in the setting sun's rays, reflected also on the opposite horizon where the moon would rise, tinting the whole sky. It was a very bloody sunset, the sky a burnished gold, and Yul felt the oppression strongly. The heat pressed down, stifling and close.

He heard them coming before he saw them.

"Goddess, we're late." It was Magus' deep voice. "Look, the sun's set already. Come on, Clip, speed up!"

Clip led the way with Magus behind carrying Sylvie. Yul's heart wrenched at the sight of her lying in his arms, her head resting on his shoulder and her hair hanging down. Magus reached the top and put her down quickly. She stumbled as she tried to find her feet and then stood like an automaton. Yul remembered how she usually behaved at this time, just before moon rise; full of energy and fidgety, jittery with anticipation.

"Remember what I said," said Clip, talking as if Sylvie couldn't hear them. "No eggs and not too long on the stone. No more than half an hour."

"Oh come on, she can do a few eggs. Just to replace the ones I've used up."

"Absolutely not, Sol! We agreed. She's not strong enough this month. You were too greedy last time. She can't take it again so soon."

"You're being ridiculous, Clip. She's fine now. Look at her. Of course she can take it."

"She's been ill most of the month! I'm warning you, Sol, you'll damage her if you overdo it. And then there'll be no

189

moon magic at all."

"Alright, alright. We'll compromise. Just one hour with six eggs. Then we'll let her off the rock. But you must promise me she'll do the full load next month, whatever happens. I've got some people interested in the eggs. Is that a deal?"

"Well, I suppose so. But if she gets distressed, I'm taking her straight home. "

Yul was sickened by their talk. Magus spoke as if she were nothing, just a commodity to be used. How could the man be so heartless? What neither had noticed was that Sylvie had slowly turned towards the sea, gazing out at the pinkness. Her arms began to lift. It was her singing that roused them both.

"Quick! It's rising!" shouted Magus, grabbing her round the waist and almost throwing her up onto the disc. Again she stumbled and he jumped up next to her, pulling her into the centre. Her arms had dropped and she stared at the horizon, making a strange mewing noise. It was nothing like her ethereal singing at Hare Stone.

"Are you coming up too?" Magus asked Clip.

"No, it was too much for me last time," he replied. "I'll wait till the moon's risen a bit and she calms down."

"Well I'm going to try and stay on this time. Here we go!"

The pink rim of the moon was just visible and Sylvie had begun to shake and vibrate, her body jerking uncontrollably, her face contorted. Yul had to close his eyes. He thought of her tip-toe dancing, leaping with the hares, skipping around in the grass, and then this – standing on the hard stone, being pounded and shaken by a force of immense magnitude pouring through her body. He understood straight away what was happening. He could almost see the moon energy being wrenched by the great stone from the night sky, thrust hard through her frame and down into the stone. She had to take the full force of it and she couldn't move. She simply had to endure. Yul felt the tears hot on his cheeks and fought down the sobs that threatened to fly from his throat. This was far worse than he'd imagined. He'd have done anything to stand there instead and take the pain for her.

Magus stood next to her, blasted with the force that came up through the stone. He shouted in exhilaration as if on a roller coaster ride, his arms outstretched and head thrown back. But a few moments later he jumped off the stone.

"Sacred Mother, that was too much! I thought my heart would give out. That is *so* powerful!"

Clip lay once again on the grass with his toes touching the stone, an expression of ecstasy on his face. Magus unlocked the chest and brought out six stone eggs, which he placed next to the disc of rock.

"I'll load her up in a minute, when it's less intense," he said, joining Clip on the grass. Yul could feel Sylvie's suffering; the sharp, shooting needles that darted through her and down into the rock below her feet. He could see her glowing, the silvery threads chasing over her skin. She'd closed herself away, gone into some tiny, hidden place where the pain couldn't touch her so badly. Yul tried to embrace her in his mind, tried to comfort her. He too almost drifted away from consciousness in his fierce attempts to reach the place where she'd hidden.

He was brought back to reality by Magus' voice.

"I think she's ready to charge the eggs now."

"Alright. How long have we been here?"

"No idea. My watch always stops up here at moonrise. But it's fine. She's doing well so don't worry."

He climbed up onto the stone and put two of the heavy eggs in her hands. Yul could see how they started to glow almost immediately as the force shot down through her arms into the greedy stone. The severe jerking had stopped, for the moon had risen above the horizon and lost its pink-gold colour; now she merely trembled and shuddered. Yul closed his eyes, trying again to reach her to offer comfort.

Magus changed the eggs over after a while and both men climbed up onto the stone, spreading themselves out on it. Sylvie remained standing, staring up at the moon with unseeing eyes. Yul was sure that an hour had passed. He felt the anger, clamped down tightly inside him, begin to bubble up. When Magus changed the eggs again, Yul realized he'd had no intention of keeping to the agreement. Clip, for all his earlier solicitousness, appeared to have forgotten about Sylvie and her suffering. He was having too good a time soaking up the moon magic. As Magus put the new eggs in Sylvie's hands, she turned her eyes to him. She'd left the hidden place and could feel the pain shooting through her body. Her arms and fingers ached terribly and Yul willed her to drop the eggs, but her fingers were frozen into position.

"Please let me stop now," she whispered to Magus. He smiled at her in the moonlight, his hair shimmering almost as brightly as hers. He shook his head and put his finger to his lips, glancing down at Clip.

"*You bastard!*" thought Yul, longing to leap out and hit him over the head with his stone eggs. But Clip must have heard, for he opened his eyes and sat up.

"Goddess, I must have been in a trance," he said. "It's really late. We've been here much longer than an hour, Sol. Why didn't you wake me?"

"Don't be a fool," laughed Magus. "See, she's fine. Much better than last month."

"Come on then, let's get her down and take her home."

"Just five more minutes," said Magus. "Remember, she does love to dance at Mooncliffe."

He laughed again and Yul found it almost impossible to control his pure, white-hot hatred.

Later, Yul followed them back to the Hall at a distance. Sylvie was delivered to her bedroom via the private staircase and both men then left. Yul could see her mother moving around in the dimly lit room upstairs. He knew there was no point going home and trying to sleep. He was boiling over with anger. He seethed with it; molten rage that ran through his veins like poison. He knew that if he were to bump into Magus now, he'd try to kill him. He wasn't rational in any way. He'd had to endure watching Sylvie being abused by Magus, used for the man's own gratification and then laughed at in her weakness. It was more than he could take.

Yul ran from the Hall and headed for the Stone Circle. In

the light of the brilliant silver moon, now riding high across the night sky, he could see perfectly. He pushed himself, trying to blot out the images of Sylvie's suffering by forcing himself to his limit. His legs pumped like pistons as he raced up the hill. The great stone dance was silhouetted against the silvery night sky, the dark shapes blotting out the stars. He slowed down just before he reached the circle and tried to calm his emotions, knowing how important it was to enter the sacred space with reverence. But he couldn't. The hatred for Magus was too intense and all-consuming to be pushed aside. He stepped into the arena with his heart pounding from the punishing run, his veins pulsing with fury and the desire to kill. He stood in the centre of the circle not wanting any energy tonight from the Altar Stone. He already seethed with excessive energy that chased around his body searching for an outlet. The moon poured quicksilver into the circle. Yul raised his face to the bright disc and howled.

The rage and frustration, hatred and blood-lust came cascading from him in a torrent. It hung in the hot night air, eddying about with nowhere to go. Then slowly he started to move, pacing around the edge of the circle. He loped softly, circling inside the circumference of the great stones still adorned with corn dollies and images of the Corn Mother. Gradually he picked up speed, jogging round touching each stone as he passed. Moonlight and shadow flickered on him as he ran faster, light and dark, silver and black, like a strobe on his face flashing into his soul. Round and round he ran, his pain and rage spiralling into the centre. A great vortex of emotion started to build, a flickering carousel of anger and passion.

He didn't see the inky clouds piling in from the west. They rolled in fast, building and climbing on each other, great towers of swollen blackness growing in the sultry August night. Still Yul ran, his body slick with sweat, curls stuck to his head. He wrenched off his restrictive damp clothes as he ran. Free and naked, the night air clung to him, oppressively hot and heavy against his bare skin. The hair on his body tingled. He felt a strange lifting in his heart as if his breath itself was charged with particles of rage.

He raced one final mad circuit of the Stone Circle, stirring the power and energy into a maelstrom of wild and uncontrollable passion. He felt it building inside him, climbing, towering, piling up. With a shout he broke away from his thread and lunged full pelt towards the Altar Stone. He sprang onto the great stone with a mighty leap and turned to face the moon. He roared and roared, the sound pouring from him in a blind flood of wrath. At that moment the heavy black clouds billowed across, blotting out the moon and plunging the arena into utter darkness.

There was an earth-shattering crack as the skies too released their fury, the elements and the boy as one. A great pillar of lightning slashed down to earth accompanied by an explosion of thunder strong enough to rouse the dead. Yul screamed in wild glory and again the lightning forked down, hitting the hills in the distance. Flash followed flash, the blue-white light blindingly intense, searing the eyeball. Pure volts of vicious energy discharged themselves from the skies and blasted the earth below with their violence.

Yul stood naked astride the stone. Arms outstretched to the heavens and dark curls cork-screwing with static, he threw back his head and laughed. He shouted, screamed, yelled, bellowed - his tiny sound drowned by the great anger of the elements, the rage of the thunder as it rolled and rumbled around Stonewylde. And then came the rain. It hit Yul's hot skin like burning nails, driving hard into every inch of him, bouncing off his skin with such force that he felt punctured. He raised his face, tipping his head right back again and letting the needles of water wash away the sweat. It ran in torrents through his curls, down his body, washing and cleansing him with its fierce drumming. He was a waterfall of rain. Gradually the downpour turned cold as the heat and energy of the storm dissipated, the force now spent. Yul's roars turned to cries and then to sobs, and he howled once more into the drenching night. Howls of pain and sorrow, howls of anguish and torment for the girl he loved but could not protect from the man who abused her.

Just before dawn, the cold boy lying crumpled and naked on the Altar Stone was awoken by a pecking. He opened his eyes blearily, unable to focus properly, and saw the crow perched next to him. It blinked and let out a loud *caw*. He pushed himself upright, his head spinning and his body wracked with tremors. Slowly he levered himself off the stone, stumbling as his bare feet hit the wet earth below. The crow flapped off and he followed it, falling and tripping, as it took the short cut to Mother Heggy's cottage and sanctuary.

After the night of the Corn Moon both Sylvie and Yul were confined to bed for a few days. Sylvie rested in her Tudor bedroom, not quite as weak as previously, for this time she'd been allowed off the stone before she collapsed. Miranda took care of her and Magus looked in to check she was alright, pleased that Hazel was not needed this month. Yul, however, was not safely tucked up in his bed. When he'd arrived in the grey light of the misty August dawn, falling through her front door shivering and stark naked, Mother Heggy had been waiting for him. She'd wrapped him in a mouldering blanket and laid him on a narrow truckle bed at the back of the cottage. She made him drink from the stone mug and then left him to battle it out. He had a high fever but she knew he was strong and in good health. He tossed and turned for two days and nights, his black curls plastered to his head, cheeks flushed and eyes glassy. He was delirious and unaware of where he was. Mother Heggy took good care of him. She forced him to drink, sponged him down with tepid water, covered him when he shivered with cold. She sent a message with a passing Villager to Maizie telling her of Yul's whereabouts. On the fourth night Mother Heggy judged him recovered from the chill and let him leave, wrapped in the blanket and with instructions to bring Sylvie to her well before the next full moon.

September began as warm and balmy as August had been. The sun was hot, and in the afternoon Sylvie decided she felt strong enough to go outside. She wandered around the lawns and flower gardens, watching newts in the great ornamental pond for a while. Then she went to the formal garden with the gravel and clipped hedges. She'd never been here alone before and strolled around looking at the stone ornaments carved in the shapes of mythological creatures. She was deep inside the maze-like garden when she heard the gravel crunching behind her and turned to see Buzz approaching. Her heart sank. Because of his injuries, he'd kept to himself and she'd managed to avoid him. But it was now a month since the fight with Yul and he was mending. His nose was out of the splint, although still swollen and unsightly. The bruising around his eyes had faded to a nasty yellow and his split lip was almost healed. The tooth was still missing; soon he'd have an implant put in.

He quickened his pace and waved for her to stop.

"Hello, stranger! I saw you coming in here from my window. I've wanted to catch you for ages."

"Hi, Buzz. Are you feeling better?"

"Yes, finally. It's taken a long time though. I expect you heard what happened? Viciously attacked by that Village thug. He thought I was having a go at his bloody sister, although she was willing enough, believe me. I mean, do I look like I have to force myself on girls? Other way round, usually. He hasn't heard the last of it."

"Really? I thought we were all waiting to see what punishment Magus decided on. It's a serious crime, trying to force yourself on an underage Village girl."

He looked at her sharply.

"No, that's just malicious gossip. Magus is looking into it and I know he'll sort it out. It's just a misunderstanding. That boy has got it in for me. It was all his doing."

He ignored her look of scepticism and put an arm around her shoulders, giving her a hug.

"Anyway, let's forget about that half-witted bastard. He's not worth it. Did you hear about my exam results? I got straight As!"

"Congratulations. But Yul's not a half-witted bastard. From what I've seen he's very intelligent."

"You're not still keen on him? I warned you about that. Do you know what my father did to him in June, while I was away sitting my exams? Yes? That proves just what Magus thinks of him. That's why I know he'll sort this mess out about the girl. He's not going to take Yul's side over mine."

Sylvie shrugged miserably. She too had been worried about such an outcome.

"And how can you say he's intelligent? Pig ignorant, more like. I wonder how many As he'd get, if he was even capable of taking any exams. He's illiterate, for Christ's sake."

Sylvie turned on him angrily.

"And just why is he illiterate? Because your father doesn't allow Village children to learn to read and write! If he'd been educated properly, he'd outstrip you in every way. Go away, Buzz! I don't like your attitude or your values."

He stopped and looked at her hard. Then he shook his head and took her elbow quite gently.

"I'm sorry, Sylvie. I always seem to go crashing in and upsetting you. Can we start again? Forget Yul and what he did to me. Let's talk about something else. Please?"

Against her better judgement, and mostly because he looked so ugly with his broken nose and missing tooth, Sylvie nodded.

"Let's go in here, shall we?" he said smoothly. "I like this part of the garden. It's very private."

He led her into a section of the formal garden she'd never seen before. It was concealed behind a tall yew hedge with a trick entrance and exit that fooled the eye into the illusion that it was solid. Inside, the dark hedges were tall and impossible to see over. There were more alcoves with benches and she could hear the sound of water. It was a maze within a maze. They walked around heading for the centre, and Sylvie glanced at the stone ornaments that also decorated this maze.

"Oh!"

She blushed scarlet. The ornament was obscene. So was the next one. Buzz laughed at her embarrassment.

"Great, aren't they? I believe my grandfather or maybe great-grandfather had them carved. They were both rogues, apparently. Loved their wine, women and song. Right Jack-the-lads, so I've heard. I think I must take after them!"

She grimaced, wanting only to get out of the horrible place.

"Come on, we're almost in the middle. There's an incredible fountain there. You've never seen anything like it! I hope you're not a prude, Sylvie. You're far too gorgeous for that. And I've heard all sorts of gossip about you."

"What gossip? And I'm not a prude. I just don't like vulgar, obscene things."

"Let's sit down here then," he said, patting a large, comfortable bench. "Come and tell me what you've been up to lately, since I last saw you in May. I can't believe it's September already."

She sat down reluctantly, trying to keep a distance between them. He placed himself close, trapping her in the corner of the bench.

"Nothing much. I haven't been very well for some of the time."

"Oh? Holly tells me you've been spending a lot of time with Magus."

She began to tremble.

"No, not really."

"Holly said you were keen on him. She said you've been going up to Mooncliffe with him at the Moon Fullness. Is that right?"

"Yes," she replied, shuddering, "I love to dance on the stone there for Magus."

He laughed at this and it was not pleasant.

"I bet you do! Who'd have thought it? You're a dark horse, Sylvie. I put you down as sweet and innocent, but there you are. We all make mistakes. I thought you were fifteen at the Summer Solstice, not sixteen. Or am I wrong about what goes on at Mooncliffe with Magus at the full moon?"

She looked away, her cheeks burning again.

"I don't know what you're on about. Can we talk about something else? Tell me what you've been doing in the Outside World."

"Oh, this and that. I went to stay with my mother after the exams. Haven't seen her in ages. We went to South Africa for a holiday, which was great. It's odd when you leave here and go back into the Outside World. Everything's so different. More exciting in some ways. I went to some clubs, that sort of thing. But in other ways it all seems a bit shallow. I don't know. I always find it difficult to adjust when I come back here."

"And what are you planning to do now?"

"Well, start my higher exams of course. And we'll all go skiing as usual this winter, after the Solstice, so that'll be fun. You'll come, won't you? We all stay in a gorgeous place in the Alps and have a ball. Superb skiing and snow-boarding there. Stonewylde's a bit grim at that time of year – cold and grey. Leave it to the peasants to toil in the mud, that's what we always say. Give me the piste any day."

"I think I'll be getting back now," she said tightly, starting to get up. He pulled her down on the bench.

"Don't go yet, Sylvie. We haven't even started. I really missed you when I was away. I thought about you a lot, and I've never done that before over any girl. I've been looking forward to picking up where we left off."

His arm on the back of the bench slid down around her shoulders, his hand stroking her arm. She noticed the bristly blond hair on his thick fingers and a new signet ring to match the heavy gold bracelet. He was sweating and she could smell his anti-perspirant as he squeezed her warmly. She'd forgotten just how insistent he was and bitterly regretted allowing herself to be persuaded into this situation. She should never have come into this more secluded part of the garden alone with him. He was bigger than ever and had that gleam in his pale blue eyes that she remembered of old. She began to feel frightened.

"Did you miss me, Sylvie?"

"To be honest, Buzz, no I didn't. I …"

"Oh come on, Sylvie, stop playing hard to get! You know I want you. I meant what I said. I really have been thinking of you. It's been hell stuck up in that bedroom and not being able to see you. I've been dying to spend some time with you and tell you how I feel."

"I'm sorry Buzz but I don't feel that way about you at all."

"That's okay. Give it time. I know you like me and that's a start."

"No – no, I don't even like you. I'm sorry."

She felt him stiffen next to her and swallowed hard. Maybe she should just pretend until they were somewhere less isolated. She glanced at his battered face and shuddered as he glared down at her.

"I see. After the bigger fish, eh? You're a scheming one, Sylvie. I misjudged you there as well. Well let me tell you this. You might have set your sights on Magus and he may seem interested now, but you're fooling yourself if you believe it will last. It never does with him. He never stays with one woman for long, not ever. By the next full moon he'll have moved on to someone else. But I'm different. One day all this will be mine. You'd do well to remember that. You and I could have a future together. There's something about you - something special. I want you and I know it's not going to wear off. I want you more than I've ever wanted anyone or anything."

She shook her head and tried again to stand but his arm held her fast. He shifted his weight so she was wedged even more tightly into the corner of the bench. With his free hand he turned her head towards his and clamped his lips onto hers, trying to thrust his tongue between her teeth. She pulled backwards but there was nowhere to go. His hand began to roam over her T shirt, grasping and kneading at her. She struggled and hit out at him but he was heavy and persistent and she couldn't push him off. She tried to scream but he took the opportunity of pushing his tongue deep into her mouth. She started to gag, repulsed by him. As he pulled back she bit his split lip. He jerked away, eyes blazing with a strange light.

"You little bitch! What are you playing at?"

He put his hand to his mouth and it came away covered in blood where she'd opened the wound. She tried to get up yet again and make a dash for it. He grabbed her and pulled her down, shoving her hard against the bench and thrusting his hand roughly up the front of her T shirt.

"You bite me again and I'll hurt you, you bitch! Really

hurt you. We can both play rough if that's how you like it. Now kiss me properly. I don't care if I'm covered in blood. That's your fault."

He closed in on her again and the taste of his blood made her retch. He started to push her onto her back on the seat of the bench, using his weight and bulk to pin her down. He was crushingly heavy, his breathing hoarse, his hands insistent. She punched at him wildly and caught him on the nose. An arc of blood spattered across her, hot and wet on her face. He yelled with pain and closed his hands round her neck, screaming at her frenziedly. She shut her eyes against the horror of his face so close, blood streaming from his nose and mouth, his pale blue eyes manic. This was it - the end. He'd lost control and there was nobody to stop him squeezing her soft throat, squeezing hard …

Buzz sat in a chair in Magus' office, a sheet around him to catch the blood that still oozed. He was white, his hands trembling, his head hanging in despair. Magus sat opposite in a large leather chair regarding him with contempt. Magus shook his head, his mouth curled with disdain at the spectacle before him.

"I am now formally banishing you from Stonewylde, Buzzard. You have an hour to pack all your belongings and then you'll be driven to your mother's where you'll make your home permanently. Your mother will receive a generous payment that will sever any need for future contact between us. I am formally cutting all family ties between us. You are not my son; I am not your father. You are no longer a member of the Hallfolk, nor part of the community of Stonewylde. You will never be permitted to return here."

Buzz began to cry; piteous, mewling sobs which made everything bleed more.

"Please, Dad, please! I beg you, don't do this! It was all a misunderstanding."

"There's no misunderstanding about assaulting a Hallfolk girl. You tried to strangle her. Maybe I should say attempted murder rather than assault. If those gardeners hadn't heard you and stepped in so quickly, you could've killed her."

"But she led me on! She …."

"No she did not," said Magus coldly, his expression implacable. "Sylvie would never do that."

"Alright, she didn't. But I wanted her badly. I've wanted her since she got here, and she couldn't stand me. She treated me like I was dirt."

"I'm not surprised. You are dirt."

"No I'm not! I'm your son! Anyway, if you can have her, why can't I?"

"I haven't had her, as you so crudely put it. She's still a child. I thought I'd made it clear how important it is *never* to break that law."

"But you take her up to Moo…"

"Silence! Don't you dare accuse me! You're the one who's done wrong," barked Magus, his face twisted with distaste. "She's not for you and never would be. Sylvie's very special. She's out of your league."

"But she's Hallfolk! You said I mustn't have a go at Village girls, but Hallfolk were alright. You said …"

"Oh be quiet, Buzz," Magus said wearily, shaking his head. "You don't have a clue. We do not force ourselves on any female, Villager, Hallfolk or Outsider. Not ever. We don't need to."

"Don't tell me you've never forced anyone!"

"Of course I haven't! Nobody refuses me. Now that's enough. You sicken me. Go and pack. You have an hour."

Buzz started to cry again. Magus hauled him roughly out of the chair by the back of his collar, propelling him to the door.

"No, Dad! Don't do this! I'll do anything …"

"Get out of my sight! You are pathetic and disgusting. When I look at you, I feel ashamed to have fathered something so worthless. I'll tell you, that boy Yul for all he's been a thorn in my flesh, is worth ten of you. I've seen that boy take more punishment than I'd have believed possible, yet I've never seen him cry. Yul has something you utterly lack. He has pride."

The talk in the Village pub and on the Green was all of Buzz's banishment. The Villagers were delighted that Magus had acted so strongly, particularly as Buzz was his own son and he could have bent the rules for him. Some would have liked to see him publicly whipped too, because Buzz had not been popular. He was arrogant and rude, and many in the community had been slighted or upset by him in the past. Rosie was hailed as a heroine for standing up to him and fending him off. Yul was everyone's hero for beating the Hallfolk at cricket and then for thrashing Buzz so soundly in his sister's defence. And Magus was once more the just and benign master who always treated them fairly.

When Yul met Sylvie a couple of days later in the woods, he told her how happy he was that Magus had finally acted. Yul was surprised but pleased that Magus had shown respect for Rosie by taking the matter of her assault so seriously. He said how he'd never expected Magus to actually banish Buzz, and was impressed by his decision. Sylvie looked at him sadly.

"Sorry to disillusion you, Yul, but I don't think that's why Magus banished him at all. You obviously haven't heard. Buzz also attacked me. Look."

She wore a silk scarf round her neck, not something he'd seen her wear before. She undid it to reveal deep purple bruising around her neck.

"Sacred Mother! He did that to you?"

"Yes. It looks worse than it is because I bruise easily. But he did try to kill me. I wasn't co-operating with him, in the same way your sister wouldn't co-operate with him. He tried to force himself on me but I lashed out at him and he went completely mad. He tried to strangle me. Luckily some gardeners heard and pulled him off just in time. A few seconds more and it may have been too late."

Yul grimaced as he stroked Sylvie's damaged throat with gentle fingertips. His face was white.

"And then Magus banished him?"

"Yes. Within ten minutes apparently Buzz was hauled into his office and told he had to leave. An hour later he was gone."

"So he attacks a Village girl and almost a month later he's still here, unpunished. But he attacks a Hallfolk girl and he's banished within ten minutes."

He shook with rage, barely able to contain himself.

"This is one more thing Magus is going to pay for," he said ominously. "One more thing in a long line. Nobody in the Village will think the banishment is because of this, even if I tell them what's happened. Everyone already believes it's on our account, because of what happened to Rosie. Because Magus is so just and fair, so caring towards the Villagers. Such a kind master who puts our welfare above his own son's. He is so bloody clever! Goddess how I hate him!"

# CHAPTER ELEVEN

Drowsy and golden, September was the month of the great apple harvest at Stonewylde. Yul, along with many others, was pulled from his normal duties and sent to the orchards to pick fruit. Working from the misty dawns until the mellow dusks, the Villagers arrived daily in the vast orchards filled with apples of every variety. The gnarled trees groaned with heavy fruitfulness waiting to be harvested, and this was overseen by two men: Stag and Old Bewald. Eating apples were taken to the fruit and vegetable store house, a stone building almost as big as the Great Barn. Cool and dark inside, it was full of different levels and racks where vegetables, fruit and potatoes were stored. Cider apples were carted straight to the Cider House, where the maunds were hauled up by a winch and pulley into the apple loft, ready for the mill.

The apple gathering was overseen by Stag, although anyone less stag-like would be hard to imagine. He was in his fifties, small and wiry, with skin like leather and a permanent squint from screwing up his eyes against the sun. He was in charge of the orchards and under normal circumstances was grumpy and morose. At this time of year he became a complete tyrant. The apple harvest was vital to the community; Stonewylde without cider would be unthinkable. The Cider House was the domain of Old Bewald, an ancient, wizened man who'd worked with cider all his life and knew everything there was to know about it. Stag and Old Bewald didn't see eye to eye. There was constant friction between the two about which varieties should be harvested next and when the apples were truly ready for picking.

The grass in the orchards, which had grown tall and lush with wild flowers to provide nectar for the hives, had been scythed for hay in June. It had been cut again for silage at the end of August and was now short around the trees so that all windfalls could be easily collected. The ladders were stacked every night near the trees, and just after dawn the tribe of Villagers gathered to begin their day's work. Yul and his younger brothers, Geoffrey and Gregory, arrived with a group. Rosie was needed at the dairy, and Maizie was busy harvesting her own back garden produce and making chutneys and preserves. Her jams were all done; row on row of jars sat on shelves in the pantry neatly labelled with a picture of their fruit. Maizie would bring down lunch for her children later, after she'd visited the baker's for their daily bread.

The younger Villagers were back in school or the nursery, but anyone over the age of eight helped to bring in the harvest. Picking up windfalls was easier for children, who could also climb up into the thinner branches which wouldn't hold an adult's weight. They ran errands and helped with other autumn harvesting; the hedgerows glistened with ripe blackberries waiting to be picked, and juicy elderberries clustered thickly on elder trees all over the estate. Cob nuts were just beginning to fall and needed to be gathered before the squirrels had their fill.

The band of Villagers stood in the soft light waiting for orders. The shadows were long and the air hazy with early morning gold. Old Bewald and Stag were away over the far side of the orchards in heated discussion about which trees were ready for today's harvest. Yul sent his brothers to collect mushrooms in the dewy grass where the blackbirds hopped. Maizie would be pleased, and if they weren't picked the mushrooms would be trampled by the harvesters. While he was waiting, Yul strapped a wicker basket tightly round his waist and adjusted the harness on his shoulders. He was still sleepy for he seemed to be working even longer hours than was usual for harvest time. Edward, the farm manager who orchestrated the labour at this time of year, was piling the duties on him, expecting him to work in the Cider House every evening after the day's picking was done.

"Come on!" grumbled one of the men. "Them two, like a couple o' women the way they nag and scold at each other."

The carters put nosebags of oats onto the horses' heads whilst they waited, and people joined Yul in strapping themselves up with a picker. Eventually Stag came stomping over to the group, whose number was growing all the time as more workers arrived. Old Bewald hobbled out of the orchard towards the Cider House muttering incoherently under his breath, a battered clay pipe clamped in his mouth and foul smelling smoke hovering around him. Stag began to direct the workers to different areas of the orchard, growling the names of the apples that were to be gathered today. The warm September sun rose higher, the dew started to dry and the day's work commenced.

Yul was sent over to the far side of the orchards and took a stack of large wicker maunds with him. He and his group began to collect the apples; the children gathered the windfalls, being very mindful of wasps, the adults picked the ripe fruit from the lower branches of the tree, and Yul set the ladder against a strong branch and climbed up to pick from the top. As an agile woodsman he was useful at the apple harvest. He shinned up and down the ladder with the full picker, tipping it into the waiting maunds, which were loaded onto the cart when it came over on its rounds. It was thirsty work and several times Yul sent one of his brothers over to fill his water bottle from the barrel.

Yul was up the tree stretching towards a branch almost out of his reach when Magus rode into the orchard. He greeted his people warmly, encouraging them and praising their efforts. On the great prancing horse he trotted over to the tree where Yul was working with his team and sat watching from the saddle for a while. Yul felt uncomfortable under his scrutiny. Magus looked up at him through the foliage and caught his eye. The man's face hardened, his eyes cold.

"I hope you're working hard, boy!" he called up. "No fooling about."

"No, sir," replied Yul, smothering his irritation. It was Magus who was the fool because obviously he was working hard.

"You're putting in the hours in the evening too, at the Cider House?"

"Yes, sir."

Yul had been right then; he was being given extra work. And it was Magus himself who'd ordered it.

"Good. There are many extra jobs to be done and I shall keep you busy from the moment you wake up in the morning until you go to bed at night. You've been a damn nuisance for the past six months and it's going to stop. I'll make sure you're so bloody tired you'll have no energy for more mischief."

"Yes, sir."

Yul kept his eyes lowered, the dark hair falling over them, but his nostrils flared and his mouth clamped tight to stop it quivering. Although he was happy to work for the good of the community, he resented being singled out for added labour. September was a lovely month and he'd have liked a little free time to enjoy it; to walk up on the ridgeway, or go fishing in the evening on the beach with the other Villagers. Not to mention seeing Sylvie.

Magus turned and trotted back through the trees to where Stag was supervising the loading of maunds into a cart.

"There'll be a group of young Hallfolk coming up after lunch, Stag," he said. Stag suppressed a grunt of annoyance at this, and managed to arrange his features into an expression of mild pleasure and anticipation.

"Right enough, sir."

"I want them to do their bit helping with the harvest. The Villagers work damn hard at this time of year and Hallfolk youngsters should do the same. They're a lazy bunch, most of them. So make sure they work, won't you?"

"Oh aye, sir," said Stag, thinking ahead as to how he could get rid of them as quickly as possible. Hallfolk were useless at this sort of thing. They had no idea what was required, they couldn't take orders, and they had no stamina. All they did was get in the way. But Magus' commands were not to be questioned.

Yul and his team made their way back to the centre of the

orchard at mid-day, along with everyone else. Maizie was waiting with a basket of food for her sons' lunch, and little Leveret skipped about chasing copper coloured butterflies. When the food and cider were finished, Yul lay back in the grass. He laced his hands behind his head and gazed at the blue skies through the branches, drowsing in the golden September heat. He was tired and would have liked a sleep. All around him people chattered and gossiped, happy with the weather and the way the apple harvest was going. Someone had brought a fiddle and started to play a harvest song, which many people sang along to. After a while, Stag hollered at them all to get back to work or he'd tan the nearest arse. Reluctantly they packed up lunch and brushed themselves down, heading back to their trees.

Yul and his team were hard at work when they heard the group of Hallfolk coming towards them through the orchard. There was a ripple of discontent amongst the Villagers. The young Hallfolk seemed to be worse than ever each year, becoming ruder and less co-operative. Yul eyed the bunch approaching and groaned at the sight of Holly and her crowd. That was all he needed. He didn't notice Sylvie trailing behind, keeping herself apart. She didn't see him either, up in the branches with only his boots visible from below.

"Is this the tree he said then? Silly old fool. They all look the same to me."

"Don't suppose it matters, does it? One apple's much the same as another. If they're ripe, they're ripe."

"I don't see why we have to do this anyway. That's what the Villagers are for. Since when did we have to supply manual labour?"

"Magus has got a bee in his bonnet about us not doing enough for the community. But it'll blow over and then we'll all be back to normal."

"It's not fair. I wanted to ride this afternoon."

"Well I was in the middle of watching a really good film and then we were going to have a swim, so you're not the only one to have their plans ruined. Come on, let's choose any old tree and get on with it."

The Villagers picking below Yul's feet exchanged glances and rolled their eyes in disbelief. Hallfolk could be very dense.

"Which tree did Stag ask you to pick?" asked one of them politely.

The Hallfolk regarded him with disdain.

"If we knew that, we wouldn't be confused. Not that it matters. They're all pretty much the same, surely."

"It does matter, sir. Some are for cider, some for eating, and some not ready yet. You must only pick the ones that Stag has chosen. Else all the apples'll get mixed up. What was the name of your apple?"

"We don't know! Some ridiculous name. He said it was near your tree."

"Well that there tree's the Onion Redstreak, and those ones over yonder are the Catsheads."

"None of those."

"This here one is a Foxwhelp, and ..."

"Yes, that's it, the Foxwhelp."

"There you are then, miss. That's your tree. 'Tis important to pick up the windfalls first so they don't get trodden underfoot, and then start on the lower branches. Apples should fall into your hand if you cup and twist. There's the ladder to use for the upper branches."

"Yes, alright, thank you. We understand how it's done."

The peaceful golden afternoon with the rhythm of reaching and picking, reaching and picking, whilst chatting desultorily or humming softly, was now spoilt. The young Hallfolk were strident and treated the event as a game. They messed about throwing apples to each other, swinging on the branches, shrieking and laughing. Sylvie kept her head down and worked steadily, filling her picker and tipping it into the maund before starting again. She was acutely aware of the Villagers' disapproval and felt embarrassed to be classed among the poorly behaved Hallfolk.

Holly was in good form. She insisted on dragging the ladder over and positioning it against the twisted trunk. It looked precarious as the tree split and divided into branches and there was no good resting place for the top of the ladder.

Wearing a skimpy T-shirt, short skirt and trainers, she acted provocatively, tossing her shoulder-length hair and brandishing her bare legs. As usual the boys in her group pandered to her ego. The other girls seemed to find it hilarious, which encouraged her further. Sylvie kept as far away as possible, picking from the spreading branches on the other side of the tree.

Holly climbed half way up the ladder, making a big deal of the boys looking up her skirt. She began to pick apples and throw them down, trying to hit people. She made a lot of noise and Yul, up his tree, was sick of it. He and the other Villagers had been working now for almost a whole day and he was in no mood for Holly and the Hallfolk. His picker was full so he climbed down the ladder and went across to the maund where he gently tipped the apples onto the steadily increasing pile. At that point he looked across and saw Sylvie reaching up into the branches above her, unaware of his presence.

He paused to admire her as he re-buckled the picker, noticing how she'd become taller and willowy in recent weeks. His mouth went dry and he felt a surge of excitement at this unexpected encounter. He was on his way over to her to say hello, trying to be unobtrusive, when one of Holly's apples hit him on the chest. Without thinking he caught it and threw it back. It bounced off her leg and she shrieked with exaggerated pain. Then she noticed who'd thrown it.

"Yul! You great oaf! That hurt!"

They all turned to look at him and he glared back sullenly, hair in his eyes. Sylvie too turned around, her heart beating faster at the prospect of seeing him. She'd imagined he'd be working in the woods as usual, not the orchards. He stood by the maund, chin raised and contempt on his face. His bare arms were well-defined with muscle and the picker strapped tightly around his waist emphasised his lean height and the breadth of his chest and shoulders. When had he turned from a boy into a man? It had happened so gradually and yet so quickly. She longed for him and shivered at the intensity of her emotions as she stood in the sunshine amongst the ripe apples, grappling with the temptation he aroused in her.

He looked away from the group of Hallfolk and straight into her eyes. His deep grey gaze flared with emotion and she read all his love and longing in that look.

"Oy! Yul! Come here! I want a word with you!" shouted Holly, still halfway up the tree. He ignored her but with all eyes on him thought better now of going over to see Sylvie. Instead he returned to his own tree, climbing swiftly and disappearing amongst the foliage. The last thing he wanted was a run in with Holly and the Hallfolk, bringing down more of Magus' displeasure. The Autumn Equinox festival was close now and he was determined to enjoy it this year.

But Holly couldn't let it rest there. She remembered how keen he'd been on her before and this complete indifference now only fuelled her interest. With Buzz gone she was at a loose end. None of the Hallfolk boys of suitable age took her fancy for they'd all been his satellites. Yul had grown up so much since the spring and she'd always recognised his promise. She was surrounded by blond, soft people; he was the complete antithesis of this. She climbed higher up the ladder and then off it altogether, getting right up into the boughs amidst a great deal of commotion. The Villagers were now ignoring the Hallfolk, for the afternoon was well under way and they needed to move on. Their tree was almost picked and they must check with Stag where to go next. There were several maunds sitting on the grass full of apples. Yul climbed down from the tree and told one of his brothers to run over to the nearest horse and cart and ask them to come over for a collection. He removed the ladder and laid it on the ground, then unstrapped the picker from his waist.

Sylvie noticed and made her way around towards him. They managed to stand close together shielded by the low-hanging branches of the tree, now bare of apples but still covered with leaves. He caressed her slim bare arm with his fingertips, looking into her silvery eyes.

"How are you, Sylvie?"

"Better for seeing you."

"Me too. I miss you. I wish I could be with you every day, every minute. I think about you all the time, Sylvie."

She nodded, her heart drumming at being so close to him and feeling his gentle touch on her skin. He moved a little closer and his hand slid round her waist, pulling her to his side. His touch burned her skin through the thin cotton of her dress.

"All I want is to hold you and kiss you!" he whispered.

Sylvie's legs weakened at the desperation in his voice. She felt at once powerful and yet also completely in his thrall.

Their snatched intimacy was shattered by a shriek from Holly, up high in the Foxwhelp tree.

"I'm stuck!" she wailed at the top of her voice. "I can't get down! Someone help me!"

One of the Hallfolk boys climbed up the ladder and tried to persuade her down through the branches and onto the upper rungs.

"No! I can't move! I'm stuck!"

Fennel said that he certainly wasn't going up there and Yul grinned at this, remembering how wobbly Fennel was on ladders. July tried too to rescue Holly, shouting at her to just put her foot on the rung and stop being so silly. But Holly wouldn't budge. She then began calling for Yul to come and rescue her. Yul stiffened. He closed his eyes in dismay at the sound of Holly repeatedly yelling his name, insisting he was the only one who could rescue her.

"You'd better go and help her," said Sylvie, her voice small and quivery. "She'll just go on and on and make it worse."

"I don't want to help her. I can't stand her."

"I know, but she won't stop until she gets what she wants. That's what she's like. Just get her down, Yul."

"Yul! Yul! Come here and help me!"

All eyes, Villager and Hallfolk, were turned on him. Reluctantly he stepped forward and stood at the foot of the ladder looking up. She was high in the tree, perched on a branch and holding on tightly. Her bare legs dangled down and her face was a mixture of imperiousness and discomfort at her situation. Yul shook his head.

"What a stupid thing to do," he said.

"It's not my fault!"

"Of course it is. There aren't even any apples up there. You climbed up that high for no good reason other than to show off. Didn't you, Holly?"

"No! Just shut up and rescue me, Yul."

"Not until I'm satisfied you see how stupid you've been. Else you might do it again. I'm far too busy to waste more time rescuing silly girls who don't know their own limits."

The Villagers and Hallfolk laughed, many pleased to see Holly getting her come-uppance. Everyone looked up at her and she flushed.

"Come on, Holly," said Wren. "It was stupid. Just admit it and he'll come and get you. I've had enough of this apple picking."

"Me too. Just agree with him, Holly. He's right; you are stupid sometimes," said Rainbow.

"Okay, I was stupid," yelled Holly. "Now get up that bloody ladder, Yul, and help me down!"

He climbed up and edged towards where she was perched, until his face was level with hers. Her knees brushed against him and he pulled away. His face was closed and cold as he looked around, working out the best way to get her down. She gazed at him speculatively.

"Since when did you become so masterful, Yul?"

He shrugged, not even bothering to reply.

"Did you enjoy humiliating me just then? You're so unfriendly nowadays. I remember how you used to be. At the ceremonies and in the Great Barn afterwards, dancing and messing about with me. Do you remember?"

"No I don't. That was all a long time ago."

"Not that long ago. In fact it was the last Equinox, I recall. I went off with Buzz and his gang and you got upset. And then they beat you up and you got into trouble with Magus."

At this he looked her full in the face, his grey eyes blazing. She recoiled slightly, quite shocked at his intensity. She noticed how handsome he was, with his high cheekbones and chiselled nose and jaw.

"I remember that, Holly. And I'm grateful to that moron

Buzz for showing me what a mistake it was. Even the punishment from Magus was worth it, to see you for what you really are."

She flushed at the insult of his words and the contempt in his voice. She'd had no idea just how passionate he was, both in love and hate. Any chance she might have once had for a bit of fun with him was obviously gone.

"Shut your mouth, you stupid Villager, and get me down from this bloody tree!" she hissed. "And don't you *dare* speak to me like that again! Remember your place or Magus will hear about it and then you'll suffer."

He shrugged at this, indicating his utter disdain for both her and Magus.

"Slide along the branch here and then slip off and stand on this bit where I am now. You can't go down the ladder facing that way, so as you slip yourself off, twist around and I'll guide you."

He edged away giving her space to move along. Down below the onlookers had lost interest. The Villagers were loading their maunds into the cart which had arrived. The Hallfolk were now busy picking. The driver of the cart had brought a message from Stag. Magus had told him they couldn't go home until they'd picked at least one tree. The only person still watching was Sylvie. She couldn't quite hear what they were saying up there but she could see them looking into each other's faces, and Holly's bare legs touching Yul. Her throat was tight and aching, seeing Yul so close to Holly. As Holly slid her bottom off the branch, Yul braced himself to balance. He put his hands round her waist, ready to twist her so she faced the right way. As he touched her she gasped and stared into his eyes, now only centimetres from hers. She felt the energy inside him; the pull of his being and the sheer magnetism flowing through his strong fingers. There was something in him - something powerful and thrilling. She could sense it dancing just behind his eyes. She was washed with a wave of desire for him and wobbled on the branch. He grasped her more tightly, thinking she'd fall. His body pressed against hers, balancing precariously on the branch. She closed her eyes and swallowed.

"Yul, Yul, please."

"What's the matter?" he said coldly. "Hold on to the branch for Goddess' sake or you'll fall. Hold on! Stop leaning into me."

"I can't help it," she whispered. "I want you. I'm sorry, Yul, sorry for everything. I was wrong. I made a mistake about you. I want to go back to how we used to be together."

"You made a mistake alright, but there's no going back now, Holly. Let's just get down to the ground."

"Wait!"

He'd started to move away, now that she was facing the right way. He planned to guide her from below onto the rungs of the ladder and get down as fast as he could. The last thing he wanted was Holly making a play for him, especially with Sylvie watching. He caught a glimpse of Sylvie's face, white and pinched. He couldn't blame her. He knew how he'd feel if he was on the ground watching her and Buzz up in a tree.

"Hold on a minute, Yul," Holly said quietly. She closed her fingers around his wrist, looking at him with an expression he'd never seen her wear before.

"Let me go," he said. "I'm not interested, Holly. That was in the past."

"Listen, Yul. I've just made a decision. It's our Rite of Adulthood at the Winter Solstice. It's only three months away. If I can't have Magus, I want you to be my partner at the ceremony."

He stared at her, a dangerous glint in his slanted eyes.

"Oh really? Well understand this, Holly. I don't take second place to anyone, not even Magus. And I have other plans for the Winter Solstice which certainly don't include you."

She gasped at the harshness of his words and the look in his eyes. She'd never seen this side of him before. She remembered the fun-loving Villager from just six months ago. The boy who loved to leap high during the dances in the Stone Circle and gallop around in the Great Barn afterwards holding her hands. The boy who used to show off and try to impress her with his antics. She shook her head, bewildered by his curt rejection.

"I don't understand, Yul. You've changed. You used to be such fun and you've always liked me. Remember how we used to play together and get up to mischief at school, before I went up to the Hall School? We used to be friends, Yul. A bit more than friends even. Why are you so cold to me now?"

He sighed and gazed up through the branches above their heads, trying to avoid even eye contact.

"It's hard to know where to begin and I really can't be bothered anyway. Far better to accept that I'm not interested in you and leave it at that. Now let's get down from this tree, please. This is just fooling around and I should be working."

As his feet found the upper rungs of the ladder and he began to climb down, she spoke once more in a voice which quivered dangerously.

"No I won't leave it at that! How dare you treat me like this? You should be honoured that I'm favouring you. I'll speak to Magus, and believe me, you *will* partner me at our Rite of Adulthood."

"Only in your dreams, Holly," he said, with a harsh laugh. "Now put your feet on the ladder and stop wasting my time."

He grasped her ankles quite roughly, not wanting her or Sylvie to misinterpret his actions, and pulled her foot onto the rung. He reached the ground and stood watching, making sure she was coming down safely. But when Holly reached half way she stopped and precariously turned around, so she now faced outwards. She smiled down at Yul. They both remembered the time in the Stone Circle when he'd done the same thing as he'd climbed down from the bonfire and tried to impress her. Then she leapt straight at him. He caught her full on and staggered under the force, just managing to keep his balance. She clung to him, her arms around his neck and her bare legs wrapping around his hips. She kissed him hard on the mouth. He pulled his head back sharply but she was like a limpet. Then she let go and sprang back from him, smiling, and he remembered how agile she'd always been.

"Thank you for rescuing me, Yul," she said brightly. "I

owe you."

Yul was aware that Sylvie had turned on her heel as Holly clung onto him and was now disappearing amongst the apple trees. He was desperate to run after her and stop her. The Villagers were following the cart back to find Stag and ask him where to go next. The Hallfolk were still picking, putting a little more effort into it now. He decided it was worth getting into trouble for, if Stag noticed his disappearance.

"I'll be back soon!" he called to the rest of his group and hared off through the trees and the other apple gatherers. By the time he caught up with her she was almost out of the orchard. There were many other people about and he despaired of talking to her alone.

"Sylvie!" he called. He slowed down as he approached her, not wanting to attract attention. "Sylvie!"

She turned slightly and saw him, but carried on walking fast.

"Wait! Please stop!" he said, grasping one of her wrists.

She shook him off and marched on grimly.

"Just leave it, Yul," she said. "I'm going home. I've got a headache."

"Please listen. Just listen, then you can go home."

Reluctantly she stopped and he turned her to face him, acutely aware of all the people milling around them. If they'd been alone he'd have taken her in his arms and kissed her jealousy and anger away. As it was, his hands were tied and there was nothing he could do. She wouldn't even look him in the eye.

"Sylvie, I understand why you're cross, but believe me, I wanted nothing to do with her. I can't stand her."

"I know."

"I hated having to rescue her. I never wanted to go up and help her."

"I know."

"I told her I wasn't interested in her."

"Oh, so you did discuss it then?"

"Well, not exactly discuss it."

He decided it wouldn't be wise to tell her about Holly's

plans for their Rite of Adulthood. Or even the fact that he'd once liked Holly.

"I just want to get home, Yul. I'll see you soon."

"But you're angry and upset. I swear to you, Sylvie, there's no need for it."

"I know. Really I do. But the way she wrapped herself around you and kissed you ... How d'you think I feel?"

"But I didn't want her to! It was horrible. Please don't be upset."

"I can't help it. Let me go."

"Just show me you're not angry with me. Please, Sylvie."

But she couldn't bear to look at him.

"I'm not angry with you but I'm starting to be. You're making a big deal about nothing when I just want to forget it. Go away, Yul, and keep out of her way."

She walked off, close to tears. Her annoyance with Yul was all the worse for knowing that her jealousy was unwarranted.

"Yul! What are you playing at? Get your arse along over here, boy! You ain't finished yet."

"Sorry, sir. I was just coming."

"Course you were. Get down the Cider House now and put in a couple o' hours on the mill. Take over from Jed, who's been on it all afternoon. You can knock off to eat when the others go home for their supper. But mind you come back straight afterwards. Edward said I can use you all evening if I want. You'll be working again in the Cider House tonight. The old cheese needs taking apart. You know how to do that?"

"I think so, sir. Unscrew the press and pull out the old sacking and pomace."

"Aye, but make sure you do it proper. Those apple cheeses are rock-hard once the juice has been squeezed from the pomace. You need three bins – one for the straw, one for the sacking and one for the dried up pomace. Leave it all clean and tidy. I want it done tonight so when Bewald comes in first-light tomorrow morning 'twill be ready to build a new one. I don't want the old bugger moaning at me. You don't go home tonight till that cheese is completely cleared. Make sure you do a good job of it. Understand me, boy?"

"Yes, sir," said Yul wearily.

Nearly three hours later, Yul stopped to go home with the other Villagers for a meal. He was bone tired. He'd fed hundreds and hundreds of apples into the mill, scooping them down from the apple loft into the large funnel that led to the mill. Turning the great iron handle that operated the mill, crushing and chopping the apples until they were macerated into a lumpy pulp, was hard work. The muscles in his arms, chest and shoulders screamed for mercy. He'd been up and down the ladder continuously, pulling a barrel in place, opening the valve to let the mashed-up pomace slide out, scraping out the mill, and then starting the process all over again. The mountain of apples in the loft that had greeted him on arrival was now considerably smaller. He surveyed the many barrels of pomace he'd made, which would sit for a day or so before being packed into a new cheese. A job well done, Yul thought, and nodded in satisfaction. Neither Stag, Old Bewald nor Magus himself could accuse him of slacking. He was very pleased to drag himself home and be greeted by a smiling Maizie and a hot supper waiting on the range.

It was hard going back to work after having sat down and relaxed. Maizie couldn't understand why he had to do so much extra work, and offered to speak to Magus about it. But Yul told her on no account must she do that. He just hoped that by keeping his head down and doing as he was told, Magus would gradually lose interest and ease off him. As he left the cottage, Maizie and Rosie had just set up the spindles for an evening of flax spinning. Maizie had ready a great bundle of long silky fibres. It was fine flax from the retting pond rather than the coarse dew-retted fibres, and would eventually be woven into the best quality linen.

"'Tis for you, Yul," she said, indicating the pale tresses of flax. Yul recalled the back-breaking task of pulling the flax crop and then gathering it all up for the retting. He was pleased that he'd benefit from all that hard work.

"What are you going to make, Mother? You've already

sewn me some new clothes for the Equinox celebration."

"Your Rite of Adulthood!" she said. "'Tis going to be the linen for your robe. You must decide soon what totem you want woven into it. Have you any notion yet?"

He smiled at her, excited at the prospect of his own robe at last instead of the childish tunic.

"I always thought I'd like a hare," he replied slowly. "For years that's what I wanted. But now I'm wondering about a Green Man instead."

"That sounds nice," said Rosie smiling at her brother. "And unusual too."

"Aye," said Maizie, scooping up some fibres and twisting them expertly. "I don't think anyone else uses that totem. Well, you don't have to say yet, though I'll need to know the colours soon because I must dye the thread afore I start the weaving. So shades of green then?"

"Probably, yes. Maybe with some gold and brown too. And my silver disc would be a sprig of mistletoe on one side for the Winter Solstice, and a Green Man on the other."

"Well my boy, you're a woodsman and you've always loved the trees. Old Greenbough says you're a natural-born man of the woods such as he's never seen afore. 'Tis a good idea."

"I must be off now, Mother. Magus may be checking up on me."

He left the comfort of the cottage and walked down the track leading into the heart of the Village. The sun had vanished in a haze of gold. Yul regretted being unable to go to the Stone Circle for sunrise or sunset and receive the green magic of the Earth Goddess. It was the Equinox soon and he must try to get up there before then. With Magus working him every hour of the day there was no chance at present to slip away. He walked through the warm night, greeting several Villagers on their way to the pub. On the Green the bats swooped in their gnat hunting, and light and laughter spilled out from the Jack in the Green. The Great Barn was also lit, and through the open doors he could hear music playing. He guessed the musicians were practising for the Equinox dance.

The drummers would be in there too, waiting to go through the rhythms they would play up in the Stone Circle at the ceremony. Sweethearts wandered around together on the Green where most of the Villagers' courtships took place. There were plenty of sheltered spots under the great circle of trees that clustered around the perimeter, just right for kissing and cuddling and making promises. Unattached youngsters looking for a partner sat on the benches outside the Barn, chatting and joking together and eyeing up likely mates.

Yul felt a pang as he realised that none of this would ever affect him. He had a sweetheart but she must be kept secret. Their relationship must be furtive and snatched. He could never court her openly like all those around him now, sauntering arm in arm in the balmy autumn night under the golden moon, kissing and laughing. She was forbidden to him and any liaison must be clandestine.

Although he knew he should hurry, Yul made a detour to the great yew tree. He slipped under the low boughs into the dark cavern of its shelter and breathed in the magic he always felt in this place. He was pleased there were no couples here, for this was where he and Sylvie had shared their first kiss. He remembered that night in exquisite detail and closed his eyes, his breath catching in his throat. He cautiously opened the lid on the treasured memory and was blown apart as always by the explosion of joy it detonated in his soul. This was their special place and he hated the thought of others intruding here. He was unaware that nobody else ever came under this tree for their assignations. People felt uncomfortable under the yew because of its association with the Yew of Death down in the valley. He and Sylvie alone felt the pull of the dark magic in this ancient place. Yul dragged himself away reluctantly and jogged along the track leading to the Cider House. He was very tired and yawned as he opened the door. It was pitch black inside and the smell of apples was overwhelming. He felt around for the matches and lantern that lived on the shelf near the door.

The soft candlelight illuminated the area immediately around it, but everywhere else was in shadows. He lit another lantern over by the cider press where he'd be working and looked woefully at the machinery. He had a mammoth task ahead of him. The great screw was clamped fully down, the flat press as low as it would go. Beneath this was the old apple cheese, a huge cube of woven straw and hemp sacking filled with compressed layers of pomace, from which all the apple juice had been extracted. This was now a deep brown and quite solid; very different from the fresh pulpy pomace he'd been making earlier.

Tonight he must unscrew the press, which was a heavy physical job, turning the great wheel above that would slowly release the press and make it lift off the cheese. Then he could begin the task of pulling the cube apart and sorting the materials as Stag had instructed. Yul dragged three bins over and then climbed up above the press where the heavy iron wheel was situated. Turning the wheel to lower the press onto a new cheese was a two man job, for there was great resistance. Raising the press, as he must do now, was slightly easier, but he must do it alone tonight. With a grimace, Yul gripped the rim of the wheel and put his back into it, forcing it as hard as he could. The wheel turned a few centimetres; the press didn't budge. He tried again, and after a minute of straining as hard as he could, the press seemed to move slightly up the giant screw. Yul paused and took a deep breath, wondering if he'd actually be able to manage the task. Was it Magus, Edward or Stag who'd decided he could do this alone? He'd only ever tightened the screw before, with the help of another man. But he knew he must do it for there'd be trouble if he didn't. So resignedly he heaved and strained, knowing that tomorrow he'd ache in every sinew.

Unbeknown to him, somebody had slipped into the Cider House and now stood silently in the shadows watching him sweat. She kept absolutely still, heart beating fast as she looked at him toiling up on the platform, his brown arms pulling for all their worth, the sinews and muscles bulging with the strain. His legs were braced and his hair fell into his eyes. In the gleaming candlelight she saw the sheen of sweat on his face, his determination and concentration as he wrestled with the heavy machine, knowing that at all costs he must raise the press. She shuddered as she watched him working; watched him pushing his body and strength to the limit, grunting with the effort. Eventually, with a roar he swung the wheel round and the press was fully raised. He shouted in triumph, flipping the lock on the wheel to hold it in position, and jumped down from the platform. The curls were stuck to his face and his chest heaved with exertion. He went over to the tap, where water was piped from the river, and filled a bowl. He drank deeply and let the water wash over his sweaty face. Then he went back and surveyed the great apple cheese, knowing he must start now to pull it apart.

But just as Yul was about to pull off the first layer of straw and hemp sacking, Sylvie stepped out from the shadows. He jumped with surprise, then his face lit up at the sight of her. Her silvery hair hung down around her bare arms, almost reaching her waist. She smiled at him, beautiful in the soft candlelight.

"Are you really here?" he whispered, echoing the words she'd spoken not long ago. "Or have I fallen asleep and started to dream?"

She laughed and came forward, taking his hands in hers.

"I've been feeling guilty all evening about how I treated you today. It wasn't your fault and I was really unfair to you. I was just so jealous, seeing you touching Holly. I couldn't bear it."

He smiled down at her, noticing that although he'd grown so much, she was barely a head shorter than him. He looked into her silvery grey eyes with the startling dark rims.

"You'll never need to feel jealous of Holly, I promise."

She nodded, letting his hands go.

"I overheard her tonight at dinner talking about you with her friends. She was saying how you didn't want to know, and how rude you were to her up in the apple tree. She's very angry about it. But Yul, there's something horrible I must warn you about. She said she wants you for her partner at the Winter Solstice, for her Rite of Adulthood. She said she can make Magus agree to it. You won't do it, will you?"

He gazed deep into her eyes.

"The only person I ever intend making love to is you, Sylvie. I know exactly where I want our first time to be, and it's not in public up at the Stone Circle, believe me. I shall be giving that a miss. It's my Rite at the Solstice too but I'll wait until you're old enough. And until you feel ready."

He watched the expressions flit across her face; embarrassment, relief and something else, which he hoped was excitement at the thought of making love with him. He smiled at her, loving her openness but realising that her inability to mask her emotions and bury her feelings deep away from prying eyes made her vulnerable. She had yet to learn the lesson he'd been forced to learn this summer.

"Good," she said. "Because I'd have killed her rather than let her have you first! Or have you at all, for that matter."

He laughed out loud at this uncharacteristic outburst.

"I'm not joking!" she said. "I hate that girl. But let's forget Holly, shall we? I can't stay long. I'm meant to be in the Great Barn with a couple of Hallfolk who came down to practise the drumming. I said I needed some fresh air. I knew you'd be here because I heard that grumpy old man ordering you about. Why do you have to work so much harder than everyone else, Yul? It's not fair. It's a beautiful evening and they're all out there relaxing and enjoying themselves."

"Magus' orders. To keep me constantly tired so I can't get up to any tricks, he said."

"He's so cruel to you. He's completely abandoned that deal I made with him at Midsummer. He's on your back all the time, isn't he?"

"Yes, but we must remember what Mother Heggy said. I've just got to bear it and hold on. It won't be for ever."

"Poor you," she said softly. "Why can't things ever be easy for you?"

They stood in the shadowy candlelight, acutely aware of each other. Yul knew he must get on with his work or he'd be here all night dismantling the old cheese. Sylvie knew that the Hallfolk in the Great Barn would be wondering where she'd got to. Their time alone together was so precious, but the very fact that it was snatched and secret made them both feel constrained.

Sylvie looked around the cavernous building with the two cider presses and the enormous apple mill. There were bins and barrels everywhere and piles of sacking and straw. Then she noticed another room leading off, dark and shadowy.

"What's in here?" she asked. She could see many barrels inside arranged in rows. She walked in, looking around the shadowy depths, and Yul followed her inside.

"This is where the apple juice is stored when it's fermenting. See these barrels have no bungs in them? They're fermenting now. They need constant topping up with more juice to keep the air out. Usually they rack them after the first fermentation – that means transferring the juice to a clean barrel. They let them ferment a bit more, then put the bungs in and leave the cider to mature. Those ones at the far end are last year's cider, waiting to be moved to the cellars in the Jack in the Green."

"I see," said Sylvie, interested but more interested in the proximity of Yul as he stood beside her in the near darkness. The strong smell of apple juice and cider was in her nostrils but she could smell him too. Every tiny hair on her body was aware of him so close to her, taut with control as he kept himself apart. Her fingertips brushed his bare arm longingly. She drew breath sharply as he tensed like a bow-string at her touch.

"Yul," she whispered. "Yul, I ..."

His body hit hers so urgently she was thrust back against a barrel with a thud. He bent his head and his mouth locked onto hers. Twisting his hand into her long hair, he held her tightly to him and released all the frustration and anger of the day into his kiss. Sylvie kissed him back with equal intensity, her lips crushed and desperate. Jammed with her back to the oak of the cider barrel and his body pressed up hard against hers, she felt a flood of longing melt her bones. She pulled him even closer, wanting to lose herself in this intense pleasure. His mouth was demanding but so giving too. He kissed her until her tongue was on fire for him and her heart must explode. He pulled away, abruptly releasing her from the fierce embrace, his breathing audible in the silence. She could make out the brightness of his eyes in the shadowy darkness and sensed rather than saw the trembling excitement in him.

Then they heard a sound outside that made them both freeze in terror – the jingle of metal and the snicker of a horse.

"Sacred Mother, that's Nightwing!" he hissed. "Magus has come to check up on me!"

She gazed at him in mute terror, scared for him rather than herself.

"There's an outside door at the end of this store," he whispered urgently. "I'll go back into the press room and talk to him. You get out and run like the wind back to the Barn. Sylvie, be careful. Don't make any noise."

She nodded and began to tiptoe into the deeper shadows of the barrel room towards the far end. He dashed into the other room and started to pull frantically at the straw of the apple cheese, flinging it in great handfuls into one of the bins. The door opened and the two lanterns flickered slightly. Magus' blond hair shimmered in the soft light, his dark eyes fathomless in the shadows. He stood in the doorway, tall and broad-shouldered, surveying the scene. If he noticed Yul's quick breathing and nervousness, he said nothing. He walked in and shut the door behind him, tapping his boot with his riding whip.

"Good evening, Master Yul."

"Good evening, sir."

Yul stopped ripping at the straw and turned to face Magus. He concentrated on not looking into the dark doorway of the barrel room, not doing anything to give away Sylvie's presence. He needed to mask any sound she might be making in her exit, so he nudged the straw bin with his foot, making it shift loudly on the stone floor.

"Stop fidgeting, boy. I've dropped by to make sure you're not slacking. You don't seem to have got very far. Stag told me you had to dismantle this cheese tonight, but you've barely started. Do you have any idea how late it is? You're going to be here half the night."

"I'm sorry, sir. It was the press. I found it difficult to turn the wheel to release it. It took me a long time."

Magus frowned at him, the lines around his mouth sharp.

"I find that hard to believe. One thing that's struck me recently is how much you've grown."

He stepped forward and reached out to feel Yul's bare upper arm, squeezing the muscles with iron-grip fingers. Yul steeled himself not to recoil from Magus' touch.

"Well, well! Even stronger than I'd imagined. I can't believe you had any trouble raising the press. Far more likely you've just been dawdling about. Don't let me keep you, boy. You've a good couple of hours' work ahead of you and you must be up early in the morning. I suggest you get on with it and stop wasting time. You're going to be very tired tomorrow with so little sleep."

He smiled at Yul and raised his whip to stroke the thin pink scar on Yul's tanned cheek.

"I see you still bear my mark. Let it be a constant reminder to you, Yul, of what happens if you defy me. You may be free of Alwyn now, but you're not free of me. Whatever you do I shall be watching and waiting, ready to correct you if you stray in any way whatsoever. I'm taking a personal interest in you, Yul, so be very careful. One step out of line and I shall come down on you hard."

He tapped his boot again with the whip, his meaning clear.

"Goodnight, Yul."

"Goodnight, sir."

# CHAPTER TWELVE

The Autumn Equinox was approaching and Stonewylde was busy in preparation. Just as in the Outside World, the Harvest Festival was a time of thanksgiving to the Earth Mother for her generous bounty. It had been a particularly good harvest this year; the granaries were full to the brim, the hayricks plentiful, and the Meadery was working flat out to cope with the honey yields. The vegetable store was packed full with even more to come. The sweet corn harvest was just starting and promised to be superb. Hazelnuts clustered thickly on the cob trees and the great walnut tree on the Village Green was daily loosing its harvest onto the grass for children to gather. Every day the blackberries and rosehips in the hedgerows were picked, and the elderberries already gathered bubbled away in most pantries to make a sweet, rich wine. The freezers were stacked with meat and vegetables, and the wool and flax crops had been exceptional too. These raw materials were stored away, waiting for the long winter nights when the Villagers would have the time to spin and weave, knit and sew. In the Cider House, Old Bewald was saying he'd never known a year like it. Many new barrels were being made by the coopers to cope with the expected cider yield.

Yul was particularly looking forward to the festival as he'd been working at full stretch all month. A couple of days before the Equinox, Edward the farm manager who'd co-ordinated the harvest labour, took Yul to one side. He told him to go back to Old Greenbough in the woods where he was needed more urgently. Yul grinned in relief at this news for he was sick of the sight of apples.

"You've worked really hard, lad," said Edward, clapping him on the back. "I'm proud of you. Magus told me to give you an extra heavy load and I have done, but you've borne it well and not complained once. It's certainly built up your strength, hasn't it?"

Yul nodded, knowing this was true. Greenbough would appreciate the change in him.

"When are you an adult?" asked Edward.

"Winter Solstice, sir."

"Well you've been doing the work of two men this harvest-time so you won't have any problems. Is your mother coping alright without Alwyn? I been worried that with him up in the hospital and you working every hour of the day for Magus, she might be struggling."

"It's difficult for her, sir. There's lots of work to be done at home, and I'm not there at all to help. Rosie's busy at the dairy, and my two brothers are still too young to do the heavy stuff. And there're the three younger ones to cope with too. She's finding it hard."

"In that case, I'll stop loading you with extra duties in the evening. I'll let Magus know, so don't you worry about that. You'll be working hard at home and he can check on that if he wants to. 'Tis not fair that your mother and family should suffer because Magus wants to punish you. I'm sure he never intended that. What had you done anyway?"

Yul shrugged, as ever at a loss of words to explain the antipathy that Magus felt towards him.

"He's just got it in for me. He doesn't need a reason to punish me."

Edward frowned down at him and shook his burly head.

"I don't like the tone of your voice, lad. Magus is always just. Sometimes hard, I'll give you that, but always just. You make sure you show proper respect for him or you'll feel the weight of my hand. Magus is a great master and a truly great man. Don't ever let me hear you speak against him, Yul. You should be giving thanks to Magus for his generosity and his bounty."

Yul bit back the retort that it was the labour of the Villagers and the bounty of the Earth Goddess that ensured their comfort, not Magus' generosity. He liked and respected

Edward and didn't want to get on the wrong side of him. Edward was very loyal and still served Magus with blind obedience, unlike Tom and Greenbough, whom Yul had sensed were becoming disillusioned with the greatness of Magus. He backtracked quickly, not wishing to make an enemy of Edward.

"I'm sorry, sir. I meant no disrespect. At some point in the past I displeased Magus. He doesn't need to justify punishing me whenever he wants, if he chooses to do so. That's what I meant. I'm sorry if it sounded like I was speaking against him."

The giant of a man looked down at him and ruffled his hair.

"Fair enough, lad, fair enough. And you're right, he doesn't need to justify himself to us. We must just obey and not question. The master is the master after all. But I stand by what I said. You stay at home in the evenings and help your mother."

Greenbough was delighted to have Yul back again.

"Thought you'd become a farmer, boy!" he growled, giving Yul a great slap on the arm. Over the past months Greenbough had grown fond of the lad. He knew what a hard life Yul had led and how unwarranted his ill-treatment was. He felt affection and respect for the dark haired boy who took whatever was dished out and still kept his chin up and the light in his eyes blazing. And Yul was a damn good worker too.

"We got the bonfire up in the Circle to start. We're going up there now and most likely tomorrow too, for 'tis the Equinox the day after. Then it's the oak woods and pigs to organise. Bloody animals! The bane of my life every autumn, they are, with their snouts rooting up everything. I'd rather collect up the acorns and give 'em a bucket full than have 'em messing up my woodland."

Yul grinned. Greenbough's contempt for the pigs was legendary, although he enjoyed his bacon and ham along with the rest of them.

Yul began to shake as he and the group of other woodsmen approached the Stone Circle. He hadn't been up here for almost three weeks, since Magus had started piling on the work. He felt an ache deep inside his soul and knew that the green magic was calling to him, needing him for its release from the dragon lines in the Earth. The other men headed straight for the site of the bonfire at the opposite end and stood around waiting for the horse and cart to bring the wood. Yul took a deep breath to steady himself and walked with a straight back towards the Altar Stone. Fortunately the painters who decorated the stones hadn't yet arrived and he was alone in this part of the circle.

He approached the stone and could feel an immense pull, a surge of the force snaking towards him, seeking him out. As he got close there was a mighty flash of green and he felt himself leap inside. The energy poured into him, drenching him, flooding him. He sprang up onto the horizontal stone, his feet barely able to make contact with the rock. He groaned aloud, overwhelmed by the sensation. He'd never known it to be this strong. He closed his eyes and thanked the Goddess. With her magic inside him he could face anything.

Then the cart arrived and the woodsmen began building the bonfire. Although still agile and now throbbing with new strength, Yul found that he was no longer able to slither up the framework like a squirrel. He'd grown too tall and heavy. A young lad who'd joined the woodsmen at Lammas was now the one who'd be sent up to the top of the bonfire with the bag of brushwood strapped to his back. Yul felt a moment of sadness. He'd always longed to be a man. He'd wanted the size and strength that maturity would bring so he could stand up to Alwyn and look after his family. Now that he'd realised this ambition, he understood one of life's hard lessons: nothing is truly gained without something being lost. The fleetness and carefreeness of boyhood was gone for ever.

The artists arrived soon after and the Villagers among them began to clean the stones of the Lammas symbols. A horse and cart had brought the buckets of water, tallow soap and scrubbing brushes, along with the ladders and paints. Merewen the potter's daughter was as usual in charge, gathering the painters around her and discussing the patterns and symbols they would use this festival. Once the stones were dry, they began to sketch out in chalk and charcoal the Autumn Equinox designs. The acorn was the main symbol. It signified the fruit of the harvest and the seed of new life already produced, ensuring the never-ending cycle of growth, death and new growth. All around they drew blackberries, apples, hazelnuts, and corncobs and the creatures of autumn: the squirrel and dormouse, the leaping deer and the hedgehog.

Busy constructing the frame of the bonfire which would be lit for the evening ceremony at the Equinox, Yul felt happy to be working with wood once again. Harvesting was all very well, but it was wood and trees that he loved best. He thought again about choosing the Green Man as his symbol and felt a sudden certainty about the choice. He knew that the Earth Magic he received from the Goddess was linked to this, and to his empathy with the spirits of the woodland. He'd tell Maizie that he'd decided on his totem. The thought of his Rite of Adulthood filled him with anticipation. He knew it would mark more than his transition from child to adult; it was also part of Mother Heggy's prediction for his future. He smiled to himself as he worked. The sooner the better. He longed to break Magus' power, and especially his hold over Sylvie. He knew he must get her to Mother Heggy before the next Moon Fullness. The spell must be broken so she could be free to dance at Hare Stone again. Magus would not drain her of the moon magic this month, Yul vowed.

The day passed quickly, for there was much work to be done preparing the Circle. Yul was aware of the painters working all around him, and kept well out of the way of the Hallfolk among them. Fennel seemed worse than usual, and Yul guessed he was enjoying a new sense of power with Buzz gone. Rainbow, Fennel's younger sister, was in the painting group for the first time. But rather than encouraging her, Fennel could be heard putting her down and criticizing her work. Yul felt a flicker of sympathy for the girl, but Merewen stepped in and put Fennel in his place. Rainbow was taken to the largest upright stone that stood behind the Altar, and Merewen told her to begin sketching out the design. It was an honour to paint this stone, the focal point during the ceremony.

"Take no notice of him," said Merewen gruffly, patting the girl's shoulder. "He's just jealous. You've far more talent than him, Rainbow, and he knows it. He doesn't like the fact that you've been coming to me for lessons either."

Rainbow smiled at the dark haired Villager, one of the few who seemed to command Hallfolk respect. Merewen took no nonsense from anyone, and as a gifted artist herself she enjoyed undisputed status at Stonewylde. She left the girl roughing out the great cornucopia that always adorned the largest stone during this festival. Glancing over every so often, Yul could see that Merewen was right; Rainbow was talented and deft. The design grew quickly under her sure hand, the cornucopia spilling out its harvest bounty in a cascade of abundance.

The sun was low in the sky when Greenbough decided to call it a day.

"Come on, men. Home we go. Don't know about you lot, but I got a tasty rabbit pie waiting for me."

They packed up their tools, leaving them stacked ready for the morning, and started to leave the Stone Circle.

"I'll see you tomorrow, sir!" called Yul. "I'm going to stay up here a bit longer."

"Right enough, son. See you back here in the morning."

The painters too were packing up their things and leaving. Yul glanced at the sky impatiently. It would soon be sunset and he needed to be here alone. Fennel wandered over to where Rainbow was fiddling with the first coat of paint on her design.

"We're off now," he said. "Are you coming or what?"

She glanced at him and shook her head, turning back to the great horn of plenty she'd spent the day creating.

"Suit yourself. It's no good sulking, Rainbow."

"I'm not sulking. I just want to finish this first coat. Merewen's really pleased with it."

234

"Well of course she'd say that. She's only trying to make you feel better about your first bungled attempts. You'll see - in the morning she'll come and add her own images until yours is almost hidden underneath. I've seen her do it before to new artists. Don't kid yourself, Rainbow."

He sauntered off, joining the others who were leaving to go down the Long Walk. Rainbow stood back from the stone looking at it critically. Then she scrambled up onto the Altar Stone to get a different angle. Yul cursed silently. The sun was a golden ball, sinking rapidly in the sky. He needed to get on the stone himself. He glanced around and realised that everyone else had gone. Frowning, he came out from behind the bonfire where he'd been waiting and went over towards the girl on the stone. She stood dejectedly.

"It's beautiful," Yul said, and she spun round in surprise.

"Do you really think so? You're not just being kind?"

"No, it's one of the best cornucopias I've ever seen. Some years they're really ordinary. Yours looks like its bursting with goodness. And I love the dormice."

She smiled at him.

"That's nice of you. You're Yul, aren't you? Holly's been going on and on about you."

He shook his head and groaned. Rainbow laughed and jumped off the stone. She quickly rinsed her brush and picked up the basket of materials.

"Well, she's one of my best friends so don't be nasty, will you? All I can say is, she's very annoyed with you. But if you're playing hard to get, then it's worked. She's talked about you non-stop since you were so unfriendly in the orchard. I wish I'd heard all that you said to her. Not many of the boys would turn Holly down. They wouldn't dare!"

With a little wave, she turned and walked off towards the darkening tree tunnel of the Long Walk.

Yul breathed a sigh of relief. He stood alone at last in the ancient circle. The sun was burrowing into the west, glittering gold in the pink sky. He could hear the soft, soothing call of woodpigeons in the oak woods nearby. The Altar Stone pulled at him, urging him to come. Yul closed his eyes and breathed deeply, feeling perfectly in harmony with the earth and the sky, the moon and the sun, the five elements and all the stars. He was part of the fabric of life and at peace with himself and the world. With a run and a leap, he landed on the stone and faced the setting sun, his arms raised to the heavens and his head thrown back. As the sun disappeared, the Earth Magic spiralled up and enveloped him. He laughed out loud with the glory of it.

Rainbow worked quickly, her soft pencil capturing the lines perfectly. She perched in the shadows of the Long Walk on one of the low stones that lined the way, sketch book balanced on her knee. She was unaware of what she'd just witnessed, but her picture told the true story. The lines of Yul's taut body arched backwards in ecstasy, the radiance about him, the joy on his upturned face. She'd caught the essence of his blessing by the Earth Goddess without even realising it. She smiled and stood up. Holly would love the picture, she knew. Not that she'd part with it. She rather liked it herself.

Many of the community gathered in the Stone Circle in the grey light before the dawn of the Equinox. The birds in the woods sang gloriously. Overnight a myriad of spiders had visited the Circle and left their Equinox gift; silver gossamer threads shimmered in cascades of silk from the stones, catching the light and dew to form a glistening skein across the soft earth floor. The drummers had been playing softly, but as the sky lightened their intensity increased. The beats bounced around the stones, leaping off the hard surfaces and into the bodies of the people of Stonewylde. Magus chanted as he stood on the Altar Stone, facing east where the sun would soon appear. Yul smiled to himself. He felt the energy; tendrils had been seeking him out ever since he arrived in the Circle. He doubted whether Magus was feeling anything at all.

As the sun appeared for this day of equilibrium between light and dark, the drumming reached a crescendo. Magus lit the kindling in the brazier and the blue flames fizzed up. All eyes were on him, but Greenbough, standing near to Yul, felt the blast of energy that shot through the boy. Yul staggered as he took the full force of it, and the old man stared at him in wonder. His gaze was speculative as the ceremony finished and the people began to make their way back to the Village and the Hall for breakfast. He knew that he'd seen something special, something of which not many were yet aware.

The day was perfect, with that misty softness peculiar to September. The skies were mackereled with wispy clouds, and as Yul lay on his back on the Village Green looking up into the bright blueness he felt completely happy. Sylvie was about, and just knowing she was close by made him feel good. They barely managed to speak a few words to each other, but both were acutely aware of where the other one was at all times. Sylvie watched him, looking taller and more handsome than ever in his new clothes. He seemed to be constantly surrounded by a flock of girls. Every so often he would catch her eye and grimace.

Lunch in the Barn was a true Harvest Festival for everything served today had been grown and harvested at Stonewylde. During the afternoon the community relaxed and enjoyed the warm sunshine on the Village Green, at the beach, and along the river banks. Magus was in fine fettle. Morale amongst the Villagers was high, for the harvest had been excellent and Buzz's banishment had reaffirmed people's faith in Magus' justice. He was fired up on the moon eggs and his energy knew no bounds. He sparkled and thrilled with it, spreading himself around and making everyone with whom he came into contact feel special. Yul watched him covertly, noticing how he pulled the community together and bound the people in a web of goodwill and contentment. But like the spider who wove the web, his intent was to create a cocoon that would entrap and allow him to feed. Yul realised that Magus needed the folk of Stonewylde far more than they needed him, despite their apparent dependence on his leadership. Fired up himself on the great doses of Earth Magic he'd received over the past few days, Yul felt powerful and wise. A revelation kindled inside him, quickly taking hold and blazing in his heart.

*I could lead Stonewylde. I could lead it for the good of the Villagers. And I'd do a better job than him.*

A large group of people headed off for the beach as the afternoon had become very hot indeed. The sea was at its warmest now after the long summer. Yul noticed Sylvie sitting under the walnut tree on the Green tucked almost out of sight. She was watching him and beckoned him over.

"I've just seen Mother Heggy's crow," she said, smiling up at him. "And Yul, I must tell you how gorgeous you look today. Although doubtless you've already been told that."

He pulled a wry face and sat beside her.

"Are you sure it was Heggy's crow? Not just any bird?"

"No, definitely hers. I can tell."

"In that case, we'd better get ourselves over to her cottage. The crow's her messenger and she sends it to summon me. And you too. I expect she wants to speak to us urgently."

Inside he was rejoicing at this turn of events. Now must be the time to remove the spell. He'd become increasingly worried about this, for time was running out.

"Why does she want to see us?"

"Let's go and find out. We'll leave separately in case anyone notices. I'll meet you by the rowan tree just before the path forks to her cottage. You go first, Sylvie."

As they approached the hovel, she slipped her hand into his and squeezed it, smiling at him happily. He felt a little guilty deceiving her about the purpose of their visit, but it was for her own good. Sylvie was delighted to see Mother Heggy again and kissed the old crone on her withered cheek.

"I'm so sorry I haven't been to see you lately, Mother Heggy. It's been very difficult. I've been ill quite a lot and everyone watches me."

"I know, I know, my little one. But you are stronger now, and 'tis why I had to see you. Do you trust me?"

She nodded.

"Of course I do."

"Then you must believe me when I tell you this. You are under a spell."

"What? A *spell*?"

Yul and Mother Heggy could tell from the incredulity in her voice that she didn't believe it. They caught each other's eye.

"Clip has put a spell on you, Sylvie," said Yul gently. "It's to do with the Moon Fullness, and it's why you don't come up with me to Hare Stone any more."

"But a spell? With a magic wand?"

"No, no, a spell to make you obey. A spell that speaks to your mind but not your soul. You do what he has commanded without question," said Mother Heggy. "'Tis an old trick and Clip has the wisdom for it. He has done the same to your mother. Mother and daughter both spellbound by that evil pair of half-brothers."

They could see she still didn't believe them. Yul took her hand in his and looked into her startled eyes.

"Sylvie, every time I speak to you about the Moon Fullness, you say exactly the same words. It's like you learnt them off by heart and you must obey them."

She frowned. Something stirred in her brain. She thought of the rising moon and the first thing that came to mind was Hare Stone. But then the fog came rolling in and she nodded.

"A black fog that blanks out everything. That's what I see when I think of the full moon."

"Aye! A black fog is right, covering all. Smothering your own desires like a blanket over the face so you no longer breathe freely. Do you know what he forces you to do at the rising of the moon?" asked Mother Heggy.

"I ... I ... I like to dance on the round stone at Mooncliffe. I must share my moon magic with Magus. It's why I was brought here."

"That's the spell!" cried Yul. "Always the same words!"

"Do I? But it's true. I do like to dance at Mooncliffe."

"Sylvie, listen, you don't dance there at all! They put you on the rock and you're frozen like a carving. I saw it all last month, Sylvie, and it nearly killed me watching you suffering. I could feel your pain. The energy pours through you into the rock and they make you stay up there for ages, holding heavy

239

stone eggs to charge them up. There's a whole crate of them. They feed off your moon magic and that's why you're so ill afterwards. They've bled you dry."

She shook her head.

"I don't remember any of that. But really, I do like to dance at Mooncliffe."

"Now we must unlock the spell," said the old woman. "Sit down, my bright one. Sit down and look at Mother Heggy. You must trust me, Sylvie. And trust your sweetheart here. We would do you no harm. You know that in your heart."

Reluctantly Sylvie nodded, her eyes scared. She looked at Yul and he put his arm around her, holding her tightly as she trembled.

"I'd never hurt you, Sylvie. I love you. They're leeches, those men, feeding off your magic. This is for your good, I swear to you."

Sylvie sat slowly in the chair opposite Mother Heggy and Yul kept a reassuring hand on her shoulder. The crone took Sylvie's hands and looked into her eyes. Within seconds Yul felt a change in her. She was somehow more rigid, less conscious, although she didn't look any different. He remembered the power he'd sensed inside the old woman; a power all the stronger for being so well disguised in the withered, feeble frame.

"You are a blessed moongazy girl," she began, her cracked voice sing-song. "Blessed by the Triple Goddess at the rising of the Moon Fullness. You are hers. She calls to you and you must come. She calls to your heart and your soul. She is in your eyes, your moonstone eyes, and she gives you wings to fly and a tongue to sing in her honour. This is what you must do at the Moon Fullness, my little one. Listen to the Goddess calling and obey only her commands. The stone at Mooncliffe is of another power – the evil power of the serpent at Stonewylde. In your heart you know 'tis a place of suffering and malevolence. You do not truly want to dance there. You must go where the Goddess herself calls you. At the Moon Fullness you must honour the Bright Lady in her special place and nowhere else. You must dance on the hill with her creatures, the hares."

She looked over Sylvie's head at Yul, her eyes cloudy.

"Will it work?" he whispered.

"Let us hope so," she replied. "She must be at Hare Stone for the Harvest Moon. She needs that red harvest magic if she is to face the dangers that lie ahead."

The evening's party in the Great Barn was riotous. This was the festival where serious cider drinking took place, and as the next day was a holiday everyone let themselves go. The cider was a special one that had been brewed the previous autumn for just this event, and was particularly potent. Yul had in past years been especially wary of Alwyn at the Autumn Equinox celebrations. The man was renowned both for his prowess at cider consumption and his brutal aggression afterwards. This year was the first Harvest Festival where Yul could enjoy himself without watching his back. After the evening ceremony at the Stone Circle the party got underway in the Barn.

There were many traditional country dances involving circles, lines and arched arms, and Sylvie found herself galloping round the Barn with several different partners. She'd hoped to be able to dance with Yul but he was monopolised the whole evening by girls, both Hallfolk and Villager, who wouldn't leave him alone. Even when he did break free of them he didn't dare make any moves towards Sylvie. Instead he found refuge by staying with his family whenever possible, and had to content himself with meaningful looks across the floor at Sylvie.

When Magus arrived in the Great Barn a little later, his additional rituals in the Circle over, the atmosphere became even more charged. The apple games, involving bobbing, peeling and passing apples down the line without hands, were a great leveller. Hallfolk mixed freely with Villagers, all laughing riotously as they made fools of themselves. After this the children were taken off to sleep, the musicians struck up a lively tune, and the dancing started all over again. It was hot inside the Barn and the great doors were flung open to the starry night. A waxing gibbous moon hung overhead, whilst the bats flickered in the night air devouring midges. People wandered in and out of the Barn, needing to cool off when the dancing and cider became too much. Several people lay on the grass completely oblivious.

Magus was on top form. His energy knew no bounds; he dominated the Great Barn and was the magnet to which all attention was drawn. He was clearly working his way around, and Sylvie's heart sank as he approached and asked for the next dance. He was very hot and perspiration sheened his tanned face. His distinctive cologne wafted around him, released by the heat from his body. His grip was firm and he smiled down at her, dazzlingly handsome. For a moment she almost forgot all that she'd learnt that day. His charisma worked its magic, even on her who knew the truth. His teeth gleamed and his dark eyes danced as he looked deep into her eyes. Close up like this, in physical contact with him, she felt an inkling of why every woman was so enthralled with him. He exuded an animal magnetism that was almost overpoweringly sensual. As he held her to him, his strong hands on her spine and her face close to his great chest, she felt his aura enfolding her, drawing her into its gravity. Her hands were awkward on the back of his damp shirt, trying not to touch him. She began to tremble, her body and mind sending different messages. But then he broke the spell.

"You're a special girl, Sylvie," he murmured, taking advantage of the softer music now playing to hold her close and speak to her as they danced. "Truly unique. I'm so pleased you came to Stonewylde. Are you still happy here? I haven't had a chance to talk to you for ages, have I? You've been quite poorly lately, what with one thing and another."

She stiffened at this. There was one thing alone that had made her ill - his greed.

"Yes, I'm still happy thank you."

"Delighted to hear it. Did you know it's the Moon Fullness in three nights' time?"

She shuddered at the mention of it, and suddenly a clear memory flooded into her mind. The moon rock and the silver snake of moonlight on the water. The needles of pain and the heavy stones in her aching fingers. She trembled violently.

"Sylvie? What must you do for me at the Moon Fullness, my moongazy girl?"

When he said this, she looked up and met his eyes. Her grey ones were filled with fear; his black ones were piercing. Just in time she remembered the spell.

"I love dancing at Mooncliffe," she said quickly. "I want to share my moon magic with you."

She saw his expression change to one of lazy confidence. He smiled down at her, then bent and kissed her head.

"You're a good girl. I'll let you dance to your heart's content and you may give me all your moon magic. You know it's why you came to Stonewylde."

She found her knees almost buckling at his words, Yul's explanation now fully confirmed. This man was evil and she knew she was in danger from him. As the music drew to an end, he hugged her tightly, wrapping his arms around her. His scent was overpowering.

"You really are special, Sylvie. There's no-one else at Stonewylde who can give me what I need. I shall have to take very good care of you."

When Magus had finished dancing with her and finally released her, Sylvie stumbled towards the doors of the Great Barn and into the cool air outside. She still shook, overcome with dread at what Magus had in store for her in three evenings' time. Yul and Mother Heggy had promised they'd prevent him from taking her to Mooncliffe, but she wasn't convinced. She was scared of Magus and his intentions. He appeared charming and benevolent, but underneath was as cold and cruel as sleet. He manipulated and controlled, and all the time he fooled everyone. She sank onto a bench outside the Barn, closing her eyes and breathing deeply in an attempt to calm her trembling. She wanted to cry but knew she must be brave. Everyone around her was having such a good time and it would look very odd if she were upset. If Magus noticed, he may even guess that the spell had been broken.

She felt the caress of fingertips on her shoulder and looked up into Yul's smiling face.

"At last! I thought we'd never get a moment together! Come on, let's go and find somewhere quiet."

"Oh Yul, we daren't. So many people might notice. Just sit down a minute here and talk. It'll seem innocent enough."

He did as she said, but looked at her in consternation.

"What's wrong, Sylvie? You seem miserable. If it's because of Holly, I promise that I don't ..."

"No, it's nothing to do with her. It's Magus."

"Why? What's he done?"

Yul had tensed and his eyes flashed as he stared at her. She could feel him bristling with anger.

"He talked about the Moon Fullness and Mooncliffe. I had to pretend I was still under the spell. Yul ... I'm so scared."

He reached across and took her hand in his.

"Don't be. Mother Heggy has said she'll sort it out. Whatever happens I'll make sure you spend Harvest Moon up at Hare Stone with me, Sylvie. I promise you."

She gave him a little smile.

"I know. But I'm still scared. The way he spoke about it ... my moongaziness, how much he needs me. He's so strong, Yul, so powerful and relentless. It's as if he owns me and I'm only here to serve him. It was terrifying."

"Oh Sylvie! Please, let's go under the yew tree ..."

He was interrupted by a shriek. Holly appeared with July and Wren in tow.

"There you are! We wondered where you were! You've got to have one dance with me, Yul. You promised earlier on, and this is it. You always loved the Flying Sheaf – it was your favourite last Autumn Equinox. Remember? Come on!"

She grabbed both his hands and pulled him off the bench, the other girls tugging at him too, almost dragging the shirt off his back. They were flushed and intoxicated, their eyes over-bright and their voices shrill. They hadn't even noticed Sylvie sitting next to him. He looked back apologetically over his shoulder as the girls manoeuvred him back inside the Barn. Sylvie sighed and wished that Holly would trip over her Flying Sheaf and break an ankle.

# CHAPTER THIRTEEN

After breakfast the next day, Magus summoned Miranda to his office. He seemed relaxed and friendly towards her and she was relieved. There'd been times of late when she felt he didn't care for her at all; that he found her dull now that she was pregnant and desperately in love with him.

"You're looking radiant, Miranda," he said, patting the leather sofa by way of invitation. She quickly sank down next to him, her heart quickening hopefully.

"Pregnancy really suits you. I meant what I said last night at the dance. I shall have to keep you constantly pregnant. Would you like a string of little blond haired children? Seven, like many of the Village women have? I'm sure it could be arranged!"

She laughed, slightly embarrassed, and snuggled up against him. He'd thrown an arm around her and his hand idly stroked her breast, fuller than usual because of her pregnancy.

"You're like a luscious fruit ripening." He felt her belly with his other hand, pressing firmly. "Have you felt the baby move yet?"

"Not yet."

"It shouldn't be long now. I was thinking last night, Miranda, that it must've been about the time of the Autumn Equinox that you conceived Sylvie, if she was born at the Summer Solstice."

She nodded, laying her face in the strong hard hollow between his arm and chest, breathing in the scent of him. She wanted his love and affection more than anything else in the world. She wished she could captivate and enthral him so he desired only her and no-one else. He felt big and powerful, that."

"He was sitting with Sylvie, wasn't he?" mused Wren. "When we found him for the Flying Sheaf. Outside the Barn on a bench together."

"No!" shouted Holly, ignoring the stares from other women. "No! Surely not? She can't have got her claws into him too!"

"I'm sure she hasn't," said Dawn soothingly. "Wren, don't stir it up. You're only speculating. Just leave it."

"Well look at her now!" exclaimed Rainbow. "That's Yul's sister isn't it? Going over to sit with her?"

Sylvie sensed someone approaching. Feeling awkward and self-conscious, she'd been huddled in a corner trying to hide herself away. She wished her mother was here so she'd have somebody to talk to. The Hallfolk girls were ostracising her openly now. Dawn was the only one still talking to her and even she kept away when the gang were about. Sylvie knew they blamed her for Buzz's banishment. Normally she didn't let it bother her. She could avoid them at the Hall, other than in the classroom. But in the Barn for the Dark Moon menstruation gathering it was impossible to act as if nothing was wrong. She tried to sew the patchwork pieces and pretend she didn't care, but the day stretched ahead emptily, and tomorrow too. She hoped maybe it was Dawn coming to sit with her after all.

But she looked up into a pretty Village girl's face and knew immediately that this must be Rosie, for she had the same dark curls and slanted grey eyes as Yul. Sylvie smiled shyly, delighted that someone was prepared to talk to her at last.

"Come and sit with me," she said warmly. "I think I know who you are."

The girl sat on the bench next to her and smiled back, picking up Sylvie's hexagons and examining them.

"No, don't look! They're terrible. I've never sewn anything before I came here. Please don't look at them. It's so embarrassing!"

almost vibrating with energy. When she was close to him like this she felt herself drowning in a dark well of want and need. She loved him with blind obsession. Nothing else mattered. His frequent indifference to her only fuelled her longing and made her more desperate for his attention.

"I think, Miranda, that the time has come for you to tell me all about it," he murmured.

She tensed.

"I think I have a right to know. So tell me now. Who was Sylvie's father? How come you became pregnant so young?"

"Please, Magus, I really don't want to talk about it. It upsets me and ..."

"I think you're forgetting something," he said very softly, his fingers still fondling her breast. "I know best and you always obey me. Remember?"

She nodded again and swallowed.

"You do not defy me or go against my wishes."

She shook her head miserably.

"No, of course not, Magus. It's just ... I find it so hard to talk about it. I've kept it all buried inside for so many years. I really can't *bear* to tell anybody. I've never told anybody everything that happened."

"But I'm not just anybody, am I Miranda? And you don't want to make me angry with you again, do you?"

Miranda felt herself splitting inside; a new force had entered the sphere of her resistance and pulled at her free will, compelling her to obey.

"No, Magus," she whispered. "I don't want to make you angry. I want to please you."

"Good," he said smoothly, stroking her collar bones and the soft skin of her throat with a rhythmic touch. "That's as it should be. So tell me about Sylvie's conception. I want to know the whole story, every detail. This is not a request, Miranda. It's an order."

"Yes, of course. I'm sorry, Magus."

Falteringly, she told him everything she could remember about that night, sixteen years ago, when she was taken into the woods by a stranger. There wasn't much to tell because the whole incident had happened so quickly. He listened carefully.

"So the full moon was red? It must have been the Harvest Moon. And you didn't see his face at all?"

"No, he wore a mask like everyone else at the party. It was a big charity function at a country house. A masked ball in aid of one of the Third World nations, I think. There were lots of business men there, colleagues of my father's, and their wives of course. Everyone was in fancy dress or at least masked. The man who ... the one who took me into the woods wore a sort of bird mask, like an eagle or a hawk."

"And he definitely had blond hair?"

"Yes. Silvery blond hair. Like yours. Like a lot of the Hallfolk."

"And he didn't say anything to you at all? Not even afterwards?"

"No, not really. He just told me to lie down on the leaves ... murmured really – his voice was soft. That's why I didn't resist him. He was nice, gentle. I didn't realise ... And afterwards, when it was over, he said nothing. Only smiled. I started crying, I remember. My mask was wet with tears. He helped me up and brushed the leaves off me and put my clothes straight. I just stood there in my fairy costume sobbing, trying to hide my face. I felt so ashamed. He was very gentle then, I remember. He said something ... I don't recall exactly. Something about me being beautiful and fulfilling his dream ... I'm not sure. Then he took my hand and led me back to the party. He left me by the open French windows and disappeared into the night. It was as if nothing had happened. In fact I often wondered, until I knew I was pregnant, whether it had all been a dream."

She fell silent, her head bowed. Magus glanced at her and frowned, shaking his head.

"I don't understand why you're still so upset about it," he said. "It was such a long time ago."

"I know. But my parents ... When they discovered I was pregnant and I had to tell them what had happened, they said it was all my fault. That I must have encouraged him. But I didn't! I was so innocent. I had no idea what he was going to do to me in the woods. And once he'd started, there was no chance to try and stop him. It happened so fast. He was gentle, almost reverent, the way he laid me down and touched me. The way he took my virginity. It didn't seem like rape until afterwards, when I was bleeding. And even then I didn't really feel as if I'd been violated, because he hadn't used force. But my parents never let me forget how wicked I'd been, how dirty."

She began to cry quietly and Magus stroked her hair.

"He had to be Hallfolk," he mused. "The fact that it was a full moon and he had our blond hair. There are so many Hallfolk out there in the Outside World. After I took over here I sent a great horde of them away. Told them to make their own living in the world instead of leeching off Stonewylde. Something like a business charity function is just the sort of thing they'd go to – a networking occasion. And one of them obviously couldn't resist the opportunity of doing what comes naturally to us at the Moon Fullness. When I look at Sylvie, she does seem to be one of us. Don't you think?"

"Yes, Magus."

"I know it was difficult for you at the time, Miranda, and your parents were wrong to make you feel so ashamed. But I'm sure that now you appreciate what a good thing it was to have had Sylvie. You wouldn't want to be without her. So really, you could forgive the father now, couldn't you? Lay it all to rest?"

"I suppose so. If you think I should."

"Yes I do. No more guilt. Sylvie is a true blessing and who can blame a man for wanting you under the Harvest Moon? At Stonewylde we know how the full moon affects your normal judgement. Moonlust, the Villagers call it - makes you throw caution to the wind. I've felt the effects of moonlust myself, in fact. I'm sure you were as lovely then as a young girl as you are now as a woman. A temptation impossible to resist. It's not as if he hurt you or used brute force. He was gentle. It was wrong of course – there's no excuse for taking a girl like that, but he was clearly carried away by the whole enchanted dream of it. A beautiful young woman dressed like a faerie queen in the woods under the red harvest moon, who perhaps seemed willing enough … at first anyway. It's understandable how these things happen. You need to see it in that light, not as rape. Try to forgive and accept."

He brushed away her tears with his thumbs, then bent his head and started to kiss her full on the mouth. He kissed her deeply, running his hand through her long red hair and caressing her rounded curves.

"Mmn, you are delicious," he muttered, his chest rising and falling. "There's a lot to be said for a woman in full bloom."

She responded readily, drawing him closer and kissing him passionately. He chuckled at her enthusiasm, resisting her mouth and eagerness.

"Enough of this! No - stop tempting me, Miranda. I can't. I don't have enough time to enjoy you properly. You know how I hate to rush these things. I've got to be off within the hour."

He pulled away from her and leaned back into the soft leather of the sofa, his eyes dark and heavy, the lines around his sensuous mouth etched sharply. Miranda gazed up at him dreamily, her breathing deep.

"Off? You're not going away again?"

"Yes, I have to go to London on business for a couple of days. It can't be helped. But I'll be back for the Moon Fullness. That's what I really wanted to say to you. Make sure Sylvie is ready for me, won't you? I have an important appointment in the morning so I can't leave London until lunch time. But that'll still give me more than enough time to get back before sunset. Just make sure she rests from now until then. I want her kept in bed and given plenty to eat so she's strong enough for the moon dancing. Do you understand me?"

"Yes, Magus."

"She's not to go out during the next couple of days or do anything at all other than rest, sleep, and eat. Make sure she's bathed and ready before sunset. Is that clear?"

"Yes, Magus. I'll make sure."

"Good."

He kissed her briefly and stood up from the sofa, stretching contentedly like a great cat.

"I'm not promising, but I might come and visit you afterwards, when I've finished with Sylvie. After all, it's the Harvest Moon. Maybe we can lay those ghosts to rest. That's all, Miranda. You may go now."

Before he left for London, Magus searched for Clip, anxious to make things right between them. They'd had a row a few days earlier about the coming Moon Fullness, when Clip had baulked at reinforcing the hypnosis and coming up to Mooncliffe again to help with the eggs. Clip had been avoiding his half-brother ever since. Magus found him up in his circular tower, nose buried in an old book. He'd brought a large biscuit tin with him and sat on one of the chairs as Clip eyed him warily.

"Are you planning on spending the Moon Fullness in your dolmen?"

"Yes I am. So don't start having another go at me, Sol. I won't change my mind. I need some time alone. I'm out of touch with everything that matters to me, thanks to you."

"I'm sorry, Clip. I appreciate all you've done to help me. I know it's not your style. I wish I had your natural abilities but I don't, and that's why I need your help. You were lucky to be born with such powers. I just wish I'd been. Anyway, no hard feelings, I hope. I've had these made especially for you – your favourite ceremony cakes. And we've added a new ingredient. I think you'll find these really special."

Clip's eyes lit up. He adored the cakes. Only Magus and Violet, Martin's mother, knew the recipe, which was a closely guarded secret. They would certainly help with his shamanistic journey during the full moon.

"Thanks, Sol. Ooh, and so many! I shall be well away on these. No, there are no hard feelings I suppose. Have a good trip to London. You'll be back for the Moon Fullness?"

Magus chuckled.

"Yes, of course! You're right; I can manage Sylvie on my

own. She's easy enough to handle and she told me only last night how she wanted to give me her moon magic. She's still compliant so I'll be fine up there alone with her. I've told Miranda to keep her in bed from now until the evening itself, and to feed her up. Hopefully that'll strengthen her. I'm going to get her to do all the eggs this time because she seemed absolutely fine last month. Up and about in no time. I expect it'll get easier for her, as I said before, with training and practice. It's probably fairer to make sure she does all the eggs every month so it's not such a shock to her system. She'll get used to it and I may even be able to gradually increase the amount she can take. Don't you agree?"

"Yes, I suppose so," said Clip, opening the tin and nibbling at one of the cakes.

"I'm actually seeing a couple of people while I'm in London about the eggs. I'm sure there'd be a huge market for them. It's an exciting proposition."

"Mmn, very exciting," mumbled Clip through a mouthful of cake. "These are superb, Sol! I've never tasted anything like them. They are so powerful! You should be selling these too."

Magus laughed.

"Somehow I don't think they'd be legal in the Outside World."

Yul was worried all day. He nearly chopped off his fingers with an axe, and later let a whole load of logs roll from a cart, which he then had to reload. He swore fluently and started again, tossing them onto the cart at top speed, anxious to finish and get away. How on earth was he going to stop Magus forcing Sylvie up to Mooncliffe that evening? He knew Mother Heggy had said she'd stop him, but how? What was the plan? Did he need to help?

"Sir, could I finish after this, please? Mother Heggy said she wanted me to drop by with some provisions today."

Old Greenbough looked surprised, but nodded.

"Course you can, lad. I didn't know you called on her. 'Tis good of you. I feel sorry for the old thing. Used to be so respected, she was. Delivered all the babies, brewed all the remedies. Everyone looked up to her. But then Magus brought doctors to live in the Hall and he opened that hospital wing. Nobody needed Mother Heggy any more."

"It must have been difficult for her."

"Aye, I reckon it was. She's always hated Magus and never hid it like some do. There was some trouble, years and years back. There was a girl who lived with Mother Heggy, a strange, wild maiden. She were the mother of Magus, and Master Clip too. Died up at Mooncliffe, she did, one Moon Fullness. Mother Heggy reckoned it was the old magus' fault and she never forgave him. She blamed our Magus too, although I don't see how it could have been his fault as well. He was only a boy."

Yul listened intently to all this. So Raven had actually *died* at Mooncliffe? His heart clenched at the thought of what Sylvie had to go through up there. Had the same thing happened to Raven? Did Elm, Magus' father, feed on her moon magic too? Why had she died? He needed to know. But Old Greenbough had little more information than that.

"All I know is when our Magus brought in the doctors, he told us we weren't to go to Mother Heggy no more. Made out she was a useless old biddy who knew nothing. Can't blame him really for she was very rude about him openly and he can't have that. She was a powerful woman with a great deal of the old knowledge. I suppose he couldn't abide someone else having such power. I wouldn't cross her myself, though. You've finished, lad. You go now, and give her my respects."

Yul found Mother Heggy hunched in her rocking chair with the crow in her lap and an ancient book open on a stool beside her. She looked up crossly when he arrived at her door.

"I'm busy!" she snapped. "I don't need disturbances. Go away."

"But Mother Heggy, how am I going to stop Magus taking Sylvie up to Mooncliffe tonight?"

"Stupid boy! Didn't I say *I'd* stop him! Leave me in peace or 'twill be too late. He's already well on the road."

"But ...."

"All you need to do is to take the girl up to Hare Stone

tonight. Let her drink her fill of the red Harvest Moon. The evil one won't be back in time for the moon rising. You must be ready to take her at sunset. That's all. Now go!"

He turned away reluctantly, unable to believe that she could do it.

But it seemed he was wrong. He slipped in through the outside door and climbed the stairs to her bedroom just before sunset, having seen from the garden that Miranda was in the sitting room. He fully expected to find that Magus had already taken her. But Sylvie was pacing the room, alive with jitteriness and jumpiness.

"Yul!" she sprang on him as he crept through the arched door. "Where have you been? I'm going mad."

"Good. It shows the spell's well and truly broken. This is normal, isn't it?"

"I suppose so. But please let's go now! I've got to get out!"

She flung her arms round him, her body rigid with tension, and kissed him hard on the mouth.

"It's so good to see you, Yul."

He grinned at her.

"And you. I've missed you at Moon Fullness. And tonight it's the Harvest Moon. We need to get going, Sylvie. The sun's low. Where's Magus?"

"I don't know! Not back from London yet I suppose. I've been stuck in this room for three days and I don't know what's going on. What about Mum?"

"I think she's sitting in the other room. I could see her through the window. Let's just go, Sylvie. By the time she realises you're missing, hopefully it'll be too late. She won't come chasing after you, will she?"

"No, but what about Magus? Won't he come and find us at Hare Stone?"

He shrugged.

"Mother Heggy said she's taking care of him. We've just got to trust her. Come on!"

They tiptoed down the wooden staircase and ran across the

garden. Then they hurried along the track to the woods, alive with bird song. The sun was setting as they climbed the hill, the evening was warm and still. The sky was a soft pink; tiny golden clouds speckled the horizon after the sun had slipped away. The light grew thicker and birds stopped singing. The hares appeared from the woods, loping up the hill to sit long and upright, their ears raised, looking about them. The leverets, now well grown, hopped around nibbling grass and playing like kittens. Yul sat in his familiar place, his back to the great stone and his legs hugged up to his chest, chin resting on his knees. He breathed a sigh of relief. It was almost moon rise and Magus couldn't possibly make it now. He shook the dark curls from his eyes and glanced across at Sylvie. Wearing the beautiful moongazy dress that clung to her slender curves, she stood a little way off facing the horizon where the moon would rise. She looked well, not so thin and pale now, and he was pleased. His own stomach growled but he ignored it. Plenty of time for food later.

Mother Heggy crouched on the filthy flagstones of her cottage. Clutching a short, smoke-darkened wand of hazel, she poked at some dried lichen, fungi and herbs which burned acridly on the stone floor. She was muttering unintelligible words to herself, rheumy eyes fixed on the distance, hunched-up body swaying and rocking. In her other shrivelled hand she held the dark glass into which she peered every so often. Her crow was missing.

The crow sat on the bonnet of Magus' car and cawed. The front of the sleek sports car was crumpled to half its size. The radiator grille was wedged against a large stone in the ditch and steam poured from under the twisted metal. Magus was trapped in the driver's seat. Apart from a few bruises he was unhurt, but the damaged door wouldn't open, the air bag wedged him in his seat and his safety belt was jammed. He cursed vehemently at the police officer who stood nearby.

"I'm sorry, sir. You can swear all you like, but there's nothing more I can do until the fire-fighters get here with their cutting equipment. They reckon at least half an hour as they're busy at the moment and you're not hurt or in immediate danger. Don't fret, sir, please. We'll have you out in an hour or so."

"That's not good enough! The sun's set! I need to get home *now*!"

"Oh no, sir," said the police officer, shaking his head. "We ought to get you checked over by the paramedics first, once we've cut you out. And how do you intend getting home? This car won't be going anywhere, will it? And I need to take a statement. I know you haven't been drinking from the breathalyser, but I need details."

"But I told you! It was that bloody crow there! Just came out of nowhere straight into my windscreen. Look at it!"

The large black crow blinked its dark eye at him. Then with a clumsy flapping of wings it took off into the darkening skies.

*Now I can dance and spread my wings, fly the spirals and sing of her magic and beauty. Together they dance, the earth and the moon. I am free of the spell, free of the stone that sparkles and sucks my magic so greedily. Come, Bright Lady. I am here with the hares!*

As the rim of the red moon peered over the edge of the earth, Sylvie rose up on tip toes, spread her moon angel wings, and with a joyful song began her dance. The gossamer silk of her dress floated around her, the silver beads that tipped the pointy hem flying out as she moved. Yul leaned his head back against the stone and smiled to himself. Mother Heggy had done it!

Later Yul raised her from her moongazy reverence on the grass. She'd been kneeling for some time surrounded by many hares. The barn owl had visited and called across the silence; an eerie sound to accompany the rising of the blood red moon. It glided in on silent white wings, staring with its pale heart-shaped face and round black eyes as it perched on the stone. Yul stood tall and strong, looking down at her with love in his eyes as he reached to help her stand. When she rose to her feet, still gazy and dazed, it was natural to fall into his arms. They kissed in the moonlight, now silvery and high. Sylvie felt the power of the red Harvest Moon glowing inside her, calling to his green and gold Earth Magic. The quicksilver enchantment of the sacred place sparkled all around them. She clung fiercely to him, excited by the steely restraint she sensed beneath his passionate kisses. Eventually he pulled away and held her at arm's length, his face hollowed in the moonlight.

"We must get back, Sylvie. Magus may've come home by now and be out looking for you. We mustn't let him catch us here. I need to get you home safely, my moon angel."

"I love you, Yul," she whispered, her eyes full of moonlight. "I wish we could stay up here all night and be together."

"I love you too, Sylvie," he replied, kissing her tenderly. "And one day we'll have all the time we need. But not tonight. Not yet."

They hurried together back through the woods and arrived at the Tudor wing. The pointed roofs and gables were silhouetted against the moon-washed skies, and a light still burned in the sitting room window. Yul quickly kissed her goodbye and she raced on tiptoe up the stairs, heart pounding with fear. Her room was dark and empty. Nobody waited for her in the shadows. She jumped straight into bed and pulled the covers up to her chin, trying to calm her breathing. She couldn't believe they'd got away with it. Where on earth was Magus?

She found out the next morning. He was like black thunder, shouting at everyone and upsetting the entire household. When he questioned Sylvie about the previous night, his dark eyes flashing ominously, she smiled guilelessly at him and told him how she loved to dance at Mooncliffe. That was all she would say, endlessly repeating it until he almost slapped her. As he turned away in exasperation, she smothered a smile. Poor Miranda was shouted at brutally for not knowing what had happened. Miranda, it turned out, had fallen asleep on the sofa after she'd got Sylvie ready and had slept through the whole evening. She had no idea whether or not Sylvie had been out moongazing. She burst into tears when Magus yelled at her and spent the next few days moping around in abject misery. Clip had been oblivious to the world in the dolmen all night long on a cake-induced shamanic journey. He'd felt a pang as he saw the deep red moon rising, thinking of Sylvie, but his mind was too muzzy to dwell on it for long. He couldn't help Magus either as to Sylvie's whereabouts, merely shrugging vaguely when interrogated.

Sylvie smiled in her school room as Magus stormed around the Hall, furious with everyone, yelling at anybody who got in his way. His beautiful sports car was a write-off. He'd been delayed even longer than expected after the fire-crew had finally cut him free from the wreckage; the person summoned from the Hall to collect him had run out of petrol in the middle of nowhere. He'd had no phone of course and had to walk miles for help. Then they'd had to wait ages for the breakdown service to bring fuel, and it had been very late when Magus had finally returned to Stonewylde. It was as if someone hadn't wanted him back that night.

October had come to Stonewylde and the leaves were changing colour in the woods. The hedgerows were bright with haw hips, scattered like blood-red garnets along the lanes. The field maples glowed brilliant yellow and the beeches a deep gold. Everywhere the trees released their fruits to the waiting earth: conkers, beech nuts, chestnuts and acorns. It was a new experience for Sylvie, brought up in a city with only exhaust-dusted trees and fenced-in parks. She loved the different colours, textures and smells of autumn at Stonewylde. Yul and the other woodsmen were busy, chopping and chopping from dawn to dusk, getting the loads of logs into the Village and stored away for winter. He found the log chopping easier this autumn and realised how much muscle he'd acquired during the spring and summer. Greenbough was proud of him and delighted that he could now give Yul a man's full workload.

One misty morning Sylvie was in the woods working on a biology project. She'd chosen to study fungi, and was looking for different types to identify from her book. She carried a camera, sketchbook and a basket for collecting specimens. She loved this type of practical learning, especially as it enabled her to be outside in the glorious autumn morning. The birds were flitting all around her, darting from tree to tree. Squirrels scampered everywhere making a surprising amount of noise as they rustled in the fallen leaves. Her foray proved quite successful. Sylvie identified a number of different fungi which she photographed and sketched, and she picked a specimen of some of the more plentiful ones. She looked in her basket and was struck by the beauty of the mushrooms; the delicate blue sheen of the Wood Blewit, the pinky-brown tinge to the re-curved scales of the Shaggy Parasol, the purple-lilac of the Amethyst Deceiver. She had a giant white puffball that she'd almost tripped over and a great orange-red bracket of Beefsteak Fungus which she'd climbed up a tree to retrieve. She loved the names too, and was pleased that she'd chosen this fascinating topic for her project. She wished Yul was with her; he'd have known all these species and many more.

She heard the faint sound of axes thudding into wood, and her heart raced. Yul may be nearby. Since the Harvest Moon she'd become quite desperate to be with him. Her feelings for him were running deeper than ever, fuelled by the intensity of his emotions for her. She thought back to that evening, only a week or so ago. She didn't remember much about the actual moon dancing, but she did remember the sight of the enormous deep red moon rising, grey shadows clearly visible on its face. The Triple Goddess had worn her red harvest robes that night as she walked in beauty. Sylvie would never forget how magical the moonrise had been. When she'd finished her dancing and moongazing she'd felt stronger than ever before. She thrummed with energy, deep red energy, which she still felt coursing through her veins. She no longer felt frail or delicate. She felt empowered.

Sylvie wandered along an overgrown path off the track, heading for the sound of axes on wood. All thoughts of fungi were forgotten. Up ahead she spotted a group of men working in a clearing. Then she saw Yul and her breath caught in her throat. He wore old trousers and work boots and had taken off his shirt. The mist was clearing into a sunny day, and Yul worked in a pool of hazy sunlight filtering down through the golden leaves. He was deeply tanned from the summer. Although the stripes criss-crossed his back, the sun had helped to camouflage the scars slightly. The muscles in his arms, shoulders and back rippled as he chopped, his movements precise and rhythmic. His chest was well-defined with muscle, his stomach hard and flat. The axe bit into the wood as he swung it powerfully, putting all his strength and energy into the task. His black curls were stuck to his face and neck with sweat and the rest of his torso gleamed too, golden and smooth. She watched him and felt herself dissolving inside. After a while, she turned away and looked in another part of the woods for her fungi. She was too embarrassed to approach him in case he recognised the hunger in her eyes.

A while later Sylvie sat on a mossy bank to have a drink and look at her pictures and notes. She closed her eyes, remembering how Magus had once told her to use all her senses in the woods. She smiled sadly as she recalled his kindness when she'd first arrived. So much had happened in the past six months. Had she really been so naïve then? She knew that this summer she'd grown up; left the innocence of childhood behind and started the rocky transition to womanhood. It wasn't easy and she wished she was still close to her mother. But Magus had spoiled that. Miranda was a different person now and Sylvie no longer felt she could rely on her loyalty. She sighed and then jumped as she heard voices approaching.

Soon she saw a strange sight coming along the path. Two old women hobbled side by side, both wrapped in grimy shawls and carrying battered wicker baskets over their arms. Their heads bobbed as they talked; they were deep in conversation and didn't at first notice her sitting on the bank.

"Good morning!" she called, not wishing to startle them as they drew nearer. Their heads shot up and both glared at her, whiskery chins jutting belligerently. They peered with beady eyes and she recoiled from the animosity in their look.

"'Tis the Newcomer!"

"Aye, sister, you speak right. The Newcomer on the bank, right by our little crop o' Fly. She better not've touched 'em!"

"No, she better not've. They're ours, them Fly. Always pick 'em, every year 'tween Equinox and Samhain, this crop."

Sylvie had no idea what they were on about but recognised their hostility. She put her things back in her basket, anxious to be off. These were the first Villagers to show any lack of civility and she was unsure of how to behave towards them.

"You stay put, girlie!" muttered one of the women. "Stay there. We want to get a good eyeful of you."

"Aye, sister, a good eyeful. We seen you afore, at the ceremonies, but never so close. Stay put, young maiden."

They'd stopped before her as she sat on the moss, both staring down at her. She felt awkward under their scrutiny. They nodded, pursing their wrinkled mouths.

"Moongazy as they come, ain't she?"

"Aye, moongazy as that one afore her. And I'll bet he loves it too."

They cackled in unison and she felt the hair on her arms prickle.

"Well, Raven, you're home again to roost."

"Aye, sister. You speak right. Roosting up at the Hall in luxury this time around."

"I'm not Raven," said Sylvie, her throat constricted. "I'm Sylvie."

"Aye, right enough. But we know, don't we sister? We know what comes around."

Sylvie started to get to her feet, but one of them stepped forward and pushed her back with a shrivelled hand.

"No, don't you go yet. We want to speak with you. Get the feel of you. We mean no harm."

"No harm at all, young maiden. Bide your time. What've you got in your poke?"

She peered into Sylvie's basket.

"Been gathering, girl? Gathering the fruits of the woods?"

Sylvie nodded.

"I'm doing a project for biology." She realised the futility of that sentence as soon as it was uttered. "I mean I'm learning about fungi. I've been looking for different types."

"And you found our Fly!"

They pointed along the bank, where a large group of brilliant red toadstools, flecked with white spots, glowed on the backdrop of emerald green moss. Sylvie wondered how on earth she'd missed them.

"No, I hadn't seen them. They're beautiful."

"Aye, beautiful for dreams and wanderings. Beautiful for helping the spirit travel far. They're our Fly Agaric. You ain't been at them?"

Sylvie shook her head quickly.

"Raven always was one for the mushrooms, weren't she sister? Always one for the gathering."

"Pah! I could show that Raven a thing or two. Too busy moongazing and singing to notice what was right under her pretty nose. Too busy dancing around with all the men in her thrall crawling after her. Never would have made Wise Woman, that one. Moongazy and feckless with her bare feet and her mass o' hair."

"Aye, sister. You were always the wiser. She never had her heart in it, not after they got their hands on her and took their fill."

They cackled again, clutching at each others' arms in glee.

"Who are you both?" asked Sylvie, her mouth dry.

"Who are we? Who are we? There's a question."

"You've been here a six-month. You should know by now. You've ate my cakes, girl."

They glared at her again and the older of the two shuffled to the bank. To Sylvie's dismay she lowered herself stiffly onto the mossy top.

"You've ate my cakes and you've seen my son, Martin. I'm Old Violet. I'm the Wise Woman of Stonewylde."

Sylvie was puzzled by this. Martin the major domo at the Hall? It seemed such an unlikely relationship. Closer up, she could see the women weren't quite as old as she'd originally thought. Their lined faces were creased with grime which made them appear more wrinkled than they actually were.

261

"I thought Mother Heggy was the Wise Woman," said Sylvie.

The women spat in unison.

"You're wrong there!" hissed the one still standing. "My sister Violet's the Wise Woman. That crone Heggy has no power left in her broken old bones. She's as worthless as wet firewood."

"If you've had dealings with her," said Violet, "then you'll be in for a spell o' trouble. She's a danger to all who come to her, that one. She'll drag you into her web of lies and spit you out when she's done. You mark my words, girl. You'll rue making a friend of her. You should've come to me, Old Violet. I'd look out for you. I'd help you find your way. Here, give me your hand. Let me read you."

Before she could snatch it away, Violet had grabbed her hand. She now sat with it clutched between hers, rubbing the palm with her filthy thumbs and peering intently, her bony nose almost touching it. She rocked slightly as she held on tightly and Sylvie was wafted by her sour odour. The other sister sat down, wedging Sylvie between them, and fingered a long strand of her silver hair. Sylvie felt trapped.

"Well blessed be!" muttered Violet. "Blessed be. 'Tis the maiden and the mother, but not the crone. Oh no, not the crone."

"Do you see, sister?" cried the other woman. "'Tis clear?"

"No, Vetchling, 'tis not clear. Like moonlight through dark clouds – only glimpses. She'll suffer, this one. How she'll suffer. Her heart will be broken. The place of the hares, that's part of it. Moonlight and the black zigzag on silver. Three of them chasing around and never finding what they seek. Not until 'tis too late. Not until 'tis far too late to save her."

She released Sylvie's hand abruptly and wiped her own dirty ones on her shawl as if Sylvie had somehow tainted her. She shook her grizzled head and stared into Sylvie's eyes. In their black depths Sylvie saw something that shocked her. She saw pity.

# CHAPTER FOURTEEN

"Look at her! Acting as if there's nothing wrong. I'd like to go over and slap her."

"Don't be silly, Holly," said Dawn. "I feel sorry for her. She's all on her own. Maybe I should go and sit with her."

"Don't! She's on her own for a good reason – nobody likes her. And I'm not surprised after what she's done. Poor Buzz! We all knew it was coming. He can only take so much teasing and then he flips. It's all her fault!"

"Come on," said Dawn. "You're being unreasonable, Holly. Sylvie says she always made it clear to him she wasn't interested."

"Oh yeah!" said Rainbow. "As if we'd believe that! Remember that time they were caught cuddling in the music room? I've seen them together, messing about on the lawns. And if she wasn't interested, why did she go into the Deep Maze with him?"

"True. That was a bit stupid," said Dawn.

"I don't know about stupid. Asking for it, more like," said Holly bitterly.

The girls sat around on the squashy cushions in the Great Barn, ostensibly sewing patchwork hexagons for quilts. But this Dark Moon, Holly's group wasn't getting much work done. Although Buzz had now been gone for some time, the incident had been raked up again that morning by an e-mail Fennel had received from him.

"I can't believe he wants a photo of her," said Holly. "Why? Somebody tell me that!"

Dawn shrugged, trying to keep her stitches small.

"He's obviously still mad about her."

"The bitch! How does she do it? Goddess, how I hate

her!"

July and Wren came to join them, flopping down on the cushions.

"You're not still on about the photo?" groaned Wren. "Get over it, Holly. It's no big deal."

"But I miss him! It's boring here without him. I've hardly seen him since May when he went off to do his exams. I've e-mailed him lots of times since he was banished, but all he ever wants to know is how Sylvie is. And now he's asking for a photo! I hope nobody sends him one."

"I thought I might send him a drawing," said Rainbow. "I've got a few sketches of her in my book."

"What? Why on earth do you want to draw *her*? Are you mad?"

"She's very beautiful," said Rainbow. "There's something about her that's hard to catch, and I'm determined to do it."

"You're so talented, Rainbow," said Dawn. "You must go to art school when you're old enough."

"Maybe. But Merewen's a great teacher. I'm learning a lot from her. I'll tell you what, Holly. Just to cheer you up I'll scan my drawing of Yul and print you a copy."

"Really? Have you got it here now? I thought you said you'd never part with it."

"A copy won't hurt. Here, it's somewhere in the middle of the book. Be careful – no grubby fingerprints."

The girls huddled around Rainbow's sketchbook and located the drawing of Yul on the Altar Stone, his body arched and arms outstretched for the sunset.

"You've captured him perfectly," said Dawn. "Hasn't he changed over the past few months?"

"He is so gorgeous!" breathed Holly. "Although I hate him too. Did you see the way he was at the Equinox dance? Just didn't want to know. When I think back to the previous Equinox in March – I had him wrapped round my little finger. He was all over me then. Why doesn't he want me any more?"

"Maybe he fancies someone else now," said July.

"What, some stupid Village girl? I don't think so. He wasn't with anyone at the dance, was he? No, I don't think it's

Rosie laughed.

"I only came over to say hello, miss. I think we went through the same nightmare with a certain person from the Hall."

For one moment Sylvie thought she meant the moondancing with Magus, but then she remembered Buzz and nodded with a grimace.

"Please - I'm Sylvie, not 'miss'. And yes, I heard he attacked you first."

"I was so frightened," said Rosie, shaking the curls from her eyes in a familiar gesture. "There was something mad about him, more than just a man wanting a bit of fun. He was vicious, like a dog gone mad."

"I know what you mean. It was horrible. It's a relief knowing he won't be coming back, isn't it? But I'm not very popular with them now. They say I encouraged him."

Sylvie nodded towards the group of Hallfolk girls spread out in the centre monopolising the large cushions.

"Oh, they're not worth bothering about, stupid Hallfolk," said Rosie, then gasped and put her hand to her mouth. "Oh miss, I'm sorry! I didn't mean …"

Sylvie laughed. "It's okay. I'm not one of them. I can't stand them either. And you're right - they *are* stupid."

They smiled at each other and then Rosie looked away in embarrassment.

"I hope you don't mind me asking, miss, I mean, Sylvie. It's just … do you know my brother Yul?"

Sylvie found herself blushing scarlet. Rosie giggled into her hand.

"We've been wondering, Mother and I, who's this girl he's fallen for. He's so secretive, won't tell us a thing. So I guessed it must be someone a bit different. He used to like that silly Holly but he's over her, thank Goddess."

Sylvie felt a sharp stab of jealousy.

"He used to like *Holly*? When? He never told me! He said he couldn't stand her!"

"Oh don't you worry, it was a while ago. Before you came here, and it was nothing like he is about you. He used to dance with her at the ceremonies up in the Circle and back in the Barn afterwards. They made a good pair, both very quick on their feet. But that's been over a long time since."

Sylvie stared at her in consternation, fighting the tears that prickled behind her eyes. Why had he never told her? Was he hiding something? Rosie glanced at her and frowned.

"Honestly, miss, he never really liked her, not like he feels about you. I never seen him like this before. My brother's completely moonstruck for you. That's what I really wanted to talk to you about. I hope you won't mind me speaking plain, but I'm worried, you see."

She took the piece of material now lying idle in Sylvie's lap and began to sew, her stitches deft and tiny.

"I'm worried about what will come of all this. Yul's led a terrible life. I expect you know some of it but I'll bet you don't know the half of it. There are some things he'd never talk about. And you probably couldn't believe it if he did. But he's suffered so much ever since he was a little boy, no older than our Leveret is now. Our father – he was a cruel man, and when it came to Yul ... Well, that's over now. This is the first time Yul's ever been happy in his whole life. And I don't want him to get hurt. He truly loves you, 'tis plain to see. But you're Hallfolk and he's just a Villager. Where's the future in that? 'Tis against our laws for you two to be walking out together as sweethearts. I don't know how you feel about him, whether 'tis just a bit of fun for you or something deeper. But please, miss, don't hurt him, will you? Don't break his heart."

During October, as the land began to draw back into itself for winter, Sylvie learned how Stonewylde dealt with its dead. She heard about the death at breakfast. People were discussing how Old Humphrey had passed away during the night peacefully in his own bed in the cottage where he'd lived all his life. He'd been a farmer and right up until the end had been doing whatever odd jobs he could manage; making himself useful around the Village and playing the fiddle at the dances. Humphrey had an enormous family and was a well-liked member of the community. The funeral was set for the following day, there being no reason to delay. Sylvie and Miranda were told they were welcome to attend as most of the community would be coming. Sylvie was a little nervous about the funeral. Death was frightening and she herself had been ill enough in the past to have felt the cold draught of mortality.

Late afternoon the next day the Hallfolk walked together down the long drive. Everyone was dressed smartly but not in black. Sylvie was surprised at the number attending, although Magus wasn't there. Clip, wearing a dark green cloak and carrying a staff, fell into step beside Sylvie and Miranda and smiled down at them both.

"This is your first Passing On, isn't it? I'll stay with you during the ceremony if you like. You'll find it very different from anything you've experienced before."

"I'm amazed at how many Hallfolk are going," said Sylvie. "I wouldn't have imagined they'd go to a Villager's funeral."

She was pleased Clip was with them. Even though Mother Heggy had insisted it was he who'd put the spell on her, and she knew he'd been at Mooncliffe with Magus for the Moon Fullness, somehow he didn't fill her with the same fear and dread as his half-brother. There was something gentle about Clip, an inner core of kindness where Magus had only steel.

"Humphrey was a popular character and he's been around for most people's entire lives. But Hallfolk and Villagers usually attend each other's Passing On. It's an important part of our culture. We're a community and you're never alone in a true community."

"So what might we expect to happen at this funeral?" asked Miranda coolly, irritated that Clip had attached himself to them.

"It's a cremation, not a burial. Our funerals reflect the philosophy at Stonewylde."

"Why do you call it a Passing On?" asked Sylvie.

"Because that's what we believe death is. Your soul passes on to a different place."

"Like heaven and hell?"

"No!" laughed Clip. "Absolutely not! That's what Christians believe. We call it the Otherworld and it's the next stage in your soul's journey. Your soul spends some time in this world and then it passes on to another world when your time here is finished. Our ceremony is simply an honouring of the person's life and a send-off to the next world. We need to dispose of the body that's left behind, of course, and comfort those who'll miss the person. But we don't see death as the end, nor as the opportunity for divine punishment or reward."

They walked some way further, and instead of turning into the Village, headed towards the higher woods surrounding the Stone Circle. They didn't go up the Long Walk but turned off at a path marked by two carved stones. Sylvie saw that the images carved in relief were crows, and she shivered. The Hallfolk had fallen silent now as they walked along the stony path. They were surrounded on either side by dead bracken of a deep gold and silver birch trees, their leaves bright yellow and their trunks papery white. All around in the undergrowth Sylvie could see different types of fungus and mushrooms. This would be a good place for her research, although she wouldn't like to come here alone.

"Clip, where are we going?" she whispered. Miranda walked in front of them, for the path wasn't wide enough for three abreast. He bent his head to answer her.

"To the Yew of Death. Are you alright, Sylvie? You're pale."

She nodded although her hands were shaking.

"I'm okay thanks. It's just a bit daunting."

He patted her shoulder.

"Don't be scared. Death isn't frightening. I've seen the other side, the Otherworld, and it's a good place to go when your time here is done. The only thing that's frightening is the unknown, and the idea that death is the end. It isn't, believe me. I promise you, nothing you'll see today will frighten you."

The path went on for some time and gradually the silver birches gave way to oak trees. Acorns clustered thickly amongst the leaves, just beginning to turn ochre. Squirrels

269

scurried up and down the trunks, leaping in the branches and bounding across the ground. The oaks were thick all around them, overhanging the path which now went downhill into a valley. The route was marked with waist-high stones, many of them carved with crows and some with skulls. There were lanterns on each stone to mark the way, although it was still murky daylight. Sylvie heard the soft beat of drums coming from the valley below and the hair on her arms began to rise. Still the procession continued in silence, travelling down deeper into the woods, and at last they came to a great clearing.

Sylvie gasped at the sight before her. At the far end of the huge open area stood a yew tree, bigger than any tree she'd seen in her life. It had many trunks all rising from a massive bole, covered with pink-brown scaly bark. She remembered what Professor Siskin had told her about the yew tree regenerating itself, and how yews could live for thousands of years. She wondered how old this one must be. Its dark green spiky slips made a huge canopy, and in places the branches hung low. The ground underneath the yew was strange; soft and powdery and littered with pebbles.

What really drew the eye, however, was the funeral pyre in the centre of the arena. It was built of a series of criss-cross rafts of wood, and stood chest high to a man. On top was a bier, and on this lay the body of Humphrey. He was dressed in his ceremony robe and his shock of white hair was bright in the gloom. His arms had been crossed on his chest and he looked peaceful, as if he was sleeping. All around his body were slips of yew, making a dark green bed on which he lay. The clearing was full of Villagers in their best clothes or ceremony robes. The long procession of Hallfolk poured into the circle and mingled with them. The drums still beat softly, the rhythms weaving in and out of each other and making a strangely comforting background to the silence. Clip stayed close to Sylvie and she was glad of his presence beside her.

"The yew is wonderful, isn't it?" he whispered to her.

"Yes! It's massive, even bigger than the one on the Green," she whispered back.

"It's special because it's the tree …"

"… of life and death and rebirth," she finished for him, smiling.

"Well done! Who told you that?"

"Yul," she said, without thinking.

"Did he now? Are you still hanging around with him?"

"Oh no!" she said, shaking her head vehemently.

He looked down at her with raised eyebrows, then pointed to the oak trees all around them.

"Look, Sylvie. See the birds?"

She was shocked to see the branches of the trees clustered with hundreds of black birds, mostly rooks and crows. They perched in silence, fidgeting slightly, and she felt a little spooked.

"Why are they here? I've never seen so many birds all together in one place."

"The crow is one of the emblems of the Otherworld," explained Clip. "Humphrey was a lovely chap. That's why there's a good turn out of birds here today."

Sylvie frowned at him – surely he was joking.

"Humphrey was brought down here at dawn. His body has lain on the bier all day with his family and friends around him. They'll have had a picnic and spent the day thinking of him, talking about him and his life; all that he's done, all that he was. Taking their leave of him. In a minute Magus will start the ceremony. As the sun sets the family will light the pyre. We believe that then, in the twilight as his body burns away, his soul will leave this world and enter the Otherworld."

Sylvie shivered suddenly and Clip looked closely at her.

"Sure you're alright?"

She nodded and looked around, trying to locate Yul amongst the great crowd. She could feel him there and knew that he was looking at her right now. She scanned the faces and then her eyes locked into his, feeling the jolt of fire behind the deep grey. She drew breath sharply as she gazed at him and again Clip watched her carefully. Then he bent down close to her.

"You'll have to give him up, Sylvie," he whispered. "For

his sake, if not your own. Magus won't tolerate a relationship between the two of you."

She was saved from answering by the appearance of Magus himself emerging from beneath the boughs of the yew tree. He wore a long grey cloak, on which was sewn a great crow with outstretched wings, defined with golden stitching. Beside him walked another cloaked figure wearing a crow mask and carrying a burning torch. Magus strode towards the funeral pyre, the crow man following, and the drumming changed beat. More instruments joined the music and suddenly the whole community burst into song. Sylvie and Miranda both jumped and clutched each other's arms at the unexpectedness of it. The sound was strange – a sort of eerie serenade, almost an ululation, and it filled the clearing. The birds shifted in the branches, preening and watching.

"Who's the man in the bird mask?" asked Sylvie, noticing the blond Hallfolk hair.

"Martin, from the Hall. He usually assists Magus at the funerals."

It was too cloudy to see the sunset but Magus seemed to anticipate the moment. The light had been steadily fading from the grey skies. At his signal, five men brought forward a large piece of heavy hemp cloth, on which was sewn an embroidered pentangle of green and gold.

"Do you know about the pentangle?" whispered Clip. "It represents the five elements. It's a sacred symbol to us."

Then he was silent as the music quietened and Magus began to speak. His deep voice rang out in the clearing, his words unhurried and beautifully spoken.

"Blessings, folk of Stonewylde!"

"Blessings, Magus of Stonewylde!" chorused hundreds of voices in perfect unison.

"Great Earth Mother who gives life to us all, in your sacred presence we gather to honour our friend Humphrey. He was a loved member of our community at Stonewylde. His time with us is now over. His soul is ready to leave our world and enter the Otherworld. We come to say farewell at his Passing On, to wish his soul good speed through the veil, and to comfort those who will miss him most."

Every face was turned towards Magus; everyone was rapt and still. Even the birds were unmoving up in the branches.

"Humphrey was good man and a true Villager. He loved Stonewylde and served our community well. He loved the land, he worked hard all his life, and he honoured the Earth Goddess in every way. We say farewell to you, Humphrey. We will remember you, and especially at Samhain when the veil is thin. We send your soul now to pass on to the Otherworld, under the green symbol of the five elements that are the fabric of life itself. Earth! Air! Fire! Water! Spirit! We say farewell to you under the boughs of the Yew of Death, the great tree of rebirth. As the yew is reborn from death, so too may your soul be reborn in the Otherworld. May you ever walk with the Goddess, she who is life itself. Farewell, Humphrey!"

As the five men draped the green cloth over the body up high on the bier, the community spoke as one great voice.

"Farewell, Humphrey! Goddess speed your soul to the Otherworld!"

The drums began a gentle beat and Magus nodded to an old woman who stood flanked by her family. She took the burning torch from the crow-masked man and lit the kindling at the base of the pyre. Sylvie swallowed hard and felt Clip's arm slip comfortingly around her shoulders. There was a whoosh as the flames caught hold, and very quickly the resin-soaked pyre was a crackling mass of red hot fire. Everyone stepped back and as the fire burnt, the music played and the people swayed gently, many with tears rolling down their cheeks.

Sylvie felt incredibly moved. She let her tears flow freely, thinking of the old man she'd never even met. She felt part of something special; a coming together of human kindness and love. As the pyre burned, people held hands or hugged for comfort and the music was gentle and calm. The body under the hemp cloth seemed to have been consumed already; there was a strong smell in the air and ashes floated upwards. Suddenly and with no warning, all the birds rose together from the trees in a great black cloud. The air was full of black wings as if someone had scattered black confetti. There was a collective sigh from the people and everyone held their arms outstretched to the darkening sky.

After a minute it was over and people began to talk almost normally.

"His soul has gone," said Clip. "Did you feel it? Whatever was the essence of Humphrey is no longer here with us in this world. The birds know the moment when the soul passes on."

"That was amazing," said Sylvie, wiping her eyes. "Wasn't it, Mum?"

Miranda nodded, also clearly moved by the experience.

"The most beautiful funeral I've ever seen," she agreed. "All I remember of the last one I attended was the plastic flowers and the stench of air freshener. I'll never forget this experience today. Magus does things so wonderfully, doesn't he?"

"What happens now?" asked Sylvie.

"We all go back to the Great Barn. We share some mead and a bite to eat, and that's it. His immediate family will probably stay in the Barn together for the evening. In the morning they'll come back down here and sweep the ashes under the Yew of Death. They'll also put a pebble under the tree to represent Humphrey's presence at Stonewylde. The next boy to be born into the family will be named after him."

Back in the Great Barn Sylvie sipped at the glass of mead and looked about her. On the tables were great basketfuls of fresh rolls, dusted with black poppy seeds and baked in the cruciform shape of a flying crow. The bakers had been busy during the day. There were bowls of butter and chutney, many round cheeses, and baskets of apples. Everyone milled about, talking and eating, and the fiddlers played softly. Sylvie found herself standing next to Cherry, whom she saw often enough but rarely to talk to. It was frowned upon to talk socially with servants at the Hall, although was more acceptable at festivals and ceremonies. Cherry was always so busy but Sylvie remembered her kindness when they'd first moved in to Woodland Cottage. She welcomed this chance for a chat, although she found it hard to get a word in edgeways.

"May I say, miss, how tall you've grown lately? I remember when you came here barely a six-month ago, a scrawny little scrap, and now look at you! Still much too skinny for my liking, mind, but you're so tall and leggy now."

"Thank you, Cherry. I'll take that as a compliment."

"Aye, well, 'tis a blessing you've lost that nasty scaly stuff on your skin too. Told you our wholesome food would do the trick, didn't I? You're happy at Stonewylde, aren't you m' dear? Not planning to go back to the Outside World, I hope?"

"Oh no!" said Sylvie quickly. "I shall never leave Stonewylde! I love it here. That funeral we've just been to ... I mean, Passing On. It was wonderful. They don't do it like that in the Outside World."

"Aye, well, 'twas a fine ceremony today, lots o' birds. He'd have liked that, old Humphrey. The Village will seem strange without him around, dear old soul that he was. But never mind; we go when the Dark Angel summons. Not before or after. And Humphrey knew his time on this earth was finished. He was ready."

"The Dark Angel?"

"Why the angel of death, m'dear. You must have him in the Outside World too. How else is a person to know when they must die? He appears when death is close. And if he summons you, your spirit must follow. We all obey him, even the magus himself. Nobody cheats the Dark Angel."

Later as they walked back up to the Hall, Sylvie reflected on the funeral. It had been simple; no drawn out speeches or tributes, no prayers, hymns nor dogma, yet all the more effective for its simplicity. The community had despatched Humphrey's soul with love and sadness, disposed of his body and comforted his family. She thought of what she'd said to Cherry about never leaving Stonewylde. If so, she would herself one day end up under the Yew of Death as a handful of ashes, with only a simple pebble to mark her presence at Stonewylde. The thought made her shiver and she took

Miranda's arm in the darkness. She felt in need, all of a sudden, of her mother's protection.

The community began to prepare for the next festival in the pagan calendar, held on the last day of October. It was the festival of the dead and also the last day of the pagan year. Sylvie was expected to take part in a big dance drama performed by all the young people, Villager and Hallfolk, at Samhain. She must make her own costume and mask and had been given material to sew. She sat alone in the window seat of one of the downstairs rooms stitching the seams, glancing outside every now and then at the misty lawns. A band of gardeners raked dead leaves into large piles for composting into leaf mulch. She could feel the death of the year approaching and felt a sadness creep into her soul. She looked up as the door opened; her heart sank at the sight of Magus. He came over and sat down next to her, feeling the material of her costume and then looking carefully at her, his dark eyes searching.

"All on your own? Don't you want to sit with some of the other girls to do your sewing?"

She shook her head.

"They don't like me much. I'd rather be on my own anyway."

"That's a shame, but to be expected in a way. You are different from them; special, like a pearl amongst pebbles. Maybe it's better that you keep yourself apart. In fact, I think it's to be encouraged. You're not one of them. I like the idea of you not mixing too much with the other girls."

He continued to watch her and his proximity, the smell of his exotic cologne, made her nervous.

"Sylvie, I need to talk to you. It's about the Moon Fullness next week."

Sylvie kept her head down over her sewing. She knew he was testing her to see if she was still under the spell. She tried to remember the exact words. She looked up directly into his deep brown eyes; they bored into her as if he was entering her soul.

"I want to dance at Mooncliffe. I want to give you my moon magic."

He smiled at her and put his hand on hers, stroking it gently with long fingers.

"You're a good girl, Sylvie. You know how I need it. And you know it's why you were brought here."

She forced a smile in return and carried on with the stitching, her hand shaking slightly under his touch. He turned to gaze out of the window.

"The thing is, Sylvie, we need to spend longer up there this month. Something went wrong last time and we couldn't go. Do you remember?"

She frowned, pretending to be confused.

"I want to dance on the moon stone for you."

"I know, I know. And you shall. But nothing must go wrong this time. Nothing. It's really important that you give me every drop of your magic this month so it's going to take longer. You'll be a little more tired than usual afterwards I expect. So because of this I need to take special care of you now. I want you as strong and healthy as possible. So there'll be no more school until after the Moon Fullness. You're not to leave your bedroom during this next week and you must stay in bed. All I want you to do is rest and eat. Is that clear? I may have to get Clip to speak to you again if you don't co-operate, but I hope you'll do as I ask. Do you understand, Sylvie? In fact, take this sewing and go up to your room now, there's a good girl."

She nodded, her mind racing. He was confining her to bed for a week *before* the night, and then she'd probably be ill afterwards for another week. It wasn't fair, making her miss two weeks of the month just to satisfy his need. Magus couldn't steal her life away like this. She was worried about how she'd get out of it this time. Surely Mother Heggy couldn't arrange an accident for him every month? Would Yul be able to do anything? Sylvie made her way reluctantly to the Tudor wing, and tried later to talk about it with her mother. She came up straight away against the spell. At this point she realised that what Mother Heggy and Yul had called a spell was actually hypnosis. Miranda was clearly repeating phrases she'd been told. It was frightening to hear her mother, the one person in the world who should be protecting her from people like Magus, saying that she would always obey him, that he knew what was best for Sylvie. She realised just how clever he was. Confined to bed now, even though there was nothing wrong with her, she wouldn't get the chance to see Yul or Mother Heggy for help. Over the next few days of enforced bed-rest Sylvie became increasingly frightened about Magus and what he had planned for her up at Mooncliffe.

A couple of nights before the full moon, Magus asked Clip to come into his office for a chat. Since the last month, Magus had made sure he kept his older brother happy. He still needed his help. They sat down and Magus rang for coffee. As they drank it, surveying each other on opposite sofas, Magus produced a tin of cakes.

"Almost forgot I had these in here. Would you like one?"

"Are they…?"

"Certainly are. Help yourself."

He watched as Clip devoured the cake, eyes closed in bliss. He didn't have one himself.

"Absolutely scrumptious! May I have another?"

"Have as many as you like, Clip."

When he could see that Clip was relaxed and amenable, he set to work.

"I need your help this month with the Mooncliffe business."

Clip waved airily.

"I'll help if you want, but you don't need me. The hypnosis hasn't worn off, has it?"

"No, I've checked that. But there are still things that could go wrong. Where I missed it last month, the moon energy has completely gone from the big stone at Mooncliffe. There are only a couple of charged eggs left and it's Samhain the week after. For some reason I'm not getting anything from the Altar Stone any more so I *must* have this power. You know what Samhain's like - I really need the extra energy. So if something were to go wrong at the next full moon and I'm up there all on my own, I'd be stuck. But if you're there I know it'll be alright. I really do need your help, Clip."

"Well, it's nice to be wanted. Mind if I have another little cake? Thanks. They're quite addictive, aren't they?"

He sat eating the cake slowly, savouring each morsel.

"I'll help you," he mumbled, wiping crumbs from his lips, "but Sol, I don't want Sylvie kept up there for hours and weighed down with all those heavy stone eggs. It's cruel and I can't stand it."

Magus sighed and shook his head slowly.

"I wish there could be some other way of taking the moon magic but regrettably there isn't. Sometimes, Clip, to be part of a community you have to make sacrifices. At the moment she's the only one we know who has this ability to channel the moon's energy, Sadly she has to sacrifice some of her own energy to do this. But she does recover fully, and I think she overdoes the suffering just a little, don't you? It can't hurt that much surely. I think there's something of the teenage martyr in her and she enjoys wallowing in it. She needs to toughen up a bit. Don't you agree? Here, have another cake. "

"Well, possibly. But her distress on the rock is genuine."

"Oh no doubt. I expect it is a little uncomfortable for her. But this time I thought we'd lie her down after a while so it's not such a strain. And more of her body will be in contact with the stone too. She can even sleep if she wants. She'll barely notice it then. Would you be happy with that?"

"Alright, alright, you've persuaded me, just like you always do," laughed Clip, his pupils dilated. He waved his hands expansively. "Just don't be cruel, will you? I hate it when you're cruel, Sol, and you so often are."

"I think the cakes have affected you, Clip," said Magus smoothly, his eyes gleaming. "I'm not cruel at all."

"Come on Sol, I've known you all your life, remember? I know just what you're capable of. Which is why I have to go away sometimes. You're too demanding, too overwhelming. I can't cope being around you for too long. I've decided to leave here after the Winter Solstice. Then you'll have to find someone else to help you out with things like this, and with the ceremonies."

"I expect I'll manage. I usually make do until you come back."

"No, this time I'm going away for an extended stay, not just a quick visit to the Outside World."

Magus looked hard at him.

"But this is a very bad time for you to leave for a long period, Clip. There's so much going on. I need you. We agreed."

Clip closed his eyes, blotting out his brother's demanding face and the ruthless eyes that bored into him so relentlessly.

"No we didn't. You know how I get when I'm trapped in one place for too long, Sol. I need to get away. That's why I handed everything over to you. I don't want all the pressure and responsibility of Stonewylde. You can't make me stay! You know I can't take it."

His voice had started to crack. He'd only found the courage to stand up to his brother because of the cakes, and even their effect was limited. Magus watched him carefully, eyes narrowed, gauging how far he could be pushed.

"Don't get upset, Clip," he said soothingly, his voice soft. "I'm sorry. Don't even think about it now. We'll talk some other time. It's just that with all my plans for expansion there are going to be some big changes at Stonewylde in the new year. I'll need you to smooth things over for me if anyone becomes difficult. You know how good you are at getting people to comply with my wishes."

He sighed, gazing out of the window at the gardeners still raking the endless fallen leaves on the misty, dew-soaked lawns.

"I don't know, Clip, I do my best for these people and sometimes I wonder if it's all worth it. I have such dreams, but does anyone appreciate my efforts? I'm going to build another school to accommodate all the children, and more cottages in the Village. I intend building the holiday homes up here for Hallfolk so we can get all of them to stay more frequently. We need their money pouring regularly into the coffers. The wind farm will have to be expanded to cope with the extra power needed. And then there's the quarry. I need that stone. Jackdaw's been worth his weight in gold. That man proved to be an excellent site manager back in the summer. He got so much work out of the men. I'm planning to re-open the quarry properly next year, with experienced workers this time. So you can see just how much I've got on my plate and why I really need your support. You're my right hand man, Clip. There's no-one else. Don't leave Stonewylde."

Clip opened his eyes and gazed helplessly at his younger brother, so vibrant and determined. He felt worn out and frail just looking at him. He knew that he must stick to his plans or Magus would talk him round, as he always did. It was so difficult to stand up to him and go against his wishes; Magus commanded obedience.

"You don't get it, Sol. I hate all that. I just want to live in a simple hut in the hills and devote my life to my calling. I'm a shaman not a business manager. All this empire building stuff – I hate it. You need to find someone who can share your passion and help you build it up. I know you were thinking of Buzz at one time."

Magus' face darkened.

"That young man was a complete waste of time. He had no backbone at all, a snivelling wretch. He cared nothing for Stonewylde. I'm better off without him."

"What about any of the others? There must be one of your children you can start to groom to help ease your burden."

Magus shook his head.

"There's nobody, not one of them who really shows the grit and force of personality needed. They're too young anyway to be of any help."

Clip sat up, his face brightening.

"Of course!" he said excitedly. "Why haven't we thought of him before? What about the Village boy Yul? They don't come much tougher than him and he seems bright and intelligent. There's something special about him, something steely inside. I know he hasn't been brought up as a Hallchild, but ..."

Magus glared at Clip, his black eyes glittering.

"Yul? But he's not my son."

"Oh come off it, Sol, of course he is! It's obvious! I know he's dark haired like his mother, but in all other ways ..."

"I repeat: Yul is *not* my son. I've been through this many times. He can't be my son. Just leave it, Clip. We don't talk about this."

"But you know he's yours! That grand passion you had with his mother all those years ago - the dark-haired Maizie, with her pretty grey eyes and joie de vivre. I remember it well. That Moon Fullness during the eclipse! You took her up to Mooncliffe on the moon stone. You told me all about it the next day - in far too much detail I recall. What a night for her first time! Come on, Sol, you must remember that night! It was that spectacular lunar eclipse. The moon turned so dark red it was almost black. And the owls – remember the wild noise? And you and Maizie ..."

"Nothing came of that union," said Magus in a dangerous voice. "Maizie did *not* conceive that night."

"But of course she did. She had Yul!"

"Oh for Goddess' sake, she *didn't* conceive that night! She couldn't have because she was already pregnant."

"Already pregnant? No, Sol, you know that's wrong. She only went with you. That night was her initiation. You told me so. She was mad about you and you were pretty keen on her too, I recall. She'd only just reached adulthood, remember? She'd been with no-one else. She couldn't have conceived before that Moon Fullness."

Magus regarded him coldly.

"You're completely wrong. Confused. Alwyn was always in the picture, sniffing around her and trying to muscle in. Maizie lied to me. Alwyn had her first. She was already pregnant with his child when we made love during the eclipse. I know for sure because Yul was born eight months later. Eight months, not nine. At Yule – remember? Midwinter Solstice? He was actually born on the Solstice itself."

"Which was special that year, I recall. I'd forgotten about all this. It was so long ago. But it's coming back to me. It was a full moon on the Solstice, and a blue moon at that. Very powerful magic – solstice, full moon and blue moon all in one. An auspicious time for a baby to be born. I remember Yul was born on the very night in the middle of the ceremony itself. Maizie gave birth in the Circle right up by the Altar Stone. Red and blue, red and blue, Mother Heggy kept screaming it out while poor Maizie was groaning on the ground. The red moon and the blue moon. Conceived under the one and born under the other. She held the baby up to the moon, and told us that one day, when your son reached adulthood, he would …"

"WILL YOU SHUT UP!!"

Magus' face was white and he jumped up from the sofa, his hands trembling.

"We don't talk about that, remember?" he shouted. "I told you years ago we'd never mention it! It's a load of utter rubbish anyway. Just a crazy old biddy's rantings that I've never believed for one moment. I don't want to hear any more, Clip! Yul is *not* my son, he is Alwyn's! Maizie was already pregnant before I had her. She deceived me. Yul was not conceived under that red moon. Old Heggy is completely mad and her insane prophecies are pure nonsense. Yul's just an ignorant Village boy and nothing more. He's no threat to me whatsoever. Never has been and never will be!"

Clip regarded Magus warily, shocked by his reaction. He'd never seen his brother quite so shaken.

"If you don't believe the prophecy, why are you so scared? Why do you hate the boy so much if he's nothing more than an ordinary Villager?"

Magus glared at him and sat down again. He took a deep breath.

"I'm not scared! But I've had enough of Yul's challenging behaviour, his defiance and disobedience. He's got above himself during the past few months. He's over-stepped the mark once too often. I'm going to finish him off before he reaches adulthood. I shall take pleasure in crushing him completely. There's no place at Stonewylde for someone who defies me the way he does. I am the magus and if he can't accept my absolute authority, his days here are numbered."

"Surely," said Clip quietly, "rather than trying to destroy him, it would be better to get him on your side?  Heggy may be wrong, after all.  Her terrible prophecies may never happen. If you had Yul as your ally, working by your side, then maybe none of it would happen as she predicted.  Maybe, when he reaches sixteen, he wouldn't rise up against you with the folk of Stonewylde behind him and overthrow you.  Think about it, brother."

"I have," said Magus shortly.  "I've thought about it a great deal.  There's something about Yul … something in him that I have to snuff out.  I could never work alongside him.  I could never, ever let him become magus after me.  I'll see him dead first."

# CHAPTER FIFTEEN

Sylvie was scared. Restricted to bed, she could think of nothing but the approaching full moon. She almost wished she was still under Clip's hypnosis and in blissful ignorance. She was virtually a prisoner as Magus had locked the outside door leading to the garden. Her mother never seemed to leave the sitting room, through which she must pass to leave their end of the wing. She deeply resented having to stay in bed when there was nothing wrong with her. She wasn't sick or weak; she felt fine. The moondancing at Hare Stone had restored her fully and she teemed with the dark red energy of the Harvest Moon, feeling stronger now than ever. Lying in bed all day, even with books to read, was driving her mad. And the food! Magus had trays of it sent up every meal time and she was expected to eat it all. There was no opportunity to work up an appetite and she felt sick from being force-fed by Miranda. She was desperate to see Yul and find out the plan to help her on the night of the Moon Fullness.

Yul too was frantic with frustration at not being able to see her. He plied Harold with questions and was told that Sylvie was being kept locked in her room with her meals sent up. It explained why Yul hadn't seen her out and about, for he'd hung around at every opportunity in all the places he might find her. He visited Mother Heggy, desperately hoping that she'd be able to help again. He was disappointed.

"This Hunter's Moon he will take her to the stone. There's nought I can do this time around."

"But why can't you stop him again? It worked so well last time."

She wheezed at him, pouring him a mug of some

concoction.

"Sit down, boy, and stop fidgeting. Drink this. No, 'tis just a drink. You have grown, Yul, did I tell you that? A young man now as the Solstice comes closer. 'Tis as well, for you'll need a man's qualities soon enough."

She sat rocking, peering at him fondly as he downed the drink impatiently. The crow was hopping backwards and forwards along the table, pecking at bits of meat with its black beak. Under the table crouched a battered black cat, tail twitching.

"Please, Mother Heggy, you *must* help! She can't go up there again."

"If there was a way clear, I'd follow it. Do you think I want her to suffer? But 'tis not yet time for the conflict. And till that day comes, he still rules and he still gets what he wants. Bide your time, my boy. Have faith."

"But, Mother Heggy, it's dangerous!"

"Aye, true enough. But she's strong now. 'Tis why I made sure she had the Harvest Moon at Hare Stone. With that red magic in her she'll be strong enough for the Hunter. She can take it."

He leapt up and banged the table hard with his fist, making the crow flutter and the cat growl.

"I don't *want* her to take it!" he shouted, his face dark with anger. "I can't bear her to go through that again! If you could see how she suffers …"

Mother Heggy nodded her wizened head, rocking fast in the creaking chair.

"I have seen. Not your bright one, but my Raven. My poor little girl. I saw how she suffered. Every moon, every single moon she was up there, for years and years. I watched her getting weaker as first one man, then another fed off her magic, bled her dry. All the life draining from her, month after month. So don't think I don't know. I know better than any what snake-stone does to a moongazy girl."

"But couldn't you have stopped it? You were powerful, Mother Heggy. You were the Wise Woman with magic at your call. Why didn't you stop it?"

She laughed harshly at this and pulled her shawl closely around her withered body, her eyes faraway.

"Do you think I didn't try? Do you think I stood by while they took my little one away? Of course I fought them! 'Twas not so bad with the first one, Basil. He was softer. He cared for her in his own selfish way, despite the forcing. He wanted only to lie with her for the Moon Fullness, and at first he took her into the woods or down to the river under the willows. But after the baby was born, he came across the secret of the snake-stone at Mooncliffe. There was no stopping him then. He tried to keep my Raven in the tower at the Hall. Tried to lock my girl away. She had to roam wild and free. 'Twould kill her to be in captivity. I got her out from there, one Dark Moon. I cast my circle and I got her out. But then the other one, Elm, he found out the secret. He saw what went on at Mooncliffe and the magic my girl could draw down to that stone. Basil was dead within the month."

Yul stared at her in astonishment.

"You mean Magus' father, Elm, killed Clip's father?"

She shrugged, plucking at the frayed shawl with bony claws as she rocked.

"I saw nothing. But one moon Elm discovered the secret of the rock, the snake within that feeds and holds the magic. By the next moon Basil was dead, fallen sick and wasted in his bed as he lay. There was dark magic afoot there, and not my magic. Someone else who wanted Basil dead. 'Twas the Destroying Angel finished him, and I know who brought *her* to the feast. There was only one other with knowledge enough."

"You mean he was poisoned by mushrooms? Does Clip know?"

"He was a babe-in-arms. If anyone knew anything they kept their silence. Elm was not to be crossed, and once he had the power of the moon magic in him too there was no stopping him. He took the mantle of magus and he took my Raven too. Every moon, up on that rock. He was a bad man, evil. In many ways like this one now, cruel and hard and only looking out for himself, never for others. Wanting everyone to worship and obey him. Destroying anyone who defied him.

This one now, he hides it better. He can make people believe he's a good master, though underneath his heart is black and deadly. But Elm - if he wanted something, he got it. He didn't plan and scheme as this one does. Oh no, he just took it. He knew I had some power. He knew I would stop him if I could, for he was far crueller to my girl than his brother afore him. So he made a pact with me. If I let him bring Raven every Moon Fullness to Mooncliffe to take his fill, he would let me keep her here and care for her all the other days of the month."

"But I still don't see why you didn't hex him. Like you did to my father."

The crow hopped from the table onto the chair back and the old woman turned to whisper to him. He dropped onto her lap and hunched there, staring at Yul with his beady eyes.

"I told you he was clever, that one. He had these papers writ. They were kept in the Outside World, locked away somewhere safe. Should anything happen to him – anything at all – the papers would be read. They told of Raven, of her moongaziness. But they twisted it. He read them to me so I knew. They spoke of her strangeness at the rising of the moon. They spoke of how she was wild, but they made her to be a danger, to be a madwoman. Elm said that men would come from the Outside World, if they read the papers, and take my Raven from Stonewylde. They would lock her away in the Outside World and she would never be free. So I could do nought. 'Twas like a binding spell. He had all the power and my magic was as nought."

Yul shook his head. It was just the sort of thing Magus would do – clever and cruel.

"I'm sorry, Mother Heggy. I didn't realise how much you've suffered already with the moon rock."

"Aye, history repeats. The wheel turns. I know well how you feel, my Yul. You want only to protect her from his evil. But Sylvie will survive this."

"I was worried. I heard that Raven died up at Mooncliffe, and I thought …"

Mother Heggy nodded, her eyes gazing unseeing at the fireplace.

"Aye, she died there, 'tis true. 'Twas an eclipse. The moon magic is strange at times such as that. Different, more powerful, yet tainted and dark. Well, she lay on the rock as always. The moon was high and he had done with her. I came up the path for her, same as every month, for she was too weak to walk alone after he had taken his fill. Then the eclipse began. The bright moon grew darker and darker as the jaw moved across, devouring it. My Raven started to groan with the pain of it. I tried to reach her, to pull her off the rock where the snake drank so greedily of this new dark magic. But the evil one held me back. He wouldn't let me near her. Said he wanted to see her moongaziness under the eclipse. She moaned and she cried. Like a buzzard riding the winds she sounded, high and keen. When the Bright Lady was all dark, all devoured, the crying stopped. My girl had slipped away."

Her shrivelled hands caressed the crow in her lap and she sighed heavily, the breath rattling in her old lungs.

"After a while he touched her and saw she was dead. He cursed and cursed, ranting and raving, calling at the dark powers with every foul name, howling at the blood red moon. He dragged her poor little body off the rock and threw her at me. I had to get her down from there, carry her all the way down the cliff path on my own."

"Mother Heggy, that's awful. I'm so sorry."

She got up and poked at the fire fiercely.

"Aye, well, 'twas a long time ago, and he got his justice in the end. And 'twas as well she passed on when she did, for her life was nought. Just a vessel to be used by him for his greed. I hated that man, just as I hate this magus. They have the same lust in them, the same desire for power. I see it clear in this one. He'll get worse, just like his father afore him. The power is a canker. 'Twill eat into his soul and turn him bad, like a maggot in an apple, spoiling and rotting him. So, my Yul, never believe I don't want to help. When the time comes, I will fight for you as I have done before. You will have every last drop of my magic when you need it. But 'tis not yet time. I know the bright one can take it, though it hurts her. She'll survive this Hunter's Moon. Raven survived years of it."

Yul stood up and the crow hopped onto his shoulder, pecking at his ear.

"Alright," he said sadly. "I'll have to accept it, unless I can think of a plan."

"No! You mustn't force a battle yet. No plan. The time is not right. The wheel has not yet turned full circle."

"But when will it be time? How much longer do I have to wait before I can destroy him? I feel strange at times, Mother Heggy. I feel this great need in me, this stirring of power and knowledge growing inside. There are things I must do and Stonewylde calls to me. I feel it at the Altar Stone when the green magic comes, but I feel it at other places too. In the woods, on the Village Green, at Hare Stone, by the river – everywhere I feel Stonewylde calling to me. This must sound strange. But I know I'm here to guard and protect Stonewylde, and Magus isn't. He's forgotten what being the magus truly means. He thinks only of his own power and glory, not what Stonewylde and the folk need. Not what the Earth Mother wants of him. That's why she no longer gives him her Earth Magic but gives it all to me. When will his rule end, Mother Heggy?"

"The Winter Solstice, my boy, that's when. *Under red and blue, the fruit of his passion will rise up against him with the folk behind, at the time of brightness in darkness in the place of bones and death.* Be patient, Yul. Bide your time, for 'tis almost come, and some of us have waited long for this. Remember what I told you. If we do it right, if we can keep on the path, those who stand against you will fall, one by one."

Sylvie stood in her room looking out of the window. It was late afternoon and the sun was beginning to sink. She knew that soon it would be time. She felt jittery and jumpy as she normally did at this point, but over-riding this was her terror of what would happen to her tonight. Miranda had made her bathe and change into the silver dress, which she now loathed. She was cold with her arms and legs bare, and pulled a cover off the bed to wrap around herself. She trembled with fear, hoping, wishing and praying that Yul would somehow manage to stop this from happening, with or without Mother Heggy's help. She knew that if it was humanly possible he would. She knew how he loved her.

She heard them coming through the sitting room, the men's voices seeming loud after the silence. They came into her bedroom without knocking. Sylvie caught a glimpse of her mother's face in the doorway smiling anxiously. Magus was brusque and business-like, glancing peremptorily at her. He took her arm and led her towards the arched door. He threw the bedcover onto the floor but Clip picked it up.

"She'll need this, won't she? It's going to be cold up there."

They both wore warm clothing, she noticed.

"Yes, alright, but let's get on with it. I've got the key."

"Goodbye!" called Miranda. "Have a nice time!"

At the cliff path Sylvie started to climb but Magus stopped her. Neither he nor Clip had spoken to her; it was as if she didn't exist as herself, only as a means for providing them with what they wanted. Magus picked her up, shifting her in his arms. She had to lie passively, pretending to be docile and still under the spell. She felt his hands gripping her and laid her head against his chest, breathing in his scent. She forced herself to relax; her body screamed to escape.

"Good," said Magus, "she's put on some weight. She feels heavier than last time. Miranda's fed her up well. Does that make you feel better, Clip? She'll be stronger now and it won't matter so much if she doesn't eat for a few days afterwards."

"Yes, I suppose so. She became so thin last time it worried me."

"Well don't be worried. And remember what I said to you before. I think there's a certain amount of malingering to get attention. She's going to have to learn to cope with it. This is what she'll be doing every twenty-nine days for the foreseeable future and she'd better get used to it."

He shifted her in his arms and she felt like a sack of potatoes, especially when he cursed and then slung her over his shoulders in a fire-fighter's lift. Her arms and long hair dangled down his back, while his shoulder pressed into her stomach. Sylvie started to cry silently at this indignity. At the top of the cliff she saw the strange glittering rock placed so unnaturally on the grass like a massive round table; she was the feast. The sun was close to setting in the watery sky. There was some broken cloud and a light breeze blew up from the sea. Magus put her down, righting her as she nearly overbalanced. She started to tremble, partly from the cold but also with fear. There was a strong feeling of unreality, not helped by her natural tension and jumpiness this close to moonrise. Clip came over and looked into her face, smiling. She managed to smile back.

"I love to dance at Mooncliffe," she said, for good measure.

"And so you shall, Sylvie," he said, patting her arm kindly. "Here, let's wrap you up whilst we wait for the moon."

He carefully put the cover around her, although her bare legs and feet were still cold. Magus was over at the wooden chest fiddling around with a padlock. Next to it lay a new chest, also locked.

"Come and give me a hand," he called. "I want to shift all these eggs up to the rock so they're ready. Then we can put them back in the chest as they get charged up."

"But there are more here, Sol! A whole new crate of them! What have you done? She barely managed the first lot. She'll never cope with all these extra ones as well."

"We'll see how it goes. We've got nothing to lose. And look, the new ones are much smaller. They won't take so long to charge. Did I tell you that I've got some people interested in buying them? The smaller ones are to sell and I'll keep the larger ones for our own use. I thought that when she can't stand upright any more, we could just lay these smaller ones on top of her. I don't know if it'll work but we can try. Remember I said we're going to stay up for a bit longer tonight."

"No, Sol! I didn't agree to that! You promised me you wouldn't be cruel tonight. You promised! I only agreed to come on those conditions."

"Oh for Goddess' sake, stop whingeing. Look what I

brought up here earlier, to keep us going. A couple of bottles of the strong brew mead and a tin of your favourite cakes with the added new ingredient. We'll celebrate the Moon Fullness in style tonight."

Sylvie stood in the slight breeze with her hair blowing around her whilst they shifted all the stone eggs to make a circle around the edge of the rock. It seemed to take for ever as they went backwards and forwards. She shook with cold and fear, not sure how she should be behaving but feeling that familiar rising within her as darkness began to fall. Finally they stood ready, all three staring out to sea waiting.

*I cannot bring the magic to Stonewylde here! The snake is waiting, the greedy one, the sparkling one. I cannot dance the sacred spiral dance here. I must be at Hare Stone! The Bright Lady comes, but I cannot be her moon angel at this terrible place of suffering.*

Yul was hidden in the bracken, also shaking. He couldn't bear to see her there, cold in the thin dress with a blanket that barely covered her, waiting silently for her ordeal to begin. He knew she was aware of what was happening. Several times, when they'd had their backs to her, she'd looked around desperately as if for a means of escape. He hadn't made himself visible to her as she may then have given his position away. The worse thing was that he didn't even have a plan of action. Despite Mother Heggy's warning, he was hoping some opportunity would present itself so he could rescue her. But time was running out and it didn't seem now as if it would. He noticed the little signs in Sylvie that the moonrise was imminent. She fidgeted, going up on her tip-toes, and then he saw her arms start to rise. On the horizon he could see the rim of the moon, half buried in the cloud. The cover slipped off as her arms rose into wings. Magus noticed and grasped hold of her.

"Here we go, Clip! Take the other side. We'll lift her up like this."

They manhandled her towards the stone but she began to struggle, thrashing around and screaming.

"What the hell's happening?" bellowed Magus. "I

thought she was still under hypnosis? Quick, grab her and get her up there!"

"Sylvie, Sylvie, you're at Mooncliffe!" said Clip. "You love to dance here."

"No I don't!" she shrieked, kicking and wriggling. "I hate it! You have no right to do this to me! I must go to Hare Stone with Yul. Let me go!"

Unsure of what to do, Yul stood up in the dead bracken, his fists clenched. She flailed her arms, almost breaking free. Magus grabbed her roughly with one hand and slapped her round the face with the other. Her head snapped sharply to the side, and with a roar of rage Yul jumped out of the bracken and up onto the cliff top.

"What the hell is *he* doing here?" yelled Magus, still trying to get a good grip on Sylvie. She fought and kicked as he struggled to lift her up onto the rock. "For Goddess' sake, keep still you stupid bloody girl or I'll *really* hurt you!"

"*Don't you dare touch her, you bastard!*" screamed Yul, leaping onto them and trying to wrench Sylvie away. Magus shoved Yul back and then in a quick and violent motion swung Sylvie off her feet and sent her sprawling onto the rock. She landed with a sharp cry, her body convulsing. In the near darkness, she began to glow with the silver threads of light. Yul was up on his feet again trying to scramble onto the rock to reach her. Magus punched him hard, catching his shoulder, and yelled at Clip who stood there uncertainly.

"Clip, get up on the rock now and stand her in the centre! Quick! The power isn't flowing properly while she's lying like that."

Clip leapt onto it and took hold of her, but dropped her again instantly.

"Sacred Mother!" he screeched. "I can't touch her! It's like an electric shock!"

"Come here and hold this boy, then. Don't let him go!"

Magus jumped onto the rock and grabbed Sylvie, his face contorting with pain as he touched her. He yanked her upright and pushed her into the centre so she faced the rising moon, every bone in her body jolting and jerking. Her face too was twisted in agony and her curtain of hair rippled violently.

"Let her go!" roared Yul, breaking free of Clip's hold. He dodged to one side, trying to get round Clip and onto the stone. Magus dived at him and knocked him hard to the ground, winding him. For all Yul had grown, he was still young and slim and Magus was a tall, powerfully-built man. There was no competition. Within seconds Yul was lying face down in the grass. One arm was twisted viciously up behind him, while Magus' knee pressed hard into the small of his back. Yul choked and gasped where he'd been winded.

"Keep still, you little shit, or I'll break your arm!" hissed Magus, giving it a wrench for good measure. Yul cried out in agony and tried not to move. He felt Magus relax, the weight increasing on his back.

"Everything's alright now, Clip," he called. "She'll be standing up there for a good hour or so until we start to load her with stones. Now all we've got to do is deal with this bloody nuisance and then we can crack open the mead."

"What's he doing up here anyway?" asked Clip, coming over to stare down at Yul.

"Come to rescue her," sneered Magus. "I've warned you before, Yul, to stay away from this girl! Just won't be told, will you? And this time you really will pay."

"Please!" gasped Yul, his face squashed into the grass and his lungs compressed by Magus' weight. "Please just let her go. It hurts her up on that rock."

Magus only laughed.

"Clip, there's a piece of rope in the new chest, I believe, from when it was dragged up here. Bring it over, will you?"

He proceeded to bind Yul's wrists tightly together behind his back, and then hauled him upright into a sitting position facing the rock. He looped the end of the rope through one of the iron rings set into the ground and fastened it securely.

"There!" he said. "You won't be going anywhere in a hurry. Feast your eyes on her, Yul, if you're so keen. She's not going anywhere either, not for a long, long time. I'm sure you'll enjoy watching her up there. Look at her! She's even dancing for you."

Yul let out a cry of rage at this.

"I *hate* you, you bastard! One day I'm going to kill you!"

Magus turned and with a vicious side swipe that Yul remembered well from his days in the byre, knocked him sideways to the ground. The side of his face was now agony, his lip bleeding freely. Magus yanked him upright to face Sylvie again.

"Not if I kill you first!" he spat.

An hour later, Magus and Clip had drunk much of the strong mead and Clip had consumed a few cakes. He lay on the grass on his back with his feet against the rock, humming softly. Magus had climbed onto the rock and lay there soaking up the moon energy. Sylvie's terrible convulsions had quietened into tremors, and the silver light still crawled all over her arms and legs. Yul was worried about how cold she must be. It was the end of October and not balmy like last time up here in August. He was chilly and she wore less than him. He'd kept quiet since Magus had hit him so hard in the face, realising how vulnerable he was. It wasn't in his or Sylvie's interests to goad Magus into a rage. But he couldn't let her freeze.

"Could you put the blanket around her?" he asked quietly, hoping Magus would take pity on her. Magus raised his head from the rock and glared at him, his face clearly visible in the silver light of the moon.

"Aah, how touching. Such sweet concern. Shut up, Yul!"

But Clip must have heard for he slowly staggered to his feet and found the cover lying on the ground. He managed after a few clumsy attempts to climb up onto the rock and drape it around her shoulders. He could barely stand and almost fell against Sylvie.

"It had better not interfere with the energy," muttered Magus.

"No, look, it's still going into the rock," mumbled Clip. "Think I'll join you now it's calmer up here. What have you put in those cakes, Sol? They are so powerful! Sacred Mother, that's a good combination – cakes and moon energy. I can feel myself going ..."

Magus sat up and reached across, picking up two of the larger stone eggs. He placed them in Sylvie's unresponsive hands and lay back down again with a groan. Yul sat silently, anger seething through his body but mingled with sharp sadness. He'd let her down. She'd trusted him to rescue her. She'd stood there waiting, not trying to escape because she'd had faith in him. And he'd failed her. He welcomed the pain in the side of his face where Magus had hit him; he deserved it. He hung his head and cried silently.

Magus continued to change the eggs at intervals once they were glowing, putting the charged ones back into the chests. Later, on his way across the grass with a pair of them, he stumbled over the tin of cakes still lying there. He swore vehemently then stopped. He came back to where Yul sat mutely in his own private hell. Magus crouched down and grasped Yul's chin roughly, forcing him to look up and into his eyes. They glittered coldly in the harsh, silver light. The strong mead had done nothing to mellow him; if anything he seemed possessed tonight by a strange wildness different to his usual tight control. Yul sensed the icy quicksilver slithering inside him, not sparkling and magical like Sylvie's, but cruel and sharp as venom. Yul quaked with fear, for he knew only too well where this man's sadism could lead. But he met his gaze squarely, trying not to show any weakness.

"How are we doing, my lad? Still feeling angry? Upset?" He chuckled. "You really should've learnt by now not to defy me, Yul. You just don't seem to learn your lesson, do you? When we've finished up here tonight, I shall have to start all over again teaching you how to behave. Just like I did before. This time I won't have your dear father to help show you the error of your ways. That's a shame, because he took such pleasure in it. But never mind, I have someone else almost as good. In fact, better in many respects. You remember our friend Jackdaw? Yes, I thought you might! He'll enjoy correcting you, especially if I give him free rein. He has a wider and more sophisticated repertoire than your father. Maybe the two of us together will succeed this time in bringing you to heel. Or finish you off altogether."

Yul's heart sank. It was two months until the Winter Solstice. Would he survive long enough to overcome this man? He closed his eyes, blotting out Magus' cruel face, and heard him chuckle again. This time there was a manic edge to the sound that made Yul's skin crawl with terror.

"You won't get rid of me like that. In fact you won't get rid of me at all, you bloody upstart! I've just had such a good idea, in view of your attempts tonight to interfere with my moon magic. How dare you come up here at the Moon Fullness! How dare you try and get Sylvie off that rock! Who the hell are you to stop me taking what I need?"

He reached across and pulled over the tin, opening it and holding up one of the small cakes. It looked like an innocent fairy cake speckled with herbs and spices. But Yul had seen what they'd done to Clip. Magus' face gleamed like white stone, the shadows deep in the hollows of his cheekbones and eye-sockets. He smiled and the moonlight transformed it to a snarl. Suddenly he seemed demonic in his gleeful excitement.

"A little treat for you, Master Yul. You're probably feeling hungry now, aren't you? I don't expect you ate tonight before coming to rescue your maiden in distress. And you don't know when you'll eat again, once I get you back into the byre. Remember last time? Five days, wasn't it? ... Well, wasn't it, boy?"

"Yes," croaked Yul, his heart lurching with dread. Magus settled down more comfortably on the grass opposite him, the tin of cakes in his lap. He took a long swig of mead and corked the bottle carefully.

"We can't have you going hungry, not yet anyway. So I'm going to feed you now, Yul. Feed you with Old Violet's very special cakes. You can join my brother on a spiritual journey, and with any luck you'll never return. When the soul wanders too far it can't always find the way back again. And it wouldn't be my fault! I wouldn't be breaking the binding spell. I'm only feeding you after all. Open wide, Yul."

Yul shook his head and kept his lips clamped shut. Magus frowned at him, cake in hand.

"Open up *now!*"

He grasped Yul's jaw in his free hand and squeezed his cheeks to open his mouth. Yul tried to struggle as Magus jammed the cake hard into his mouth.

"Swallow it! I SAID SWALLOW IT!"

Yul spat the cake into Magus' face and was rewarded with another of the violent back handed blows, knocking him to the ground again. Magus reached over and hauled him upright, breathing heavily and wiping the crumbs from his face in disgust. He grabbed a handful of Yul's curls and wrenched his head backwards, leaning in close and snarling into his face. In the silver moonlight, Yul saw the writhing fury and hatred behind those black eyes.

"That was a very stupid thing to do, my boy. Now I shall have to feed you even more. So let's start again. I'll put this delicious little cake in your mouth. You'll chew and swallow it. Then I'll give you another one, and so on. We'll continue until I decide you've had enough. If you don't obey me, I'll take that blanket off Sylvie. If you still won't obey me, I'll take her dress off. She'll get very cold standing up there naked, won't she? So, will you co-operate now?"

Yul nodded, a sob of frustration and fury escaping his lips.

"Good!" chuckled Magus. "I thought you might. Now open wide."

Yul swallowed the first cake, and then another, and another in quick succession. He started to choke on the dry crumbs. Magus held the bottle of mead to his lips and forced him to drink deeply of the strong brew. His eyes were merciless and Yul saw again that strange vicious light. As he poured the mead down Yul's throat, watching him struggle to swallow it, Magus threw back his head and laughed. Then he fed him more cakes, far too many, cramming them relentlessly into his mouth one after the other and washing them down with mead.

"Swallow!" he cried encouragingly. "Well done! And one more! You can take one more, I know you can."

His breathing was heavy with excitement, and Yul whimpered at the sensations in his stomach. Everything started to tilt as the burning pain spread inside him. Magus knelt over him, another cake ready in his hand. Yul groaned pitifully and tried to pull away.

"Please!" he gasped. "Please … no more."

Magus sat back on his haunches. As Yul raised his agonised eyes he sensed a shadow standing beyond. The shadow was unnaturally black; much blacker than the night around it. Magus too seemed to sense something for he glanced around and then flung the cake away in panic.

"No more cakes, then!" he gabbled. "I've fed you well. No more, you greedy boy. How many did you eat?"

Yul had lost count and didn't care anyway. The dark shadow had faded as quickly as it had appeared and only Magus remained, silver and black. The night became very strange. Yul was aware of laughter, loud and harsh, which came and went in waves towards his head. He blinked to stop it but his eyelashes weren't strong enough. It smashed over him in pounding waves, drenching him with mirth and madness.

Magus, the man with silver hair and black eyes, stood up like a great monolith. He began to move, going back and forth, back and forth so many times, carrying glowing eggs in his hands. Yul knew they came from a magical bird who cried, who begged to be allowed to stop. He could hear the bird calling and crying. Such sad birdsong. It seemed to go on for a long time. He wished he could help the lovely bird. She was a strange creature with silver feathers covered in moons and stars and long white arms and legs. But he couldn't help her and she continued to call; to call and cry into the empty night. The Magus cat just laughed and purred.

He saw the glittering snake inside the stone coiled up and glowing with pleasure. The snake had been well fed by the magical moon bird and was now fat and satiated. It lay in sparkling ecstasy, pulsating with pleasure at feeling so full and satisfied. The beautiful creature still cried, sobbing piteously now, begging to be released. But nobody listened or cared. The snake wriggled with contentment and settled its slack coils for a long sleep. The eggs were still being created. There were so many of them and the cat was tireless. He prowled around with them in his paws looking very pleased with himself. The cat with black eyes. The cat with silver hair. The cat who hated him and was going to kill him. But not quite yet. The cat loved to play with his prey first, just to prolong the pleasure.

He sighed and saw the moon like a bright silver penny up in the sky. He heard the flapping of great wings and then another bird landed on the cliff top. It was a raven, a big black raven who strutted across the grass and stared at him. He saw the raven's sharp eyes and beak transform into a beautiful girl's face. She had delicate features and such exquisite grey eyes, the irises pale and ringed darker. Her long silver hair was wild and full of tangles and knots, but still lovely. She smiled at him and her teeth were tiny and pointed. She reminded him of someone he loved. She leant over and stroked his face gently with a small, rough hand. He saw such kindness in her eyes. She bent and kissed him on the forehead, whispering in his ear. He wished he could understand what she was saying.

Then another cat came along, an older larger one, much uglier than the beautiful, sleek Magus cat. It was fat and bloated, with thin silver hair and a blotchy face. Its teeth were discoloured and its eyes bloodshot. It pounced greedily on the raven, grunting with pleasure. Holding the bird between its paws, it lowered its head and began to feed voraciously. Before his eyes the Elm cat ripped into the raven, tearing it apart and devouring it, then spitting out the feathers when all the flesh was gone. Yul started to scream at this, scream and scream at the horror of it. The younger cat came over and laughed. The Magus cat laughed and laughed and then kicked him hard, until the screaming stopped and the groaning began.

A little while later, the magical bird fell down on the rock. The cat tried to stand her up but she seemed to have no bones in her white legs any more. He knelt over her and spread her out flat on her back. Then he began to cover her with stones. He piled them up all over her in a crushing, heavy blanket.

She lay very still, buried alive by the stones. There was a tiny, hungry snake inside each stone. The snakes wanted the silver bird to feed them; all clamoured for her special nurture. After a long time they too began to glow, for the kind bird had managed to satisfy them as well. The cat was very pleased and replaced them with yet more stones. The cat and the snakes were insatiable in their need. The poor bird was nearly empty now. She had little more to give them.

A strange creature rose up from the snake rock, a long creature like a worm with wispy silver hair. He moaned and shook his head. He covered the bird with a blanket that must have come from her nest. Then he lay down again in a heap and went on a long journey to a place faraway where wolves howled and eagles soared.

Much, much later, everything had turned into solid cold stone that wouldn't bend or move. All was held together with rope tied around the branches. The twigs couldn't move and the trunk was tied to the ground. The tree was captive and was turning to stone. The Green Man inside the tree was dying slowly. He hung his head as his halo of leaves changed into stone carvings about his face. The black shadow had returned and waited just in the corner of his vision. All around it danced the blackness, like the raven's feathers only thicker and deeper in their darkness. It was cold – so very cold.

Then the worm rose up again and spoke to the cat. The worm was angry and frightened. The blanket was pulled off the magical bird and they could see the stones glowing quite well. The worm rose right up and together, he and the cat gathered the stones and put them in the big boxes. When all the eggs were stored away safely in the wooden nests, the Magus cat came over and stared. His eyes were black in a silver face. The face kept changing, melting and reforming into a different face, each one more horrific than the last. But the eyes always stayed the same – black and cold like death itself. His mouth was moving and he seemed to be shouting. No words came out at all, only a stream of black wasps that buzzed angrily in the air. They swarmed towards the shadow and merged into its depths, making the blackness even deeper.

Then the Magus cat lifted the silver bird from the round white moon where she lay and threw her over his shoulder. She was limp and hung there, floppy and lifeless. Her poor feathers were quite bedraggled. Her magic was completely gone, drained away. They had all fed from her and fed well. Everyone left and it was lonely up on the cliff top. Lonely and cold. Only the dark shadow remained, hovering nearby, waiting so patiently. The dark one. The dark one with great black wings. He could feel his own tiny bird inside his chest beating its wings feebly. The beating became slower and slower as the little bird sank down inside him, no longer able to fly. The shadow moved in closer.

Magus kicked open the arched door and strode into the bedroom. He was slightly out of breath from carrying Sylvie all the way home and then up the stairs, but so fired up on moon magic that he barely noticed. He laid her on her bed and looked down at her. She was pale and completely still. A wild surge of power throbbed within him at the sight of her, exhausted and defenceless and entirely at his mercy. She was the magical one and yet he was the one getting all the special energy. He'd learnt how to tap the source and he'd never be without moon magic again. He laughed softly at the thought and pulled the blanket from beneath her body to cover her up. She was very cold. He stroked her cheek with one finger. She was beautiful, exquisitely so, and not a girl for very much longer. He held his breath for a moment, gazing down at her with different eyes. That boy Yul, whom he'd left out in the cold night up on the cliff, loved this quicksilver girl. Despite all the warnings and threats he'd carried on loving her. But no more. They would never see each other again. Magus had a very different future lined up for his moongazy girl.

Magus left the room by the stairs, not wanting to deal with Miranda tonight. He thought about going back up to Yul on the cliff top. He ought to bring the boy down to the byre now. But he didn't relish the prospect of that shadowy cliff top again, knowing what was lurking there. He'd leave the boy up there alone. Or maybe not alone. It was out of his hands and nothing to do with him anyway. He'd done nothing but feed the hungry boy after all. Besides, it was the night of the Moon Fullness. He brightened at the prospect, determined to put all thoughts of Yul and his fate aside.

As Magus skirted the silent building he slipped through the porch into the entrance hall and picked up a phone. Time to call in reinforcements. If Jackdaw drove through the night, he'd be at Stonewylde by morning. He could have the tedious task of bringing the boy down from the cliff. Alive or dead. Magus smiled as he made his way in the brilliant moonlight down to the Village. His earlier cruel frenzy had passed, vented on the boy who sat tethered to the ground stuffed full of the special cakes. Now all he felt was the moonlust, strong as ever in his veins. The night was still young and he tingled with anticipation, feeling omnipotent. So much moon magic this time – the best yet. He thought again of the pale girl he'd just left, lying silent and unmoving in her bed. He thought of the gift she'd given him.

"Bright blessings, Sylvie, my moongazy girl," he said softly to himself. "You've served me well tonight."

In the tumbledown cottage the black cat leapt off the table and huddled by the fire. Mother Heggy gazed unseeing into the meagre flames, moaning softly. She knew the boy was in danger. She'd warned him not to force a battle tonight. It was not yet time and he couldn't win. As she looked into the flickering firelight, she knew the awful truth. Despite her binding spell, despite the cloak of protection she'd wrapped about the boy since birth at such great cost to herself, he was in mortal danger. Somehow the evil one had stepped around the spell she'd cast so long ago; the spell that had been the only thing between the boy and death all these years. Magus was clever - too clever. What had he done to Yul tonight? How had he managed to put the boy's life in danger but without the consequences to himself? She sensed dark magic afoot and knew it must be that other one, the one who fancied herself as Wise Woman. She'd played a part in this. Magus had surely used her dark powers tonight. Why had the boy not listened? The prophecy was foretold but it was one path of many; nothing was fixed. Must the bright one walk alone and face the evil times ahead without him by her side?

Mother Heggy shook her wizened head and muttered. She made the sign of the pentangle and called upon the Moon Goddess as Mother to protect the boy tonight. To banish the black shadow that hovered close and threatened to summon him. She called upon the powers that were left to her, old and withered as she was and with her magic all but used up since that Solstice so long ago. She rocked in her chair and tried to keep hope alive in her heart. The cat turned and stared up at her, blinking its yellow eyes and purring hoarsely.

The raven swooped down again to the cliff top and looked sadly at the figure huddled on the cold grass. This boy was the future, the only one who could make everything all right again. He alone could stop the events that would unfold, the cruel times ahead for the folk of Stonewylde. He was the guardian of the Earth Magic, the one whom the Goddess favoured. On his young shoulders rested the future and all bright hope. But he was fading. His hands were bound tightly behind his back and the rope held him fast to the iron ring. His deep grey eyes gazed up at the moon but he saw nothing. His head was an inchoate mass of images, completely out of control. She pecked at him gently. There was no response. Slower and slower his heart beat in his chest. The powerful hallucinogens from the cakes he'd been forced to swallow coursed through his body, poisoning his system.

Yul sat near the bright disc of snake-stone as if made of stone himself, slowly petrifying as the night grew colder. Above him the Moon Goddess blazed in silver glory, her magic spent. Beneath him lay the Earth Goddess, her spirals weak at this place of suffering. Nearby stood the Dark Angel, watching and waiting to summon his soul. The tiny bird inside him grew more and more feeble as the stars danced through the night. Yul's head dropped slowly to his chest. All around him, Stonewylde shivered silently in the silver moonlight ...

Read the next book in the Stonewylde Series:

**SOLSTICE AT STONEWYLDE**

**There will be five books altogether in the series.**

For more information about Stonewylde
and Kit Berry's book signing events and talks,
visit the website ***www.stonewylde.com***

You're invited to leave a comment in the guest book
and subscribe to the Stonewylde newsletter.

Join other readers in the Stonewylde Community at
***www.stonewyldeforum.com***

# STONEWYLDE

For more information about the Stonewylde Series visit the website:
*www.stonewylde.com*